SEPARATION GAME

A SEASONED ROMANCE.

ROMANCE GAMES, BOOK ONE

DARCI ANN BAKER

PEAR LAKE PRESS

Edited by Lila LaBine, LaBine Editorial

Cover Design by Deborah Gruchalski

Cover Photograph by Carlo Fornitano

Content Warning: This book contains adult themes which may not be suitable for sensitive readers including on-page sex scenes, swearing, and mild violence.

Real novel guarantee: This author does not uses AI at any stage in her writing process. Thank you for supporting human authors!

 Formatted with Vellum

.

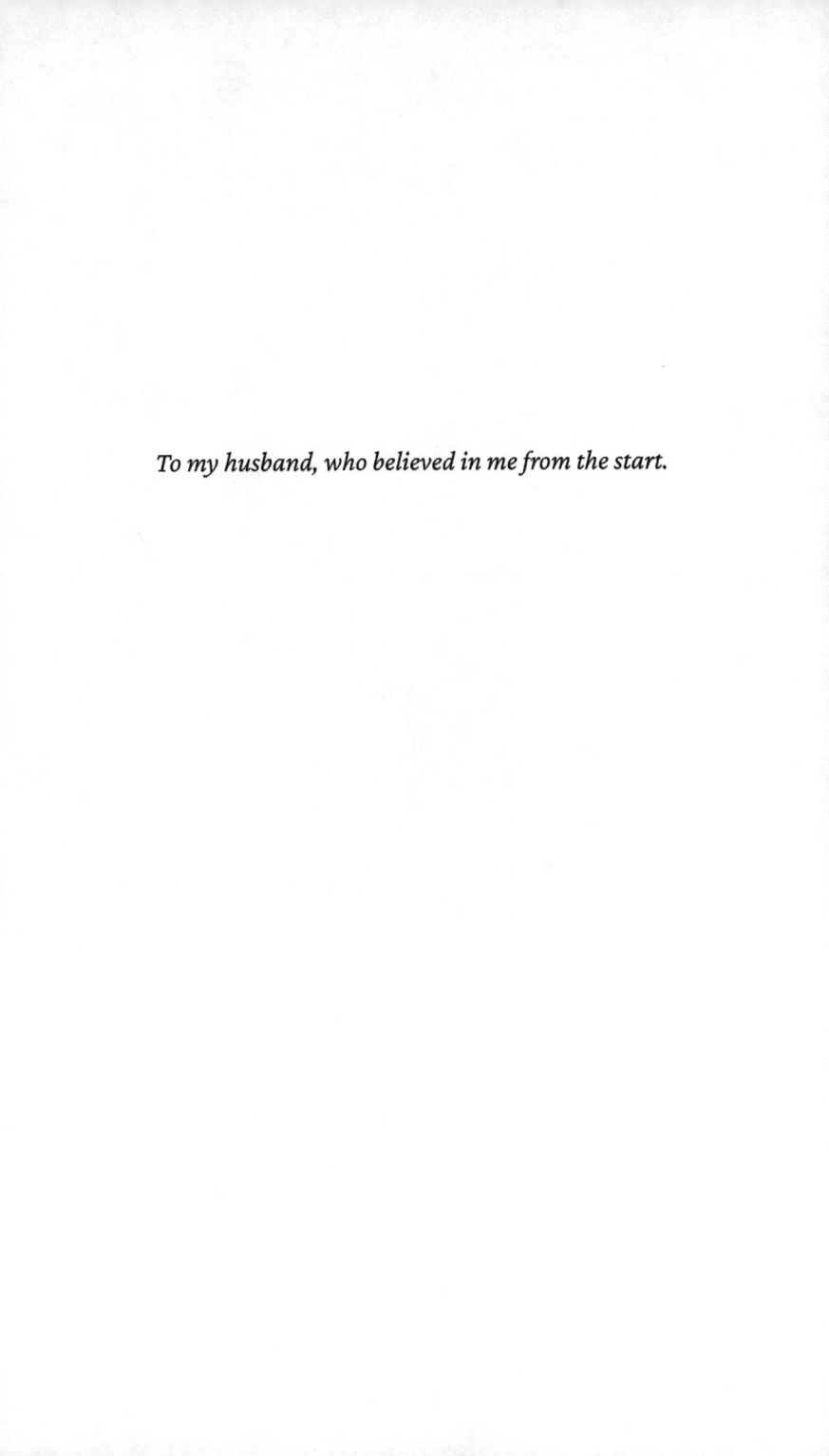

To my husband, who believed in me from the start.

CHAPTER
ONE

The mudroom door slammed. I froze, the spoon in my hand stilling in the pot of soup along with my breath. The fine hairs at the back of my neck rose as unknown footsteps strode evenly across the slate floor one room over. My heart stumbled, then raced as a shadow blocked the strip of light under the solid oak door not ten feet from where I stood.

Who the hell...

My son, Mark, was still at soccer practice and my husband was in DC. No one should be here but me.

The knob turned in a classic slow-motion-nightmare style. My mouth dried, and my attention darted to the knife block, just out of reach from my spot at the stove. Then out the French doors that led to the backyard.

Run, you idiot!

"Nicki?"

Derek's voice halted my escape as I made it past the island. I turned around and let out a shaky breath as fear gave way to a combination of frustration and confusion.

"Jesus, Derek, you scared the shit out of me. What the

hell are you doing home?" Not the most welcome way to greet my husband, but he shouldn't have been home on a Wednesday.

I glanced at the calendar pinned to the fancy corkboard my assistant hung above the small kitchen desk area in order to keep me organized. I might have been known to lose track of time on occasion, but I'd never lost whole days. And just as I thought, it was Wednesday. I'd spent the day at the library, teaching ESL to future citizens of this country.

And as of last week, the Senate had ended its summer recess. My husband should have been in our nation's capital, not our suburban Illinois kitchen.

"If you'd turn on the goddamn alarm—whatever." He aimed a finger toward the mudroom door, but then midpoint dropped his hand and shook his head, cutting off his standard lecture on the dreaded security system for once. "Where's Mark?"

"Soccer practice. Then dinner at Brian's. I left the alarm off for—"

"We need to talk." His stern expression caused a knot to form in my stomach. If he was willing to forget about the alarm, something must be wrong.

Besides the fact he was home on a Wednesday—one of his busiest days, packed tight with committee hearings, floor votes, constituent meetings, and public appearances. Derek hadn't missed a day in the past thirteen years. Not one.

He motioned toward the great room. "Turn off the stove and come sit down."

My mind raced through the possibilities as I headed across the kitchen and down the two steps into the adjoining great room. My phone had been with me all day. I hadn't received any emergency calls. And it was midweek. No chance I'd forgotten any of Derek's social engagements requiring my presence.

I frowned, taking in my husband sitting across from me in his favorite chair. He wore stonewashed jeans and a light blue checked button-down. Blue check? What the hell was going on? Derek hated patterned shirts. Crisp white, maybe cream, the occasional French blue if he was feeling adventurous, but never checks or stripes. *Where did he even get that thing?*

"...it's nothing personal, but I just can't do this anymore."

"Sorry, what?" I shook my head like a dog shedding water as I sifted through his words. Distracted by that shirt, my brain refused to cooperate, or maybe Derek wasn't making sense. *What can't he do anymore?*

He huffed, dragging his fingers through his still-thick hair the same way he'd done for the past twenty-odd years whenever I frustrated him. "Divorce, Nicki. I want a divorce."

Divorce? He couldn't be serious? The next moment my thoughts turned into words. "What? You can't be serious," I sputtered, but he really didn't need to answer me. It was written all over him.

For a man who wielded body language like a weapon, his hunched shoulders and the way he stared at his clasped hands hanging between his knees spoke volumes. He raised his head and our eyes met. Just for a moment, I saw guilt in those ice-blue depths. Then he straightened and his face hardened.

"Let's not get emotional over this, Nicole. We've lasted longer than most marriages."

My lips parted, but no words came out. *What?* I blinked

at him for a second as the last two minutes hit me like a CTA bus.

"*Longer than most marriages?* What are we, just some Goddamn statistic? Should I be happy we ended up as an outlier?"

A dam broke inside me. My blood surged, pounding into my ears and every cell in my body. I stood, my hands curled into fists.

"You can't do this anymore?" I spat out. "After all I've done? Supporting you through law school, standing by you through all your campaigns, standing next to you like the *good little wife.* You said we were a team."

God, how I wanted to hurt him. The smug, fucking asshole, sitting there as if this was just business as usual. As if I was just unfortunate collateral in a policy he supported.

The knives sat all the way across the room on the counter. Castration was out, unless I used my hands. That was doable. Mount his balls above the fireplace mantle. Could I get them in the divorce settlement?

Whoa. The reality of that thought shook me, but that's what we were talking about. Separation, then divorce. Lawyers and judges. Alimony and child support. By the steely look on Derek's face, he had already thought all this through. I was steps behind him.

"How long?" I hissed, taking a step closer to the bastard. "How long have you been planning this?"

"I don't know. A month maybe." His left eye twitched— a subtle movement no one would notice unless they'd spent twenty years watching him. Up until now it'd been useful for trivial things, like who ate all the mint-chip ice cream. But now...

"I didn't actually set out for this to happen, Nicki. It just did."

"Who is she?" I asked through clenched teeth. If only I had the power to strike him dead with a look. It had to be a *she*. What we had was good, solid. You didn't throw away twenty years of marriage for nothing. "Do I know her?"

He laughed, as if my accusation was preposterous. "There's no other woman. I just need out."

My attention zeroed in on his left hand as he waved it in front of me. His bare left hand. The ring we'd spent hours choosing twenty years ago was missing. The absence of that little gold ring was like a sucker punch to the gut.

"Liar. Get out." I turned away, fighting the sudden nausea. "Take your shit and leave before you're sorry."

"Don't make this ugly, Nicki. I'll have my lawyer call yours. We can make this quick. Just keep this quiet and civil, and we'll both get everything we want."

I wanted to go back ten minutes and forget this conversation. *I* wanted our happy marriage back. *I* obviously wasn't going to get everything *I* wanted.

My shoulders dropped with sudden exhaustion and I let out a quiet sigh. "You don't care about what I want, you selfish bastard."

He let out his own sigh and shook his head as if I was being irrational. "Nicki, don't do this. You know I can make things a lot worse for you. I don't want to, but I could."

Was he threatening me? The mother of his children? I rolled my eyes and turned away again, ignoring his ridiculous warning.

He stepped around to face me, towering over me—or trying to. It had always bothered Derek that I was only two inches shorter than him. For the first time in years, I stood straight and stared him in the eye.

"How much worse?" I closed the gap between us until I could count the stray hairs between his eyebrows. He

5

flinched as my fingers traced the edge of his still-sharp jaw one last time. At forty-four his tawny, blond hair had lightened to silver, and years of fundraiser dinners and lobbyist luncheons had taken their toll, but my husband was still a handsome man. A catch for whoever she was.

I shook my head in resignation and dropped my hand. "Whatever. I could ruin you with one phone call, one social media post, but I won't. For the kids' sake. But you? Go fuck yourself, Senator Robinson."

Gathering my last stores of energy, I stormed up the stairs. I could feel Derek's eyes on me as I rushed across the bridgeway that spanned between the great room and the foyer, connecting the two upper wings of the house. Down the hall, I slammed the double doors to our bedroom—*my bedroom*, my mind corrected—behind me with enough force to rattle the windows. My breath caught. The top of his dresser lay barren of his things.

I stepped across the room, my skin tingling with apprehension, my heart lodged in my throat. Pushing the closet door open, I gasped again. The bastard must have been here all day while I was out. The proof of his calculated act sat on the empty shelves and rods that occupied his side of the massive closet.

A cold hand gripped my heart as my knees hit the soft carpet. What the hell was I going to do? A mother of two with a frivolous liberal arts degree. My last job was over a decade ago. I had become completely dependent on my husband.

Derek was right. He could make things much worse.

CHAPTER
TWO

My body shivered the second my bare feet hit the icy wood planks of the small balcony just off my bedroom. The cold lake breeze stung against my cheeks and brought tears to my eyes. At least I was willing to blame the wind on my tears, not the heart-breaking view in front of me. Why would I cry about majestic oaks and dappled sunlight, or the diamond-tipped waves crashing against the rocks on our shoreline?

Twelve hours since I'd discovered my marriage was ending, and the thought still ran through me like I was standing in water, holding a bare electrical wire.

It's nothing personal, Nicki. I just can't do this anymore. One last lungful of crisp morning air and I stepped back into the warmth of the bedroom, shutting the French doors behind me. Derek's words repeated in my head for the thousandth time since he had spoken them. Their sharp edge hadn't dulled in the last twelve hours. How long would it take until they did?

A sob broke from my chest, that I couldn't possibly blame on the cold, echoing across the bedroom as I collapsed onto the chaise. If I'd thought I'd run out of tears last night, I was mistaken.

Nothing personal. Like twenty years of marriage was nothing personal. Like two kids and a lifetime of sacrifices was nothing personal. Felt pretty personal to me.

Stop!

I swiped at my useless tears. I had to hold on to the anger that burned inside me. If I succumbed to the anguish and self-pity that threatened, I'd be lost.

In the next moment, the hum of the garage door pulled me from my pep talk. I rushed to the front windows, my stomach knotting with guilt. Brushing back the heavy drapes, I watched Mark's bright blue Jeep Wrangler make its way down the driveway.

Coward.

I had lingered upstairs on purpose, unable to face my son this morning. It would be cruel to spring this kind of news on him before school, and he would realize something was wrong the minute he saw my face. I didn't need to look into the mirror to know my eyes were unlikely to conceal a night's worth of tears.

Tonight. I would tell him tonight.

And what about Brooke?

My daughter was away at Harvard. The last thing she needed was family drama interrupting her studies. Not that I could keep this from her forever.

I turned away from that thought and snatched the can of cinnamon spice air freshener off the nightstand, laying down a heavy fog as I walked around the room. Last week I'd bought it to celebrate the beginning of September and the unofficial start of fall. Now, I just needed it to mask Derek's Tom Ford cologne that seemed to have permeated our entire bedroom. I gave the mattress an extra heavy coat along with a disdainful look.

Might have to burn that. But that could wait. I had more important things to do.

HOURS LATER, I stumbled through the mudroom door, heavy bags tugging down my arms, my phone ringing demands from somewhere deep inside my purse. I mumbled out a jumbled string of curses involving cell phones and traffic and shopping and no-good husbands, and then turned toward the annoying chirp and evil green glow of the security panel.

"Not today, you..." I growled while stabbing the alarm code into the keypad.

The readout on the wall flashed INVALID CODE. Of course it did.

I let out a quiet sigh and closed my eyes, ignoring the ticking time bomb that taunted with another chirp in front of me.

The anger-fueled adrenaline that had kept me going all day was dwindling. In its place, alongside the exhaustion that weighed on my limbs, a ball of ice-cold fear formed in my stomach. No matter how hard I tried, the direness of my situation insisted on invading my self-imposed facade of normalcy.

Dropping the bags to the slate floor, I punched the numbers in again—this time slower—breathing out a measured breath to stop the trembling in my fingers.

The solid green light on the panel told me I'd been successful this time. I pushed my bags out of my way with my foot and headed into the kitchen, fumbling for my now silent phone that was wedged in the bottom of my purse next to a half-melted chocolate bar.

I hit the return call button and opened the fridge to grab a much-needed bottle of water, dropping the chocolate on the shelf for later.

"Nicole. Fucking. Robinson." The raspy but feminine voice on the other end had me smiling for the first time in almost twenty-four hours.

"Cynthia..." Her name came out on a shaky breath as the tension I'd been holding all day melted like candle wax.

Eighteen years ago I'd been a new mom looking for a few hours out of the house, away from a mountain of dirty diapers and the increasing stress of Derek's early campaigns. The ad for a part-time receptionist at a real-estate office in town seemed perfect. Two minutes into my interview, Cynthia and I became instant friends.

Dangerous with a veneer of sophistication—kind of like a bowling ball hidden inside a Louis Vuitton bag—Cynthia was the only person I trusted at the moment.

Shortly after Mark had left for school this morning, I called her. But of course she had been busy. That was the problem when your only friend had a type A personality and planned to take over the world.

"What's wrong? Your message sounded frantic." Her heels tapped a rhythm on the floor in the background.

I sank down on a stool at the island and put my phone on speaker. "Derek's left me."

Tears sprang to my eyes—again—and I laid my head down on the counter, the cool granite solid and steady under my cheek.

The click of her shoes stopped. "What?"

"Last night. He asked for a divorce." My voice was

surprisingly calm and steady considering my insides were anything but.

"You're fucking kidding." Her voice lowered. "Jesus Christ, what an ass. I'm so sorry."

"Thanks, Cyn," I said, my own voice dull in my ears. Forcing myself to sit up, I took a sip of water.

"Nicki..." She paused. "What do you need? Whatever it is, you know I will move mountains to get it for you."

I snorted a little laugh at her exaggeration. "Mountains?"

She laughed back. "Don't underestimate me. I know people. More people than Derek, which means..." She paused for a second and I heard a door close in the background. "Whatever you want, sweetheart."

In the last twenty years, Cynthia had gone from small-town realtor to big-city real-estate developer and broker. She had been one of Derek's biggest donors, and was on a first-name basis with most of the others. The dark edge in her voice said she was willing to do a lot of damage.

"Thanks for the offer, Cyn, but maybe we should put that *offer* on hold right now. At least for the kids' sakes? I honestly have no idea what I need. I don't even know what's happening."

"Fine. I love my godchildren too much to throw away their future along with their father's." Her breath gusted across the line along with a groan. "God, this is hard. A really big part of me wants to call him every name in the book right now, to fly out to DC and wring his damn neck, or at least egg his fucking Cadillac. But I know you are hurting—"

I choked out a laugh. Things had to be pretty bad for Cynthia Jacobs to restrain her opinions. "Don't hold back on my account. I'm pretty sure I've called him every one of those names since he left last night. And I hated that Cadillac."

We both laughed for a minute. He had always been so anal about his cars.

"Someday that asshole will realize what he's thrown away. But by then it will be too late, and he will spend the rest of his pitiful, lonely life regretting this decision."

"Thanks for the pep talk, Cyn, but I'm pretty sure he's found someone else. He's not coming back."

After a moment's silence, she barked out, "He *actually* admitted that?"

I snorted, rolling my eyes. "Not in so many words, but I asked him, and well... after twenty years of marriage, I know when he lies."

"Bastard." She huffed. "We will make him sorry."

I shot a glance at the pile of packages sitting inside the mudroom and an unhinged giggle bubbled up in my chest. "I may have done that. Gave a few of our credit cards a workout today."

I was still pinching myself that Derek hadn't closed the accounts. Yet.

She coughed out a short laugh in return. "You didn't."

"I needed a few things." I turned away from my morning's splurge, grabbed the phone, and headed toward the great room. "Single women don't wear beige underwear and low heeled shoes do they? I figured Derek owed me this makeover." And a new bed. And lace-topped thigh-high stockings the saleswoman insisted were integral to every new divorcée's wardrobe.

"That's my girl."

"After shopping, I cashed out a healthy sum. Opened a new account with the money. Derek never said anything about the bills." Not that I'd been in the mood to discuss those details last night. With the yelling and the name calling and the threats, the important stuff had gotten lost in the moment. But then this whole thing had been Derek's fault. "There's the mortgage, utilities, insurance, Mark's car payment. And so many other things."

Just the thought of those *other things* made my stomach drop.

"Well, fuck him, then. Like I said, if you need anything..."

Cynthia had reached the level of success that most could only dream about. And she was more than generous with her wealth and time. But no way in hell was I about to become one of her charities. Not if I could help it.

The pictures lining the great-room mantel mocked my resolve. I'd eat my pride before I let Brooke and Mark suffer because of Derek's thoughtlessness. Did Derek even think of them when he was making his plans to leave?

"God, Cyn. I'm just so angry. How could he do this? Not only to me but to the kids?" I turned away from the fireplace with a frustrated sigh. "I hate to ask, but I'm really gonna need your help."

"I told you. I know people. They'll know just where to bury the body."

"As enticing as that sounds, I was thinking about a job."

I held my breath for a moment. We'd been friends forever, but I'd only worked a handful of years for Cynthia before Derek decided I should stay home with the kids. Had I proven my worth in those years?

"Funny, I was *just* thinking of bringing on a partner. I'm busy as hell and I'd rather have you than some unknown. Please tell me you kept up your real-estate licensing?"

I froze as her offer penetrated my thoughts, along with uncertainty. I hadn't sold a house in almost fifteen years, but

I'd been faithful in keeping up my license. Every two years. Taking the classes and paying the fees even though Derek had complained. At the time I'd told myself it'd been a matter of pride, a sliver of the old me I'd been loath to forget.

"I did, but partner? Are you sure? It's been years since I sold a house. And commercial real estate? Maybe I could just answer phones or bring you coffee or something."

Back into the mudroom, I grabbed my heavy bags from the floor. Mark wouldn't be home until much later, but I needed to hide the evidence of my shopping trip before I forgot. It was legendary in this house how much I hated shopping. With Brooke away at college, explaining my purchases would be difficult.

So will the divorce.

"Please. You're brilliant. And I already have someone to make coffee and answer phones. I need you and you need me. This will be fun. And before long, Derek might be begging *you* for alimony."

My smile died on my lips. I was getting a divorce. No matter what Cynthia promised, I couldn't escape my new reality.

"Where the hell am I going to get a lawyer? All the ones I know are friends with Derek." I paused at the top of the stairs, absorbing the silence. The loneliness. Was I about to turn into a cliché? My friends were Derek's friends. Given a choice, I knew which side they'd take. Besides Cynthia, I had no one. "Shit, Cyn."

"Stop panicking. I know just the man." Cynthia paused. A masculine voice mumbled something on her end and she laughed.

"Listen, I have a busy schedule today. How about drinks and dinner tomorrow?"

She rattled off the name of a bar in the city, and I decided right then that Derek could have all our other friends. The only one I needed was Cynthia.

I NUDGED a dark navy stiletto in line with its mate and then stepped back from the shelves to survey my bounty. A rainbow of new shoes sat on the empty shelves that had once held Derek's dress shoes, loafers, and running shoes. If I looked close enough I could see their faint outline in the cherry shelves, like ghost footprints. But I did my best not to dwell on that, or the empty drawers and hangers on that side of the room. Even if I enjoyed shopping, it would take me years to fill this closet.

The bastard must have been home the entire previous day. He knew my schedule as well as I knew his. And of course he knew I'd be at the library. It had been his idea— not the ESL classes but volunteering.

It'll give you something to do and make me look good.

I had laughed off the second half of his comment at the time. Brooke had just started high school, Mark had reached that independent age, and I was becoming obsolete. I needed something to fill my time. Something fitting the wife of a senator.

But who would help my students now? My heart squeezed tight. Holding down a full-time job and maintaining my volunteer hours would be impossible. I would have to call Barbara at the library.

I dropped down on the sitting room love seat just outside the closet, my head spinning. Why was it always the woman that made the sacrifices in a divorce? I'd certainly made enough of them in the marriage. More than I wanted to acknowledge at the moment.

God, I'd been stupid. Why hadn't I seen the changes sooner? Changes in Derek, changes in our marriage. They say hindsight is twenty-twenty, but maybe if I'd been paying attention?

Did I even notice how long it had been since we'd made love? This summer he'd barely been home. His reelection was still years off, but he'd been campaigning hard for the presidential race. There was a possibility of a cabinet post, he had told me. Another step toward his own long-term dreams of the White House.

Was that even a goal for him anymore? The only divorced president I could recall was Ronald Reagan, but that had happened early in his life. Why would Derek take the risk? Not that I wanted to play the token wife for his ambitions.

Was that all I'd been for the past twenty years?

I stared at the silver-framed wedding photo on the end table, searching for answers I would probably never find.

I swiped at a stray tear and then shoved the photo into the table drawer next to the TV remote and a stack of silver coasters.

Several hours stood between me and Mark's return from school. It was too beautiful a day to be sitting inside wallowing in self-pity. A glass of wine by the pool sounded like a better option.

Pulling the sedate one-piece swimsuit out of my drawer, I blanched.

Was this why Derek didn't want me anymore? Over the past fifteen years of campaigns he had molded me into someone I didn't even recognize. Frumpy clothes, frumpy hairstyles, even frumpy underwear and bathing suits. Well,

I took care of the frumpy underwear this morning. And the hair.

If Derek still cared, he would have a fit over the edgy chin-length cut I'd gotten this morning. He always insisted that I keep my blonde hair long. Wholesome.

The rest of my wardrobe had to go, but this time I didn't need to spend a penny. Down the hall, there was almost an entire closetful of clothes my daughter had left behind when she took off for Harvard in August. Unlike me, Brooke loved to shop, and Cynthia was more than happy to indulge her need for the latest fashion trends.

The look on Brooke's face when she took in the two feet of closet space in her dorm had been comical. Mark had often joked his sister could go a year without wearing the same thing twice. As I stepped into her closet, I realized Mark hadn't been far off in his assessment.

"Jesus..." I whispered, taking in the rows of dresses and skirts and blouses. It was like a department store inside the space that was almost as big as mine and Derek's closet. Had it always been this big, or did the mirrors just make it look bigger?

A minute later those same mirrors dared me to try on the string bikini that had her father hyperventilating two months ago.

I stripped off my clothes before I could chicken out, slipping into the tiny strips of fabric, then turned toward the glass with a cringe at the ready.

Huh. Okay, well, I wouldn't be caught dead on a public beach in this thing, but...

My blue eyes stared back at me, pleasantly surprised. Not quite as thin as my college days, but still... My almost flat stomach and long, lean legs were proof of the hours I'd put in with my personal trainer. A few stretch marks and a couple of dimples couldn't be helped when you were a forty-three-year-old mother of two.

What had turned Derek off?

Back downstairs, I glared at the ridiculous double wine cellar my husband had to have. *One side for the reds and one for the whites,* he'd explained when we remodeled several years back. I never understood his obsession with wine.

Focus on what's important, Nicki. Red or white?

That was a good question. I tended to lean toward white, but a cabernet from the year we married caught my eye. *Seems fitting.* I could almost hear Derek yelling at me to let it breathe or some shit, but I poured a healthy glassful and took a sip.

Not bad. My husband—correction, soon-to-be ex-husband—would probably drone on and on about how the tannins had mellowed with age and some crap about the taste of tobacco and chocolate. *Fuck it.* I tipped my head back and swallowed the whole glass in one gulp, picturing his furious glare. I smiled and poured another glass, downing it only slightly slower.

I filled my glass to the rim for the third time, snagged my now firm chocolate bar from the fridge, and headed out to the pool.

The sun blazed hot on my skin. For early September it was a perfect day. Not a cloud in the sapphire-blue sky, the crisp lake breeze from this morning mellowing to an occasional puff just in time to chase away the heat.

But days like these were numbered. And so was my time in this house if Derek didn't feel charitable.

Would he really do that to me? Or his son?

I took another sip of wine and then settled back onto one of the chaise lounges we had bought just after putting in the pool, and considered the odds. The husband I knew would never have forced me to sell this house. But that husband would never have walked away from twenty years of marriage either.

If only he had waited. We were only two years from paying off the mortgage. The taxes would be a stretch, but I could budget. Turn off the lights more. Turn down the air conditioning in the summer, same for the heat in the winter. Clip coupons.

Get rid of my personal trainer. And my assistant. I didn't need a stylist anymore. Or a publicist. The groundskeeper and his crew. Invest in a lawn mower instead? Don't forget a snow blower. Could I get Mark to cut acres of grass and clear the long driveway?

Rosa. No. Absolutely not. I winced, thinking about doing without my housekeeper's help the three days a week she whipped the place into spotless order. She was almost a part of the family, really. But could I afford her salary?

Damn him. In one impulsive decision Derek was sending a small village to the unemployment line. Not that he cared.

The pool. I stared at the crystal-clear water of the dream oasis we had created years ago until my eyes blurred. I dropped back onto the chaise and closed my eyes, letting the warm sun sink into my skin. The soft burble of the waterfalls drowned out the anxious voice in my head for a moment.

Shit. There was no avoiding the expense of the pool. The chemicals and mechanicals overwhelmed me. Gabriel was the best in the business. Irreplaceable.

I drained the last of the wine from my glass, spitting the nasty sediment back with a grimace. *Better get used to cleaning bathrooms, Mrs. Robinson.*

I set my glass down just as the back gate rattled. In

19

walked Gabriel, almost as if I had conjured him with my thoughts. But no. It was late Thursday afternoon. He came every Thursday like clockwork.

Shit. I glanced down at the tiny scraps of fabric that barely covered me. Gabriel did not need to see this. Too late, though. His wide-eyed expression said as much.

I pictured my daughter laughing at my embarrassment. She made no secret in our house of her opinion of Gabriel. His blond surfer looks, beefy muscles, and hint of a southern twang in his deep voice. She talked about him for hours after the first time he showed up; she practically swooned every time he came after. Derek always reminded her he was way too old for her—which he was.

"I'm sorry. I'll get out of your way. I completely forgot. The day just slipped my mind," I babbled stupidly.

"No need. It's a beautiful day. Not too many left." He set down his equipment, offering me a small smile.

"I—I'll just... go inside." The warmth of my face suggested my skin had turned a brilliant crimson. I stood up and grabbed my empty glass, wanting to be anywhere but here.

The next few seconds were a blur. I spun around to head toward the patio doors, hoping for a quick exit. The three glasses of wine on an empty stomach, combined with the heat of the afternoon, had other ideas. The backyard swam and the patio tilted. As I reached for the back of the chaise in attempt to regain my balance, my wine glass slipped from my hand shattering everywhere. Everything slowed down, like one of those disaster films. Slow but inevitable. There was nothing I could do to stop my foot from landing upon the shards of glass sparkling in the sun.

CHAPTER
THREE

"S hit." I squeezed my eyes shut, my hand clenching the back of the chaise. I jerked my foot back, but the searing pain shooting up my leg along with the blood dripping on the stone patio told me it was too late.

"Hang on," Gabriel shouted a second before dashing across the pool decking, sweeping me into his arms.

My face turned molten and I issued a protest, trying my best not to notice the heat of his very hard body pressed against my bare skin. I was definitely not noticing the firm curve of his pecs or the way the sleeves of his T-shirt stretched to accommodate the circumference of his biceps. Or the thickness of his neck. The guy could have doubled as a pro footballer. Not that I was paying attention.

"I'm fine. Really." Or I would be once I limped inside and died of humiliation, then started a new life where I would swear off bikinis and day drinking.

Gabriel shoved open the French door, ignoring my assurances with a skeptical snort. He strode across the kitchen and set me on one of the stools at the island. "First aid kit?"

"Gabriel, please." I whimpered, wishing he would just disappear, or that the floor would swallow me up. "I'm fine."

He didn't budge. The pain in my foot seemed to increase. Sweat beaded on my upper lip, and my head started to spin. My stomach did a warning flip that said the bottle of wine I'd consumed hadn't been the best idea and that this staring contest might not end well.

"Powder room, top shelf of the cabinet." I pointed a shaky finger toward the hall, squeezing my eyes shut.

"Y'gonna be okay for me to leave ya?"

I leaned against the back of the stool and breathed slowly through my nose to quell my stomach, the uncomfortable decorative ironwork pressing into my back. *God, I hate these stools*. Pretty sure Derek picked them out.

"Be right back, then."

I blew out a shaky breath once he disappeared around the corner, then looked down to survey the damage.

Splotches of wine sludge dotted my shins, catching on the fine hairs. The one day I skipped shaving...

I twisted my foot and winced at the sight of a bloody glass shard sticking out of the ball of my foot. I wasn't normally squeamish, but...

A curse hissed out between my clenched teeth as I tugged on the large chunk—a vicious curved piece lodged just below my big toe. Once free of the obstruction, blood oozed from the opening, running toward the opposite edge of my foot.

My head swam. Crimson drops spattered against the marble floor like tiny Rorschach tests on the bright white marble. My mouth flooded with saliva. My stomach offered a warning lurch. Slapping a hand across my mouth, I did a mad hop across the kitchen, retching the best of Napa Valley 1999 into the sink.

Wiping tears from my eyes, I shot a quick glance down the hall, but there was no sign of Gabriel. Thank God. Leg hair and vomiting. Could this day get any worse?

I performed a quick but thorough rinse of the sink and then an even more thorough one of my mouth. Those mellowed tannins and hints of tobacco and chocolate weren't quite so smooth the second time around.

"Whatcha doin', Mrs. Robinson?"

I jumped and caught myself on the edge of the counter as the room spun again. In a heartbeat Gabriel was at my side, slipping his strong arm around my waist to steady me.

"A minute ago y'were about to fall on your face." Once again he slipped his free arm under my knees and lifted me against his chest. "Are you trying to damage yourself?"

"Think I already did that," I mumbled as he set me back down on the stool.

"Let's gitcha patched up, then." He paused for a second, giving me a narrow look, one probably reserved for difficult clients or stubborn algae. "You aren't gonna try and get up if I walk away again, are you?"

"No," I grumbled.

His warm and slightly rough hand closed over my shoulder, and he gave me a small smile. "And please don't go fallin' over."

My skin heated uncomfortably. Unlike my daughter, I'd grown impervious to Gabriel's good looks over the past five years. But up close? Nothing could prepare me for the full attention of his dark blue eyes creased with concern. Or the heat radiating off his deeply tanned skin. *And lord help me*, the way his crisp white T-shirt stretched across his muscled chest, forming to every ripple in his stomach?

He removed his hand and stepped back, a grin spreading across his face while mine turned blast-furnace hot. I may not have noticed before, but the quirk of his brow suggested he was aware of my noticing now.

I gave him a slow nod. *Get a grip, for goodness sake.*

I was too young for hot flashes, but that's what this had to be. Hot flashes and too much wine. Definitely not sexual chemistry. I could be Gabriel's mother for Christ sake. Or aunt. A young, sexy aunt. *Who's bleeding all over the floor.*

His eyes stayed on mine, as if he didn't trust me at my word.

"I'm not drunk."

He set the first aid kit and the powder room's decorative wastebasket on the floor in front of me and then winked, his smile widening. "Didn't say you were."

I frowned as he turned away, headed over to the sink, and started washing his hands. What was with that wink? Didn't he believe me? *You drank a whole bottle of wine, what is there to believe?*

"The sun was hotter than I'd expected." I swiveled in my seat as he headed back, ignoring the way my head floated like a balloon on a string. "Really, I can take care of this, Gabriel. You should get back to work. I don't want to get you in trouble."

His lips twisted and his navy-blue eyes narrowed as he slowly knelt in front of me. "Keel over in the process, too." Lifting my foot, he tipped his head, squinting to get a better look. "Even sober you'd have to be a contortionist to get these out. And I'm my own boss, so I promise I won't go firing myself."

Gabriel. Angel Pool Services. I could almost hear my daughter's sarcastic *duh* in my ear. How had I never made the connection in the past five years? Had I thought the company only hired employees with angelic names? That there was a Uriel and a Raphael running around somewhere with plain white T-shirts with the company logo complete with angel wings on the pocket, leaving pools blessedly clean?

I leaned back against the hard seat and silently cursed myself. This was all my fault. All of it. How much of the past twenty years had I been content to let these little details slip by, blissfully unaware of the bigger issues hiding under the surface?

God, I was stupid.

At least Mark wasn't expected home for hours. My humiliation would have been complete if he walked in on this embarrassing little scene. He and Brooke would never let me hear the end of this, that was for sure.

"It's not so bad, Mrs. Robinson." I flinched as he pulled the first shard out. "I think you lucked out. This shouldn't take too long."

Lucky was the last thing I would have called myself at that particular moment. My husband had left me. My sexy pool guy was probing my foot with a pair of tweezers while his large and very masculine hand wrapped around my hairy ankle. Sweat trickled down my back and beaded across my hairline. I probably smelled. But at least I didn't feel like puking anymore. So I guess I was lucky on that count.

"Oh good, my humiliation will be over soon. Then we can forget all about this, right?"

He grinned up at me. "Ain't nothing to be humiliated about. Accidents happen. Knew a guy, walked into a plate glass window. Broke his nose, then fell on his ass and fractured that too. Now that's embarrassing."

I flinched as he pulled another piece out. "Was he drunk?"

Gabriel shook his head and then winked. Again. Maybe he was just a winker. But it was a damn sexy wink all the same. "Stone-cold sober, just like yourself."

I let out a heavy sigh. "Fine. You got me. But it's been a really shitty day."

He paused in his search for glass and looked up at me, his eyes sympathetic. "We all have shitty days. No one's judging you, Mrs. Robinson."

God, I hated that name. Mrs. Robinson. From almost the beginning of my marriage I had been the butt of jokes referencing that movie about an older married woman who has an affair with a younger man. The insinuations had been insulting and ridiculous. I never would have considered an affair. But obviously Derek didn't have the same high morals.

"Thanks. But could you, maybe, call me Nicki?" I let out another sigh. "Derek and I are getting a d-divorce, so shitty might be a bit of an understatement."

Spilling the news for the second time today wasn't any easier. And to my pool guy? Chalk up another humiliation.

Gabriel's eyes softened, most likely with pity. "Sorry t'hear that. He's a fool for leaving you."

"How do you know I didn't leave him?" I flinched as he pulled another piece out. My words came out sharp. I didn't want pity.

His lips curved into a soft smile. He stood and walked to the sink. "If you'd left him, you'd be gone. But here you are."

"Very perceptive. Thank you for this," I amended, guilt sitting heavy on my shoulders. He could be done with my pool by now. He had to have better things to do than waste time with me.

"His loss, not appreciating the intelligent, beautiful woman he was blessed with." He scanned my face as he bent down and washed my foot, and then used the damp cloth to wipe the blood off the tile.

"And if you want my opinion, you're better off without him. Men like him..." He shook his head, a scowl hardening his handsome face for a brief second, before he stood and returned to the sink. Derek could be unpleasant at times, and I was sure in that moment Gabriel had had personal experience with Derek's less than cordial side. "Well, trust's something you don't ever get back once it's lost."

His gaze held mine as he sank to his knees in front of me again, his words stabbing deeper than the glass he pulled from my foot. They hurt more too. Would I ever trust another man? Did Derek set me up for a life of mistrust and loneliness? I tried to push those thoughts away, focusing on the pain in my foot. That I could handle.

"I think I got it all," Gabriel said, continuing to run his thumb across my foot. "You feel anything?"

Boy, did I feel something. The warmth of his strong fingers wrapped around my ankle, his other hand pressing gauze to the bottom of my foot. Maybe I'd been neglected for too long, but the combination of his caring touch and the way his gaze locked onto mine set off inappropriate sparks of lust.

"Nope. Nothing," I lied, my voice shaky.

"That's good." He nodded, his tongue running a lazy path along his bottom lip. God, this man was sex on speed dial, and the sooner he got out of here the better. For both of us.

I watched, mesmerized, as he applied salve to my foot and then slowly wrapped it in a bandage. For such a large man his touch was gentle, and I couldn't help but imagine those gentle fingers elsewhere on my body. Damn Derek for leaving me needy and vulnerable. It would probably be years before I dated again.

Gabriel gave my ankle a final squeeze and then stood. "All set?"

I nodded, and then before I could react, those warm and gentle hands closed around my waist, guiding me to my feet. Or, at least, one foot.

He wasn't much taller than Derek, but Gabriel had a good fifty pounds of muscle on my soon-to-be-ex-husband, with shoulders as wide and corded as a linebacker.

"Lemme help you over to the couch. Or maybe you want me to carry you to your room?"

His eyebrows quirked up in some kind of invitation, or maybe it was my imagination, my alcohol-soaked brain interpreting his kind intentions for more than what they were. But what the hell did I have to lose? With the warmth of his hands sinking into my bare flesh, and his less than innocent gaze traveling down my body—burning the places he wasn't touching—and that innuendo of something unspoken in his offer. If I was mistaken, I could blame it on the wine, Derek's betrayal, or maybe just Gabriel's tenderness, but I didn't think I was mistaken. And really, what did I have to lose at this point?

I leaned into him and wrapped my arms around his neck, pressing the entire length of my body against him like a feral cat, the delicious feel of his body heat radiating into my exposed skin making me purr.

He pulled back a fraction, his blue eyes darkening, a small smile curling at the edge of his mouth. "Whatcha doing, Mrs. Robinson?" At my scowl he added, "Nicki?"

"What does it look like, Gabriel?"

Jesus, maybe I was mistaken. Maybe he had a girlfriend? Or a wife? He didn't wear a ring, but maybe with the chemicals? *Shit.* "Forget it. I'm ridiculously old, and you can't possibly be single, or interested. And I just added another humiliation to the list today. So..."

I started to pull back, but he tightened his hold on my waist.

"I'm very single, and you're not ridiculously old." He trailed his fingers along my jaw. "You're a fucking knockout."

I breathed out a self-conscious laugh. Maybe those pool chemicals had affected his vision. "How old are you?"

"Twenty-eight."

"Jesus." I exhaled out a groan, tucking a strand of his blond hair behind his ear in an awkward motherly gesture that felt very inappropriate considering my thoughts were anything but.

"Gabriel," he whispered back, a grin spreading across his face. "Just Gabriel. Now tell me whatcha want, darlin'."

I ducked my head, my face warming. A list of dirty pleasures rose in my mind, not that I would share them with the man in front of me. In the past twenty years, I hadn't shared my desires with the man I married, the man I trusted. I certainly wouldn't share them with a stranger.

A stranger. Jesus fucking Christ. Was I really considering having sex with a stranger?

It's nothing personal.

"Revenge, Gabriel." I stared up into his handsome face, my embarrassment changing to anger as my husband's words filtered through my head. "I've been faithful for twenty years, and for what?"

He nodded his head, a crooked smirk pulling at his lips. "My granny always said there ain't nothin' like a nice glass of justice and a thick slice of revenge to put everythin' right."

"I like the way your granny thinks."

Ignoring the faint scent pool chemicals, and the voice screaming in my head this was a really bad idea, I bridged the minuscule distance between us and brushed my lips against his.

His arms tightened around my back, pulling me against him. Hard. His strong muscles tensed. I felt every one as my body melted against the contours of his impossibly solid frame.

His lips crashed down on mine, and then his tongue breached the seam of my lips. He closed his fist around my hair and held me against his hungry mouth. Tipping my head and changing the angle of our kiss, he plunged his tongue deeper into my mouth, stealing my breath.

Heat pooled between my thighs and I wrapped my leg around his waist to get closer. To feel the thick ridge of him where I needed him. I could easily come this way, but I wanted more. I wanted all of him.

"Goddamn," he growled, his mouth closing over my bikini-clad breast.

His teeth scraped over my nipple and I squealed, my core clenching. Derek had never been this rough, this aggressive, and there was a part of me I didn't recognize that responded to Gabriel's treatment.

He pulled away with a gasp, his darkened eyes scanning the kitchen and great room. "Where?" his voice rasped.

"What?" I asked, my brain fuzzy.

"I presume you don't want me taking you on the kitchen counter. Where'd ya like to go?"

"Oh, right." My face heated with embarrassment. I definitely needed to work on the whole sexy-divorced-woman thing. "Upstairs."

I pointed the way and he swept me into his arms. Up the stairs and to the right, the opposite direction of my bedroom. The space I'd shared with Derek for almost two decades felt wrong on some level. Forbidden. Not that any of this was acceptable.

The first guest room on the right was sufficiently neutral. Nicely decorated but no personal items. Gabriel pushed open the door. The sage green was supposed to be calming, or so I recalled the designer saying. It wasn't working. I trembled, my brain warning me of my reckless decision.

Gabriel gently stood me on the plush carpet. I pulled him down, fitting his hungry mouth to mine, ignoring the doubts screaming in my head, shoving my uncertainty out in the hall, and then slamming the heavy bedroom door with my hip for good measure. This was happening and I looked forward to seeing the expression on Derek's face when I confessed my sins.

Someday.

CHAPTER
FOUR

I paced across the great room—well, not quite paced. More like limped. My foot throbbed like a son of a bitch, but sitting still was out of the question. The backyard was empty, but every time I let my eyes wander toward the pool, a cold shiver ran down my spine.

What the hell had I been thinking?

Just like this morning, I had lingered upstairs. Watching and waiting for Gabriel's van to pull out of the driveway.

He finally left a little over a half hour ago, and then I jumped into the shower. Scrubbed every inch of my body twice and then slipped into one of Brooke's tops and a pair of her New Religion jeans. Threw the guest room sheets into the wash on the hottest cycle. I would burn Brooke's bikini at some point.

I opened the fridge and then closed it almost immediately. Mark would be home any minute, and the thought of making dinner was almost unbearable. Better thought, crawling into bed for a month or six seemed reasonable. As Brooke repeated on our weekly phone calls, *Adulting is hard*.

She had no idea.

I poured another glass of wine from the almost empty bottle I salvaged from the patio, then set it down untouched. Flashbacks of the wine glass shattering, and everything after, turned my stomach sour. Maybe I'd switch to scotch or gin or beer. I was never a big fan of wine to begin with.

The door slammed behind me and made me jump. I winced, putting more pressure on my left foot than intended as I turned.

Mark's crystal-blue eyes widened. "Jesus, Mom. Your hair. Dad's gonna freak. And are those Brooke's clothes?"

Laughter bubbled up in my chest, breaking out and expanding into gut-busting hysterics. A tear rolled down my cheek, but I brushed it away. The stress of the last twenty-four hours was getting to me. They'd be carting me away soon.

"You okay, Mom?" Mark's brow creased with concern. I limped toward him, and his eyes widened in alarm. "Geez, Mom, what happened?"

"Stupid accident," I said, waving it off and pulling myself together with effort. "Come sit down. Tell me about your day."

"It was okay," he replied in his standard forthcoming teenage-boy way. Details had to be dragged out of him. "Better than yours, I guess."

He had no idea, and he never would.

"I'm starved. What's for dinner?"

I slid the pizza menu across the counter and Mark's frown deepened.

"On a Thursday?"

I lifted a shoulder, smiled, and gave him my best James Cagney impersonation. "It's just you and me, kid. Rules are for losers."

He narrowed his eyes at me while pulling his phone out of his pocket. "Who are you and what did you do with my mom?"

I pasted on a contorted grin. "Alien abduction."

"You still like anchovies?"

Another laugh burst out of me, but this one was cathartic. "Always."

He groaned and then grabbed the menu to order. My love of fish on pizza had been a long-standing joke in the family. Good-natured for the most part, except for the one time when Derek had been coming down with the stomach flu and blamed his nausea on the scent of my pizza. He'd been a bit of an ass that night, but then he was always unbearable when he was sick.

Now he's someone else's unbearable.

"Twenty to thirty minutes," Mark said, pulling me out of my thoughts.

I took a deep breath and set my hand on his shoulder. Closed my eyes and sighed. No time like the present. *Gather your courage and jump in.* "We need to talk."

"What's up?"

I shot a glance toward the great room, but no. The memory of the previous night still lingered in the air. Instead I gestured for him to take a seat at the island. *Better get this over with.* As soon as I finished telling him about his father's decision, Mark shot up out his seat.

"Seriously?" he asked, his fair skin turning ruddy. Behind him, the heavy wrought iron stool tipped precariously. "No way!"

I gave him a half-hearted shrug, my own emotions overwhelming me to the point of speechlessness. My lower lip trembled and I swallowed the lump forming in my throat with difficulty. Mark marched over, hugging me hard. Tears spilled over, running down my cheeks. Again. I wasn't much of a crier, but today seemed to be my day.

"We'll survive this, honey." I breathed out a steadying breath. "I'm not a quitter."

"I know Mom." He pulled back, shaking his head. "Hell with Dad. Who needs him."

"Mark..." I cupped his cheek and gave him a sympathetic look. "He's still your father. This is between him and me. He still loves you and Brooke."

"Right." He rolled his eyes. The intercom rang, interrupting our discussion.

I stumbled to stand, wiping the tears from my face. "Pizza's here."

"I got it." Mark walked across the room and pressed the intercom button.

"Rossi's pizza delivery," the driver's voice came across the speaker.

"Yep, come on in." Mark hit the button to open the gate. He grabbed my purse off the counter and brought it to me.

"Thanks." I pulled out cash for the tip and handed it to my son.

"No problem, gimpy Mom. Just don't do any more damage while I'm gone. You're all I got." He kissed the top of my head and then headed toward the front door while I wiped away more tears.

When did my kid become so sweet? Okay, it totally helped my bruised heart that he was on my side. Not that this was a contest. Not at all. But if it was, so far I was winning.

I grabbed plates, glasses, and silverware and headed for the patio. The night still held some of the day's warmth. It felt like early August, not September. I glanced at the spot where I had dropped my wine glass earlier. No evidence remained, not one tiny shard of glass sparkled in the bright patio lights, no drops of blood trailing to the doors. Guilt sat on my chest for a moment. Gabriel had cleaned everything away, as good as his word. He was probably a good man, but I just couldn't. Not with him. Probably not with anyone. Not for a long time.

Mark fell on his pizza as if it were his last meal. My son always ate like he was in the middle of a growth spurt, not that he needed to do much more growing at six-three. Wasn't it just yesterday he lay on the great-room floor playing with his Matchbox cars?

Hard to believe just six months ago he'd shot past his father's height, and a few months later he had his own driver's license and his own car. In less than two years he would be off to college, like his sister.

"What'd Brooke say?" he asked, as if reading my mind.

"I haven't told her." I set down my pizza, my flimsy appetite disappearing for good. "She's got enough pressure with school. I hate this." I let out a heavy exhale. "Maybe I should go out there. This isn't something to spring over a phone call."

"Show up in her clothes. That's sure to make things interesting." Mark pointed at me with his pizza. His lips twisted into a scowl. "She's Daddy's girl. Probably take his side."

"Too bad Daddy's too much of a coward to tell her," I said with more vitriol than intended. Mark set down his pizza, fire in his eyes. "Oh shit. I should not have said that."

"Asshole," Mark muttered.

I lowered my head, pulling my hair until it stung my scalp. "My intention is not for you to hate your father. You shouldn't feel you need to choose sides. This isn't a game with winners and losers. Somehow something just went wrong between us. The last few months have been stressful for me. Maybe I was so busy getting your sister off to college, I just didn't see the warning signs. Nothing should change between your father and you."

"Fuck that!" He exploded off his chair. The metal legs screeched back on the stone patio in protest as he shot to his feet. "Everything's changing. Don't deny it. What values did you always teach us? Trust, honoring our promises, our word is everything. Is Dad doing that? Fucking hypocrite. What would his voters think?"

Mark stomped away. At the doorway he stopped and turned. "I love you, Mom. But don't tell me Dad isn't the bad guy here. I'm smarter than that. Unless you want me to agree with his morals, let me hate what he's doing right now."

LATE THAT NIGHT I stared at the ceiling, an iron band wrapped around my chest. Every breath took effort. Sleep far from my turbulent mind, Mark's words haunted me. My morals didn't look too good right now either. Would Mark take my side if he knew about my afternoon with Gabriel?

What was I thinking? Sleeping with my pool guy hadn't taken away the pain and anger of Derek's betrayal. If anything, this afternoon added to my troubles. How would I look at Gabriel every Thursday? Would he be expecting more from me now? That wasn't possible, but what if today jeopardized our work relationship?

Jesus, what a mess. All because of Derek. After twenty years, why did he decide he had enough?

Every time I sifted through the past looking for an answer, I came up empty. I'd been a good wife, deferring to his decisions, never arguing even when I thought I was right. And we had so many good times—or I thought so.

Derek had been everything to me from the start. My first, my one and only. My mother's old-fashioned values had been drilled into me from the moment I reached puberty. *Save yourself for the one.* A handful of years later, I'd met the dashing Derek Robinson at a party thrown by one of my parents' friends. I was starting my sophomore year at Illinois Wesleyan, and he had been in his final year at UC. I'd been impressed by his maturity, swept off my feet by his classic good looks and polished charm. I knew instantly he was the one.

For the second night in a row, I tortured myself into a sobbing mess as the darkness turned to twilight and then dawn.

Pictures flashed through my mind. Memories of Derek's face when the kids were born. His happiness and pride. Christmas mornings, birthdays, they all came back to haunt me. When did he stop loving me? When did I stop being enough?

What happened? We were a team. The golden couple— everyone called us—at our Drake hotel wedding that had cost my parents a fortune. Not that my parents couldn't afford it.

My stomach soured at the thought of my mother's reaction. I could almost hear her now, accusing me of not being supportive enough, sympathetic enough, *available* enough. *Men have needs...*

I'd been plenty available. It wasn't me who'd shunned sex for the last... Shit, how long had it been?

CHAPTER
FIVE

The weight of exhaustion anchored me in bed long after the gentle chimes of my phone's alarm told me it was time to get up. At least the scent of Derek was gone with freshly laundered sheets. I had to look at the positives in my life. If I got up, maybe I could spot some.

My new reality wasn't pretty, but avoidance was futile. No time for a pity party; life moved forward with or without me. I showered and dressed quickly, prepared to battle my way through another day.

"Sorry about last night, Mom." Downstairs, Mark looked up from his cereal. "The swearing, you know. Just... sorry."

"I understand. Did a lot of swearing myself Wednesday night. Let's just do better." I gave him a crooked smile—the best I could manage—and set my coffee down next to him. "That means focusing on your grades, not your parents' troubles. I got that covered. Deal?"

"Deal. Just don't ask me to vote for him in the next election." He gave me a wicked grin that reminded me too much of his father in his younger days.

Less than two years from now my son would be eighteen and free to make his own choices. Hopefully better ones than I was making at the moment.

I shoved that thought aside and sent him a matching grin. "Maybe I'll join you."

"Maybe you should run." He stood up and gave me a hug. "Got to go."

"Don't say anything about this at school." I winced at the thought of all his friends' parents' reactions and was tempted to head back to bed. "At least not until I talk to Brooke."

"Seriously?" He tipped his head and leveled me with a piercing stare. "Last thing I'm talking about with my friends is Dad screwing around. But when it gets out, you'll be a sure thing with the sympathy vote."

I raised my eyebrows. There was so much wrong with Mark's comment I didn't know where to start. "I never said he was screwing around, Mark."

He gave me a skeptical look that matched my gut feeling.

"Right," he said, walking away. "Senator Mom."

"Oh, I'm meeting Aunt Cyn tonight. I may be late. And Mark?" He paused at the mudroom door and turned back. "I'm not sure we'll be able to afford to keep Rosa. Can you maybe take care of your bowl?"

His smile deflated. Rosa had been with us for over a decade. We would all miss her.

"'Kay, Mom." He nodded and then put his bowl in the dishwasher, landing a kiss on my cheek as he passed me on the way out.

Back in my bedroom, I started a to-do list in my head.

All my frumpy clothes were headed to the donation center. Except my suits. They'd go to the tailor. Their boxy cut would need an update if I was going to work beside Cynthia and her cutting-edge style.

I loaded up the back of my Cayenne. At least it was paid off and in my name. I flashed back to Christmas four years ago when it sat in the driveway, big red bow on top. To say I'd been shocked would have been an understatement. Derek was a firm supporter of American cars.

I quickly slapped that memory away. Several months ago Derek suggested trading it in, getting me something new. I argued that Mark needed a car first. I could wait. A car payment was one less worry now. *Had he been unhappy then?* Would he have been planning a divorce and offering to buy me a car at the same time? *Guilt car,* a small voice supplied. Was that even a thing?

I spent the rest of the afternoon moving half of Brooke's closet over to mine. Derek's empty half slowly disappeared, filling up with bright colors and trendy styles. I'd reimburse my daughter later. Or maybe Derek could. Either way no more beige for me.

I WALKED INTO MAYBES, the bar in River North where Cynthia had suggested we meet the previous day. It was small, dimly lit, filled to the brim with a twenty-something after-work crowd. Loud with conversation and some popular music I vaguely recognized from one of my kids' playlists.

Customers milled around a rustic maple bar that stretched along one brick-clad wall. More people filled the plush, chocolate leather and wood booths along the other wall—this one covered in thickly textured plaster colored an aged-barn red.

I paused, the feeling of being completely out of my element urging me to turn around. Get the hell out of there before I made a fool of myself among those young and hip patrons. What was Cynthia thinking?

People turned to stare from the middle of the long, high table, lit by some industrial fixture consisting of rusty pipes and Edison bulbs, spanning the full length of the room—or maybe it was my self-consciousness that made me feel as if I was the center of attention.

Did they even use the word hip anymore? God, I felt old.

I hung my trusty Burberry coat over my arm and, with my free hand, smoothed down the warm cable-knit dress I'd borrowed from Brooke's closet. The soft, fuchsia fabric might have hugged my waist a tad bit more than my daughter's, and I was definitely flashing way more cleavage than Brooke had. The dress was fun and a bit sexy—definitely what I needed on my first night out as a sort of single woman.

Glancing down, I gave my low-heeled black equestrian boots a disappointed frown.

Back home I had barely taken one step in my brand new stilettos before my injured foot told me the four-inch heels would be out of the question. Only my most comfortable footwear allowed me to make this trip downtown tonight. They weren't quite as casual as my pair of Uggs, but I definitely wouldn't be winning any fashion awards. At least I wasn't limping. Not much, anyway. And in this dark and crowded bar, would anyone be checking out my footwear?

And crowded, it was. I skirted around a waitress who was busy passing out her tray of drinks to the table, and continued deeper into the space. The bar was larger than it first appeared. Long and narrow, with additional tables and booths tucked away in a jog behind the L-shaped bar. Cynthia was nowhere to be seen. I doubled back and then slipped onto the last open stool at the corner of the bar, tugging down the short skirt in an attempt at modesty. How did my daughter wear this dress, for God's sakes?

I set my purse down on what appeared to be a clean section of the bar and then pulled out my phone.

I'm here. Where are you? I texted Cynthia.

A minute later her reply appeared. *Running late. Be there shortly.*

I caught the bartender's eye for a second as he rushed past me and stopped to drop off a drink a few patrons down. Then he grabbed a bottle off the shelf behind him and poured shots for the waitress, laughing at something she said before she walked away. Then he headed down to the other end of the bar. I sighed. A drink would be nice, but it looked like I would have to be patient.

I glanced back at my phone. *Come on, Cyn.*

A man slipped in at the end of the bar next to me and waved his hand at the bartender. It seemed to do the trick. The bartender rushed over as if the man held up a hundred-dollar tip. I breathed out a frustrated sigh. So much for patience.

"Craigellachie with a splash of soda," the man ordered.

I smiled to myself, my frustration forgotten for the moment. His order of scotch reminded me of the charming Senator Mitchell. Jack Mitchell was as obsessed about scotch as Derek was wine. We always had a bottle of something expensive on hand for Jack. The bottle would be wasted now. It was unlikely he would ever visit again.

The man placed his hand on my shoulder and I flinched, tipping my head back to meet his eyes with an annoyed stare. He was tall, or maybe it was my perspective from my spot on the stool. And good-looking. Not that it mattered. "Excuse me?"

"You look thirsty. What would you like?" He bent slightly closer to my level, sending a wave of bergamot and other exotic spices in my direction.

I shifted my focus on the bartender, who was now giving me his full attention. "Um, rum and coke, please."

"Privateer and coke," the man amended, generously upgrading me to top shelf, then handing his credit card over to the bartender and instructing him to set up a tab.

He leaned casually against the bar, facing me. "My name's Trent, by the way. What's yours?"

I returned his small, polite smile with a stiff one of my own. I'd had enough of men to last a while, even generous ones who smelled good. "Thank you very much, Trent. I really should buy my own drink. I'm meeting a friend in a few minutes."

"Wow, that's the longest name I've ever heard. What does this friend call you for short? And is this friend male or female?" His forest-green eyes sparkled and his smile widened, revealing deep dimples accenting his cheeks.

When did I become a magnet for men in their twenties? Trent couldn't be over thirty. His dark, slightly wavy hair shone in the bar lights with no sign of thinning or gray. No creases around his eyes or laugh lines bracketing his mouth. His razor-sharp jaw showed no hints of softening, either. He was in the prime of his life. Why he was talking to me when there was a bar full of women his age was a mystery.

"Nicki." I rolled my eyes. "And my friend is a woman."

"Well, *Nicki, I really should buy my own drink,* I'm meeting my brothers. Who should be here…" He glanced at his watch and then shook his head. "Whenever the traffic gods decide, I suppose. So, I probably have time. But even if I only have the next thirty seconds with you, I want to buy you this drink."

"Fine, but I'm a bit old for you."

"Why are you trying to chase me away?" He let his gaze drift over me, making my skin heat and my dress suddenly seem way too small. "I highly doubt you're older than me."

I clutched my phone like a talisman, silently begging Cynthia to arrive and save me. This place was a meat market and I was chum in the water. And yes, I was mixing my idioms, but I was twenty-some years out of practice at this sort of social encounter. And as my kids liked to point out, I wouldn't know cool if I googled it.

Chances were I was about to embarrass myself again. Only this time it would be in the middle of a packed bar instead of my backyard.

Trent's easy charm unnerved me, and his penetrating stare sent a flurry of unwanted sensations through my veins. I fidgeted with the band of my watch. Then slid my right hand over my left, covering the deep groove left on my ring finger where my wedding rings sat until yesterday morning.

Trent leaned closer and smiled his easy, dimple-generating smile.

"And if you are older, how can you be sure that wouldn't be a turn-on?"

Holy shit.

I gave him a wide-eyed look of shock and he chuckled while my heart stuttered. My skin bloomed with perspiration that had nothing to do with early menopause.

A stool opened on the other side of my corner spot and Trent sat down, giving me much-needed breathing room.

The bartender returned, setting our drinks down. I concentrated on stirring mine to give myself a moment to collect my thoughts.

Was this how the dating scene went? Confident men with bold pickup lines? If so, I would probably have a heart attack before I turned forty-four. I'd never see my kids married. Never be a grandmother. All thanks to Derek.

"What are you... twenty-eight, twenty-nine?" I asked, staring into the icy darkness of my glass.

He laughed, placing his arms on the bar and leaning toward me. "Ha! I'm thirty-seven, *ma'am*. And I'll have you know I'm a great-uncle."

He whipped out his phone and pulled up a picture of a sweet baby girl with short ringlets of glossy brown hair hugging her head. Her blue eyes stared back at me with an intensity that made me wish for a time machine. I would have given anything at this moment for my past filled with a loving husband and babies to care for, instead of the mess in front of me.

"She's very pretty. Great-uncle you say?"

"Yep. My sister's a grandma. I'm never letting her live it down." He grinned with an evil glint hinting at good-natured sibling rivalry.

"I bet." I couldn't help but return his smile. Not over his sister's situation. She was probably my age. If Brooke or Mark—no. I couldn't even consider the possibility. My divorce was enough drama.

"Life's unpredictable that way, though."

I lifted my glass to my lips and smiled. "You have no idea."

His gaze drifted to my left hand and he nodded. "Not all change is bad. Sometimes it's an opportunity. A door to a new adventure."

Once again his eyes locked onto mine with an intensity that had my heart hammering against my breastbone. He looked down at his drink for a second, then returned his focus to me.

"You ever been to the Grenadines?" he asked, his voice lowered.

I raised my eyebrows, curious about where this was going. Clearly he had another smooth pickup line rehearsed. "Can't say I have."

"Beautiful little chain of volcanic islands just north-northeast of Venezuela. Brilliant blue skies, mountains, white sand beaches. Paradise." He traced his long finger through the moisture on the bar as if drawing a map, and my eyes followed, transfixed. "There was this one tiny island, barely a beach and a couple of palm trees. Too small to be marked on the charts. It was like something out of a cartoon. I think the waters around it were the same color as your eyes." He paused, his nicely manicured fingernail poised over the spot as he pierced me with his stare. "But I'd obviously have to take you there to be sure."

My mouth dropped open. As pickup lines went, that one had to win awards. A little over the top, but wow. If I were younger and a little more gullible, he'd be reeling me in right now.

Before I could come up with a response, my stool spun around. Cynthia's dark pixie-cut hair flashed in front of me, then a hug squeezed the life out of me. Cynthia Jacobs, just in time.

"Holy fuck, Nicki!" Cynthia screamed, alerting the entire bar of her presence. She pulled me off my stool, spinning me like a mad ballerina. I shoved my skirt down as it twirled dangerously high on my thighs.

"You look fabulous. You should have gotten divorced a long time ago."

My face burned as Trent watched with rapt attention, along with half of the patrons in our vicinity.

"Doesn't she look fabulous?" Cynthia asked, noticing Trent's obvious interest.

"The most beautiful woman in the place," Trent answered, unfolding himself from his stool and offering Cynthia his seat.

He was damn tall. My mouth dropped open again as I took in his full height from my standing perspective. Derek's six feet put me a hair below eye level, but with Trent I was more around the knot of his tie. A very nice tie. Brilliant red with a subtle tone-on-tone stripe that stood out against his crisp white shirt and charcoal suit.

Calculating from my viewpoint, he had to be at least six-four.

"What can I get you to drink?" Trent asked Cynthia.

"Ooh, you found a *gentleman*." Cynthia pressed her elbow into my ribs, her eyes raking over the man who stood opposite me. "I'll have a dirty *gin* martini, shaken, with three olives, thank you."

Trent turned to flag the bartender down. Cynthia's eyes danced. Our nonverbal conversation headed past R-rated as she gestured toward Trent shamelessly.

"So... girls night out?" Trent turned back, grinning as he glanced between us.

I made formal introductions and then took a desperate gulp of my drink, doing my best to ignore Cynthia's roving eyes. Trent didn't seem to mind. Probably used to women cataloging his assets. Before long he and Cynthia were chatting about city politics and sports as if they were old friends.

Cynthia waved a hand and scoffed. "The Bears are a lost cause and the Bulls will never be what they were a handful of years ago."

Trent's eyes narrowed with the fervor of a die-hard fan. "You're probably right on the Bears, but Williams has serious talent for a rookie. Along with Samuel, Gage, and Fredricks, they're going to take us all the way this year. Mark my words."

He turned and winked at me. Cynthia disputed his comment with stats and comparisons. I was going to have to pull these two apart shortly.

Trent turned as a man slapped him on the shoulder. Then the two did that handshake, arm slap, hug thing men did with those they were close. One of the brothers, I assumed.

"Ladies, this is my brother, Troy."

Troy stood a few inches shorter; his hair was a fraction of a shade lighter. His few laugh lines didn't detract from his looks in the least. When Troy smiled, only one dimple stood out on his left cheek.

Trent's brother shook his head, and gave his sibling a long stare. "Two beautiful women? How do you do it? Wait, I don't want to know."

"We've been arguing about sports." Cynthia laughed. "He's a real charmer, this one."

Troy scoffed at his brother and then turned back to Cynthia. "I apologize for this ones social skills."

Trent made a similar noise of derision. "My social skills are fine, thank you very much."

"Are they?" Troy glanced at Cynthia for what I assumed was conformation of the fact.

"I don't think I'm the target of his charms tonight." She gave me a significant look, making my face warm.

I hadn't blushed in probably a decade, but I was obviously making up for it tonight.

Trent leaned toward me. "You sure I can't tempt you away for a quiet dinner with absolutely no abuse from these two."

"Just wait until TJ shows up," Troy said with a chuckle.

"TJ?" Cynthia asked, raising a curious eyebrow.

"Oldest brother. Makes my teasing look like amateur hour," Troy informed while patting his younger brother on the back in what might have been a comforting gesture.

Cynthia twisted her lips, her gaze shifting between the two men. "Somehow I think you two give as good as you get when it comes to teasing."

Trent and Troy sent each other matching grins.

God, they were both adorable in a mischievous sort of way. Their mother probably had her hands full with them growing up.

Cynthia glanced at her watch before pulling me from my stool. "Well, as much as we'd like to meet this *infamous* TJ, sorry boys, us girls have reservations. Steaks don't eat themselves."

I stumbled as I stood, wincing as my full weight landed on my injured foot, sending a bolt of pain up my leg.

Trent slipped an arm around my waist, steadying me. "Careful, beautiful."

"Thanks," I muttered, shoving the memory of another man's arms around me just a day ago out of my mind. Gabriel and Trent were nothing alike. Gabriel's weightlifter build and golden-boy looks didn't hold a candle to Trent's tall, lean frame and dark handsome features. I'd had enough of blonds to last me a lifetime.

Not that it mattered. After yesterday, I had no interest in any man.

"How old *are* you?" he whispered, raising a dark slashing eyebrow.

I shook my head slowly. "Old enough to know better." *This time.*

"I like that about you. Your answers always leave me wanting more." He slipped his card in my hand. "Call me, *Nicki, I really should buy my own drink.*"

CHAPTER
SIX

Cynthia shot me a frown. "Why are you limping?" I rolled my eyes, tucking my hands deeper into the pockets of my wool coat as we stepped out of the bar. The night had turned decidedly cooler with an icy breeze blowing off Lake Michigan a few blocks away.

"Long story."

She snorted, slipping an arm around my waist in an attempt to support me. Which probably looked ridiculous. I had a good six inches on Cynthia. But she had twice my stamina on a good day. Today she had me beat by at least several double espressos' worth of energy.

"We've got all night, you cougar bitch. First night out as a single woman was a definite success. Way to go!" She laughed, pulling me along the sidewalk at a sedate pace. I had no idea where we were going, but the sharp pain in the bottom of my foot warned a long stroll through downtown wouldn't be fun.

"Trent was hot. More than hot. I saw him slip you his card. You definitely need to call him."

"No way, Cyn. The last thing Derek said before he left

was to keep this quiet." I had shoved Trent's card to the bottom of my purse without even a glance. The thing was doomed to mingle with all the other bits of my disorganized life. The next time I pulled out that small bit of card stock it would likely be covered in lint, sticky candy wrappers, and exploded pen ink. "I'm pretty sure picking up strange men in bars doesn't fall under *keep this quiet*."

"Seriously? You're letting the guy who left you for another woman make all the rules?" Her glare said I was out of my mind. "You need to find yourself a fuck buddy. Trent would make a great fuck buddy."

I was about to suggest we get a cab when she veered across the sidewalk toward Black's, cutting in front of several people in the process.

"I need a lawyer, not a fuck buddy, as you so elegantly put it. I want Derek to pay, and I want it to hurt. I don't want to do anything more to mess this up."

I bit my lip and flashed a quick glance toward my friend in hopes she didn't catch that slip. No such luck. Her eyes narrowed and she practically screeched to a stop in her four-inch heels, her dark brows drawn down in a frown.

"Anything more? What have you done so far?"

I let out a slow exhale, my shoulders slumping. I gave the confused doorman an apologetic smile and pulled Cynthia forward toward the open door.

"My pool guy. God, Cyn. I don't even want to talk about it," I whispered.

Cynthia screamed, doubling over with laughter. I covered my face with my hand and shushed her. Not that it did any good.

"Your pool guy? You didn't," she whispered back while giggling. "Is this why you're *limping*? Oh God, I need details. You have to tell me fucking everything."

"Shut up." I ignored the doorman's smirk and lowered my voice even more. Not that the man hadn't seen and probably heard way worse in this spot. "It was a complete disaster. I'm not cut out for this single life. One day and I fucked everything up."

She patted me on the back and grinned. Then sobered up and headed toward the hostess desk. Black's was all hushed elegance. Crystal chandeliers and mahogany-paneled walls. Fine china set on linen tablecloths. The complete opposite of the bar we'd just left.

The hostess seated us at one of the plush high-backed booths that offered the illusion of privacy and then took our drinks order.

Cynthia's eyes danced with curiosity, and as soon as the woman left she pounced.

"Describe. Name, age, distinguishing features. Performance on a one-to-ten scale. Although your limp tells me it wasn't a complete disaster." She counted off her fingers, then pointed at me. "This is your interview. Make it good."

"So unfair. I hate you, Cyn." I groaned and gave her a brief outline of the previous day in all its unattractive glory. "It *was* a complete disaster. As soon as we were naked I lost all motivation."

"So it was like sex with your husband." She gave a dramatic shiver and then grinned. "Poor Nicki."

"Ha, ha. Funny. No, it was really bad. Gabriel was all eager to please in this sort of aggressive-frat-boy style that I kinda liked for about a minute, but... then I was all... shit—" Cynthia cackled and I tossed my napkin at her. "Not funny. I had to fake it. I wanted to cry, but it probably would have put him in therapy for life."

She bit her lips together and struggled to hold in her

laughter as our waiter dropped off our drinks and read us the specials.

"Okay," she said as soon as the waiter left. "First of all, revenge sex needs to be done in the heat of the moment. You don't wait until you've had time to simmer down. If Gabriel had shown up right after Derek left the other night..." She snapped her fingers. "...no problem."

I drummed my fingers on the table while Cynthia sipped her drink, her eyes crinkling with humor. I took a long swig of my rum and coke and sat back. I was pretty sure she hadn't finished blessing me with her nuggets of wisdom just yet.

"But really, you picked the wrong guy." She pointed at me with her swizzle stick loaded with olives. "The pool boy, really?"

"Pool *guy*," I corrected, wincing at the word boy. My son was a boy. "He's twenty-eight."

She tipped her head to the side, a skeptical look on her face. "Twenty-eight is a boy at our age." I opened my mouth to remind her of the five years she had on me, but she waved me off. "Whatever. He was hot. And maybe you've been subconsciously craving the *man* for years. But you were drunk."

I rolled my eyes. "Don't remind me."

"I'm being serious here. You polished off an entire bottle wine for fuck's sake. A gentleman would have patched you up, tucked you in on the sofa, and then suggested a raincheck when you were able to make a fuck-ing. Sober. Decision." She punctuated the last three words with a stab of her finger against the table, her jaw stiff with what I assumed was anger.

"You make it sound like he took advantage of me. You're forgetting I seduced him." I wince at the volume of my voice, but a quick glance around the restaurant told me no one was paying attention.

Cynthia lowered her voice. "You didn't even get a decent orgasm. Not only is your pool boy an asshole, he's a selfish one. Unlike Trent."

I laughed. "Fifteen minutes of conversation with the guy told you that?"

"More like twenty minutes. In that time he offered me his seat, bought me a drink—top shelf, mind you—and even though most of the conversation was between him and me, he couldn't keep his eyes off you. Any idiot could see I was the easier score, but Trent wasn't interested in just scoring."

"I'm not used to that kind of attention, Cyn. The way he looked at me, all dark and... and intense." My skin flamed and my stomach dropped just thinking about the way his forest green eyes penetrated mine.

Cynthia chuckled. "Like he wanted to spread you on the bar and make a banquet out of you? Get used to it."

"Cynthia!" I pressed my finger against my lips. The quiet din of the restaurant, soft music, clinking of silverware, and hushed conversations seemed inadequate to mask my friend's exuberant comments.

"I speak only the truth." She shrugged off my reprimand but at least had the decency to lower her voice. "He would be the revenge you're looking for. Hot as sin and rich. Derek would shit if he saw you with Trent."

"Just because he orders top shelf doesn't make him rich."

"You really have been out of it, Nicki Robinson. His cologne was Clive Christian, his watch was an Omega—expensive, but not flashy—and his suit? That thing didn't come off the rack at Manny's Big and Tall. Gerard's on

Diversey if I'm not mistaken. He does this interesting little stitching detail on the lapel, subtle but distinctive. His suits cost a king's ransom, but worth every penny."

"If you say so," I said, sipping my drink that was a pale comparison to the one at Maybes. Trent's choice in liquor was impeccable. "Just stop calling me that name and I'll agree to anything."

She hummed a few bars from that Simon and Garfunkel song. "Robinson? Are you *tired* of being Mrs. Robinson?"

"If I had a dollar, Cyn, for every Mrs. Robinson joke." I shook my head slowly. "I know the divorce is a long way off, but from this moment on I will only answer to Nicki Adams."

"Fine, Nicki Adams. I promise no Dustin Hoffman jokes if you call that man."

"You promised me a good lawyer," I said, desperate to switch to a tamer subject.

Our waiter interrupted to take our order. Cynthia ordered a New York strip, rare, and I ordered the Dover sole. My friend gave me a look of disappointment and then changed my order to match hers.

"Trust me." As the waiter left, she pulled a card from her purse and slid it across the table. "Best divorce lawyer in the country," she said with a suggestive wink. Cynthia had never been married. Driven and independent, she'd had a string of lovers. All wealthy, with an appreciation for Italian loafers, bespoke suits, and beautiful, independent women not interested in commitment. "Randall Harris. Don't sleep with him unless you want to be tied up and… well, just don't sleep with him."

"Did you?"

She lifted one shoulder in a casual shrug. "I was curious."

She went on, supplying me with more information on Randall Harris than I probably needed to know. Would I be able to look him in the eye? Possibly not.

Cynthia patted my hand like a knowledgeable grandmother. "My dear, you've lived a sheltered life with your missionary man. It's time you learned what you've been missing. Trent will open up a whole new world for you." She gripped my hand harder when my eyes widened in alarm. I opened my mouth to argue with her. "Not that world. Trent isn't Randall. I promise you that."

"How do you know?" I asked just as the waiter set down plates of rare steak and the usual sides.

She gave me a steady stare that suggested it was better if I hadn't asked. "One just knows. Now eat. Your *boss* is hungry."

We discussed the status of Cynthia's life and the future of mine over dinner. Over the past decade we had caught up like this a few times a year. With her work schedule, and mine with the kids, it was hard to see more of each other.

Derek always hated those nights I ran off with my best friend. Said she was a bad influence on me. He had never hid his feelings about Cynthia. *She has too much money and not enough morals.* Yet her morals were just fine when he needed money to finance his next campaign.

Listening to her fill me in on city gossip, I couldn't help but grin. I looked forward to us working together again. Being around Cynthia was a bit like orbiting the sun. Warm and brilliant, she tended to throw off flaming bits to keep you on your toes. Life would never be dull.

"You know, with that haircut, the makeup, the clothes, you look at least ten years younger. No wonder Trent couldn't keep his eyes off of you," Cynthia said while peeking over the dessert menu. "I wish I could be there the first time Derek sees you. He's going to swallow his teeth."

"I'm overwhelmed, Cyn." I set down my own menu, no longer in the mood for dessert. "I go to bed and my mind just starts spinning with questions."

"Don't worry. Randall will take care of you. He's brilliant and ruthless when necessary. In the meantime. I will keep you busy. Pretty soon you will make so much money, you will buy and sell the Derek Robinsons of this world." She sat back, relaxed, sipping her coffee. Black. No messing around with sweetness, she once told me.

I added cream and sugar to mine. "I don't know. He's not the same man I married. The other night... he was cold. He threatened me not to make a mess. And if he finds out you helped me? There could be consequences."

"He messes with me, it will be the *sorriest* day of his life. He would do well to remember those donors whose wallets he relies on are also my clients. I'd like to think I make them happier than he does." She waved off the threat with her hand. "How are the kids taking this?"

"Mark is angry. And I don't know how to tell Brooke. What if she blames me? She was always closer to Derek."

She let out a frustrated noise. "I don't know. He doesn't deserve either of them. You just have to tell her the truth and hope for the best. Let me know if Aunt Cynthia needs to have a heart-to-heart with her goddaughter. We bitches have to stick together."

"You haven't changed, have you?"

"No. Men haven't, why should I? Use them for their dicks. It's the only thing they're good for." She smiled, a wicked gleam in her eye. "You need to remember that. Stop freaking out about the Gabriels and Trents of this world and enjoy them."

CHAPTER
SEVEN

"Morning, Nicki," Ava Marquardt chirped before sitting down next to me on the cold metal bleachers.

Friday night's chilly temperatures lingered the following morning as I sat huddled under my wool throw waiting for Mark's soccer game to start.

"Morning," I returned, ignoring the curious looks I was getting from her and the rest of the home crowd around me.

Mark had been on one soccer team or another since he was in grade school. At first Derek had been disappointed. Soccer wasn't really the all-American sport like football or baseball. But for the past decade, Derek had done his best to attend every weekend game.

Until today.

Derek's absence felt like a big red flag to everyone in the stands. A warning that something wasn't right in the Robinson family. I could almost feel the rumors starting.

Why couldn't he have come for his son?

I turned to Ava with a friendly smile. "How's Alex doing?"

We'd known each other since Brooke and Alex's kindergarten days, volunteered for field trips and class parties together. Her youngest, Sam, was down on the field with Mark.

"He hasn't been arrested, hasn't maxed out my credit card, and Princeton hasn't kicked him out yet, so I guess good. How's Brooke?"

"She's settling in. Still accepting my calls every Saturday afternoon, so I guess she hasn't forgotten me just yet."

"Must be nice. I wish Sam would let me call him every Saturday." She let out a brittle laugh. Then her eyes shifted to the empty spot next to me. "Is Derek sick?"

I glanced to my left as if he would magically appear. No such luck. "Problem at the townhouse. Pipe leak. He had to stick around for the plumber."

Ava's face scrunched up. "That stinks. Mark must be disappointed."

I turned toward the field. My lie would only get me through this game. What if Derek didn't show up next week, or if Mark was out there telling a different story? Not that his friends noticed whether his parents were in the stands or not. But we should have gotten our stories straight, just in case.

I wasn't cut out for deception.

"Hard to say. He's so busy with his friends I don't think he even pays attention to us anymore."

She laid a hand on my shoulder. "Welcome to my world. I had to fight Alex for a hug before he left. Sam's the same way. Pretty soon it's going to be very quiet around here. You sure look good, though. I love your hair."

"Thanks. It was time for a change."

Ava's eyes lingered and an uncomfortable wave of suspicion washed over me. She'd divorced years ago, shortly after the kids had started school. Derek had been helpful at the time. Inviting her boys on his yearly camping trip with the kids and then helping her find employment with a small law firm in the area. But had he just been being friendly?

Suddenly his friendliness took on a new, darker light. All the times I found her and Derek sipping wine by the pool while the kids swam.

Ava was petite and curvy, with long dark hair and warm brown eyes. She was beautiful, but for some reason she had never remarried. Had she been waiting all this time for Derek to leave me? Was she the other woman?

My lungs constricted at the thought. She had mentioned once that her ex-husband had cheated. How could she possibly do that to another woman? And to a friend at that?

Stop.

I took a deep breath. How many kids had been invited to play in our pool? I wasn't home every day in the summer, but Derek was. He could have slept with dozens of women. And he'd given plenty of people, both men and women, job references over the years.

Before long I'd be looking at every woman with suspicion, and did it really matter?

My phone rang, breaking me out of my paranoia. The readout showed a photo of Derek from our last vacation in Hawaii. Speak of the devil.

"Hey, honey," I answered, choking on the false sweetness in my voice.

"Nicki. What the fucking hell did you do?" His voice was low and angry, not an ounce of sugar to be found.

"I'm fine, honey. Mark's game is just about to start. How's things with the plumber?"

He paused for a second and then barked out, "Fifty thousand? You charged fifty-fucking-grand on the credit cards?"

Oh, that. I couldn't help but grin. I could almost picture the steam coming out of my husband's ears, imagine the way his skin flushed face first, then spread slowly down his neck. Angry Derek was fascinating to watch as long as you weren't the target of his rage. At the moment I was grateful there were over six hundred miles separating us.

"That's great news." I gave Ava a thumbs-up and she smiled back. "Listen, they're about to start the national anthem. Why don't we talk later?"

"You bet we'll talk, Nicki. This was fucking uncalled for."

"I know. Well, sometimes things just don't go as planned. But it could be a lot worse." I could have hit the black card with no limit.

"We'll discuss this later."

"Looking forward to it. Love you," I said, somehow without gagging on the words, and hung up, my stomach churning.

Not for the first time I questioned the intelligence of my impulsive shopping spree. But once the first purchase went through and I realized Derek hadn't closed out the accounts... well, I could hardly be blamed for taking advantage of the opportunity.

Ava plucked a strand of her wavy dark hair from her lipstick and gave me a smile. "You're so lucky, Nicki. Derek's one of the good ones. You can't imagine how rare they are these days."

Unfortunately, I could.

THE EMPTINESS of the house seemed to expand with every minute. Reading held no interest, and the sound of the TV irritated. I paced around like a caged animal at the zoo, too much energy and nothing to do with it.

I stared at my phone, waiting for it to ring. *Ring dammit!*

Every frustration I had built up since Wednesday night sat inside me waiting to burst out. Derek thought he was angry about a couple of credit cards? Try leaving me to explain to our children why their father no longer wanted to be a part of this family, or how I was to figure out how to pay the upcoming mortgage with nothing in the checking account, or maybe trying to explain to all the soccer parents where Mark's father was this morning? There was also the fact I now had to scramble to support myself on a moment's notice—thank God for Cynthia. Derek didn't even know angry. But I was more than willing to show him.

Unfortunately, my phone stayed silent.

"You fucking coward." My voice echoed off the vaulted ceilings of the great room and I winced. I wasn't a yeller, but there was a lot I wasn't until recently.

I snatched Rosa's cleaning products out of the main-floor laundry and headed into the powder room off the back stairs. Since I was now the housekeeper, I wasn't the kind of person who could afford to sit around waiting for the phone to ring.

Turned out battling water spots and smudgy mirrors was a good way to burn off anger. And a clean toilet? I had just aimed my newfound skills on the second bathroom when my phone rang. Not Derek, Brooke.

Shit. The screen said it was half past seven. I had forgotten all about our call. Not that I was ready to talk to my daughter, but ready or not...

I took a deep breath and swiped to answer, taking a seat on the great-room sofa. "Sweetheart, I'm so sorry. The day just got away from me."

"I can't imagine," she clipped out, her voice full of sarcasm. Brooke lived on a schedule. I'd probably thrown her whole evening off.

"I'm sorry. After Mark's game I just got distracted."

"Distracted? By what, Mom?" The unusually sweet tone in her voice sent cold dread slithering down my spine. She knew. Somehow she knew.

"What have you heard?"

Music played in the background, drowned out for a moment by the sound of laughter.

Brooke lowered her voice, the sharp edge replaced with a raw note of disappointment. "Mark told me Dad left. That he cheated on you. Why did you tell Mark but not me?"

Shit.

My throat closed and my eyes stung. When I had warned Mark not to tell anyone I had never thought to include his sister. How was I supposed to know they even talked?

"He didn't cheat." I gritted the words out between my teeth. At least, I didn't have solid proof of that fact, nor did I want my kids entertaining that idea. "And I was going to come out. Tell you in person. It didn't seem right—"

"And when was that? Thanksgiving?" She huffed. "After the networks speculated on the cause of your split and

65

Stephen Colbert turned my parents into jokes? Was I to be the last to know?"

"No. Sooner. I've been busy—"

Wrong thing to say. I knew it as the words left my mouth. But it was too late.

Brooke growled out a strangled noise of frustration and I closed my eyes tight, cursing her father to the depths of hell.

"Well, I know now, so you can save your time and your airline miles."

"I'm sorry, but if you'd just give me a minute—" But that was unlikely. The line was already dead. She'd hung up.

I stood and tugged down the hem of my daughter's sweatshirt, then sighed. At least we hadn't been on video chat.

EIGHT

E very painful throb from my injured foot seemed like an accusation. My kids were speculating on their father's infidelity, but I was just as guilty.

After Brooke's call, I'd gone to bed and stayed there most of Sunday with one of the latest suspense novels to keep me company. My current list of romance novels waiting on my e-reader would have to wait. I was in no mood to be swept off my feet. At the moment my tastes ran more toward murder and payback and grisly justice at the hands of guys like the hero, who happened to look a lot like Trent. At least, in my mind he did.

I glanced up from my book as the train slowed in its approach to Union Station. Only fools and masochists drove downtown during rush hour. With my most comfortable pair of running shoes and softest socks doing their best to cushion my walk, I drifted with the crowd and headed out of the station and into the crisp, almost fall morning. The four blocks' walk to Cynthia's high-rise would be a piece of cake, I silently encouraged. *Easier than the rest of the day in those stilettos waiting at the bottom of your bag.*

My best friend greeted me as I walked off the elevator on the thirty-sixth floor in her usual style, squeezing the life from my lungs in a hug.

"Nicki, this is Sonya." She turned and smiled at the woman behind the glass and steel reception desk. "Sonya, this is Nicki Adams. Sonya works here part-time while she finishes law school. Maybe you can help me convince her to stay once she graduates. We could really use another good lawyer on staff."

Sonya laughed. "I'm waiting to see your best offer."

Cynthia chuckled. "Good. I've taught you well, then. Can you track down Greg and tell him we need coffee?" She turned to me. "You need coffee, right? Tell him to bring cream and sugar."

She steered me away from the reception area, her hands kneading my stiff shoulders. "Relax, this week you're just going to shadow me."

Of course her office was gorgeous. Framed in deep red molding, the floor-to-ceiling corner windows showcased the dark Chicago River as it ribboned its way between the glass and steel canyon of the city.

Cynthia sat down behind an ebony and steel desk that had to cost as much as your average car and stared at me.

"Nicki? Have you heard a word I've said?"

"Sorry. Distracted for a moment. This view... It amazes me every time I visit."

Cynthia had begun her career as an agent at Lake Realty, a small agency located in Winnetka. By the time I came on, she'd taken over as manager. Shortly after my kids started school, she opened her own office just north of downtown selling both residential and commercial properties. A decade later, here I was, staring out the window of one of the most expensive office buildings in the city.

"Get used to it. There's one just like it in your office."

I stepped away from the window. "Office?"

"Where else would I put my second-in-command?"

I opened my mouth to voice my doubts. I'd been out of the real-estate business for over a decade. Was I ready for this much responsibility? But before I could say a word, Cynthia continued, "We have a busy day today..."

She listed off her schedule. A closing first thing this morning, then a visit to a prospective listing, then a sales presentation with a real-estate investor in the afternoon. In between a million calls.

Cynthia's assistant, Greg, came in bearing a tray of coffee and a plate of biscotti. Cynthia made the introductions and then handed off a stack of documents to her assistant. I watched him leave, closing the door behind him.

"He's handsome," I commented, taking a small sip of robust coffee before added in enough cream and sugar to cut the bitterness. "Does he do more than make coffee?"

"He keeps me on schedule and corrects my grammar. And he has a husband, so if you're implying something sordid, don't." She scowled at me while biting into her cookie. "Jesus, what happened to my sweet little friend?"

I grinned over my cup, recalling her sage advice the other night about men's usefulness. "She slept with her pool boy, remember?"

Her eyes crinkled with humor. "Always the innocent ones... but we have rules here. No fucking the clients. No fucking the employees. We're here to rule the world."

I gave her a salute. "Got it, boss."

She slid a thick folder across the desk. "This is a presentation for the client I'm—we're—meeting later. Place is on Dearborn. High-rise, twenty-three floors. You need to get comfortable with everything in here. Be ready to answer questions because some of the dumb fucks we work with don't have the patience to read all this. We need to be prepared."

I nodded and gave her a confident smile I didn't quite feel. Then opened the file, and the listing price sent my blood pressure soaring. *Jesus Christ.* The rest of the numbers blurred and names blended together as Cynthia explained every document in detail.

I pulled a pad of paper from my bag and started taking notes. There was no way I'd remember everything. Tenants and vacancies. Turnovers. Rental agreements. Leasing contracts. Property managers. Maintenance costs, improvements, return on investment. Profit estimates. Unlike my previous job, the clients were investors, not families looking for a home. People who expected to make money. And so many attorneys. Everyone had an attorney. My hand cramped and my head swam. *How am I going to keep everything straight?*

My heart thudded loud in my ears. The years that stretched between my last real-estate deal and this moment seemed like a lifetime.

Cynthia steepled her fingers under her chin. "Stop panicking. You're brilliant. I have faith in you."

I exhaled a nervous laugh and closed the file. "Glad one of us does."

"You'll be fine." She pulled the file out of my hand and set it back on the desk, waving off my apprehension. "So how was your weekend?"

"Too long." I smoothed the fabric of my skirt, and then adjusted the file to line up along the edge of her desk. "Too much time to think without Derek home, which is crazy. If he'd been home…" I shook my head at the stupidity of that comment. "Brooke called. Mark beat me in breaking the divorce to her. Of course she was angry and hurt. Once she scolded me, she hung up. I tried calling back a few times, but she sent me to voicemail.

"Brooke holds grudges longer than anyone I know. Probably got it from Derek's mother." I paused, a smile tugging at my lips. "There's a positive thought. I'll never have to spend another Christmas with his family again."

"Never could figure out how Rosemary Robinson could shit with that stick up her ass." Cynthia grinned. "There's always a silver lining. You just have to look hard enough."

"Oh, and Gabriel texted last night." I grimaced. "Just a *hi, how are you*, but still. He's never texted before."

"Ignore him. With men the effort has to justify the reward. Once he realizes there's no reward in pursuing you, he'll expend his efforts on someone else." Cynthia set her cup down and reached in her drawer, pulling out a cell phone. "But just in case you decide to seduce any more of your maintenance men, I got you this. For work, but also any calls or texts you may not want Derek to know about."

Jesus. I made a mental note, while slipping my new phone into my purse, to check the next phone bill for any unusual calls on Derek's line. Not that I'd noticed on the previous bills. But then I hadn't known to look for anything a month ago.

My head swam.

"How did Derek do this? Cheating is hard. I feel guilty, and my husband already asked for a divorce. He did it when we were happily married, or so I thought."

Cynthia reached across the desk and patted my hand. "Men are wired differently. They see a gray hair and all of a sudden they need to know they still have *it*. Even at the expense of their morals, in some cases. Although, being a politician, the moral thing probably wasn't a big problem for Derek."

I collapsed back into the chair with a sigh, finding it all hard to believe.

"You need to call Randall. It's your first task this morning," Cynthia said, straightening the documents Greg had dropped off with the coffee. She opened a drawer and filed them away.

"I know. Somehow that makes this whole thing more real. Which is stupid. This is real. But maybe if I just hold still for a bit..." I shook my head slowly. "I know, I know. Call Randall Harris."

"Standing still isn't the answer." She looked at her watch and picked up her phone. "Make the call. We leave for the closing in twenty."

RANDALL HARRIS'S office sat on the converted first floor of a graystone off of Dearborn in the Gold Coast neighborhood only a few blocks from Cynthia's place.

"Relax," my friend said for probably the hundredth time of the day as I got out of her Escalade. "I promise a stiff martini and Mario's lobster ravioli will be waiting when you get finished."

"You don't want to come in? Maybe say hi?"

She gave the building a long look and scrunched her nose. "No thanks. Just tell him I said hello, if he asks."

Inside the front door, the large foyer split in two directions. The pocket doors on the left were closed, but the right doorway stood open, revealing a large front parlor of the unit that still held its period charm.

Deep crown moldings framed the ceiling and intricately

patterned parquet wood tiles graced the floors. A substantial desk sat just inside, occupied by a young man in a suit. He looked up from his computer as soon as I walked in. From what Cynthia said, I didn't think this was Randall Harris.

"Mrs. Robinson?" He gave me a polite smile.

"Yes?" It came out as more of a question, as if I wasn't sure. I repeated myself with more confidence. "Yes, I'm Nicole Robinson."

"I'm Seth Eislen, Mr. Harris's assistant. Please have a seat. He's just wrapping up with his previous appointment."

He gestured to a large seating area to his right. Two Stickley sofas covered in a rich ginkgo tapestry fabric sat facing each other flanked by a brick fireplace with decorative tile accents that echoed the ginkgo theme. A leather ottoman—I'm sure no one dared put their feet on—separated the two sofas.

I sat down, calculating the value of the furniture in the room. Would I even be able to afford Randall's retainer?

Perfectly spaced magazines sat on top of the ottoman. Generic interests; *Time, National Geographic*, and *Condé Nast Traveler*. The last one's cover showed a virgin white sailboat on an impossibly blue sea. The caption read *The Aegean Dream*.

I breathed a quiet laugh to myself. Not too many people in my spot would be dreaming of the Aegean. Or maybe they would. Running away sounded attractive right about now.

A moment later Seth led me across the foyer into the office.

"Mrs. Robinson." Randall Harris met me just inside the room and shook my trembling hand, looking me over with his dark eyes narrowed, as if judging me. I smiled with a fearlessness I didn't quite feel. "Please have a seat."

The office was about the same size as the waiting room and filled with the usual assortment of office furniture on one end. The other side was furnished with another Stickley sofa and coffee table, and in the far corner a small conference table. An elaborate chandelier hung in the center of the room, remnants of the home's original design.

I took a seat across the heavy oak desk from Randall, folding my hands over my purse. Did he actually work here? The surface of the desk gleamed within an inch of its life, and almond polish mingled with the smoky scent of its owner's cologne.

Maybe he buffed between clients?

Randall himself was just as polished. From his perfectly styled dark brown hair, to his crisply ironed shirt and precisely-knotted silk tie, to the knife-edged crease in his trousers; everything about him seemed obsessively conforming. Even the way the magazines had been precisely spaced on the ottoman in the waiting room. I pictured Randall measuring them with a ruler as he spaced them out—or maybe Seth did, like a Victorian butler setting a table.

"Thank you for seeing me so quickly."

His desk held only a Montblanc pen and my folder, sterile compared to my desk after only one day with Jacobs Realty Group.

His lips quirked up a fraction as he looked down at my file. "A friend of Cynthia's... Now, I've been in contact with David Hersch, your husband's attorney. I have a clear picture of your husband's goals—"

I exhaled a dry laugh. "I bet you do."

He looked up, his eyebrows furrowed. Interrupting him

did not sit well, if his expression was any indication. "Mrs. Robinson, my time is money. *Your money*. Maybe we should discuss that first. You will be less likely to waste it."

He pulled a sheet of paper out of a drawer and slid it across the desk. *Jesus Christ*. Any guilt I felt about the credit cards vanished while scanning over my lawyer's fees.

"Now, first question. Do you feel your marriage is irreparably broken? No chance for a reconciliation?"

"Yes." I answered without hesitation. "To the first question. No, to the second. I can't imagine taking him back after this. He's left me for another woman, not to mention—"

"Yes, Mrs. Robinson," he said in a bored voice, interrupting me this time. I didn't object. "Save your anguish for your therapist. I'm here to get you what you want, not hold your hand or listen to you complain. Try not to cry on me. I hate crying."

It was my turn to narrow my eyes. Had Cynthia really slept with this jerk? Maybe there was a warm and fuzzy side to the man outside this office, but I was having a hard time picturing it.

But, unlike Cynthia, I didn't have to sleep with the man, just pay him to do his job.

"I can assure you, Mr. Harris, I won't be crying."

"Good." He paused only a fraction of a second, then continued. "An uncontested divorce would be the quickest, most uncomplicated way to resolve this. It's what your husband is proposing. You just need to sign a few documents and we can proceed without you being served a summons. The details can be negotiated out of court, saving you money and months of frustration. The process of mediation can be somewhat painless," he explained. "If not we could be looking at years."

"I don't want years. Let's just get this over with."

"Good. Now, item by item, let's go over your financial requirements."

Earlier today, he requested an itemized list of every living expense. To say it was an eye-opening experience would be an understatement. Money had flowed out of the house without any thought as I paid the bills each month. To tally everything up in the bank records had been a shock. I slid the spreadsheet across the desk and he barely blinked.

"Your husband's not being that generous, but I think we can get close to that figure."

"I just started working on commission. I have no idea what my salary will be. I really only want him to pay for the kids' tuition, Mark's car payments, and the mortgage. I'm hoping I can handle the rest."

He shook his head while jotting something down on the spreadsheet. "Never admit what you'd settle for, Mrs. Robinson. Your life has drastically changed. I'm here to make sure your lifestyle doesn't." He flipped a page, then looked at me. "Now, tell me about your recent shopping trip. From what I've heard you went on a bit of a binge."

"If Derek didn't want me to use our credit cards, he should have closed the accounts. I think I showed considerable restraint, given the circumstances. I only bought what I needed and then deposited a bit of money into an account in my name. Derek never said anything about support when he left, and I panicked. With a son to feed and bills to pay. It was the only thing I could think to do, and I really only have about three months of Derek's income. I figured—"

He held up a hand. "Mrs. Robinson, speak to me before doing something so impulsive." He wrote something down in his folder again, then looked up. "I could have requested temporary support to tide you over. We want to appear cooperative in these negotiations. Frustrated spouses are not generous spouses. Maxing out credit cards tends to frustrate husbands. From what I understand Mr. Robinson may need to take out a loan to pay off the cards. That loan will need to be figured into your joint debts."

Bullshit. There was no way Derek took out a loan. I opened my mouth to argue but thought better. Every minute in this office was costing me money I didn't have. "I want the house. He can have the DC townhouse, but I think he should continue to pay the mortgage on our home. And I want half his trust fund, minus the fifty grand I *suppose* I owe him. ` `

"Anything else you want?"

"Derek, buried in a deep hole. Bonus if it's filled with fire ants." Randall frowned, but I continued on, albeit a little more reasonable with my demands. "Fine, I want this over with, as soon as possible. I have a career to establish, hot men to meet, the single life to explore."

Okay, maybe I couldn't remove all the sarcasm from my voice. My single life was more likely to involve dinners for one in front of the television than hot men.

"Might be best to put the *meeting hot men* on hold for a bit."

"Why?"

Randall sighed, rubbing his temple. "Mrs. Robinson, your husband wants the appearance of an amicable divorce. A mutual decision between the two of you to end your marriage. In exchange for your cooperation—"

"My cooperation? Pretty sure he's cheating on *me.* There's nothing amicable about that."

He picked up his Montblanc and then slid the paper detailing his fees back toward him. "I can call in a private detective. Time, airfare, lodging, food. It would be expensive, and if he does prove your hunch correct, we wouldn't be looking at an uncontested divorce. You can forget about getting this over with as soon as possible, but it's up to you."

He slid the paper back, now with a bold circle drawn around the itemized list of fees for a private detective. "I understand your frustration. But you *are* still Mrs. Robinson, and this has the potential to be a high-profile divorce unless we're careful. Reporters, television coverage nonstop. Neither of you want that, believe me. But your husband more so. And therein lies our advantage." He gave me a smirk that hinted at the truly ruthless lawyer Cynthia promised me. "For now I need you to behave like the perfect wife and mother, just like you have for the last twenty years."

I shoved the image of Gabriel's face flushed with pleasure out of my mind. Would he trade his career for the bragging rights of sleeping with a senator's wife?

Randall stood and shook my hand. "And whatever you do, don't talk to your husband without me present. Better yet, don't talk to anyone."

CHAPTER
NINE

I had made a mistake, crossed a line, and now I was paying for it with crystal-clear water and the relaxing sounds of a cascading waterfall. My pool was beautiful, but yesterday I had left a message on Gabriel's voicemail. The pool needed to be shut down. September was almost over. The night temperatures had turned decidedly chilly, and I couldn't afford to keep the heater running into October. Not with the measly allowance Randall Harris had squeezed out of Derek.

But here we were, Thursday night and my pool was still full.

I let out a groan. "Why me?"

It wasn't as if I was avoiding Gabriel, like his most recent text had accused. Not exactly, at least. Okay, maybe I had called at the crack of dawn yesterday in hopes of him not answering. But I wasn't ignoring him. It wasn't as if I was buried with work every Thursday just to avoid him.

Weeks ago Cynthia had promised he'd eventually give up if I ignored him, but obviously it was going to take time.

Mark stepped out of the house and moved to my side,

giving the pool a frown. "Didn't you say this morning that Gabriel was draining the pool?"

"I left him a message. Maybe he didn't get it." I turned and headed back inside.

"Well then, can I have a pool party on Sunday?" Mark asked, hot on my heels. "You know, a last farewell." I shot him a confused look and he added, "Never know where we'll be living next year."

"We will be living right here," I snapped, then let out a sigh and offered my son an apologetic smile. "I have no plans on moving."

He grabbed an apple off the counter and bit into it with a frown. "I just thought... well, it's an awfully big house for just the two of us. But then maybe you'll get married again. Maybe someone with daughters?"

I laughed at the way Mark wiggled his eyebrows, forgetting about Gabriel and the pool for the moment. "Don't talk with your mouth full. And don't you have a girlfriend?"

He took another bite, chewed, and then swallowed. "Just keeping my options open. Speaking of, Brian's having a party tomorrow. It's gonna be late, so I'll probably stay over."

I narrowed my eyes. "Staying over at Brian's?"

He took another bite of apple and nodded. "Where else?"

My mind went to Trent and his sister and his adorable niece. "I don't know. Please be smart, Mark. I'm way too young to be a grandmother."

He started to cough. His eyes bulged and he slapped a hand over his mouth. I rushed toward him, ready to administer the Heimlich or whatever, but he held up his free hand.

"Jesus, Mom. You trying to kill me?" he asked once he regained control.

"No. Just..." I shook my head and sat down at the counter, my knees shaking. "I have enough stress in my life."

"Poor Mom." He patted me on the head. "Don't worry. I'll be responsible."

My DOUBTS MULTIPLIED as I sat alone the next night. I trusted my son, but I had been seventeen once. Had dated a seventeen-year-old boy back then and knew how their thoughts ran. One reckless moment...

Kennedy Waltham was probably a levelheaded girl. Not that I could be sure. Her family had just moved into the area, and I hadn't met them. But I doubted they were the kind of parents to allow their daughter to spend the night at a co-ed party. No parents of girls would allow that, right?

I paced across my bedroom and then back. If only Derek were here. He was always better with the teenage-boy issues than me. Always better at getting into the mind of his son.

Even if this wasn't a sex problem, I was pretty sure there was a problem. Mark had never been much for sleepovers, yet here we were, three weekends in a row spent at Brian's. First, it had been a movie night in the Larsens' new theater room, then there'd been a study night for some physics exam, and now this party.

Maybe weekends at home without Derek are too painful?

Shit. I hadn't considered that, but that made more sense than him running off with some girl. At least I hoped so.

Either way I needed answers. Calling Derek was out. Randall would have my head. And my husband hadn't seen his son in weeks. How was he to know what was going on inside Mark's head?

Phoebe Larsen, on the other hand, would. She and I had known each other since the boys had been in diapers. We had almost been second mothers to each other's kids. She was reliable and responsible and likely to have picked up any problems Mark was having.

"Phoebe? It's Nicki," I said as soon as she answered. Things were quiet in the background. No sound of a party. Maybe the kids were outside or she was upstairs. Their house was as big as ours; it was easy to escape noise if you wanted to.

"Nicki..." She hesitated. "What a pleasant surprise."

"I'm not interrupting, am I? I know you have a crowd there."

She laughed and I heard a door close. "Right. No. I'm not busy."

"Good. I wanted to talk about Mark. I'm sure he's mentioned the divorce, and I'm kinda concerned he's spending so much time at your place. Thought maybe he's not processing this as well as I hoped."

"Um. Yeah. I think he's doing okay." The hesitation in her voice sent alarm bells off in my head. Maybe I was wrong. Maybe he was just a reckless, hormonal teenager whose mother was going to kill him.

I closed my eyes. "Is he around?"

Please say yes, please say yes...

"He's out right now." She cleared her throat. "He should be back soon if you want me to have him call you."

"He's not at the party?" The silence on the other end

spoke volumes. "Phoebe, where's my son? What the hell is going on?"

She sighed heavily into the phone. "I told him not to play games behind your back. It was only going to cause trouble. No one ever listens to me. Just so you know, I was against this."

"Against what, Phoebe?" I asked, panic choking my voice as thoughts of unprotected sex and the consequences ran through my head. Derek had been out of his son's life for a little over three weeks and everything was fucked.

"Mark's with his dad. Second week in a row. I told them both to tell you. Warned Mark you would find out eventually. I don't know why he's doing this."

Dead. They were both dead.

"Thanks, Phoebe. Call me when he gets back," I said through my teeth and then hung up.

I dialed Randall Harris and, of course, got his voicemail. Left a lengthy message that would probably raise my bill, but I didn't care.

I screamed my frustration until my throat hurt. I wanted Derek dead and the GPS tracker on my son's phone —the one I swore I wouldn't use unless it was an emergency—showed me just where to do the deed.

Bastard's head would look good mounted on the fireplace above his balls.

I pulled my keys out of my purse while rushing down the stairs. Halfway down, my purse slipped from my hands and tumbled to the bottom, nearly taking me with it.

Shit, I was getting clumsy. First, cutting my foot on that stupid wine glass, now nearly taking a header into the front stairs newel post. This divorce was going to kill me yet.

I winced as I lowered myself down on the foyer floor, rubbing what was likely to be a spectacular bruise on my hip. I needed to calm down. What would hunting the pair down accomplish? I wasn't actually going to kill Derek no matter how attractive that sounded at the moment, and any other recourse I could think of would put Mark in the middle of an unpleasant situation.

Mark was safe with Derek, I conceded to myself while staring at the contents of my purse spilled across the foyer.

Too bad you can't clean out your life like your purse.

I laughed at the thought while sorting the junk from the necessary stuff that had been hiding in the depths of my handbag. I pictured tossing Derek and Gabriel alongside the old dry-cleaning receipts and mint wrappers.

A loose business card sat off to the side. I pulled the case from my purse that corralled the dozens of them I had accumulated in the past weeks of work. Somewhere on my to-do list was to organize them into a file.

This one was different, though. The handwritten number on the back caught my eye, and I turned it over. Then smiled.

Trent Richards. His image came to mind in a flash. Those intense green eyes, those dimples. It had been weeks, but I could still conjure up that combination of spices and sex appeal. Cynthia told me what his cologne was, but I didn't recall the name. *Expensive*, she had said.

In truth, he intrigued me. The chemistry between us in that short time had been overwhelming. If the ghost of Gabriel's touch hadn't been lingering on my skin, who knows what might have happened?

Instead I had stuffed his card in my purse and forgotten that night in the chaos of my life. But now I ran my thumb over the iconic red and black logo of one of Chicago's favorite sports teams. I knew nothing about basketball.

Besides Mark's mandatory soccer games, sports weren't my thing. I suppose I should have been impressed, but I wasn't.

I turned back to the handwritten number. Nice script. Only psychos had bad handwriting and forged business cards, right? It had to be real. Trent wouldn't have passed out a fake business card in front of his brother. That would have been stupid.

Oh, hell. I was thinking too hard.

Ten twenty on a Friday night. He was probably out partying or whatever semi-famous sports people did on the weekend.

I pulled my work phone from the detritus of my purse and dialed anyway. As the phone rang, a little voice warned of my impulsivity. I ignored it.

A deep, smooth voice answered.

I attempted to clear the nervous lump from my vocal cords and replied, "Hello. I'm not sure if you remember me, but this is Nicki from, um, Maybes?"

"Nicki? *Nicki, I really should buy my own drink*, who should have called me weeks ago?"

I laughed. God, the guy was ridiculous.

"Nicki Adams, actually," I corrected once I found my voice. "And I apologize for the wait."

"Ah. A last name. I'm making progress." He paused for a second, and in the silence, my pulse beat loud in my ears. "Are you just getting in from a very unsatisfactory date and looking for something better?"

"No. Are you?"

"Hmm. Maybe. Are you offering? Something better that is?"

My skin tightened with his suggestion. "Maybe. Where are you right now?"

"I'm grabbing my car keys. Tell me I'm not being presumptuous."

"Depends on if you're willing to drive to the suburbs. I assume you're in the city." I bit my knuckles and shook my head. *What am I thinking?*

"Three weeks, Nicki. You've made me wait three weeks. Tell me where to meet you. I'll drive all the way to Wisconsin if I have to."

"We can't meet in public," I blurted, which was stupid. Weren't you always supposed to meet strange men in public?

Not when your lawyer tells you not to.

Before I could talk sense into myself, I rattled off my address and the security code to the gate.

"I'll be there in thirty."

"Park inside the garage and close the door. Go past the mudroom to the kitchen and out the patio doors. I feel like a swim tonight." My heart fluttered like a trapped bird against my ribs. Who the fuck was talking? It definitely wasn't me.

"Clandestine meeting. I love it, Nicki. I'm assuming swimsuits are optional." His dark chuckle sent a delicious thrill down my spine.

"Optional is a good word for it." I pulled the scotch from the cabinet, pouring a healthy slug in the crystal glass.

"Make that twenty minutes." An engine roared with a throaty masculine growl that suggested something fast and expensive, then the line went dead.

What have I done?

I tipped my glass back and swallowed. The fiery liquid burned a path down my throat and settled in a pool of molten weight in my stomach. Tears stung the back of my eyes as I wheezed, trying to breathe past the inferno. I poured another couple fingers in my glass, knowing full well by tomorrow I might be looking at the bottle of Oban with as much shame as I did the wine in Derek's cellar. But I needed more courage than even this amber potion could offer. Setting down the glass, I dialed my only help.

"Nicki, what's wrong?" Cynthia asked, her voice strained with concern.

"No one's dead," I blurted out. "At least not yet. I may have just done the craziest thing in my life. I need you to call for a straightjacket."

She sighed on the other end and I pictured her rolling her eyes. "Calm down. What did you do?"

"Trent is on his way over. I may have given him the distinct impression I would be waiting naked in the pool." My voice squeaked out the final words. Just saying it out loud caused my heart to kick into a gallop. "Oh God, Cyn. What do I do now?"

The tinkle of her laughter mocked the dire nature of the situation.

"Cyn! This is serious," I snapped, my nerves vibrating with anxiety. How could she laugh at a moment like this? "I invited a strange man over to have sex with me. What if he's a psychopath or something?"

"Trent... *Oh, Trent!* Tall guy from the bar. Bravo, Nicki. If it was me, I wouldn't have waited this long to get naked with *that* man."

"I could barely look him in the eye at the bar. He... he was perfect with clothes on. I don't think my heart can handle what's underneath. What the hell was I thinking?" Walking over to the back doors, I looked out at the dark depths of the water. Could I drown myself in the next twenty minutes? That would solve everything.

"Please. You're overreacting. Take a deep breath, maybe

make it two. I'm sure he has really ugly feet. Take notes. I want to know. Size, shape, grooming habits. Focus on his feet, if you know what I mean." I rolled my eyes as she paused. "Now take a deep breath and relax. The pool is a great idea, by the way. Your boobs will float and look young and perky. Now go get naked. Do not disappoint the man."

I frowned at the phone. That was the difference between me and Cynthia. She worried about her boobs, I worried about consequences—a little too late, which was turning into an inconvenient habit, but still. "Seriously, this is your advice? Thanks for your concern. If I'm dead, I won't show up for work Monday, you know."

"Relax, Nicki. That man candy was hot. Taste your freedom. Like toffee, sink your teeth into him. Absolutely no day off. I expect a full report on my desk Monday morning." She sighed, probably rolling her eyes at me again. "Okay. If he starts acting funny, let him know you told me he was coming over. Even psychopaths don't want loose ends."

"I'm sure that will protect me." This time I rolled my eyes. "Cynthia, I'm serious. I don't want to die."

"Fine. Fine. Did you google him?"

"Did I what?" Was that the thing now? God, I was twenty years out of practice.

"Christ, Nicki. Always google men. Check their socials. Make sure they haven't posted any odd ravings or a manifesto."

"A what?" I took another sip of scotch. What had I gotten myself into?

"Hold on." The line went silent this time as I waited for her to return, giving me time for my dark thoughts to take wings.

If I died tonight I'd never get financial revenge over Derek. He'd play the grieving widower. His mother would do that fake crying thing that fooled no one. I'd be buried in a beige pantsuit.

Cynthia's dark chuckle pulled me from my thoughts. "Trent is not a psycho. The only thing at risk is your perception of great sex, and that needs correction."

"If you say so," I replied, my voice dry.

"I say so. Now why are you still on the phone? Get in the fucking pool!"

CHAPTER
TEN

This is a stupid idea. The backyard was freezing. Mid-fifties at the most, with a strong lake wind that had my eyes tearing. Just the thought of taking my robe off sent a shiver down my spine. I had cranked the pool heater up on high after I'd hung up with Cynthia—electric bill be damned—but eventually Trent and I would have to get out.

Pool lights on or off? I flicked the switch back and forth trying to make up my mind. With the underwater lights on I would be completely exposed. But off... I shook my head and grimaced. In the dark, the natural boulder-lined oasis we had installed over ten years ago had me shivering for a completely different reason. The mature laurels and Japanese maples cast dark moonlit shadows that moved across the water with the wind, giving the usually tranquil space a horror-movie quality.

Lights on, then.

I eyed the stack of towels and extra robe I'd pulled from one of the guest rooms, lying on the chaise. My stomach dropped at the thought of Trent naked in that robe. But he was well on his way. It was too late to change my mind.

Time to get in the fucking pool.

The warm water instantly enveloped me, not quite bathwater warm, but close. I held my breath and let the water close in around me. Then pushed off the side, stretching my tense muscles as I did a slow lap across the pool. Then another. And another. My slow pace had my lungs screaming in protest by my fifth lap. Years ago we had contests to see who could hold their breath underwater the longest. I'd won easily, but now I was obviously out of shape. Or maybe it was the scotch. I surfaced at the far end of the pool, the curtain of water that dropped from the rocks splashing in front of me.

The hair on the back of my neck prickled and I turned. Then gasped.

Trent stood like an illusion, leaning against one of the thick patio columns, his arms crossed, watching me. He had been handsome in his suit, but now in snug jeans and a plain gray T-shirt that formed to his broad shoulders, he was even more perfect.

His gaze locked on mine and my stomach plummeted.

"Nicki Adams Robinson." He chuckled, stepping closer to the edge of the pool. "This is some place. I was starting to suspect this was all part of a cruel joke."

I blew out a deep breath in an attempt to calm my racing heart. "Coach Richards. How do you know my last name?"

"It's on the mailbox."

God, I was stupid bringing him here. Randall Harris would have my head if this got out. I could almost see the headlines. *Senator's Wife Has Affair With Pro Ball Coach.*

"You'd do well to forget that. For your sake and mine. I'm pretty sure neither one of us needs the publicity."

"I know how to keep my mouth shut," he said, folding his tall frame onto the chaise, then toeing off his loafers. I was too far away to judge his feet from my spot at the far end of the pool.

I could almost hear Cynthia's voice inside my head. *Grow a fucking pair and get over there!* Taking a deep breath, I lowered my head beneath the water and pushed off from the smooth tile wall.

Trent's attention was still on me when I surfaced a few feet from him, a small smile curving his lips, his dimples flashing under a day's worth of stubble that hadn't been there when we last met. The addition made him look even sexier if that was possible.

"Hi." I smiled up at him, resting my chin on my arms along the rough pool edging.

"Hi." His voice held a hint of sexy gravel, sending a shiver across my skin that had nothing to do with the chilly evening air. "It's nice to see you again."

He paused slightly on the word *see*. Even with the slight mist rising above the water, my little trip across the pool in the glow of the underwater lights would have revealed what I was, or wasn't, wearing. I would have to talk to Gabriel about installing a dimmer.

Or maybe not.

Trent reached back to pull off his shirt, and I shoved all thoughts of my pool guy out of my head.

Damn. I was going to have to learn to appreciate basketball a lot more.

I watched, transfixed as the soft gray fabric rose, revealing firm tanned skin that hadn't faded much from his time in the summer sun, and a dark trail of hair that vanished beneath the waistband of Trent's jeans, hinting at something altogether different. The dark trail thinned as it continued higher, past the ridges of his taut abs. Then the fine hairs spread out, dusting across a well-defined chest. I'd never been with a man with chest hair before. Derek could barely grow a beard, and Gabriel. Well... I didn't want to think about him or his grooming habits at the moment.

"You're going to give me a complex, staring like that," Trent said, breaking me out of my thoughts.

He stood, reaching for his fly, and all thoughts of other men fled as my heart jumped into my throat.

"Want me to turn around?" I sort of squeaked out.

Trent chuckled, shoving down his jeans and underwear in one smooth move.

Guess that's a no.

He shook out his jeans, pulled his wallet from the back pocket, thumbing a couple of brightly colored condom packets from the interior and then setting his jeans and wallet on the chaise next to his shirt.

I drifted back away from the wall, treading water as he stepped closer.

Eyes on his face.

I swear I tried, but it was impossible. Trent Richards was all man. Tall and lean, with plenty of well-defined muscles he definitely got from a gym. God, he was huge— every inch of him.

He knelt down, setting the condoms on the lip of the pool. Then pressed his palm on the tile edge and, in a single athletic motion, hopped in. We were at the ten-foot end of the pool, and Trent disappeared completely under the water. A second later he surfaced with a grin, shoving his hair back with both hands.

"Nice. I've been in some fancy pools before, but this has got to win a prize."

"Thanks. There's a slide behind the waterfall and a hot tub over behind the rocks. I had thought that might be better, but you never would have found me there. But if you want we could go—"

He cupped my face with both hands and kissed me, effectively cutting off my nervous babble. I slipped my arms around his neck and melted against his hard, slick body. He snagged the condoms and pushed off the wall, sending both of us drifting to the other side of the pool.

Trent tasted of warm cinnamon, and his tongue was soft velvet against mine. He was a really good kisser. A way better kisser than Derek, who had over the years turned kissing into a tiresome chore he often passed over on his way to his ultimate goal.

I stifled a groan of frustration as we passed into the darkness under the waterfall. This comparing-every-man-to-Derek thing was going to have to stop.

Trent grinned, his eyes taking in the secluded little alcove behind the waterfall. Once inside, the wind died and the heat of the water warmed the air to an almost comfortable temperature.

This was my favorite spot, this small, sheltered grotto. The water rose only up to my shoulders here, and the ledge at the far end was the perfect place to curl up with a book during the day. At the moment it was dark, the pool lights just beyond splashing a diffused pattern against the rock wall, the sound of rushing water surrounding us. This pool had been installed twelve years ago, and I was only now realizing how romantic this spot was at night.

Trent pulled me closer, sliding his warm and very large hand down my back and settling it on the curve of my ass.

His erection pressed hard and hot against the crease of my thigh, making me clench in anticipation. There were no second thoughts this time.

"Do you know how much sleep I've lost over you these past weeks? How many times I've come in my hand with you in my head?" He set the condoms on the cement behind me and then pressed me against the cool tile wall, guiding my legs around his waist and lifting me up enough to capture my nipple between his lips. "These tits..."

"God, Trent." I gasped, my hands curving around his corded shoulders for balance. Then squealed as his tongue flicked against my sensitive flesh. The man had a talented mouth, which I couldn't help but hope he used to its full advantage. It would probably be the death of me, but I would at least die happy.

He switched to the other side, giving that nipple the same toe-curling treatment. I sifted my fingers through his wet hair that was even thicker and softer than I had imagined, holding him against me.

"I should have gotten your number. Should have blown my brothers off and crashed your damn dinner."

I couldn't help my breathless giggle. Not because he'd masturbated to some fantasy of me. No, I was trying really hard not to picture that. But dinner with him and Cynthia?

His hands settled around my waist and in a heartbeat he lifted me onto the pool ledge. He spread my knees apart. Despite the chilly air, heat flooded my face in equal parts embarrassment and desire while Trent stared at my completely exposed privates like it was the eighth wonder of the world.

"And how about you? Would you have loved that? Tell me you want me as much as I want you right now."

"Y-yes," I answered, the combination of self-consciousness and desperate need choking my words. I couldn't recall Derek ever looking at me with this much hunger.

Trent's gaze locked onto mine while he slid his thumb along my seam and made a slow circle over my clit. My thighs trembled as he drew his thumb through my folds, before returning back to where I needed him. My breath rushed out in pants as he continued. I couldn't remember the last time a man made me come, but it was going to happen soon if he kept this up.

"I promise by the time I leave, you're gonna wish you had called me sooner," he said while plunging two fingers inside me, making me shudder. "Damn, you're so fucking tight. I can't wait to get inside you. But first..."

He closed his warm hands around my knees, spreading my legs wider. Then dipping his head, he dragged his teeth along my thigh.

I braced my hands behind me and leaned back to give him better access. The side of my palm brushed against the sharp corner of one of the condom wrappers, and I glanced down at the bright orange package.

Had Gabriel even used a condom? The answer came like a punch in the stomach. *Jesus fucking Christ.*

I'd had my tubes tied sometime after having Mark. For the last half dozen or so years, Derek's and my idea of safe sex was not getting caught by the kids. I hadn't even given contraception a thought with Gabriel. But why hadn't he? Was he that careless? *Was Derek?*

That thought had my stomach lurching.

I pushed back before it was too late. "Trent, stop. Please stop."

His brows drew down. "Did I do something wrong?"

"You. Nothing. I-I just. I want to... more than you know,

but..." I let out a long sigh that turned into a strangled sob. *Why me?*

I didn't know who to be more angry with, myself, Derek, or Gabriel. Derek was coming in first but I was in a close second. Hadn't I warned Brooke about unprotected sex? If Derek had only stayed faithful I wouldn't be here, trying to explain why I couldn't do the thing I'd invited this man over for.

"I'm so sorry. It's not you. It's... You see, my husband cheated on me, and... and..." I covered my face in my hands to hide my embarrassment. There was a possibility I'd been exposed to any number of disgusting sexually transmitted diseases, but I still had my dignity. "It never occurred before. I don't know how long, or how many, and, shit..." I took a deep shuddering breath and spilled out my humiliation, "I r-really need to see a doctor."

"Hey, it's okay." He lifted me back into the warm water and then pulled me against his solid chest, his hands gently stroking my back. "I understand."

I didn't cry in front of Derek the night he broke my heart. And as much as I wanted to, with Gabriel and all his sweaty eagerness, my eyes stayed dry. But right now I was sobbing all over Trent. I should have just drowned myself earlier.

I lifted my shoulders in a pitiful attempt at a shrug. "My life is so pathetic. Can you believe in all the time I've lived here, I've never once had sex in this pool?"

"That's a shame. If you were my wife..." He pressed a kiss to the top of my head instead of finishing that thought. "Honestly, I need to buy you more than a lousy drink before we get naked again. I want to take you out, get to know you properly. I want there to be more between us than a night of lust-fueled passion."

I gave Trent a hard stare as he guided me back under the waterfall, and then toward the rock-lined stairs. He wanted to see me again? Besides the cold breeze stinging my wet skin and the shiver running down my spine, this was not how I pictured the night progressing. And I was sure Trent hadn't made the trip from the city for a brief swim.

But he actually wanted to see me again?

Trent wrapped me in a towel, pressing a sweet kiss to my lips before grabbing a towel for himself. His tenderness almost had me crying again. When was the last time someone had taken care of me?

Randall Harris would have my head. But I wasn't doing anything different than Derek. I didn't need to pay a private detective to prove what I knew in my heart. Life was fucking unfair, and I was so tired of it. Why did I have to obey the rules while my cheating husband got to break them?

I slipped into my robe and then held out the spare to Trent. "I'm sorry I dragged you all the way here. Can I at least make you a drink, you know, to ward off hypothermia?"

Trent chuckled, then pulled me back into his arms now covered in plush terry cloth—at least, halfway to his wrist. I was going to need a much larger robe if we did this again.

"You're worth every mile, Nicki Adams. And I'm the one who should be sorry. Expecting more from a respectable woman. Oh hell, why not." He kissed my forehead and stepped back. "May as well mooch a drink off of you while I'm here. But only if you promise to let me do things my way from now on, and that involves dinner and conversation."

"You've lived here eighteen years?" Trent asked once he settled on the sofa in front of the large fireplace in the pool house. I handed him a glass of scotch and soda, remembering his order from the bar weeks ago, and took a small sip of my glass of straight scotch. He frowned up at me. "How old were you when you got married? Fifteen?"

Turning on the gas, I lit the fireplace to chase the chill out of the large room and to allow myself time to form an answer. I gave him a small smile and shook my head slowly. There might never be enough time, but there was no way around the truth. "A little bit older than that, I'm afraid."

Would my age bother him? Thirty-seven seemed a lifetime ago, not just six years. But then it felt like a decade had passed, not just a few weeks, since Derek left.

His eyes settled on the family photos sitting on the mantle. I'd fallen behind on updating the pictures out here. Most of them were older. Mark looked around ten and Brooke twelve in the most recent ones; the earlier ones showed them around toddler age with their chubby bellies and carefree grins.

He paused to sip his whiskey, then looked around the room. "You have kids?"

"Oh, Trent." I sank down on the soft upholstery next to him and breathed a heavy sigh. "You might decide a hasty retreat is in your best interest."

He glanced down, threading our fingers together. Butterflies fluttered in my chest, then took flight when his eyes settled on mine, making me wish we could stay locked in this fantasy world void of kids and age differences just a little longer.

"Let me be the judge of that."

"Okay. I got married at twenty-two." I held up my hand, watching him do the math in his head. "We bought this place two years later. And I have two kids. Brooke is nine-teen and away at college. Mark is sixteen, almost seventeen, and with his father right now."

My voice was surprisingly calm as I mentioned Mark and Derek. I'd done my best to shove all thoughts of the insubordinate pair from my mind. *Time enough to deal with them tomorrow.*

Trent nodded his head in silence. Shock, I assumed. Luckily, he was athletic and healthy. I hadn't brushed up on my CPR in years.

"Oh, and yes, my husband *is* Senator Derek Robinson, in case there was some confusion." I reached for his rock glass. "You can run now, if you like."

He pulled his glass out of my grasp, downing the rest in one gulp. I knew the feeling well. My life had been one unpleasant surprise after another this past month.

So when Trent snaked his hand behind my head and sealed his lips to mine, it took me more than a second to respond. I was cursing that delay when he pulled away, cutting what was an amazing kiss way too short.

"You did understand everything I just said?" I asked, rubbing my tingling lips with my fingers. Maybe he was hard of hearing, or the pool water had clogged his ears.

"There's only six years between us. My last coach in LA was married to a woman more than twice that difference, only younger. Why does everyone think that's okay, but when it's the other way around, suddenly it's a big deal? It's not a big deal, Nicki. You're bold, sexy as hell, and smart. Now unless you have other reasons for pushing me away, I'd rather you accept that I'm sticking around."

I took a deep breath and let it out slowly in an attempt to loosen the knot of apprehension in my chest. I could almost hear Randall Harris yelling at me. Was Trent worth the hassle?

Derek had proven tonight that he had no respect for rules. Why should I?

"Tell me about your career."

Trent paused for a second, as if he wanted to continue arguing his point. Then he let out a sigh of what might have been defeat, but I doubted it. Trent Richards didn't seem like the kind of man who'd give up that easily.

Over the next half hour he told me of his time at Syracuse, playing ball and earning a degree in sports medicine before signing on to play with Boston for three years. After, he'd been traded to LA, where he spent eight years and had chalked up what sounded like an impressive record. A handful of years later he'd been traded to Chicago, a move he was more than happy to make.

"When I'd announced my retirement four years ago, management convinced me to stay on as an assistant coach."

I stood to refresh my drink. "Want another?"

Trent shook his head and then stood as well. "As much as I'd love to, it's late and I have practice first thing tomorrow morning."

I followed him back out onto the patio and headed into the house with our rock glasses. From the kitchen window I watched as Trent dropped his robe, taking note of the way his back muscles flexed and stretched as he bent down to pick up his clothes. The dark shadow of his testicles peaked between his smooth, taut ass for a moment before he stood. A small voice scolded my invasion of privacy, but a much louder one noted the sexy hollow in his hip and the modest tan line just above his knee. Trent definitely wasn't a Speedo man.

I forced myself away a moment later when he slipped on his jeans. The show was over and I had glasses to put into the dishwasher. Two whiskey glasses on the counter would raise questions, as would the towels and robes on the patio. I'd have to do laundry before bed. So many details to remember. Would I be able to keep up this secret life until the divorce was final?

Suddenly, Trent's heat radiated behind me. I turned into his arms, and his warm lips brushed against mine.

"Tell me how I get to see you again," he whispered against my lips, his forest-green eyes intense and demanding.

"My lawyer has forbidden me from dating. Says it could complicate the divorce. We'll need to be careful. No restaurant dinners for a while, I'm afraid."

"Breaking the rules. I like that." His lips brushed a spot behind my ear, making me whimper. "Come to my place. We don't need to go out."

"I need to think on this." Without two glasses of scotch in my system, or his lips on my skin.

He captured my hand, leading me into the mudroom.

"Shhh. They're sleeping." Finger to his lips, he slowly opened the door to the garage.

I frowned at him, confused, then peeked out into the brightly lit space and laughed. Parked in the bay next to my black Cayenne sat a bright red Boxster.

"See, we were meant to be together. You can't keep them apart." Trent kissed my cheek and walked away.

I cringed as he pulled out of the driveway. The masculine purr of Trent's car seemed to echo across the quiet drive. My insomniac busybody neighbor, Carol Jordan, would assure it was the talk of the neighborhood. The woman never slept.

CHAPTER

ELEVEN

Cynthia's red heels tapped across the marble-floored atrium as she walked toward me Monday morning, a Cheshire cat grin spread across her face. "What do you think?"

I looked up and turned slowly, taking in the stunning six-story black marble columns ending in a dingy, vaulted glass ceiling that was possibly the crowning gem of the art deco building we were standing in. Once it was cleaned, that was. "It's a lot of work."

The Argyle Hotel hadn't been occupied since the early 2000s. At least, that's what the file Cynthia left on my desk, along with a note instructing me to meet her here, had said. I was pretty sure the burgundy and forest-green plaid sofas, tubular brass side tables, and the black-and-gold lacquered reception desk were straight out of the 1990s. Or maybe the '80s.

"The seller is motivated. We just need to find a buyer with vision. I have a few in mind."

Hopefully their vision needed corrective lenses. Sixty aging hotel rooms, leaky plumbing, questionable electrical, and a reputation for being haunted—the last detail possibly its only selling feature, or not, depending on the buyer. But Cynthia knew her market better than I did.

"I see you made it through Saturday night without being chopped up and thrown in Lake Michigan. So how's Trent?" She raised an inquisitive eyebrow.

I glanced around the lobby. Despite the abandoned condition of the dark and hushed space, I knew we weren't alone. I wasn't thinking about the ghosts. Philip, Cynthia's property coordinator slash photographer was around here somewhere, probably accompanied by a property manager. "I'm touched you were worried about my safety."

She shot a quick look around as well and then slipped her arm through mine, guiding me past the reception desk. "You have to see the bar. It's original."

It was. Sort of. We stepped through the frosted double doors that had a thick coat of burgundy paint slapped on them to match the lobby sofas. The etched mirror behind the mahogany bar, with inlaid brass accents and railing, was cracked, but the black marble top was exquisite.

"Now, talk," Cynthia said, closing the frosted doors behind us.

"You're right, the bar is gorgeous. But the rest needs a lot of work. Are you sure you can find the right buyer?"

She narrowed her eyes and tapped her foot. "Funny. Keep it up and I'll turn the Collins account over to you."

I turned back from my perusal of the room and gave my friend a wide-eyed stare. The Collinses were residential clients. A favor for a friend. After months of showing them every house in their price range, they had yet to find a place that checked off every one of the boxes on their very long list of must-haves. "You wouldn't."

She sent me a chilling smile. "Try me."

"Fine." I dropped my bag on the bar and dusted off a stool before taking a seat and giving her every minute detail from the moment I spotted Trent in my backyard to my mad dash around the bushes after he left, searching for a condom wrapper.

Cynthia shook her head, groaning. "What were you thinking having sex with your pool boy without protection?"

"Obviously I hadn't been thinking. I'd been drunk, and not in my right mind that day. And to be fair, Gabriel was just as at risk. Who knows who Derek's been sticking his..." I waved my hand around, grimacing at the thought I'd been trying really hard to avoid yesterday.

Cynthia's laugh echoed around the large and mostly empty space. If there had been any tables or chairs in the bar they were long gone. Maybe in a storeroom somewhere, or possibly sold?

"His dick, cock, penis, schlong, johnson, stick. God, you're precious, but if you want to play with them you're going to have to learn how to call them by their name."

"Whatever. Once I realized the situation, there was no way I could let Trent... um... continue. I feel filthy, Cyn."

"I'll give you the name of my doctor. She's discreet. I'm sure you'll be fine, and then you and Trent can fuck like hamsters."

"I think the expression is rabbits. Fuck like rabbits."

Cynthia dusted off her own stool and sat next to me. I had the urge to request a drink even though it was a little after nine in the morning. Maybe the ghost could bring some coffee.

"Nope. Never saw rabbits mate. Had a pair of hamsters once when I was a kid, though. Horniest animals ever. Always at it. Used to keep me up at night."

"Interesting." In all the years I'd known Cynthia I couldn't remember her ever mentioning her childhood. "But I'm not sure about me and Trent."

"I sensed a but in there somewhere." She leaned toward me, eyes narrowed. "What's the problem? He's perfect."

"He is perfect, but Randall will have my head. He explicitly said no men. And then... I don't know. Do you think I'm too old for him? Trent says it's not an issue, but it might be. Someday." I smoothed the invisible wrinkles from my skirt, trying to straighten my thoughts. "I probably should have told him Saturday night about my tubal ligation. He could want children—"

Cynthia threw up her hands between us. "Slow. Down. You invited this guy over for a casual fuck, and now you're thinking about having his children? That's not how this works. *Have fun.* Live in the moment. Stop thinking about relationship problems, because this is not a relationship. And for God's sakes, don't worry about a stupid condom wrapper. Weren't there gale warnings on the lake Sunday? The thing is probably washed up on some Michigan beach by now."

"I know. It's just a loose end. I'm not good with loose ends." I closed my eyes and rubbed the spot on my temple where a headache was beginning to throb. "My entire life is turning into a loose end."

Cynthia squeezed my shoulder, her brown eyes warming. "It's going to get better. Just hang on."

"Doesn't seem like it. I didn't tell you, but Mark's been sneaking off behind my back to see Derek."

Cynthia started to stand but then sank back onto her stool. "What?"

I nodded, fighting back the tears of anger as I recounted my call to Phoebe Larsen.

"Shit. I thought he was your sensible child. Did you ask him why?"

I shook my head, pulling a tissue out of my bag and dabbing at my eyes. "I didn't have the heart to ask. He came back Sunday like nothing had happened. Not that I have any objections to them having dinner together. It's just... why did Mark think he had to hide it from me?"

I stood and brushed a few fine particles of dust off my navy jacket. "Whatever. I left a message for Randall. If Derek is instigating this kind of secrecy between me and Mark, I'll have his head on a pike."

"Atta girl. Don't wait for Randall to call you back. Get on the phone as soon as we return to the office. Tell him I said he needs to crucify the bastard." She grabbed her bag off the bar and headed back toward the double doors. "Now let's go have a good look at this old bitch. I got a feeling she's going to make both of us fucking rich by next year."

I TUGGED the edges of my Pendleton blanket down from where the itchy wool irritated my neck. Mark's game had just started. There was a nasty bite in the air, and the dark clouds promised this would be a miserable morning.

How convenient that Derek once again couldn't make it.

For the father that cheered the loudest at all of his son's games the previous years, his absence this season was equivalent to an asteroid hitting the bleachers.

A previous engagement. Or so his text said, when he set up his first official weekend visit with Mark as set forth in our shiny new temporary custody agreement. Forget the fact he'd illegally kidnapped his son the previous two week-ends. He was getting this one as well.

Do you want to press charges? Randall had asked when I demanded something be done about my husband's actions. *I don't think it would be in your best interest, if you want my opinion. The opinion you're paying me to give you, may I remind. We still have the upper hand here. He's been warned that a repeat of this type of behavior will have serious repercus-sions, Mrs. Robinson.*

"Ms. Adams," I mumbled.

"What's that?" Ava sat down next to me on the bleachers and I let out a pent-up sigh that misted in the chilly air and shook my head. Four weeks in and Phoebe knew. How long until the rest of the school was privy to Derek's and my split? Which was fine by me. I was running out of believable stories.

"Russian terrorists..." Ava gave out her own misty sigh and patted my arm. "You have my sympathies."

"What?" On the field Mark had successfully batted away an aggressive attempt at a goal. We both stood with the rowdy crowd around us as the refs considered a misconduct for one of the other team's players. The winner of today's game would go on to the playoffs, and it was looking to be a rough one. Too bad Mark's father wasn't here to see it.

Ava tipped her head, bringing my attention to the opposite side of her where a group of moms huddled halfway down the stands. Women I knew from one of the kids' activities or another over the years. Acquaintances more than friends. They looked away the minute I glanced in their direction, a sure sign I was the topic of conversation.

Ava leaned closer. "Latest rumor. Derek's been

kidnapped by terrorists, which is better than the cancer thing last week, I suppose. But there is the possible beheading. You're holding up well." She grinned, then rummaged through her bag for a second before extracting a large thermos and a couple of mugs. "Cocoa? It has schnapps."

"I knew there was a reason I hung around you." I debated for a second on inquiring further into these rumors. I could use a good laugh. At the moment anything involving Derek's grisly demise would offer me some much-needed amusement.

Instead I told her everything while she poured the cocoa, Derek's quiet divorce be damned.

Ava had been in the thick of her own divorce not too long after we first met. My kids had always referred to her as one of the cool moms. You know, the ones that allowed their kids to stay up late, and always had the best snacks and plenty of soda, and swore. I never swore, at least not until recently.

I didn't think Mark hung with Sam much anymore, but Brooke still mentioned talking to Alex. At least she did the last time we had an actual conversation.

"Damn men." Ava squeezed my hand and huffed. "Isn't it always the way? Never good enough what they have at home. I'm so sorry. How can I help? I know a few good lawyers. Are the kids okay?"

I laughed at her outpour of concern. It felt good to have another person on my side.

"I have a lawyer, but thanks. And the kids..." I paused. It would take longer than this game to unpack all my issues with my family. "Brooke's not talking to me, and Mark... I don't know about him either. Derek's actually having a car pick him up to take him to the airport right after the game.

He can't even leave Washington to see his son. And he's keeping him until Monday."

Damn teacher's institute days. I was going to lose my mind, alone in the house for three days.

Ava shook her head. "Sounds like my ex. He actually hired a nanny to take care of the boys during their visits."

I took a sip of hot cocoa and sighed as the cool mint of the schnapps cleared my sinuses and the heat of the liquid warmed everything else. Or maybe it was all from the schnapps. Ava definitely hadn't skimped on the liquor.

"That sounds like Derek's mom. I bet his parents threw a party when Derek told them about the divorce. They always hated me."

"Then good riddance to them. You know, a few of us single moms go out a couple times a month. You should join us."

Everyone around us cheered as our team scored a goal. I took another sip of cocoa and smiled. "Maybe I will."

MAYBE MARK WAS RIGHT. This house was too big for two people. At the moment, all 12,366 square feet of the place echoed with loneliness.

Mark had barely had time for a shower before a very familiar black town car pulled up to take him to the airport. Jack, or maybe it was Zack, had been Derek's personal driver for almost a decade. Probably should have found out his name since there was a good chance he'd be a permanent fixture in my son's life. At least until Mark went off to college.

That unpleasant thought must have been obvious on my face. The older man had offered me a small sympathetic smile as he opened the back door for my son, and then a minute later the two disappeared down the driveway, leaving me alone with my thoughts.

Even though Mark had been gone the previous two Saturdays, this one felt different. Like some shift in the normal balance of our lives had taken place.

A whole weekend with nothing to do. I was going to go mad.

Cynthia had mentioned a lunch date with Roger, an investment banker with silver hair and gray eyes, just before we left work on Friday. Poor man probably didn't know what he was getting himself into. Or maybe he did by now. In any case, calling her was out of the question.

I wandered over to the patio doors and looked out at the back yard, smiling at the memory of a naked Trent hopping into the pool a week ago. The earlier clouds had cleared, but there was still a brisk wind, and the temperatures hovered in the mid-forties. Not a day for swimming.

Trent had been in Orlando midweek for a preseason game but had texted every day. Nothing much more than a *hi* and *I'm thinking about you*, but it was enough to leave me giddy the rest of the day. I sent him a more lengthy text this morning along with a copy of Cynthia's doctor's test results —all negative—but I hadn't heard back from him since.

Maybe that was too forward?

I made myself a cup of cocoa—no schnapps—and settled onto the couch with a throw and my latest book in the Jack McCann series. The Trent look-alike was currently guarding the gorgeous Charlotte from her dangerous stalker, her ex-husband's creepy best friend. They had taken refuge in a secluded cabin, and of course by this time Charlotte had become completely smitten with Trent. I mean Jack. I didn't blame her in the least.

I double-checked to make sure the back door was locked and then headed into the mudroom to engage the alarm.

Gabriel wasn't a dangerous stalker. Just a little persistent. The note left on the patio table was stupid as hell. *I'm not enjoying your evasion,* it had read. At least he had the intelligence to put it into an envelope, and thank God Mark thought it was just a bill. But if my son had opened it... I didn't think I could convince him Gabriel's message was just pool talk. Mark wasn't an idiot. Just the thought of him connecting the very obvious dots had a large rock forming in my stomach. Or maybe it was the words on the paper itself. No, that had left my skin crawling.

There was no question; I would have to find another pool service.

My scheduled call to Brooke went straight to voicemail, and I spent the next few minutes trying to reason with her messaging system for the third week in a row.

A second later my work phone rang and I jumped, spilling cocoa across my hand. I wiped the hot liquid on the old pair of New Trier sweats I'd found in Brooke's closet, then sprinted back into the kitchen.

There were only two people who knew this number, and it wasn't Cynthia.

"Hi," I answered, bubbles of happiness bursting in my chest, chasing away any disappointment over my daughter's continued silence.

"Hey, you." Trent's deep voice had me grinning so wide it hurt. "What are you wearing?"

I couldn't help but giggle at the suggestive tone in his sexy voice. "Nothing interesting, I'm afraid. A long-sleeve T-shirt and my daughter's high school sweatpants. But I can change if you want?"

Conversation interspersed with a bit of long-distance phone sex sounded like a nice way to spend a long night alone. Cynthia would be proud.

"You would be sexy in burlap, but I do need you to change. Warm clothes. Layers. Coat, hat, gloves, running shoes."

"Okay..." I laughed again, a little unsure this time. Unless Trent had a long game of strip poker planned, that many clothes didn't sound like fun. At least not the kind of fun I had in mind.

"And an overnight bag. It's been a long fucking week, and I need you for more than a couple hours."

"Trent—" I sighed out his name. I needed him too, but...

"Trust me. I've thought this through. I've got your need for secrecy totally covered. But we need to do this now."

Did I trust him? I didn't even need to think twice about it. He'd seen me naked, with all my embarrassing flaws and mistakes exposed. Even all my baggage hadn't scared him away. Trent still wanted me. Of course I trusted him.

"Okay," I said with more confidence and possibly a smidge of giddy excitement in my voice. I'd been fantasizing about Trent all week fantasizing about me. In truth I was a little more than excited at his proposal, whatever it was. "Where am I going?"

The phone went silent for a second, and then a chime rang in the background followed by muffled voices. A car horn blared.

"Where are you?"

"Parking garage. Give me a second and I'll send you coordinates. If anyone sees this text on your phone they won't know what it is." He paused and I heard the chirp of his car alarm. "See, I've got this whole clandestine-encounter thing all worked out. Call me when you get there and I'll give you further instructions. And Nicki?"

"Yes?"

"I'm serious. Dress warm. Someday I'm going to have you on a beach in a bikini, but it won't be today." I heard the distinctive meaty thunk of a car door, then the rumble of his engine. "See you in less than an hour."

The line went dead and a second later a string of numbers came through on a text. I punched the coordinates into my phone's GPS and grinned as the pin revealed my destination.

CHAPTER
TWELVE

The brisk lake breeze blew errant strands of my hair across my face. I tucked the pesky bits inside my knit beanie and approached the sturdy metal gate that blocked the entrance to a wide dock. Glancing back down at Trent's last text, I reread the instructions. *Enter 264242 in the keypad. I'll be waiting on* Argo.

I squinted across the long, wide pier. A light mist sparkled in the filtered late afternoon sunshine, leaving the far end of the pier shrouded in a slightly ominous haze. Several seagulls screeched overhead, but otherwise the harbor was deserted of life as far as I could see.

Cynthia, you better be right about Trent.

I sent her a text, letting her know where to search for my body if I didn't show up for work Monday morning. Then chided myself for being suspicious. If Trent wanted to kill me, he'd have already done so.

I punched the code into the keypad attached to a post next to the gate. The lock let out an electronic click and I gave the knob a turn before pushing the gate open.

Beyond, the wide pier branched off into narrower individual docks. Except for a few fishing boats, most of the slips were empty. I tried to picture Trent behind the wheel of one of the hulking vessels with their nets and poles sticking out at all angles and failed. *Maybe his father liked to fish?*

I examined each boat's name as I passed. *Catch of the Day*, *Knotty Thoughts*, even an inspiring *Ever Faithful*, but no *Argo*.

I passed the last fishing boat and the mist cleared for a brief second, giving me a glimpse of a lone sailboat, her tall mast stretching toward the hazy gray sky. I recalled our conversation on the Grenadines the night we met. Why had I even wasted my time checking the names of the fishing boats?

I hiked my bag higher on my shoulder and picked up my pace, my chest ready to burst with excitement. I hadn't been sailing since college when a friend had invited me to their place on Long Island. It had only been a weekend, but I loved every minute. I would have given anything to have a boat, but Derek could get seasick just staring into the bathtub. A boat on Lake Michigan had been out of the question.

I was almost running by the time I reached the sleek and sexy vessel that I knew without looking bore the name written in my text. Even on this brisk autumn day, with leaves blanketing the ground, mixing the damp smell of the lake with their earthy fragrance, an evening on the water sounded like heaven.

A small set of stairs sat on the dock next to the boat. I climbed the three steps and hopped aboard. "Trent?"

A niggle of doubt set in for a second. Maybe I should have double-checked the name.

"Come down, Ms. Adams." Trent's voice floated from below and a small wave of relief washed over me.

His hands circled my waist as I descended the steep set of stairs. Grinning like a fool, I dropped my bag and wrapped my arms around his neck, crashing my lips against his. His tongue thrusted into my mouth. His rough stubble scraped my skin as he kissed me hard and deep. My skin flamed hot under the layers of clothes Trent had instructed me to wear. The unused condom from last weekend burned in the bottom of my purse. *Hope he has more.*

"Take it easy, baby. We may never leave the dock. We'll be stuck eating the stale granola bars and whatever beer's still in my fridge."

"Or each other." I flashed him a reckless grin and he raised his eyebrows, cleared his throat, and then set me on my feet.

"Quick tour." He linked his fingers with mine, scooping up my bag with his free hand and pulling me further into the boat that smelled of the sexy man who owned it. "It's not that big, so don't blink."

Not that big turned out to be thirty-eight feet of gleaming teak luxury. A small U-shaped galley sat just off the stairs. The miniature kitchen was equipped with a stainless double sink, fridge, and two-burner stove. I immediately planned on cooking breakfast for the two of us the following morning. *Need to stop somewhere to buy groceries.*

Beyond that, a deep blue upholstery seating surrounded a large wooden table, with more blue upholstery across the aisle from that in the form of a comfortable-looking built-in sofa that would be perfect to curl up on. Or pull out into a double bed, as Trent informed.

"The head," he announced, pulling open an arched door. "It's small but has everything necessary."

I nodded. If he was expecting me to be impressed, it

wasn't going to happen. There was barely room for one person to turn around in front of a toilet that definitely required instructions. The sink was so small you probably had to wash one hand at a time, and the shower... well, there would be no showering together.

His cabin was much more impressive. Trent set my bag on the bed, leaving no doubt as to where I'd be staying. The space followed the tapered curve of the boat's bow, the bed itself covered in a homey quilt and plenty of thick pillows. A small closet and dresser sat just inside the arched doorway, and a large hatch was set into the ceiling, giving us a view of the gray sky. If the clouds decided to lift, we could watch the stars tonight.

I sank down onto the bed and gave a little bounce.

"Comfortable." I grinned, lifting my eyebrows suggestively.

Trent grabbed my hand and pulled me back up. "I have plans. Don't spoil them."

I gave him a cheeky salute. "Aye, aye, captain."

There was a flash of something wicked in his grin. In the next second it was gone and he was pulling me back through the cabin. He gave my bottom a less than gentle pat, then pointed toward the ladder. "Let's shove off."

At Trent's urging, I *shoved off* my dirty expectations and climbed the stairs back into the crisp afternoon air. It was our first date, for God's sake. I could control myself for a few hours.

"So where are we going?"

"Kenosha. Unless you have objections," Trent said while starting the engine.

I didn't and said as much, but couldn't help wondering what he'd do if I did. Would we stay here and eat granola in bed?

"Good. I know this place. Amazing food." He tucked my hat down over my ears and pressed a quick kiss to my lips. "You'll love it, I promise."

A large fishing boat passed behind us. I turned away as Trent waved at the men on board. Silly, probably. Bundled up in a coat and hat, chances of being recognized were slim. But Derek had wanted me to take a visible role in his career. *A supportive wife is an asset to any campaign. When she's as beautiful as you, she's fucking priceless.* I'd been in too many campaign ads, spoken at too many rallies to take a chance someone might recognize me.

I breathed a sigh of relief when we pulled out of the harbor and put some welcomed distance between us and the shoreline.

Trent motioned me over and, before I could protest, positioned my hands on the large wheel. Various instruments stared back, all displaying information and an array of intimidating buttons. A large compass in the center of it all was the only thing I recognized, but I hadn't had much practice with one of those since my Girl Scout days.

"Just keep the boat pointing in this direction," was all the instruction he offered before leaving me in control of his very expensive boat.

The next second, Trent pulled on a line and a large white sail rose above us. A mixture of fear and excitement bubbled up inside me as the sail snapped in the wind. Trent returned and adjusted my death grip on the wheel. The boat turned and the sail billowed. The deck tilted and Trent grasped my waist to steady me.

"Almost done." He pressed a kiss to the base of my neck, leaving me shivering with delight, and then stepped away again.

He shut off the engine, and a moment later he had a

second sail up. Water rushed beneath the hull and the wind stung my cheeks. I felt my shoulder muscles unknot as the silence enveloped us.

"You're a natural." He returned to my side, giving my fingers an encouraging squeeze, the warmth of his hands soaking through my knit gloves.

"Your hands are going to get cold." I gave him a quick side-eye, not wanting to take my attention from whatever the hell I was supposed to be doing with this wheel. The distraction was hard to resist. Trent was hard to resist. The rumble of his voice, his oh-so-sexy scent, the way his thick fisherman's knit sweater fit across his broad chest—when I gave myself permission to look away from the empty lake in front of us. His ruddy cheeks belied the oatmeal tweed wool's warmth. "And where's your coat?"

"Us tough old salts don't need a coat," he said with a pirate accent and a wicked glint in his green eyes that were even more vivid in this diffused light. Or maybe it was the contrast of his orange-and-blue Bears hat.

"You're too young to be an old salt."

He pressed one of those buttons on the instruments in front of us, then pulled my hands from the wheel and guided me over to the bench.

"Autopilot," he said by way of explanation when I gave the abandoned wheel a panicked look. He spewed something technical about wind and heading I didn't understand, but we seemed to be keeping course and I trusted Trent not to kill us.

He slung an arm around my shoulder and pulled me into his warmth. Maybe he was right about not needing a coat. The man was a furnace. Not that I was complaining. It would be some time before we arrived at our destination.

The sun would set before then, sending the temperatures on the lake plummeting.

Trent pointed out the state line, or at least an approximation, I assumed. There was no welcome sign like on a highway, just more of the same rocky shoreline interspersed with a mix of houses.

The diffused sun dipped closer toward the horizon, tinting the clouds in vibrant shades of pink and orange and purple. Trent entertained me with tales of his and his brothers' childhood sailing adventures with their grandfather. A retired Coast Guard captain, then later a delivery captain, transporting vessels all over the world. But according to Trent, he loved sailing with his grandkids the most.

Trent had become addicted. Argo was his third boat.

"She's a little big, but something about her caught my eye every time I passed her. I kept bugging her neglectful owner, but he kept turning down my offers. Then two years ago he gave in. Probably shouldn't have been so eager, or I might have gotten a better deal, but..." He grinned, his adorable dimples winking in his cheeks. "I can be sorta determined. And once I see something I want, well, I usually get my way."

Obviously. I chuckled, then asked the question burning in my mind since I got here, "So Argo? Does that mean you're Jason?"

"Off on the quest for the Golden Fleece? Nah. Just a night away with the siren who bewitched me."

JUST AS THE sun sank beneath the waves, we slipped into

another snug harbor inside a similar stone break wall to the one we had left.

Trent secured the boat and then he took my hand, leading me a few blocks from our dock to a lively pub. Irish music, along with the savory scent of food, spilled out as he opened the door. The cozy establishment was decorated in knotty pine, neon beer signs, and a large TV featuring what must have been a popular ball game of some sort considering the large crowd gathered at the bar.

My stomach growled and a pleasurable shiver ran across my chilled skin. Even with my multiple layers of clothing, the sail over had been nippy, and lunch was a distant memory. I considered hugging the yellow-and-green clad hostess when she led us to a cozy high-backed U-shaped booth directly across from a blazing hearth.

Trent hung up my coat on the hook just outside our private booth and then slid in next to me, tugging my hat off my head.

I smoothed my hair with my fingers and settled back on the cushioned seat.

"See, nothing to worry about," he said, echoing my thoughts. Besides a cursory glance from a few Packers fans seated at the bar, we had walked in unnoticed.

I pulled off Trent's Bears hat, tucked it between us, and gave his messed-up hair a straightening as well.

A young, fresh-faced waitress by the name of Katie trotted over. Trent ordered both of us a local brew and what he swore was the best shepherd's pie in the country.

"To my first date since my twenties," I said, as soon as the waitress dropped off our drinks.

I raised my glass and smiled the smile of freedom. At least for tonight I had no worries, or at least none I cared to think about. Besides the man in front of me, the rest of them could go to hell.

"To *our* first date," Trent corrected, tapping his glass against mine. "One of many I hope."

I smiled but refrained from making any promises. My divorce was nowhere near finished, my freedom far from being granted at the moment. And did I really want to jump into another relationship so soon?

A short time later our waitress dropped off steaming ramekins of shepherd's pie and a loaf of crusty bread. Trent requested refills on our beers.

He shifted over on the bench to give us room to maneuver, and then cut into the warm rustic baguette with the provided knife, handing me a large slice.

"This is nice." I paused that thought and concentrated on plunging my fork into the pie. Steam billowed up, promising this would be a leisurely meal unless we planned on incinerating our tongues. "I don't remember the last time I was at a restaurant without the kids. Except political dinners—God, those were exhausting. But I'm done with that now."

"Silver linings," Trent said, then shifted his focus on his dinner.

I paused to blow on the steaming forkful of beef and vegetables hovering an inch from my lips, then let out a little moan as the tender meat melted in my mouth and the thick gravy coated my tongue, rich with the flavor of dark beer and thyme.

"Good, right?" Trent asked around his own mouthful.

I nodded with enthusiasm. Was there a chance the chef would share the recipe?

"How was Orlando?" I asked.

He let out a groan, making me laugh.

"That good? At least you had nice weather."

Most of the week it had rained the kind of rain that felt like needles on exposed skin and left you chilled the rest of the day.

He shook his head slowly and took a sip of beer. "I should be thankful. I've got a career in the field I love, with people I respect, and a more than comfortable income. But my body aches a little more each year. It's hard work, and just the thought of my schedule right now makes me exhausted—which is not a good way to start the season."

I gave him a sympathetic smile while scooping up another forkful of beef and carrots—and rutabaga?—this time with a layer of browned mashed potato on top of the filling.

I'd done my fair share of flying back and forth over the years at Derek's request. Nothing as demanding as Trent's job, but I could commiserate. Just thinking about Trent's schedule made *me* tired, and he'd been at it for well over a decade.

"I can understand. Back when the kids were little I had an excuse to stay home, but the past few years it was a constant 'hey, Nicole, we've got this dinner' or 'that fundraiser.' And I'd have to hop on the next plane. A little secret, I hate flying."

"I'll keep that in mind," Trent said before shoving a forkful of steaming food straight from the ramekin into his mouth and chewing thoughtfully.

"Mark and Brooke are way better at the whole drop-everything-for-Dad's-campaign stuff, but then as they keep reminding me, they are way better than me at a lot of things."

"I don't believe that." He narrowed his eyes, giving me an appraising look. "Kids' lives are just more flexible."

I sent Trent an appalled look. "Are you suggesting I'm old and inflexible?"

"Not at all. But for what it's worth, my nieces and nephews are always pointing out how ancient I am."

They'd probably think I was downright geriatric, but I kept that negative thought to myself. We'd gone over our age differences enough for me to know Trent's opinion on it. If he didn't care, neither did I. It wasn't like we were going to get married or anything.

I'd done that once, and once was enough.

"It's nice that you have such a supportive family," I said instead, before popping a gravy-soaked hunk of bread into my mouth. Definitely thyme and a touch of rosemary. Possibly a hint of cayenne. I scratched ingredients down on the mental recipe card in my head with plans on making it next week for Mark.

Trent laughed. "Me and my brothers get along now, but when we were younger..." He paused as if searching for the correct words. "They were demons, always ditching me to hang out with their friends or pummeling me when I annoyed them. My mother'd feel sorry for me, bring me into the kitchen, and bake me cookies."

"That's sweet." I could almost picture a sad, young Trent, having been dismissed by his older brothers. I would have baked him cookies too.

"My mom is sweet." Trent let out a slow exhale, twisting his lips in what might have been regret. "Have to admit though, I was probably an obnoxious brat. Always barging in on my brothers. I could never figure out why they wanted to spend so much time alone with girls. When I finally got a clue, they were heading off to college. TJ never moved back, and by the time Troy returned from law school, I was gone. Funny how we've gotten closer the farther we've moved apart."

"I think we all were obnoxious at a certain age."

We both fell silent for a moment, choosing to focus on finishing our meal before it went cold. I added a few more ingredients to my mental recipe. It would be perfect for me and Mark after his next weekend's playoff game.

Trent sent me an expectant look, and I realized my mind had wandered off.

"What?"

"I've been going on and on about my family. Tell me about yours."

A resigned sigh slipped out, the same one I always gave whenever I was forced to talk about my family. "I'm an Adams."

Trent's eyes narrowed. "I don't follow."

"Daily, Wirtz, Adams..." I laughed bitterly. "My grandfather started Adams Transport, my father married a Colby. My sister sits on the Illinois Supreme Court. And I... well, let's just say my only claim to fame was marrying a Robinson. My mother informed me the other day not to expect an invitation to Christmas unless I patch things up with Derek."

"Bullshit." Trent's expression softened into something dangerously close to pity. "I've only known you for a couple weeks, but I can tell you have a lot more going for you than who you married. You're an amazing woman and mother. You're smart and funny and resilient. And to hell with your mother if she can't see that." My heart warmed with his enthusiasm. "And did I mention how sexy you are? You're a knockout, Nicole Adams."

I couldn't help but laugh. "Pretty sure my mother doesn't put a lot of value on that quality."

"I do. And on that note, I think it's time to get out of here." Trent gifted me a smoldering look, sending a shiver down my spine. He held up his hand to flag down the waitress. She rushed over and he handed her his credit card and then excused himself to use the washroom. I headed toward the ladies room as well. There was no way I was using his tiny bathroom if I didn't have to.

My phone chimed with a text as I returned to the table. Not Cynthia. She hadn't called me on my personal number ever since she handed me the company phone.

Possibly Mark wishing me a good night, or maybe Brooke? It'd be just my luck she finally felt like talking. I slid back into the booth and pulled my phone from my purse while Trent went to the bar to pay the bill.

Two messages waited. Ava, knowing I'd be alone this weekend, invited me over for lunch tomorrow. *How sweet.*

My smile quickly faded as I read my son's message. Expecting a 'Goodnight Mom' or few words expressing his boredom, my heart stuttered when I absorbed the meaning of his text. "Nooo. No, no, no."

"Everything okay?" Trent asked, sliding onto the bench next to me. I shook my head and handed him my phone as if saying the words out loud would make them more real.

His frown matched mine. "Your son's on a flight home?"

I sent Trent a wide-eyed look of total panic. With the number of times I'd flown to DC and back, I didn't need to do the math to know I was in trouble. "He's going to be at O'Hare in less than two hours, expecting me to meet him. What am I going to do?"

Sailboats didn't move fast. It had taken almost two hours to make a trip that would have taken a half hour by car. I was screwed.

"Relax." Trent kissed my forehead, then pulled out his phone and hit one of his contacts.

"Davison." He flashed me a small smile. "I'm at Everly's."

Trent paused for a second while the other man spoke. Then chuckled and shook his head. I glanced at my watch, trying to calculate my chances of making it to the airport in time. Who was I kidding, there was no chance. Maybe I could get a hold of Cynthia? She'd kill me for interrupting her date, but once I explained, she'd understand.

"No. No, I'm not buying you a drink, you cheap son of a bitch. And you still owe me, remember? I happen to need a favor." He scoffed and offered me a reassuring smile as he explained my situation to the man on the line.

"Thanks. How soon can you get here?"

Trent hung up, and I narrowed my eyes at him in curiosity. "Who was that?"

"Matt Davison. Former teammate. Lives maybe ten minutes from here. He'll drive you back to your car. You should be able to get to the airport in time."

I opened my mouth, but I had no words. Disappointment rushed over me like a wave. Our perfect night was over. "I'm so sorry."

His hand cupped my face. "Don't be. It's not your fault."

"But." I glanced around the rowdy bar and sighed. "This isn't at all what I had planned."

"Plans change." He stood. "Come on. Matt'll be here soon."

Outside the night had turned downright cold and the mist had thickened to pea soup. "You going to be okay sailing back alone in the fog?"

Trent pulled us off the main sidewalk and wrapped me

DARCI ANN BAKER

in his arms. "Don't worry. I've got GPS and radar. I've sailed in much worse."

I offered him one of my stern motherly expressions I'd given the kids when they were contemplating something risky.

"Fine. If it will make you feel better, I'll head back in the morning."

"Thank you. It would be one less thing on my mind tonight."

The wind rushed past, sending a crumpled paper of some sort blowing across the dead grass. The bar entrance opened and a group of men staggered out. They barely offered us a glance as they passed by, too focused on a heated debate over the game that must have just ended.

I exhaled a long sigh of regret. "Promise me a rain check?"

His lips lifted in a crooked smile. "I'm off to Phoenix tomorrow afternoon and they're pulling the boat out of the water Monday." My face fell along with my heart. Trent brushed his knuckles under my chin. "But I have other plans."

Headlights flashed across where we stood, followed by the throaty growl of a sports car. Trent pulled away with a curse, and I turned just as a bright yellow Ferrari pulled up to the curb. The window lowered and the man inside whistled.

"Hop in, sweetheart."

Trent stepped forward. "You couldn't have brought the Range Rover?"

"I could have taken the Harley." The man I assumed was Matt chuckled. "You must have struck out pretty bad for her to want someone else to take her home. Good thing I'm around to save you." He tipped his head around Trent's

130

body and directed the last part to me. "Matt Davison at your service."

"Davison," Trent sighed out the man's name, finishing with a low growl.

I checked my watch and then stepped forward. As much as I appreciated the favor, I didn't have time for their good-natured bickering. "Trent, Mark's going to be waiting."

"Take her to my marina, make sure she gets into her car safe. And do the damn speed limit." Trent guided me around to the passenger side and opened the door. "He's a bit cocky sometimes, but I'd trust him with my life."

I started to nod but then gasped. "My bag. Shit. It's still on the boat."

"Is there anything important in there?" Trent asked. I gave a hesitant shake of my head. The Louis Vuitton bag had been an anniversary present from Derek years ago. Expensive but emotionally worthless. Inside was Brooke's mohair sweater —also an expensive present, from Derek's mother. My daughter'd kill me if I lost it.

Trent's smile flashed in the dark. "Guess you'll have to see me again."

I gave him a lingering kiss in agreement and then dropped down into the seat of the sports car. *Way down*. My ass felt like it was scraping the ground. Trent reached in and fastened my complicated seat belt and pointed a finger at his friend.

"Take care of her like your life depends on it. Because it does."

CHAPTER
THIRTEEN

Cynthia lounged in her usual spot on the sofa in my office when I arrived Monday morning. A pot of coffee and all the fixings, along with whatever pastries Greg thought to pick up on his way in, sat on the table in front of her. This morning it was scones, cranberry from the looks of them.

Normally I greeted her with a smile and a hello, and then we'd spend a few minutes gossiping about our weekend. I was in no mood for gossip this morning.

I set my purse on my desktop and dropped down in one of the comfortable chairs facing the sofa, breathing out a tired sigh.

"Can we do this some other time?" I asked, my voice sluggish from lack of sleep. The last thing I wanted was to rehash my disaster of a weekend.

She narrowed her eyes at me as she sat up and poured both of us a cup of coffee, doctoring mine the way I liked it. "Drink up. Then tell me why you have shadows under your eyes."

I took a decent gulp of the expensive brew, singeing my tongue in the process.

"Trent and I headed over the Wisconsin border in his pretty sailboat. He'd planned a nice romantic evening. Unfortunately, Mark and Derek got in a huge fight. Then while Derek was busy on a call, Mark snuck out of our DC condo, grabbed an Uber, and hopped on the next standby flight home. I'm thinking we raised our kids to be too independent." I covered my mouth as I yawned. "I rushed back just in time for my son to step off the plane. Derek didn't realize he was gone until after I picked him up. Long story short, I'm angry, Derek's angry, Mark was all broody and indignant this morning."

Cynthia's eyebrows rose and a grin spread across her face. "Interesting."

"Not interesting. And not funny." I set my coffee cup down and leaned back into the chair. Big mistake. The thick cushions tempted me to close my eyes. If I didn't know Cynthia had her usual to-do list waiting for me, I could've used a nap.

After Mark and I returned home just after midnight Sunday morning, I'd shut off my phone and gone to bed, but my mind had been too active to sleep. It hadn't been much different last night.

"Why can't we talk about your weekend for once?" It had to be more satisfying than mine.

Cynthia's grin wilted. "Highlight of my evening was watching the Bears win from the fifty-yard line. Roger has season tickets. Everything went downhill from there. Turns out his niece is selling her Gold Coast condo, and he was hoping I'd take on the listing. For free."

I bit into one of the buttery, glazed scones, my eyes

drifting shut in delight—not cranberry, but plum with a hint of cinnamon. "Sorry to hear."

"Is what it is." She pierced me with her blue-gray stare. "So what exactly were you and Trent doing when Mark interrupted you?"

"Nothing naked. Just dinner." I gave her a brief synopsis of my date with Trent and my interesting ride back over the border with the charismatic Matt Davison, followed by a more hair-raising drive to the airport.

"Mark refused to tell me what they argued about, but I can probably guess." I did my best to stifle a yawn. "The little idiot. He's lucky I love him so damn much."

Cynthia set down her coffee cup and chuckled. "He's defending you, which is commendable."

"Of course Derek accused me of being a bad influence on his son."

"Fuck Derek. It was his decision to leave. Did he think everything would be sunshine and rainbows? Wait, don't answer that. Of course he did. Has there ever been a moment in his life that didn't go exactly as he wished?"

"Maybe once or twice." There was that time when he insisted on bringing a two-and-a-half-year-old Brooke to a fundraiser dinner. "I need to call Randall. I don't know what Mark and Derek said to each other, but he's refusing to see his father now."

"They can't force him to go, can they?"

"I don't know. He's sixteen and a hundred sixty-three pounds of angsty teenager. And after his and Derek's very loud conversation last night, I'm pretty sure any time spent together won't be fun for either of them." I took a sip of my now lukewarm coffee. "Oh, and I need to find a new pool service."

Cynthia grinned and settled back in her chair. "Problem

with your pool boy's performance? His job performance, that is. We already know—"

"You promised he'd give up if I ignored him."

"I don't think I actually promised."

I gave her a dirty look. "Thanks. There was a thin layer of ice covering the pool this morning."

She tipped her head. "Might want to turn up the heater if you're planning to revisit the skinny-dipping thing with Trent."

"I'm not. I instructed Gabriel to close the pool down weeks ago." Rummaging in my purse, I pulled out his latest note, destined for the shredder under my desk just like the previous ones, and tossed it across the coffee table toward Cynthia. "This was waiting on the patio for me last Thursday, so I know he's been at the house."

Cynthia's face scrunched in what I assumed was disgust. I was definitely disturbed by what Gabriel had written in his notes.

"Good lord, the grammar."

"And arrogance." I took a sip of coffee to get the nasty flavor of revulsion out of my mouth, then shook my head. "The guy's unhinged and I'm done with him. But the bigger problem is, I have a pool full of icy water now and winter's coming. By last night's freezing temperatures, sooner than I hoped."

"Let me ask around. I'm sure I know someone who has a pool—and a pool service to recommend."

"Thank you." I stacked my plate and cup on the serving tray and stood. "Well, time for me to earn this office, unless you have some other bit of wisdom to impart."

She stood as well and headed toward the door. "I have a meeting at eleven. Lunch in my office, say, one? I'm in the mood for Angelo's pumpkin lasagna."

And I was in the mood for an easier life. Unfortunately, only one of us was getting what she wanted.

By MIDWEEK I was running on stress and caffeine. Demanding corporate CEOs and building managers, angry divorce lawyers, and lecherous pool boys all made nightly appearances in my fitful dreams.

And I hadn't heard from Trent all week. Sure, he was busy, but I had gotten used to his short but sweet messages. His silence left an uneasy feeling in my gut.

Several times I'd been tempted to text him, even typed out a few awkward words before erasing them. I either sounded like his mother—*Did you make it back safe?* Or worse, clingy.

The last time I dated texting wasn't even a thing. There should be a course for newly single women. How Not to Embarrass Yourself in the Dating World 101.

After last Saturday's fiasco, had Trent just decided I was too much trouble? I couldn't really blame him. Even so, a call would have been nice.

Or was this what the kids called ghosting?

If Brooke and I were communicating with more than one-sided voicemails on my end and one or two word text replies on hers, I could've asked her. Although, probably not.

I left a futile message with the last pool service on my list—the sixth one over the past two days. There weren't many, but I only needed one to call me back. Which they hadn't. But there was no way I'd be begging Gabriel to come back. Not after the nasty message I'd left on his voice-mail. And the harshly worded email I'd sent him for good measure. That bridge was thoroughly burned. I was done with Angel Pool Services and its owner. I'd figure something out, even if I had to pull up how-to videos and drain the damn pool myself.

I glanced at my desk clock and did my best to ignore the unpleasant free fall of my stomach while straightening my workspace. *Time to go.*

In less than an hour, Randall Harris and I had a video conference with Derek and his lawyer. Randall had already warned me canceling Mark's visits with his father was unlikely. Unless I had proof Mark was in danger, and wanted to involve child social services, request an investigation, let a judge decide, and spend even more money I didn't have. What Mark did was foolhardy, but it wasn't Derek's fault. I had insisted Mark swallow his pride and apologize to his father, and I was planning to do the same this afternoon, even if it killed me.

"How's it going?" Cynthia asked, peeking into my office.

"Almost done." I closed out my computer and then pulled my purse from the drawer. "I still have to call Tom Brenner on the Overton deal—"

"That's not what I meant. Stop stressing. You're going to get wrinkles," she said as if that were the worst thing that could happen. Walking behind me, she dug her fingers into the tense muscle in my neck. "Lose the hunched shoulders and shaky hands. They don't go with your impeccable suit."

"Yes, Mom." I let out a shaky breath and smoothed down the black wool lapel of what I considered my lucky suit. If only it were that easy.

I exhaled another stress-filled breath while fastening the top button of my blouse that kept slipping open.

Cynthia batted my hand away. "Leave it."

"It's too much." I frowned down at the neckline of the silk blouse showing an inappropriate amount of cleavage. "I don't want to give the wrong impression."

Cynthia rounded my chair, leaning her hip on my desk next to me, her hand still resting on my shoulder. "Why do women always worry about how everyone sees them? You think men stare in the mirror, worried people will be offended because their tie is a fucking arrow directing everyone's attention to their dick?"

My eyes widened and an unhinged laugh burst out of me.

"It's true. And you have great tits, so stop covering them up."

Trent had thought so too. I shoved that bittersweet memory to the back of my mind. I needed to focus on the problems I could fix, not the guy who'd ghosted me most of the week.

"If you say so."

"I do." She nodded, confident grin firmly in place. "Men like to believe they're in control, but all we have to do is flash a little skin and they're on their knees, doing whatever we ask."

I doubted Derek would do whatever I asked just because of a bit of cleavage, but I kept that thought to myself. I didn't have time to debate the point with Cynthia.

"I love you, Cyn." I stood and headed toward the door, turning back at the last minute to toss a kiss to my friend.

"Love you, too. Now go show those men who's boss, tiger." She meowed.

~

THE FOLLOWING AFTERNOON, I walked out of the office and into the bright fall sunshine, slipping on my sunglasses while lifting my face toward the warmth. A weary smile sat on my lips. Progress considering twenty-four hours earlier I'd considered running off to the frozen wastelands of Siberia or possibly a cattle ranch in Wyoming.

The previous evening's meeting had run on forever. Derek and his lawyer went on and on about how I'd poisoned my son's mind and irreparably damaged the father-son relationship, while I calculated the cost of my husband's rant. Eventually he ran out of steam as he usually did. I had done my best to, well, if not somewhat convince him I had nothing to do with his son's actions, at least appear compassionate to his plight. Twenty years experience coddling the man who couldn't even meet me face-to-face had its benefits. All Derek really wanted was a few promises to not badmouth him in front of Mark— which I didn't think I had—and a little sympathy. I could easily give him the former, if only for Mark's benefit, but the latter had been a bit more difficult to swallow. I might have moved past being angry through to acceptance over everything, but in the end Derek had brought all this onto himself. Once the divorce was over I was done bailing him out with his kids. Eventually he would have to live with the consequences of his decisions.

After Mark went to bed, I spent half the night chatting with Ava Marquardt. Comparing notes and generally bashing men. It felt good to talk to someone who had been in the trenches and made it out.

The woman was a lifesaver. By the time we hung up, she had given me the name of her pool service. By ten o'clock this morning I had a new contract with Joe Ramirez and Crystal Clean Pools and an appointment set for next

Wednesday. By then my swimming pool worries would be over and Gabriel Roth could find some other woman to bother.

Life was looking up.

Word from Trent would have been nice, but I couldn't have everything. Not that his silence didn't sting. It did. We had a good time on Saturday and I was looking forward to more good times. But that didn't look likely at this point. Of course I was too much trouble. With my kids—who would always be my first priority—and the divorce, I wouldn't blame him.

I would have to take my victories where I could find them and accept my losses. Even without Trent, my wins had outnumbered my failures this week, a sure sign my situation was improving.

A black stretch limo idled at the curb just outside the building. Some exec heading to the airport most likely. I inspected my reflection in the mirror-like finish of the paint as I drew closer. The hem of my dark red shirt dress hit just above the knee, and even in my comfortable loafers my legs looked damn good.

I made a mental note to get my Cayenne washed this weekend as the driver rounded the front of the car. My eyes widened a fraction as I took in the older gentleman's formal tuxedo and white gloves. The polish on the man's dress shoes rivaled the wax on his car. Not a livery driver, then.

I flashed him a smile and then shot a glance over my shoulder to get a glimpse of the hotshot this private car belonged to, but the wide space between the street and the building was empty.

"Good evening, Ms. Adams. My name is Harvey." The man smiled and opened the back door, his berry-blue eyes twinkling.

I returned his smile with a hesitant one. "Hello, Harvey. I'm afraid there must be some mistake."

Harvey paused for a second, his smile drooping only slightly, then turned his attention to whoever was inside the limo. "Is this not Ms. Adams?"

"Get in the damn car, Nicki," a familiar deep voice said from within. "You want discreet, but if I have to stare at your legs for one more second, I'm climbing out and stuffing your ass in here."

CHAPTER
FOURTEEN

"Trent?" I tipped my sunglasses down to peek into the vehicle's darkened interior while telling my excitement to settle down. The man had been MIA for the past five days.

"Now, Nicki." He flashed me a smile that shone in the dark.

"Mr. Richards did mention a schedule, Ms. Adams. He seems a bit... eager," Harvey added, shifting his sleeve up to peek at his watch.

I let out a resigned sigh, my willpower slipping. Hadn't I spent too much time over the past month being angry? Trent was here. In a damn limo, for Christ's sake.

Pocketing my glasses into my purse, I bent to get into the car and headed toward the seat across from him. "What is all this about?"

"We have unfinished business, Ms. Adams. Now get your pretty little ass over here." His hands circled my waist and he pulled me in the opposite direction of where I'd been headed.

The hem of my dress hiked indecently high as my knees

parted to make room for Trent's muscular thighs. The soft wool of his trousers slid across my tender skin, setting off hot sparks of desire. His hands cradled my face and his warm, soft lips pressed against mine.

The soft whomp of the car door closing filtered into my consciousness. Air rushed over my exposed thighs, letting me know there was a good chance Harvey had just gotten an eyeful. Not that I cared. Not with Trent's hot mouth moving against mine.

His thumbs caressed my face as if he were trying to memorize the feel of me, and the warm spice of his signature cinnamon flavor sizzled against my tongue.

He pulled away slowly with a low groan. "I've been dreaming about doing that all week."

"I approve of your dreams," I returned, a little breathless.

He frowned for a second, his eyes shifting between mine. "I'm sorry for not calling. I wanted to. Really. But this week has been hell."

"Tell me about it." My life had turned into a sort of hell over the past month. I'd meant my comment as commiseration, but Trent continued.

"As soon as we were settled on the bus to our hotel in Phoenix, Henderson vomited everywhere. Literally. Then a half hour later, Billings and Redstone were sick as well."

"Oh no."

"Our first thought was food poisoning, but the team doc diagnosed the stomach flu. By morning, four more were sick. Fun times, trying to decide who was well enough to play that night."

Mark might have mentioned something about them losing badly Tuesday morning.

"I never want a repeat of our flight to Tampa, Wednesday, and I'm sure the flight attendants don't either."

"Sounds unpleasant."

"I didn't have a minute's rest until the flight home this morning. It was nonstop running from hotel room to hotel room, handing out electrolytes and anti-nausea meds. Thought I might be getting it Wednesday night, but I think it was just exhaustion. Coach ordered me to my room that night—the first night I had to myself. I'd planned on calling you, but my phone wasn't in my carry on bag, where I shoved it before we landed."

"You lost your phone?" The knot of anxiety that had built over the past five days of silence loosened as he nodded.

"Apparently. I called it a few times, but no one answered. I'd planned to send my assistant out for a replacement Thursday morning, but the flu bug struck the poor man overnight. And with a game only hours away, I had no time to run out myself. I'd considered borrowing someone's phone, but I didn't want to leave your number in their call history."

I couldn't decide whether to appreciate his forethought or curse my lawyer for making me into his dirty little secret.

He winced, his gaze searching mine, possibly gauging my schooled reaction. "If I hadn't experienced it, I wouldn't believe my story either."

Okay, maybe I was enjoying making him sweat. A little payback for my week spent fighting the crushing doubts over his silence.

"I ran out this morning and picked up a new one before our plane took off, but then I decided you deserved a face-to-face explanation. And maybe a nice dinner as well as an apology? I am truly sorry, Nic."

I couldn't help but grin at his story. Our house had been in the thick of the stomach flu more times than I wanted to remember.

I sifted my fingers through the short crisp hairs at the base of his neck as my smile wilted. "I worried that you didn't make it back to your harbor safely. Or maybe you'd changed your mind about me."

He sucked in a quick breath, his brow creasing along with the corners of his eyes as he frowned. His arms tightened around my waist, and his head dropped to my shoulder. "Never. Fuck, Nic... You feel so good in my arms, I may never let go this time."

He slid a hand up to the base of my neck and branded my lips with a kiss that left no doubt how he felt. The car swayed into a turn, then thumped over a pothole. Trent tightened his hold to steady us.

"So, are we just driving around?"

"I have better plans than a quickie in the back of a limo." He tucked a strand of hair behind my ear and grinned. "Not that it isn't an attractive option for the future. But I did mention dinner, didn't I?"

The cold leftovers waiting in the fridge at home couldn't compare with whatever Trent had planned—even if it was just driving around. But fear threatened to send me back to the safe confines of my home. No matter how much I wanted to be with Trent, yesterday's confrontation with Derek proved what a dangerous game I was playing.

"You know, the whole public dating thing is still forbidden—"

"I know." His lips curved into a slight smile. "No one will see us. Trust me."

I couldn't help but return his smile. Five nights ago I'd

put my trust in him, and I had one of the most memorable dates of my life—even if it was cut short.

I nodded, running my thumbs along the soft wool lapels of his suit jacket. This one was a stunning double-breasted in a dark navy, paired with a pale blue striped shirt and a dark red water-stained silk tie that was almost a perfect match to my dress. How could I resist his plans when he was dressed for victory?

"You're quiet. What's on your mind, Nic?"

"I'm trying to decide if I prefer you in suits or jeans." I tugged on his lapels, bringing him to my lips. He was completely edible either way, but at some point tonight I wanted him naked.

"Let me know. I'm here to please." His forest eyes raked over me, causing heat to bloom under my skin as if he'd touched me. "I can say in all honesty, I like your badass corporate look."

He flicked open the first few buttons on my dress with nimble fingers, making me curious how many times they'd performed that task.

"Badass?" No one had ever called me badass in my life.

He paused for a second as if to think, then shoved the top of my dress down my shoulders, revealing the red lace balconette bra the sales assistant at Agent Provocateur swore would make my boobs look amazing. The way Trent sucked in a breath told me she was right.

"Definitely badass. And sexy as hell." His hand curved around the underside of my breast. He flicked his thumb over the hard peak of my nipple, straining against the almost sheer fabric that might've actually been worth the outrageous price tag, making me gasp.

I hadn't planned this little encounter, but if I had, I defi-nitely would have worn this sexy little bra-and-thong set that had set my husband back almost a grand the day after he left me.

"Fuck, Nic. These tits..." He lowered his head, closing his mouth over my sensitive flesh clad in lace while his free hand slid over the curve of my ass, pulling me against him. Heat spread across my skin like fire at the feel of his hot tongue, my core clenching as he guided me over his hard length. Chances were I was making a mess all over his expensive slacks, but I didn't think he cared about dry-cleaning bills at the moment. And neither did I.

I dropped my head against his shoulder and hummed in pleasure. "I thought sex in a limo was off the table tonight."

I wasn't completely averse to the idea. Over the past eighteen years of parenting, in the early years of my marriage, I'd learned how to be quick and quiet with the kids' nursery within hearing distance. But with Trent, that might be difficult.

The car accelerated, and Trent braced me as we made another turn. On the other hand, less abrupt movements would have been nice.

"Damn." He pulled back with a strangled groan, then buttoned up my dress to my disappointment. "I'm losing my mind over you, you know that? You're all I think about; you're in my dreams. And now I'm turning into a fucking teenager who can't even keep his dick in his pants."

I couldn't help a giggle from escaping, and when Trent shot me a glare, I laughed harder. "Sorry, at forty-three, I'm taking that as a compliment. Speaking of teenagers, how long do you plan on keeping me? Mine will be expecting me home soon. What should I tell him?"

Trent gave me a peck on the lips before shifting me to the seat next to him. Then straightened his tie. "Tell your son the truth. Tell him you're having dinner with a friend."

I rested my chin on his shoulder and grinned. "Is that what we are? Friends?"

Trent frowned for a second as if thinking hard about the question. "I don't know. But you definitely can't tell your son you're having dinner with the man who is obsessed with fucking you."

I laughed, shaking my head. Then Trent lifted my hand and placed a tender kiss in the center of my palm in a way that had my laugh evaporating and sent my insides tumbling. "It's more than that. I like you, Nicki. I like you a lot."

"I like you, too." A smile tugged at the corners of my lips while I reveled in the giddy feeling inside me.

"You know I'm not really fond of these, though," he said after a pause. He lifted my feet onto his lap and frowned at my unfashionable loafers I'd been unable to banish to the donation box a month ago along with all my other frumpy clothes. They were just too comfortable even though they were ugly as hell.

"I was expecting to walk four blocks to the train. Fashion has nothing to do with it," I defended as he slipped my shoes off my feet.

Trent dug his thumb into the ball of my foot, and I couldn't help the little moan of pleasure that slipped from my lips. His eyes darkened, and I watched as his large hands easily swallowed up my equally large feet, which I'd always been a little embarrassed about. Petite I wasn't, and neither were the size ten and a half flippers keeping me upright. But I'd spent most of my day running around, in heels, and right now I wasn't saying no to his magic fingers.

The tinted glass barrier lowered a fraction. "Sorry to disturb, sir. We're almost to our destination. Thought you would want to know."

"Thank you, Harvey," Trent said before the glass slid back up.

Reaching into my open bag, he pulled out my black Jimmy Choos. "I like these better."

"Where exactly are we going?" I hesitated, glancing out the window. The high-rise buildings fronted with high-end shops and trendy restaurants identified this as the Gold Coast. Prime Derek Robinson voter territory. I'd be recognized within minutes, if not seconds, of stepping onto the sidewalks here.

"Trust me, Nicki," he repeated as the car slowed, then turned. Outside the windows, the daylight vanished and the car turned again, heading down a ramp. Trent slipped my shoes on my feet, giving me a slight glimpse of how Cinderella felt. Unfortunately, it wasn't just a couple of angry stepsisters catching me at the ball I had to worry about.

The car stopped and the slight jostle and thump of the car door told me our trusty driver had gotten out.

A few moments later my door swung open and Harvey appeared.

"The coast is clear, sir, and I've called for the elevator." His voice echoed in the cavernous space of the parking garage where we were stopped. He held out his hand. "Ms. Adams. May I assist you?"

Trent walked to the back of the limo, pulling a suitcase out of the open trunk and shouldering a backpack. He thanked Harvey before ushering me toward a bank of elevators, the middle one open and empty.

"Trent?" I looked up at him in confusion. "Where are we?"

"Nicki. I've been to your home. Welcome to mine."

149

THE MAHOGANY-PANELED elevator's wall of buttons stopped at the forty-eighth floor. Above that a key slot and additional buttons LP, UP, and PH sat slightly apart from the rest. Trent inserted a key into the panel and pressed PH, and the elevator surged up with a hum.

His eyes locked on mine for a beat, then his bags thudded against the elevator floor and he closed the gap between us in one long stride.

"What is it about you? I just can't stay away," he whispered before angling his lips against mine in a kiss that erased all thoughts of work and the kids and pools and the damned divorce. Trent was like the brightest star in the sky. Everything else dimmed in his presence.

The elevator dinged, announcing our floor, and Trent pulled back. My eyelids fluttered open, and I slowly licked his spicy cinnamon flavor from my lips. He shook his head, his eyes squeezing shut as he let out a pained sigh.

"I have very respectable dinner plans tonight, Nicki, but if you keep looking at me like this, I won't be held responsible."

I couldn't help but stare at the evidence of his *threat* tenting the front of his dress slacks, then let my gaze take a leisurely stroll up the rest of his magnificent body before reaching his eyes.

"Feed me first, then we'll see who will be held responsible," I whispered before pressing a quick kiss on his lips, ignoring the husky growl coming from behind me in order to take in what looked to be a very nice foyer.

My heels clicked against the pale gray veined marble floor while I studied a stunning contemporary sculpture comprised of a trio of twisted black columns. Two doors stood on opposite sides of the room with brass plates set in the center of the upper panel, marking the two penthouse units.

"My sister, Teresa redecorated this room after my neighbor moved out a couple years ago," Trent said while he led me to the door on the left side of the room. "Before that... well, let's just say Jim and Nancy's tastes were interesting."

"How long have you lived here?"

"Four years." Trent slid his key into the lock of unit A and opened his door. "Come on in."

Stepping inside, I gasped at the aqua-green expanse of Lake Michigan stretching out from one side of the penthouse to the other in a completely unobstructed view that was worth millions. I couldn't help but grin. The rest of the place wasn't too shabby either. Masculine but comfortable.

Trent set his bags down and hung up my coat before slipping his shoes off and sliding them in the small coat closet by the entrance. I started to kick my heels off as well, but he stopped me with a hand on my shoulder.

"Keep them on."

I followed Trent past a large cream leather sectional that sat upon a shaggy charcoal rug. The former was loaded with plush pillows in a contemporary pattern of grays and browns. The biggest TV I'd ever seen hung opposite, taking up most of the pale gray wall. Trent picked up a remote and, a second later, soft piano music played on a hidden sound system.

I wandered closer to the floor-to-ceiling windows and stared out at the whole north shore of Lake Michigan. The evening rush hour flowed up and down Lake Shore Drive in miniature. Navy Pier sat just to my right and Ohio Street

Beach? right below me, deserted except for a man and his dog.

"Wow." My breath fogged the glass for a second.

Trent's reflection appeared in the window. His head dipped down to place a kiss at the curve of my neck, making me shiver with pleasure. The heat of his body soaked into my back as he pressed up against me, his hand splayed across my belly pulling me closer. I leaned back as my knees went weak with desire.

"Trent..." I let out a breathless sigh, tipping my head back against his shoulder to give him better access.

"I can't wait to get inside you. Should we start here?"

"Yes, please." I'd spent the last week regretting the way Saturday night had ended. Regretting all the missed opportunities to know this man on an intimate level. I didn't care at this point if everyone below us donned binoculars and watched. Nothing would stop us tonight.

He pulled back, his hand closing around the curve of my waist, turning me from the view. "First here, then my bedroom. Or maybe I'll feast on you on my desk, then my bedroom. I haven't worked the specifics out in my mind yet, but I want the memory of us burned into every room for when you're not here with me."

"There's a lot of rooms." If he owned half the floor, this would be a long, pleasurable night.

"There are." His fingers threaded with mine, pulling me away from the windows. "But first, dinner."

Along the backside of the sectional sat two chrome Barcelona chairs upholstered in black leather facing a fireplace set into the twelve-foot-high wall dividing the living space. Obviously not a real fireplace, but a long narrow box currently crackling with flames above a bed of black glass shards.

The artwork sitting above the fireplace caught my eye and halted my step. A stunning photo of two racing yachts passing each other at impossibly sharp angles sat in a simple frame. The colors were eye catching—the vivid red and blue of the two hulls, the yellow and orange of the sailors' jackets, the pristine white of their sails angling across one another against the azure sky. The turquoise waters surging with foam-topped waves reminded me of the lake the morning after our last date.

"You like?" Trent asked from over my shoulder.

"Very much. You can almost hear the ocean roar."

"I thought so too." He took my hand again, guiding me farther into his home.

On the other side of the wall sat a small dining room. A cascade of thin vertical black rods hung from the ceiling, the light spilling from the ends reflecting softly on the small glass table with two place settings of crisp white china. As accommodating as the sectional had been, the table in here held only four chairs. The intimate space was separated from the kitchen by a long island and nestled in the corner of the building offering views of both the lake and city. A romantic spot—especially now with the lights dimmed and the glow of the setting sun sparkling on the water in between the shadows of the surrounding buildings.

On this side of the dividing wall, more artwork hung above the crackling fireplace. The subject was also a sailing theme, but this one was vastly different. A lone sailboat sat on a clear blue ocean. Tiny, the boat was a mere triangular speck on an endless sea, giving off a sense of isolation and insignificance but also peace. For a moment I flashed back to that magazine cover in Randall's office, *The Aegean Dream*. It was similar, but this view was far removed as if God, or Neptune, was supervising their safe passage.

"I might have exaggerated when I said I was going to make dinner," Trent said from the opposite side of the kitchen island.

"Oh?" I gave a good natured laugh at his uncomfortable expression. It didn't matter to me if we ate take-out pizza in bed, or on the fluffy rug in his living room, or wherever.

"I could have, if I hadn't spent half the day wrangling a basketball team back to Chicago." He picked a plain white card off his dark gray granite counter and gave it a quick read before tossing it back onto the work surface, turning on the oven and rolling up the sleeves of his dress shirt. "I called in a little help from our team chef. You mentioned something about liking lamb, right?"

Before the last week of silence, Trent and I had spent countless hours talking about everything, from our favorite color, to memorable moments in high school, to what we'd choose for our last dinner. We both favored red, Trent's teen years were way more exciting than mine, and his last meal would be his mother's homemade macaroni and cheese. It had been over twenty years since I'd eaten the family cook's Easter lamb, seasoned with rosemary and lemon. Derek hated lamb, turned green even from the smell of it, so Mom switched the menu to ham shortly after we'd married.

"Yes. Do you need any help?"

"I got it." His head disappeared inside his refrigerator for a second before reappearing with a bright red casserole in one hand and a bottle of wine in the other. "Just have a seat and watch my incredible talent for reheating dinner."

I let out a snort of laughter. "It's an underappreciated talent."

"That it is." Trent set two wine glasses on the counter in front of me, and pulled the cork from the wine bottle with the skill of someone who'd performed the task a time or ten, while I watched the muscles of his forearms flex. "Honestly, I don't know shit about wines, but I trust Michael. He manages the food for all the fancy team events."

"Whenever we had dinners at the house, I let Derek pick the wine. He's sort of a snob when it comes to—" I dropped my head into my hands and let out a groan. "I'm sorry. I shouldn't be ruining tonight with talk of my almost ex."

Trent poured a pretty pale pink rosé into both of our glasses, handing me mine. "We could pretend you didn't have a life before we met, but that would be unfair to both of us. Whatever you and Derek had, it's shaped who you are today. If he can't see the incredible woman sitting in front of me now, it's his loss and my windfall. And in my opinion, food and drink should be enjoyed, not judged by some weird standard."

My face warmed with his compliment and understanding. "Thank you. I agree."

"Now keep in mind, there are times I'd rather not hear about your ex..." He sent me a flirty wink that left no doubt what situations he was talking about. My face heated further, for an all together different reason. Would I ever get used to discussing sex—even masked behind innuendo and innocent gestures—with this man?

Trent sipped his wine with an appreciative hum, completely oblivious to my embarrassment. "Not bad. Now let me throw the lamb shanks into the oven." My stomach made its own appreciative and all-too-embarrassing grumble. "Along with roasted vegetables and individual apple cobbler for later. If you couldn't tell, I'm trying my best to impress you."

"Color me impressed." What with the limo and the foot massage and now dinner, I appreciated his effort.

He slid the casserole dish into his bright red monster of a Viking range. Then grabbed a canister of what looked like homemade crackers off the counter and dumped them into a bowl. "Blue cheese and garlic. They're a staple in the luxury boxes and insanely addictive. We've got twenty minutes until dinner, why don't we take these back into the living room."

Dishwasher loaded, Trent's glass-topped dining table restored to it's sparkling splendor, the smell of dessert perfuming the air. I didn't know where I was going to put it. Dinner had been better than anything I could remember, but my full and happy stomach said it was willing to find room.

I hopped up on the island counter like a teenager, watching as Trent finished up at the sink and then washed his hands.

Outside, the lights of the city twinkled, and I couldn't help but hope I'd be around long enough to see the view blanketed in snow. Maybe help decorate the tree I could almost picture fitting perfectly in the windows of his living room. Which was ridiculous. I'd be spending my holiday with my kids, and unless Randall performed miracles, Trent wouldn't be invited.

Trent dropped the dish towel onto his pretty granite counter and headed across his kitchen toward me. "Eighteen minutes until the crisps are done. Then another twenty for them to cool. What do you think we should do in the meantime?"

My legs parted and he stepped between them. "I haven't a clue," I said with as much innocence as a forty-three-year-old future divorcée could muster.

Trent slipped the top button of my red shirt dress open with his nimble fingers. Then the next, and the next. "I have some ideas."

"You're very good at that."

His eyebrows rose, his dark, hooded expression suggesting we had better things to discuss than his history of disrobing a woman. I had to agree.

He made quick work of the sash at my waist, tossing the strip of fabric over his shoulder. Then the rest of the buttons were loose, and he was peeling my dress back, exposing my matching lace undergarments and the sheer, thigh-high stockings I was still on the fence about. Trent's slack-jawed expression said I wouldn't be going back to my old control tops any time soon.

"Fuck, Nicki. Are you trying to kill me here?" He ran his fingertips back and forth over the sensitive skin of my upper thigh, tracing just above the lacy edge of the stocking. I let out a gasp at the heavy sensations his touch created inside me.

"That wouldn't be in my best interest, would it?"

He skated his hands inside my dress, gripping the curve of my hips, sliding me to the edge of the counter and against him. I couldn't help but whimper at the press of his hard length still encased in slacks.

"I think you're a little overdressed for this party," I whispered against his lips, my fingers closing over the loosened knot of his tie.

"Help me out, then."

The strip of cool, fluid silk slid against my fingertips like water as I worked to loosen the knot. "You know Cyn has a theory about men's ties..."

"Oh yeah? And what's that?"

I let my gaze travel down to the part of his anatomy that, at this moment, needed no assistance garnering attention. The man had a python in his damn pants for God's sake. Not that I wasn't aware of that fact already.

My face warmed as I blurted out, "She says it's meant to draw attention to..."

Trent chuckled as I flicked my gaze down again. "I work with a bunch of men. I'm pretty sure I don't want them noticing my dick."

"Yeah, well, that's Cyn's theory." I turned away to lay his tie down on the counter.

"She sounds like a bad influence." His hands closed around my waist and he rocked against me with an appreciative hum. "One that I approve of most heartily."

I tore at the buttons of his shirt, shoving the crisp cotton off his wide shoulders while he rushed to unfasten the cuffs, then carelessly tossed the garment over his shoulder and onto the floor.

"You have too many clothes." I fisted my hands onto the waist of his neatly tucked undershirt and yanked up, pulling it out of his slacks with maybe a little more force than necessary. But the dress shirt had taken too long, and I was a little more than impatient to see him naked again.

Trent chuckled as he lifted the T-shirt over his head and dropped it on the floor. "I like you aggressive."

My face heated with a rush of uncertainty. Was I stepping too far out of my comfort zone? Would I regret my eagerness come tomorrow? Would Trent?

"I never was. Aggressive, that is. But with you..." I

fumbled to find the right words to convey this crazy need I had for Trent. Only Trent.

"Nicki..." His teeth closed over my earlobe as he spoke, and his hands—Jesus, his hands. Everywhere he touched sent a blaze of heat across my skin. "I love having this effect on you."

I was just as lost. Every innocent touch, every glance across the dinner table from Trent, made me desperate for this moment. Truth was, my need had sparked to life the moment I got into his limo, surged with promise in the elevator. From the second I stepped into his penthouse, the fuse had been lit—a slow burn of foreplay leading up to this.

Trent slanted his lips over mine. His hand slipped to the back of my neck, holding me in place. Not that I was going anywhere. Not when his mouth claimed me with a hunger I was more than willing to match.

He groaned out a long exhale as we parted to take a breath, chests heaving, skin flushed. His hot gaze raked over every inch of me before returning to my face. "Damn, you're so fucking beautiful like this."

"You make me like this." I shoved all thoughts of my flaws to the back of my mind. In the bright lights of the kitchen, Trent had to see them. The dimples, the stretch marks, my far from flat stomach—thanks to dinner and two pregnancies. I didn't want to even think about how many young, beautiful women had warmed his bed over the past decade. Women much more beautiful than me. But for some reason he wanted me. I told the critical voice in my head to shut up. To stop worrying about the imperfections Trent obviously didn't care about.

"You're not too bad yourself, mister. But you're still way

overdressed," I pointed out while tugging on his belt with less than nimble fingers.

"An unforgivable social faux pas. Damn dress codes. I'm always fucking up," he whispered while stepping closer and forcing my thighs wider. "Thank God you're here to help."

I shook my head and faked a long-suffering sigh, as if undressing this incredibly handsome man was a hardship. "I'll do my best, but there's a lot to work with here."

"There is." He kissed me while skating his knuckles over my dark nipples pressing hard against the flimsy lace of my bra, effectively distracting me from the workings of his belt buckle.

He pulled back and watched with rapt attention as he hooked his fingers over the scalloped edge of my bra and tugged the fabric down. My breasts spilled out and his eyes widened with what I could only describe as delight. Like it was Christmas morning and Santa had brought him everything on his list.

His tongue slid across his lower lip a second before he dipped his head, taking one of my nipples into his mouth, effectively cutting off my view of his complicated belt buckle that still refused to open.

Sparks of pleasure shot straight to my core as his teeth scraped over my tender flesh. I gave up on my task of getting him undressed—at least for the moment—and leaned back on my hands to give him better access.

The ill-timed timer chimed, and he stepped back. "Hold that thought."

I grinned, watching him don the pair of puffy crab claw oven mitts I would have to know the story of at some point. Trent pulled the oven door opened and a rush of heat warmed my skin. The pungent scent of apples and cinnamon and butter filled the kitchen better than any potpourri I'd ever purchased.

He turned back, his lips curving up. "Damn. This is a sight I'll be replaying in my head for a long time."

Before I lost my nerve, I reached up and ran my finger around one hardened nipple. "What, these old things?"

"Fuck, yeah." He shifted back, leaning his weight against the range behind him, while gripping himself through the front of his slacks. "Keep going, Nicki."

In for a penny, as the saying went. I sent him a flirty smile and skated my finger along the dusky perimeter before taking a stiffened nipple between my fingers and squeezing hard enough to make me gasp. In the dark of the night, after Derek had satisfied his needs and drifted off to sleep, I'd lie awake and touch myself like this.

"Slip your other hand inside your panties."

My free hand hesitated for a second. I'd never put on a show before, never wanted to, to be honest. Maybe if I had... but no. I wasn't going to consider the *what ifs* of my marriage, not with the way Trent watched me with the kind of uncontrolled lust I'd never witnessed in the twenty years of my marriage.

I slipped my hand down over the slight rise of my stomach, then paused. "Remove your slacks first."

Trent let out a low chuckle but flicked open his belt buckle, then undid the fastener at the top of his slacks. The snick of his zipper echoed in the quiet room, along with the whoosh of his dress slacks as they hit the floor.

My core clenched at the sight of his thick penis peeking out from the waistband of his boxer briefs. It had been almost a month since the last time I'd seen Trent naked, and I paused to appreciate what was standing in front of me. The curve of his hard pectorals, the ridges of his abs, the V of muscles above his hips that disappeared into his boxers.

Without a second thought my fingers breached the elastic of my own panties. I couldn't remember the last time I'd been this turned on. This wet. There was a good chance I'd detonate within the next second, so I detoured past my hard, sensitive bud and dipped a finger inside me.

"Tell me what you feel like," Trent whispered, his voice gravelly. His own hand had found its way into his boxers, giving me a glimpse of him with every leisurely stroke.

I barely recognized my own voice as I replied, "Hot. Slick. Goooood."

"Are you about to come?"

"God, yes." Sparks of pleasure danced inside me, making my eyes drift close. Even without touching my clit, I was seconds from orgasming.

"Not yet." My eyes sprang open as Trent's hand closed around my wrist, pulling it from my underwear. My mouth dropped open as he guided my fingers into his mouth, sucking them clean. "Fucking delicious, just like I expected."

His hand curved over my shoulder, guiding me down onto the counter. "Lie back for me."

The cold granite pulled a shiver from me. Or maybe it was Trent's fingers hooked into the sides of my panties, guiding them down my legs. A second later my legs were draped over his shoulders and he was feasting on me like dinner never happened.

I made an incoherent noise of encouragement as his tongue speared into me. Another as his lips closed around my clit. My back bowed off the counter as his long, thick finger slid inside me, while his other hand found my breast, pinching and pulling the way I had moments earlier.

He added a second digit, dragging his fingers across my G-spot with every stroke, while he sucked my hardened bud into his mouth. My hold on reality vanished. Wave after wave of pleasure washed over me until I felt like the rung-out dish rag on the other side of the kitchen.

I came to as Trent pulled his wallet from his slacks and then thumbed a condom from inside. Before he could open the package, I grabbed his wrist.

"No."

His eyes narrowed. "No?"

"I had my tubes tied. Fourteen years ago. After Mark." He'd seen my medical report, but I couldn't remember if that little detail was in there. "We're both clean. I can't get pregnant."

His eyes lit up with something like glee. "You sure?"

"Very. I want to feel you."

"Fuck, Nic." He tossed the condom over his shoulder, yanked his boxers down and off, and my thoughts fled.

Damn he was gorgeous. Every inch of him. Hard and veiny and completely intimidating. That night in the pool I'd been too shy to look at him, but now I cataloged every detail of him.

A shrill ring of a phone pierced the silence, derailing my thoughts. Not my ringtone. We both froze for a second before he shook his head.

"Ignore it," he instructed, pulling me toward him.

I spread my legs wider to accommodate him, giving him a nod and reminding him of where we were.

We both looked down as he grasped his shaft—glistening with pre-come—in his fist, dragging the wide crown across my wet entrance, then up.

I gasped as he brushed my clit, my hips jerking forward.

My core flooded with moisture, coating the tip of Trent's cock.

"Like that?" he asked, sliding back down and then back up again.

"God, yes. More." My voice shook. I'd have to cut off my fingers to count the times I'd come more than once with Derek, but there was a good chance I would be coming before Trent entered me if he kept that up.

The phone rang again, and Trent stilled with a sigh.

"Maybe you should get that?"

"No." He gripped my hip and then plunged forward until our pelvises met. My mouth dropped open with a silent cry as I watched him retreat and then slide home again.

"You okay?" he rasped out.

I was more than okay, but I'd lost the ability to speak, so I nodded.

The phone quieted, but a second later started to ring again. Trent dropped his head onto my shoulder and let out a groan.

"Just one second. I promise... don't move." He pointed a finger at me, and stepped back. "I mean it."

"Marcus..." he growled out from the living room a moment later. "This better be fucking good."

"What," he hissed after a minute. "I can barely hear you. Speak the fuck up."

I breathed out a sigh of disappointment, the same disappointment I could hear in Trent's voice. "You're gonna owe me big time, brother. Don't fucking cry. I'll be there soon."

He reappeared, his penis slick from my body but wilting fast. "I'm sorry. I need to go."

I hopped off the counter on shaky legs and picked up my panties. "Emergency?"

"Something like that. Gotta save a stupid rookie from himself..." He dragged a hand through his hair while letting out a growl of disappointment and frustration. "...got himself in a situation. Stay. This won't take long. I promise."

"I should go. Mark will be home, and..." I wasn't looking forward to explaining the vague text I'd sent him earlier.

I stepped into my underwear and then wrestled my boobs back into my bra. *Why isn't there a sexier way to get dressed?*

"Let me grab some clothes," he said, then headed back the way he'd come.

A minute later, I stood in the living room, fastening up the last of my buttons and tying my sash. Trent appeared in jeans and a sweatshirt with the team logo on the front. "Come on. I'll drive you home when I'm done."

He handed me my coat, opened the door, and we headed toward the elevator.

"Trent. You can't take me home. My car is parked at Kenilworth Station." I turned as we reached the elevators and gave him a sad smile. "Just drop me off at Union Station. I'll ride back."

"No." He motioned me into the waiting elevator car. "We had a date. Only an asshole would drop his date off at the station at this time of night. Wait in the car while I take care of Marcus, then I'll drive you to your car. But someday I plan on driving you all the way home."

CHAPTER
FIFTEEN

A short time later, Trent walked out of a sketchy-looking neighborhood bar with four men. Two were clearly wearing police uniforms, another was a Black man, slightly taller than Trent—Marcus, I assumed—and lastly, a squat, round man, much shorter than the rest. And way more agitated given the way the man was shouting while waving his arms around like one of those blowup characters set in front of car dealers during a sale. *Overcompensation for his lack of height, maybe?*

A bar fight was all the explanation Trent gave me before leaving me in the car to worry, at least until the police pulled up.

One of the cops placed a hand onto shorty's shoulder in what I assumed was an attempt to calm the man. A second later Trent pulled out his wallet and handed the man something. Cash, possibly? Whatever it was did the trick. Next, all four of them shook hands and then dispersed. The officers headed back to their car. Marcus lumbered off, folding himself into a shiny black BMW parked a few cars down the block. Trent stood on the sidewalk for a moment watching him drive away and then headed across the street, while shorty disappeared back into the bar.

Trent slid onto the driver's seat with a groan. He leaned his head back against the headrest and closed his eyes. "I'm getting too old for this."

"Everything's okay, though?"

He rubbed at the corners of his eyes and nodded.

"You look tired. Want me to drive?" I inspected the five-speed gear shift on the console between us with trepidation. The last time I'd driven stick had been back in college, and that had been a four-speed Honda with a wonky clutch, but how much harder could one extra gear be?

"Nah. I'm good." Trent smiled my way and then started his car and pulled onto the street. "A bit crazy at first, but everything's good."

"I wasn't going to leave you, you know." I shook my head as I stared out the front window at the mix of houses in various states of disrepair. A group of men hung out on a porch, shouting something unpleasant to a car driving in the opposite direction. My familiarity with Chicago neighborhoods wasn't great, but even I could tell this wasn't a place to linger. "Whatever you thought could go wrong, I wasn't about to leave. So what exactly happened, or is it none of my business?"

Trent gave me a hard stare as we pulled up to the red light at Irving Park. "Are you angry?"

I stared back. "No. Just... maybe a little stressed. Sitting in the car, worried you might get hurt or worse."

He lifted my hand off my lap and pressed my fingers to his lips. "I'm sorry. Marcus said he was just defending some woman from an obnoxious asshole who didn't know the meaning of no. Next thing he knew, asshole and his friend's fists were flying at him. Chairs were thrown, tables smashed. By the time the bar owner intervened, the two perpetrators ran off, leaving Marcus to deal with the mess."

"And you, obviously."

"And me. Nothing like a thousand dollars and floor seats to smooth things over, and convince the owner not to press charges."

I dropped back into his soft leather seat with a groan. I'd put my nice, quiet divorce in danger for some twenty-one year-old kid with a hero complex. *I* was too old for this shit.

"I'm his coach," Trent continued. "It's not written anywhere, but it's part of the job. Mentor, cheerleader, sometimes punching bag, part-time parent, friend. You name it, I've done it. Tough kids, innocent kids, kids from bad neighborhoods and good families; suddenly they have more money than they ever dreamed. Marcus grew up in rural Indiana. His father died when he was little and his mother worked three jobs to send him to Purdue, and feed his three younger sisters. They're counting on me to keep him safe."

I suppressed my motherly instinct to lecture him on his sense of responsibility. Trent was a grown man, and I was just... What the hell was I? We'd somehow skipped over that conversation tonight.

"Although I'm gonna be pissed at him for some time." He shifted gears and then set his hand on my thigh. "I wanted tonight to be special. And now I have to get on a plane again in the morning. Sometimes..."

His disappointment hung heavy in the car. Tonight had been nice, but it was hard not to imagine what we'd be doing right now if Marcus hadn't called. How many orgasms could this man have coaxed out of me? Time and our own personal commitments seemed to be wagering against us. When would Trent realize there were less complicated women out there?

"At least you have your phone this week." And chances of the stomach flu striking twice in two weeks was unlikely.

Trent's grin flashed in the dark. "I promise to call every night. Maybe even video chat."

My body pressed into the seat as we hit the highway. The engine growled, low and masculine, rocketing the car past the speed limit in a flash while he skillfully shifted through the gears. The quick acceleration made my stomach flutter with a combination of fear and excitement.

"So this is how you made it to my house in twenty minutes that first night?"

"Does it scare you?"

"We both have things to lose here." I frowned, watching the outskirts of the city fly by, letting him know I wasn't just talking about reckless driving.

He let up on the gas and slowed down a fraction. "I want to see you again. And again. I won't let anything happen to you."

"Maybe I'm being selfish. You're the one thing in my life that doesn't have to do with the kids or the house or what's right. I realized the other day, I haven't been truly happy in a very long time, but I think I'm heading in the right direction. Finally."

"Maybe you deserve better than me, but I'm selfish too," Trent confessed as he concentrated on maneuvering around the sparse traffic. "I'm not giving you up."

My stomach fluttered again.

The rest of the ride was spent in quiet contemplation. I wasn't stupid enough to take Trent's words as a declaration of love. Neither of us was looking for love. Just... what?

DARCI ANN BAKER

A handful of minutes later the car slowed as he moved onto the off-ramp.

"We're off to Houston in the morning. Spending the weekend there," he said, pulling next to my Cayenne way too soon. "Then LA, Monday, Wednesday... *Shit*. We're home Friday. Then back on the road Monday."

"Mark's got a game Saturday morning, then he's off to DC to visit his father. We have mediation Friday. The divorce is so close, maybe we should exercise patience."

Thoughts of how exquisite Trent felt inside me competed with the worry I'd experienced moments ago. Waiting was the last thing I wanted, but the longer we played this game, the more I saw Trent, the more I feared we were pushing our luck.

"If I have to go weeks without you..." He shook his head and sighed, and then turned to look out his window. "You're under my skin, invading my thoughts. It's physically painful, imagining not seeing you for that long."

He slipped out of the car and opened my door. End of discussion.

"I don't want that either." I smiled slightly as he helped me out of his car. Despite the risks, I didn't want to give this up, even temporarily. "This evening was a nice surprise even if it didn't end quite as planned."

He followed me over to my car, then peered inside the lit interior once I opened the door.

"I'm glad," he whispered, pulling me close for a goodnight kiss. Then another. And another, making my blood hum. If I had been twenty years younger, I would have considered pulling him into the back seat, but forty-three-year-old, not-quite-divorced women didn't do those things. Trent stepped back, putting space between us before I could convince myself otherwise. "Next time I promise to shut off my phone."

SIXTEEN

"How are you?" Cynthia asked the second she answered her phone.

"I don't know." I slammed on my brakes as the traffic in front of me came to a sudden halt. Again. I stopped inches from the car in front of me, tires screeching. The man flashed me his middle finger. I scowled back, but refrained from offering any crude gestures.

It was just before six on a Friday night. An insane time to be on the roads. *Hope Derek is having as much fun driving back to the airport.*

"Tell me everything."

I inched forward a scant car-length and then stopped with the traffic again, stretching my stiff neck from side to side. It was going to take forever to get home. And so was this conversation. "You want the long version or the abridged?"

"I've got time." I heard the clink of what sounded like ice hitting the bottom of a glass, then Cynthia added, "Just let me grab my drink and get comfortable."

I gazed at the sea of brake lights in front of me until my

eyes blurred. This morning I'd considered taking the train, but there was no way I was going to Uber all the way to the South Loop building where our mediation was being held, then Uber back to Union Station. The trip would have cost a small fortune, something I could barely afford with my strained budget. Driving had seemed like a wise choice this morning. But now...

"I could use a drink too. Unfortunately I'm driving."

"You're not home yet?"

"The meeting ran longer than expected. So long my ass went numb from the cheap plastic chairs. I hope like hell Derek's hemorrhoids flare up."

Cynthia's chuckle seemed to echo around the car. "I'll drink to that." She paused for a second. "Okay, I'm ready, now spill."

"Well, besides the uncomfortable chairs, things were... weird."

"Weird how?" Cynthia asked when I pondered my next words too long.

"Weird, as in not what I expected. Considering the last time I spoke with Derek he'd issued veiled threats, I was braced for cold, arrogant Derek. Instead I got politician Derek. He was all smiles and jokes like this was some big donor event, not the end of our marriage." My stomach soured with the memory. "The lack of hostility was a relief, but a little remorse would have been nice."

I flipped on my turn signal and slid into the center lane in hopes of escaping this mess. My new lane was moving faster just a second ago, but of course, the minute I moved over the traffic slowed to a crawl, while my previous lane zoomed ahead.

I forced out a weak chuckle to hide the cracks in my voice. I would not cry, dammit. My soon-to-be ex-husband had gotten enough of my tears. He didn't deserve anymore.

"Derek didn't even blink at the one point five million in alimony per year, for the next five years or until I marry. I get the house—and the house payments—my car, obviously, and half our personal investments. I guess me and Mark won't starve or freeze to death this winter after all."

"That's good, right? That's what you want."

I let out a shaky breath and then another more steady one. "Honestly, I'm torn. Seven point five million is a lot of money, but considering all I've done for Derek in the past twenty years of marriage? All the dinners and press events and campaigning, not to mention raising his kids, managing the household, and putting up with mediocre sex." Thanks to Trent I had a new perspective on that front. Even if our limited time together yielded more frustration than satisfaction, he'd opened my eyes to the possibility I'd been missing out all these years. "It doesn't seem like a fair trade. How do you even put a value on half a lifetime of loyalty and support? But then maybe I'm being greedy."

"You deserve a fuck-ton more just for putting up with mediocre sex."

I laughed in earnest this time, wiping the moisture from the corner of my eyes which I chose to believe were happy tears. Leave it to Cynthia to lighten my mood when all I wanted to do was crawl in bed and forget the past two decades.

"The whole thing was so anticlimactic. Sign here and here, and twenty years... gone like it meant nothing. I've seen Derek show more emotion when negotiating the price of a car."

"I'm so sorry you had to go through that. But it's over. Go home. Find the most expensive wine in Derek's fucking wine collection, pour yourself a glass, and then run a nice hot bath."

"A hot bath sounds perfect right about now. Unfortunately the traffic here is insane. And I have to stop at the market." I whimpered out my misery. A vision of the almost empty fridge sat in the back of my mind. No milk and no eggs meant no breakfast for my hungry teen tomorrow morning.

"And it's not over. Not yet. There's a few loose ends to tie up. Mark's visitation for one. This back and forth every other weekend is exhausting the poor kid. I asked that Derek be allowed more time in summer and winter breaks if he reduces the weekend visits to once a month during the school year. His lawyer vetoed that, citing the importance of the father-son relationship. Which is a joke. The man hasn't even shown up for one of his soccer games this season.

"Then there's the matter of Derek's trust fund and his parents' assets. Honestly I don't want any of it, but the kids... According to the agreement, and I quote, after death, any and all assets of Derek Alexander Robinson are to be divided equally among his natural children. It didn't specify Brooke and Mark, just natural children. Meaning if he remarries and his next wife pops out a half dozen babies, my kids go from an even split to only one-eighth of their father's assets."

"How is that right?"

"My thoughts exactly. So now we wait while our lawyers haggle over the sticking points—and charge us a fortune while they do it. Which is stupid. Derek wanted a quick divorce, and now he's the one holding it up."

"Trust Randall."

I agreed to, and then we moved on to discussing her

disappointing meeting with a client we'd hoped was interested in the Argyle Hotel but wasn't.

"Sorry it didn't work out," I said while watching the traffic move forward. Up ahead the sign for my exit loomed. I flipped on my turn signal a second before darting back into the right lane in front of a lagging semi truck.

"I've got someone else in mind. I'll call them after we hang up."

"Speaking of, I'm at Willow Road. Finally. I'm gonna let you go so I can start a grocery list."

"Sounds exciting," she deadpanned. "It's a Friday night. Where is that handsome man of yours?"

I couldn't help the smile pulling at my lips that had nothing to do with leaving the expressway. "Says the woman who's making business deals after six-thirty on a Friday night. Whatever happened to the charming restaurateur?"

She let out a sharp laugh. "Lately it's been more fun to live vicariously through your love life."

I couldn't help but laugh as well. *How is my love life more interesting than hers?*

"For as often as I've seen Trent naked, there's a disappointing lack of carnal activity. I'm hoping that all changes this weekend. Mark leaves for Derek's right after his game tomorrow. Trent has his nephew's birthday party, but he promises to stop by after. Which is nice, but am I being selfish to want more than a few hours before he hops onto another plane?"

I stop at the light and let out a stress-filled breath. Traffic hadn't lightened much since getting off 94, everyone rushing to get home or off to their evening plans. I released a silent prayer that the grocery store wouldn't be crowded.

Since starting with Cynthia I'd yet to find a time the stores weren't packed.

"Not really," Cynthia answered. "But it's not like either of you can do anything about it. Sometimes we have to accept life doesn't always go as we'd like."

"Preaching to the choir, Cyn. Nothing in my life has gone as planned recently. The way my luck's been? I'm not holding my breath on our weekend together."

The light turned green and I accelerated forward. Willow Road narrowed into the residential neighborhood. The parkway trees burst with a kaleidoscope of fall colors, reminding me how much time had passed since Derek's betrayal.

"Maybe the universe is trying to tell me something," I said, doubt staring back at me as I looked into the rearview mirror. "Maybe I shouldn't be jumping into another relationship now. After sitting in a room with Derek, the man I thought I knew... I don't know. I'm just wondering if I should take a step back."

"You want my honest opinion?"

I turned left on Green Bay Road, weighing Cynthia's question. *Do I want her opinion?*

"Of course," I finally answered. Chances were she'd give it to me even if I said no.

"Today sucked. Derek was an idiot—not much of a surprise to those of us he's been an idiot to before, but for you it was a shock. I get it. Those we love the most hold the most power to hurt us. But Trent's a good guy, and if he makes you happy... you need that right now whether it's just a fling or something more. So whatever you do, don't let Derek steal that from you."

I narrowed my eyes, trying to decipher the hidden meaning in Cynthia's words. Not for the first time, I sensed my friend's harsh exterior was just a thin veneer. What lay underneath was a mystery.

"Thank you," I said, ignoring my curiosity. Cynthia was a deeply private person and would most likely shut down any questions I'd ask. "I just pulled into the grocery store, so now I really have to go."

We hung up and I glanced down at the dry-cleaning receipt winking from the cup holder, with a groan. Another stop. *Great.*

Ominous clouds gathered as I ran into the store. Rain had been predicted, but not until later. *Not much later by the looks of it.*

The store was packed with people seeming to have no agenda except getting in my way. I ground my teeth, wistfully reflecting on my not-so-distant past. Rosa did most of my grocery shopping, or she had. *Damn you, Derek.* The long line for the cashier inched forward. The sky outside the store windows turned black and angry. At this pace I was going to get wet.

Lightning lit up the sky as I rushed to the back of the lot where I'd parked. Electricity snapped in the air, and the smell of ozone was so thick you could taste it. I packed my bags into the car and hopped in.

The dry-cleaner receipt teased from its spot in the cup holder. Not that I'd forgotten, but—

My phone rang shrill in the silence of the car's interior. I started the engine and waited for the bluetooth in the car to connect with my phone. Trent's name flashed on the car's screen. Excitement blossomed, sending tingles all the way to my fingertips. Cynthia was right. Why should I let Derek spoil my happiness?

"Hi, gorgeous. I've missed you."

"Same here. Where are you?" I asked, attempting to ignore the way the sky had darkened to almost midnight, dashing my hopes of making it home dry. Lightning flashed. My headlights automatically turned on, and the interior was cast in the glow of the blue dash lights. "Hopefully not driving in this storm."

"It's not raining yet. I'm thinking I might make it to my parents before the worst hits. But I could pick you up." His voice held a note of hope I hated to squash. But I had no choice.

"Mark's going to be home in thirty minutes, and dinner's in the back of my car." I tried to keep the disappointment out of my voice, but wasn't sure I was successful.

"You're welcome to have dinner with me."

"And your family?"

"Too soon?" He chuckled. "Sorry."

I exhaled a frustrated sigh. I *had* planned on telling Mark about us tonight. Planned on today's mediation marking the end of my marriage and of Derek's control over my life. *You know what they say about plans...*

"It's a delicate situation."

Lightning arced across the sky, a pure white flash burning its jagged zigzags of light across my eyes.

"I get it." Trent was silent for a beat, then said, "Looks like a muddy game for Mark tomorrow."

The tension in my shoulders loosened as he shifted to a less turbulent subject. Not that I didn't think about Trent and Mark together. Hanging out. Laughing and joking. My gut told me Mark would like Trent. But what if he didn't? What if Mark was as disappointed with me as he was with Derek? It'd only been a month since Derek moved out. Would my kids be shocked that I'd somehow gotten over my twenty-year marriage in weeks and moved on to a new man? Put like that, I'd be shocked too.

"And Derek arranged for his driver to pick him up immediately after the game. No time to shower. Barely enough to change. It's like he forgot how disgusting his son gets after eighty minutes of constant exercise." Although, come to think of it, it was my car that ended up smelling like a gym locker for a week, not Derek's.

"Us boys are a stinky lot," Trent said with a chuckle.

"After spending the afternoon watching Derek ignore me while his lawyer tried to screw me, it would serve him right if his driver banned Mark from riding in his car because of the eye-watering fog of body spray Mark assumes masks his body odor."

"I'll make a note of that." Trent paused, then mumbled as if to himself, "Body spray does not cover BO."

"Funny. Can I call you back? I'm almost to the cleaners."

The dry cleaners' squat green building sat on my left. I ended the call with Trent, promising to call him right back. Drizzle spattered the windshield. I flipped on my turn signal and waited for traffic to clear.

The rain was coming down in earnest by the time I made my turn into the parking lot. I threw my car door open and sprinted for the entrance.

The chain of tiny bells attached to the door jingled as I pushed it open.

"Mrs. Robinson!"

I cringed at Doris's greeting. I had corrected her a million times, insisting she call me Nicki. But it was always Mrs. Robinson. The only one who called me that anymore was Randall Harris. *Legally you are still Mrs. Robinson.*

"Doris, please, it's Nicki," I tried again with a patient smile, handing her my ticket. Thunder rumbled, loud enough to shake the panes of glass in the front window. "Haven't seen you in a while."

"My daughter had her baby. I've been elbows-deep in diapers for the past month." She laughed from somewhere in the racks of clothes. "I'm glad to be back. I can finally sleep. Looks like we're really going to get it out there."

"I think so. What did your daughter have?" I asked, only half engaged in the conversation. Lightning strobed out the window as Doris hung my garments on the hook by the register.

"A boy. My son-in-law was ecstatic, but then most men are." She raised her voice above the clamor of thunder, beaming with her announcement. "Not that they're not happy for a girl, but..."

My thoughts immediately rewound back to when Mark was born. It was impossible to connect the tender father who cried as he held his son with the indifferent man in the conference room today.

"You paid when you dropped off, so you're all set," Doris said, pulling me out of my tortured memories.

"Oh, wait, before I forget," she added with a snap of her fingers. I set the hangers back on the hook and turned back to the counter. She rummaged through the drawer under the register for a second and pulled out a bag containing something small and black. "I found this in your husband's pants before the baby came. Meant to give it to you, but then I left. I put a note on it for my sister-in-law, but I guess that was too complicated for her. Not the brightest, that one. My apologies."

"Don't worry about it." I forced a smile, pocketing the small flash drive. I'd been forwarding my husband's mail for over the past month like a damned unpaid secretary. Now this.

The wind whipped the trees outside. I had better things to worry about, not some copy of a speech he no longer needed.

"See you around," I said before dashing out the door.

In the car, I dropped the bag into my cup holder with plans to give it to Mark, who was always needing flash drives for school, then instructed my car's hands free to call Trent back.

"I hope you're driving careful," I said once he answered, sounding more like a mother than a girlfriend in my head. *Am I his girlfriend?*

Big, fat raindrops hit my windshield with a plop. My wipers sped up as cars rushed past me kicking up the water already puddling on the sides of the road. Motherly or not, the idea of Trent speeding down the expressway in his little sports car caused a nervous knot to form in the pit of my stomach.

I turned onto Sheridan, glancing for a second between the trees and houses lining the street. Harsh waves crashed against the shoreline and the wind buffeted the car. My day had been just as rough and it wasn't getting any better.

I frowned, picturing a quiet afternoon all alone while Mark flew off to his father's and Trent played the doting uncle. I'd give anything to join the fun. "When's your flight out again?"

"Sunday at 2:10." Trent paused. "So fill me in on your mediation today. What went wrong that we have to wait two more weeks?"

I gave him all the gory details of my afternoon with Derek and the lawyers, repeating, almost word for word, the same story I'd given Cynthia a short time ago.

"I'm sorry, Nic, but your ex is an asshole. Definitely send Mark in his muddy cleats."

I grinned while hitting the opener for the gate, then waited impatiently as it slid open at a snail's pace. "Nice thought, but probably not since I have to work with the asshole in order to come to an agreement on these last few obstacles. Important obstacles that will affect my children's lives. I'm not backing down. However long it takes."

Thunder shook the car and the rain poured down in sheets. Even on high my wipers couldn't keep up.

"Then tell me what you're wearing."

His deep voice drifted across the speakers, leaving my skin tingling as if he'd touched me. I smiled at Trent's tendency to switch subjects without warning. Not that I wanted to hash out the details of my divorce further. Not when I'd perfected the art of seduction during our phone conversations this past week.

"My navy suit, very conservative and lawyer approved. The red blouse, maybe not so much. Cynthia insists the top buttons are a waste."

"I agree with Cynthia. Go on. Tell me more."

"You've already seen my loafers."

The warm, dry garage beckoned like an oasis after the long drive. I exhaled out my relief, shutting the car off. Behind me rain poured off the garage roof, obscuring the driveway. I opened the middle bay door for Mark before closing mine, then got out.

Trent's voice lowered. "Get to the good part, woman. I want to know what's underneath that lawyer-approved suit."

I laughed, hooking the heavy grocery bags with my fingers, ignoring the green light on the security panel that said I'd forgotten to engage the alarm when I left this morning. With the stress of today's meeting with Derek on my mind, I'd been lucky to remember my name. "You want me to describe my underthings?"

I left the door open despite the chill in the garage. It would take at least a few more trips before I emptied all the bags from the back of my car.

"Actually, I want you to go upstairs and take off your suit. Send me a picture to tide me over. If I can't come over, give me something."

"I have groceries to put away," I teased while setting the groceries on the counter. Outside, the rain streaked the patio doors, the trees bent in the gusting wind. I flinched as thunder crashed nearby. I'd never been a fan of thunderstorms, and this one was beginning to test my nerves.

He breathed heavily into the phone. "You're killing me, Nic."

"Cynthia says anticipation is the best fore—"

Lightning lit up the back yard and a split second later thunder crashed loud enough to shake the house. Adrenaline zinged along my skin. Something heavy hit the patio door with a loud thump. I turned and screamed.

CHAPTER
SEVENTEEN

"Jesus fucking Christ," I choked out, pressing my hand against my panicked heart.

A soggy Gabriel Roth stood on the other side of the door, blond hair hanging like dark seaweed, his rain-soaked T-shirt clinging to his muscular chest.

"Lemme in," he yelled as lightning illuminated the backyard again.

"What's going on?" Trent asked, his voice drowned out for a second by the following roar of thunder.

I paused, my mind searching for an appropriate answer to Trent's question.

"My—my pool guy's on the patio." Former pool guy, but that was the last thing Trent needed to know. *Ever.* I breathed deep, trying to slow my racing heart. Trying to think. "Can I call you back?"

"Your pool guy?" Trent asked as Gabriel rapped on the glass again. "You told me last week you'd closed your pool down for the season. Why is he there?"

Shit. There was no logical answer to Trent's question, none I'd be able to give him at least.

"I—I don't know. Maybe I missed a bill. Or he wants to discuss next year's contract," I hedged, while Gabriel stared at me from the other side of the door. "Let me find out and call you back."

"No. Wait," Trent shouted through the phone. "Why wouldn't he call? Send an email with a quote? Knock on your front door? Something doesn't feel right here."

"Trent," I sighed out his name. My protective knight wasn't welcome at the moment. Not when I needed privacy to deal with whatever Gabriel wanted.

"I'll be passing your exit in a minute. Don't let him in until I get there."

"No." I gasped in horror at the thought of the two men coming face-to-face with each other. Gabriel slammed his palm against the glass door, making me flinch. "Trent, the poor man is drowning out there."

"Let him wait inside the garage. Lock the doors, I'll be there in fifteen minutes."

And Mark was due home in less than twenty. This was a disaster in the making. Unless I took control of the situation, and fast.

"You're being paranoid. Go to your mom's. I'll be fine." I ignored the voice in my head questioning my common sense. How well did I really know Gabriel? "I'll call you later."

Did I want this man in my house? No. But the image of Mark coming home to finding Gabriel on the back porch had me flipping the lock on the back door, despite my misgivings and the half dozen uncomfortable messages Gabriel had left me over the past month.

"Nicole Adams Robinson," Trent shouted in my ear. "Do not open that door."

Gabriel pushed the door open, forcing me back as he rushed in, along with a gust of rain-saturated wind and the fresh scent of the storm.

"Everything's fine. Stop worrying and enjoy your nephew's party." I winced as I ended our call. I'd apologize later. When I had time. Or when he showed up. *Please don't let him show up.*

I glared at the dripping man taking up way too much space in my kitchen. "How can I help you, Gabriel?"

Thunder roared and the overhead lights flickered for a second.

"Who's been workin' on my pool?" Gabriel scowled back, his eyes angry blue flames.

I held in a tired sigh. Not that I hadn't half expected a confrontation at some point, but with Trent's angry voice still echoing in my ear and Gabriel grumbling in front of me, how was I supposed to think?

I shut the door to give myself a moment. I didn't need any more rain in the house. As it was, a puddle spread around Gabriel's boots. Thunder boomed once again, loud enough to rattle the windows.

"Let me get you a towel."

"Don't need a towel. We need to talk." Gabriel's whole body shivered and his lips had started to turn blue, but whatever. The sooner he said his piece, the sooner he'd leave.

"So talk."

Lightning flashed, followed immediately by a roar of thunder. *Jesus, this damn storm.*

"You canceled our contract," Gabriel yelled over the storm. He inched forward, invading my space.

I took a step back, narrowed my eyes, and pointed out

the rain sheeting against the patio doors, obscuring the pool beyond. "Because you *refused* to do your job. You gave me no choice. For weeks, I called. Left you messages instructing you to close down the pool. You ignored them. And then those notes. Jesus, Gabriel. You're lucky Mark never read them. Were you even thinking?"

Another flash of lightning had the lights flickering for more than a second. *God, don't let the power go out.* The last thing I needed was to be stuck in the dark with this man.

My phone rang. Trent, of course. I swiped down on the answer button, sending him to voicemail, then flipped my phone over on the counter to silence any further interruptions. I'd make it up to him later—hopefully not fifteen minutes later.

One problem at a time, Adams.

"We had somethin'." He closed the gap between us and lifted his hand toward me, his eyes full of foolish desperation, making me want to slap the stupid out of him.

Like that's going to help? I needed him out of here, which wouldn't happen if I started an argument.

"We had an *afternoon*," I raised my voice over the roll of thunder. Stepping back, I put space between us once again. I couldn't decide what was more irritating—the storm or this stupid dance we were doing. "An afternoon, nothing more. With the divorce and the kids and the struggle to rebuild my life, the last thing I need is a man at the moment."

Gabriel pointed to my phone. "Is that what you told him?"

"Him?"

Gabriel's eyes narrowed and the muscle in his jaw pulsed. He flipped my phone over, revealing the photo I'd attached to Trent's contact at some point, along with his name. It was the night we'd sailed up to Kenosha—the sunset glowed in the background while he pressed a less than innocent kiss to my lips. "You and this Trent guy look awfully cozy."

Shit. If I kept running into situations that required lying, I was going to need acting lessons. Or CIA training.

"I may clean pools for a living, but I'm not dumb."

"Of course not." I slipped my arm through Gabriel's and guided him toward the door to the mudroom, and hopefully out the garage to wherever the hell he'd parked his van.

His skin was cold and damp, his soggy clothes dripping a wet trail through my kitchen. I'd have to mop before Mark got home.

I glanced at the time on the microwave as we passed, my heart stuttering. I had, maybe, twelve minutes until then. Fewer, if Trent had decided to head this way.

Gabriel needed to go. No matter what empty promises I had to make to get him out the door and out of my life.

"Listen, when the divorce is final, who knows. But for right now, there's too much at risk."

His lips twisted with what I feared was disbelief. If I were him, I probably wouldn't believe me either. "What you're sayin' is, getting caught fuckin' your *pool boy* would be a risk."

I let out a sarcastic little laugh. Before we reached the mudroom doorway, Gabriel planted his feet and turned to face me. "Although, imagine the revenge."

His wicked grin sent a wave of fear washing through me. "There's revenge, and then there's stupidity, Gabriel."

He tsked, brushing a damp lock of hair away from my

face with his chilled fingers. "Then it would be smart of you not to anger me."

He dipped down to kiss me, but I turned my head at the last second and his lips met my cheek.

"What are you saying?" I had a feeling I knew what he was saying, but a part of me hoped I was wrong.

"I'm sayin'—" He pressed a kiss to the side of my neck, his fingers digging painfully into my hips, preventing me from escaping—"you need to be a good girl." Another kiss, this time behind my ear. "And take me upstairs for a repeat of last month."

I shoved at his chest, but I may as well have been pushing against a cement wall for all the good it did. "Mark's due home any second."

A long rumble of thunder cut through the silence. Quieter than the previous ones. Although the rain pelting the windows was almost as loud. But at least the storm was ending.

"Then we better move this somewhere more private."

"No." I shook off his hand. Was the man insane?

"You don't call the shots anymore. Now, we can do this the easy way or the hard way. I know which one I'd choose, but you may not like it as much."

He grabbed my hand, attempting to tug me away from the doorway. I fought for traction on the wet marble floor, but so did Gabriel. Twisting my wrist, I slipped from his grasp. "I said no, Gabriel."

A lightning flash preceded a loud roll of thunder. The lights flickered for a second before going out for a beat, then returning. *So much for the end of the storm.*

He gripped my arms and slammed me against the edge of the island. I cried out in pain. I'd never feared Gabriel before, but I was beginning to.

"As much as I like your hard-to-get game, it's gettin' old, darlin'."

Lightning flashed. Thunder boomed, drowning out the frantic hammering of my heart for a moment.

I whimpered as his finger tangled painfully in my hair, tugging my head back. "The hard way it is, then."

EIGHTEEN

O ut of the corner of my eye, a large body rushed toward us. *Shit, Trent.* The next second, Gabriel's head jerked back as my protector's fist made contact with his jaw. Gabriel released his hold on my hair and stepped back, swearing.

"I told you not to open the door. If you'd listened…" Trent glared, shaking out his hand with a curse. "Call the fucking police while I take care of this piece of trash."

Gabriel grinned at Trent, his teeth bloody. "You do that, *Mrs. Robinson.* Call the police."

"No, Trent. Not the police." I sent him a desperate look. The last thing I needed was the police asking questions. Questions Gabriel looked more than happy to answer. "This was just a misunderstanding, *right,* Gabriel?"

Gabriel stared at Trent for longer than was comfortable. I could almost hear the dangerous calculations going on his brain. Finally he chuckled, wiping a trickle of blood from his chin with the back of his hand. "Oh, yeah. But things are crystal clear now. My apologies, ma'am."

He tipped an imaginary hat and then strode out the

mudroom door while I clung to Trent's arm to keep him from following.

Trent shook me off once the garage door closed. "What the ever-loving fuck was that, Nicki?"

I strode across the kitchen into the mudroom, then out the garage door. Gabriel was nowhere in sight.

Lightning lit up the sky, highlighting the large oaks that bordered the driveway.

A cold dread settled around me. The quick de-escalation of events left me unsettled and twitchy. Not to mention the sudden, unexpected violence from a man I'd trusted with my kids. The storm didn't help either. Somehow I'd come out mostly unscathed from this battle, but I'd be a fool to think this was the end of my war with Gabriel.

The rumble of thunder and the torrential rain pounding the driveway drowned out any other noise. I sprinted to my car and opened the back. "Since you're here, I could use a little help."

Trent walked over, a frown etched on his handsome face. I handed him a couple of grocery bags and then scooped up the rest before shutting the hatch.

"Are we just ignoring what happened?" Trent asked while following me back into the house.

"Like I said, a misunderstanding. And thank you for your help, but now, you really need to leave before Mark comes home."

He leaned against the counter, watching me unpack the groceries with less than steady hands. "A misunderstanding? Is that what we're calling your pool guy pinning you against the countertop?"

I opened the freezer and stashed the two pints of ice cream on the shelf. One for me and one for Mark, although given the events of today, I might dig into both of them.

Marginally healthier than the alcohol I'd turned to in the first few weeks after Derek left. Less likely to make me do impulsive things.

I grabbed a bag of frozen corn and shut the freezer door. "Okay, so it was a little more than a misunderstanding. But he's gone. It's over."

Trent raked his hand through his damp hair, his frustration obvious. Gabriel obviously wasn't the man I assumed he was. Not even close. But what would Trent think of me if he knew I'd slept with my twenty-eight-year-old pool boy? Even I was disgusted with myself.

I applied the bag of corn to Trent's now swollen knuckles with care.

"What if he comes back? We need to call the police."

"And then what? They come, we tell them what happened, which is next to nothing. Next thing you know, reporters arrive in swarms, asking uncomfortable questions. Somehow the truth would come out about us, because it always does. There goes my quiet divorce, to say nothing of your reputation."

If team management frowned upon players getting in bar fights, I was sure they'd have issue with a coach's affair with a senator's wife who was also involved with her pool guy. Maury Povich could never have dreamed up such a sordid scenario.

"Should I be frightened that you have this all figured out?" he asked, his eyes narrowed. "For the record, what I saw wasn't nothing, Nic."

I pulled the mop from the mudroom closet and strolled past Trent with more composure than I felt. Thunder rolled in the distance. I focused on cleaning up the lake in the middle of my kitchen floor, instead of the angry man in front of me, probing for answers I couldn't give. "Okay, the man has an anger problem. And he's obviously delusional if he thinks my divorce gives him a green light to make a move. But he's gone."

"What if he comes back?" he repeated with more force.

"Trent..."

"Don't Trent me. I get the reason why you don't want to involve the police. I don't like it, but I get it. But I can't get the scene I walked in on out of my head. Divorce or not, you had to have some idea of the man's interest."

I what?

"You're kidding, right? Are you actually blaming me for his actions? Get the fuck out of my house."

First Derek, then Gabriel, now Trent. Three assholes in one day was too much. Cynthia's suggestion of a hot bath never sounded so good.

"No. Wait. I'm sorry. Stupid thing to say, obviously. But I'm still processing here." He peeled the frozen vegetable off his knuckles with a wince and then dropped the bag on the counter. In the next moment he pulled me into his arms. "I'm sorry. Of course I don't blame you."

"I swear, in the past five years he's worked for us, he's never given indication of any interest in me. He was polite, friendly, but he never crossed any lines."

My heart slowed as I wrapped my arms around Trent, breathing in his clean masculine scent combined with the rain. The next second, the rumble of Mark's Jeep pulling into the garage had me jumping back.

"Out. The patio door. Quick." I darted past Trent, back into the kitchen. Then turned back, realizing he hadn't followed. "Trent!"

"I'm not leaving, Nic." His expression said I'd have better luck moving a mountain.

I tossed the bag of corn back into the freezer and

straightened my clothes. My pulse thundered inside my head, ticking off the seconds until my son walked in with his own set of uncomfortable questions.

"Fine. Fine. You can't say anything to Mark about Gabriel. Not a word. I don't want him worrying. And, and, um, you're a client." I couldn't lie, but I could spin the narrative. Bend the truth to my benefit. I'd seen Derek do it a thousand times. How hard could it be? "Sit down and pretend you've been here for a while."

My hands wrapped around the mop handle as if it were a lifeline.

"You want me to take off my coat? Chug down a half a beer?"

"Um…" They weren't bad ideas, but the slam of Mark's car door said it was too late.

Trent laughed. "You're precious when you freak out."

"I'm serious." I threw my hands up in frustration. "I was showing you a house in the area, but the storm interfered with my internet connection, so I brought you back here to send off the contract."

Trent chuckled again. Ignoring my instructions, he pulled the mop from my grasp and cupped my face with his free hand. "And you're mopping, why? I thought you said you hated lying to your kids."

"Desperate times…" I relieved him of the mop, setting it against the wall next to the patio doorway. Back in the mudroom where it belonged would be better, but there wasn't time.

"You can't lie for shit, Nic."

I smoothed down my damp skirt for a second time, shooting a glance toward the mudroom while my heart threatened to climb up my throat and choke me. "I'll work on that. Now please sit down before—"

The garage door slammed making me jump.

"Hey, Mom," Mark's excited voice came from just beyond the kitchen. My heart stuttered and I stared wide-eyed at Trent, who hadn't moved an inch and was standing too close to believe he was just a client. "Who's car—"

My son dashed through the kitchen door and then stopped, his eyes going wide as I took a step away from Trent.

"Hey, I'm guessing you didn't buy me that Porsche out there as an early birthday present?" A slow grin spread across my son's face as his eyes bounced between Trent and me. His hand rose in an awkward wave. "Hi."

My face warmed. "Mark..."

"Don't worry, I got this," Trent whispered under his breath while my son's expression went from shock to suspicion. He strode across the kitchen where Mark stood. "I'm Trent Richards—"

Mark's eyes went wide and he burst out laughing. "Holy shit. Are you kidding, Mom?"

I started forward, leaving Trent behind me. "I can explain."

"Trent Richards? *The* Trent Richards?"

I shot Trent a confused look while my son started to laugh again.

"The one and only." Trent grinned, offering his hand to Mark.

"What?" I glanced between my son and Trent.

"Mom." Mark dropped his backpack onto the floor and shook Trent's hand. "Have you any idea who this is?" Before I could go on with my impromptu client story, Mark continued, "This is Trent—Three Point—Richards. The best shooting guard Chicago has seen since MJ. Man, that full-court shot in the playoffs four years ago. Unbelievable."

"Yeah." Trent let out a chuckle. "I couldn't believe it either."

"And you're in my house. My friends are gonna shit."

"Language," I interjected. "And we should probably keep this a secret. You know, to keep the crowds of fans from gathering."

Trent turned and shot me a confused look that said I wasn't making any sense.

"Wait. What *are* you doing in my house? Not that I'm not totally stoked." He paused his eyes darting between the two of us, and then he grinned. "Well, I know you're not dating my mom. She's not that cool."

I said, "Of course not," at the same time Trent said, "Sure she is."

I sent him a what-the-fuck look. What happened to sticking to my well-thought-out client story?

"Huh." Mark froze. "No way. You know she doesn't even like sports."

I forged ahead because I had to salvage this. Stepping between the two, I smacked Trent on his shoulder. "He's kidding. A real jokester. Like there'd be anything between us with my lack of sports knowledge. Actually, Cynthia asked me to show him some houses in the area. She was busy, and I was... well, obviously not. Then the storm came, and the thunder and lighting, and the internet went down at the house we were viewing..."

Both of them stared at me like I had two heads. My face heated with discomfort.

"I thought you had a meeting with Dad and the lawyers?"

Trent closed his hands over my shoulder and gave me a pitying look. "Your mom's a little shaken up. She thought there was an intruder in the house. We were on the phone, and I raced right over."

Mark's eyes went wide. "An intruder? Shit, Mom. Did you forget to turn on the alarm this morning again?"

"Again?" Trent shot me a hard look that said we'd be discussing my security lapses later.

"I might have. But I was mistaken about the whole intruder thing. Trent checked the house and found nothing. In any case, lesson learned."

Mark walked to the fridge and pulled out a water, tossing one to Trent. "I'm so confused. Someone please explain."

Trent mumbled as he shifted next to me. "Told you. You can't lie for shit."

"I was doing fine until you brought up the whole intruder thing," I muttered back.

"No, you weren't." Mark crossed his arms over his chest. "And you're right. She can't lie. My dad's surprise fortieth birthday party proved that."

"Fine. Trent's not a client, but we actually did meet through Cynthia." Sort of. "The night we had dinner in the city. And we were on the phone when I came home and heard a noise."

Mark cleared his throat and turned back to Trent. "Will you be staying for dinner?"

"Trent was just leaving. He has his nephew's birthday party." As expected, Mark's expression showed his disappointment. "His family is waiting."

"The party isn't until tomorrow," Trent corrected with an infuriating wink. "And dinner tonight is just with TJ and my parents. I invited your mom and you—"

"Mark has an English paper to finish and a chemistry exam to study for before he leaves for DC tomorrow."

Mark opened his mouth, an argument at the ready. I sent him a warning glare. We'd had this discussion every weekend he was scheduled to fly out to see his father.

By the time he returned late on Sunday night he'd be tired and in no mood to face his school work. The three of us agreed weeks ago his visits wouldn't interfere with his grades. Not that I could trust either father or son on that promise without a little guidance. Clearly Mark regretted that at the moment.

Outside, the rain pelted the patio door glass, but the wind and lightning had died down. This was not how I pictured their meeting.

"So dinner?" I prompted, because it was easier than arguing with Mark and Trent. I'd had enough fighting to last me a lifetime.

"I'll give my folks a call, let them know I won't be able to make it until later. I'm sure the roads are a mess."

"Great." Mark smiled wide.

"Mark, why don't you and Mr. Richards order dinner while I change out of my work clothes." I shifted my attention to Trent, who was looking downright smug. "We usually do pizza on Friday. But we have Chinese, Thai, Mexican... whatever you want. You're the guest, so you choose."

Mark pulled out the menu folder from the drawer and spread out the collection of trifolds we'd amassed over the years.

"I like pizza," Trent answered. Mark slid the Rossi's menu across the granite counter to where Trent stood.

"I warn you, my mom likes anchovies." They both laughed, and Mark gave me the same disgusted face I got every time we ordered pizza.

"We all can't be perfect," Trent mumbled while giving the menu a quick scan.

"I'm still here, you know."

"I normally go for a garbage pizza. How 'bout you?" Mark asked.

"Make that two garbage pizzas. And I'm paying. It's the least I can do for barging in uninvited." Trent pulled his wallet from his back pocket.

"I invited you," Mark corrected, and then glanced my way for confirmation.

"My son invited you." *May as well make the best of the situation.* It wasn't like I had a device that would erase everyone's memory of the past five minutes.

Mark waved a hand in my direction. "See."

Both of them smiled as if all was right in the world. Maybe it was.

"I think I'm just going…" I pointed up the stairs. My clothes clung, damp and uncomfortable against my skin, and the strange scent of Gabriel's cologne lingered in my nose. A bath would have to wait, but a hot shower sounded good.

Halfway up, I paused on the landing, just out of sight. Eavesdropping and lying. Could things get any worse? I should have been ashamed, but I wasn't.

"So are you actually dating my mom?"

"You should ask her." Trent paused, and then he added, "You know we could pick up the pizzas. It would be faster."

"Can I drive your car?"

Mark and cars. That it had taken this long for him to bring up Trent's shiny sports car was a surprise.

"Sure."

My eyes widened and a small voice urged me to rush

back down, put an end to their plan. I probably wouldn't win any appreciation awards from my son. But fact was, I trusted Trent. And offering up his car was a brilliant distraction. I could only hope my son's excitement lasted through dinner.

"Seriously? Awesome." Just how awesome could be heard in Mark's voice.

"Seriously. In fact, let's call in the pizzas and then head out for a drive."

"Oh, man. My mom's gonna freak."

"She'll be fine. The rain's stopped, and it's not like we're getting on the expressway and opening her up."

Mark laughed, then quieted for a moment. "You know, it's okay if you want to date my mom. Even if she is a little boring."

CHAPTER
NINETEEN

"What?" Twin stares of concern watched me from across the kitchen table. I'd zoned off. My mind couldn't help but wander while Mark and Trent continued to discuss gear ratios, horse-power, and other things about engines and cars I knew nothing about.

Before that it had been sports, basketball in particular. Mark's rap playlist poured out from the sound system while Trent waxed on about his days in LA and later with Chicago, my son riveted to every word. Mark was an avid basketball fan, and his father had taken him to more than a few games over the years. I made a mental note to check the ball in his room, see if Trent's signature was on it.

As much as I wanted to brush off what happened with Gabriel earlier, his words kept coming back to me.

Imagine the revenge.

It would be smart not to anger me.

I needed to call him. Smooth things over before he did something stupid. Something that could ruin my and Derek's lives.

Mark gave Trent a sharp glance. "Are you all right, Mom?"

I shifted my attention away from my untouched slice of pizza, now cold and unappetizing on my plate. Not that it had been more so hot. My stomach had settled into an uneasy knot.

"I'm fine, just tired. It was a long week." I struggled to contain my yawn. The cup of herbal tea Trent had waiting for me when I returned downstairs did little to help.

Trent's lips pressed together, and he shot me a knowing glance. Then shoved a slice of pizza into his mouth, probably to keep from making the comment I could see written on his face.

"You said something about your birthday earlier?" Trent asked instead.

Mark forgot all about me while he filled Trent in on his birthday plans with his friends and the surprise present his father had promised would be waiting for him this weekend.

I stared at the dark wood grain of the table until my eyes blurred. I couldn't remember a time when Mark and Derek had bantered so easily. Was that a good thing or bad? Should I have had reservations over Mark and Trent bonding? Probably. But there was little I could do to stop it now. My son wouldn't let me if I tried.

I made another mental note to warn Mark sometime before he left for his father's tomorrow. The last thing I needed was Derek finding out I was entertaining a famous pro basketball player in my house. Former, but still...

After a bit of grumbling on his part, threatening on my part, and a little encouragement from Trent, Mark headed upstairs to do his homework.

"You okay, Nic?" Trent laid his hand over mine, squeezing lightly.

"Yeah. I'm okay," I lied. Then broached the subject weighing on me all night. "You know Mark is vulnerable right now? With the divorce and his anger toward Derek. I can see you two had a great time and all tonight. Just... please be careful, okay? I don't want him getting hurt."

Trent winced. "Sorry if I got carried away. Mark was excited and it just felt natural. I didn't think how it could affect him."

"Mark was definitely a bit starstruck." I gave him a small lenient smile while gathering up the dishes. Trent's exuberant nature wasn't something I could fault. "You've won him over, but just take it slow. He's going through a lot right now."

"I understand. Which is why I wish you would have let me call the police. The kid's worried about you. I'm worried about you and him. You know I'm not going to sleep a minute while I'm gone. Knowing that guy could come back here..." He ran his fingers through his hair, blowing out a frustrated breath. Then pulled the dishes out of my hands. "I'll do those."

"Just load them in the dishwasher, I'll turn it on before I head to bed."

"You're changing the subject."

"We already discussed the subject. And Gabriel's gone. What would I tell the police? I had an argument with my former pool service technician?" I opened the fridge, sliding the leftover pizza on the shelf and grabbing two beers. I handed one to Trent. "I doubt they'd do anything but laugh at the silly rich woman with too much time on her hands and too vivid an imagination."

"I didn't imagine what I walked in on. And you're not silly. Jesus, Nic, I have a bad feeling about the guy."

I sent him a doubtful look I didn't quite feel. Gabriel was trouble. The question was how much trouble?

Trent held up his hands. "Fine. I'm staying the night, then."

"No." I shook my head to emphasize the point. "A sleepover is out of the question. I have an impressionable son to think about."

He pulled me into his arms, his warmth chasing away the chill that had lingered all night. "Not a sleepover. Not that I would refuse your bed. But you're right about Mark. That's why I'll be crashing on your couch."

I turned and stepped back, putting space between us. Then gave the couch in question a dubious glance. I'd napped on it more than a few times. It was plenty comfortable, but then I wasn't six-five.

"Trent... we're fine." I shook my head once, hoping he'd believe me. "How would I even explain you staying to Mark?"

"Tell him I had a few beers and you insisted I stay. Give him a lesson in responsibility and me some peace of mind." Trent slid his arm around my back, drawing me closer once more. I shot a glance toward the stairway, but it was empty. "Just between you and me, your son was a little freaked out by the whole intruder thing. It'll ease his mind knowing there's someone here keeping an eye on things. Probably sleep better. So will you."

Before I could argue, his lips pressed against mine, warm and tender. One kiss led to two, and then three, each punctuated with a soft, "Please..."

The thought of Gabriel lurking around sent fear down

my spine. But would he risk coming back? Would he hurt Mark?

"Fine." I sighed in resignation. "But you don't need to sleep on the couch. You can stay in one of the guest rooms."

CHAPTER
TWENTY

"Okay, let's have it," Trent said as we watched Mark's limo disappear around the curve of the driveway the following afternoon.

"I don't know what you're talking about." I turned back toward the house and away from Trent to hide my anger.

I should have set my alarm clock this morning. By the time I'd woken, Trent and Mark had laid out an elaborate breakfast of fluffy scrambled eggs, thick-cut bacon, cinnamon French toast, and fresh-squeezed orange juice, along with plans for Trent to come watch Mark's final soccer game of the season. In the stands. With hoards of gossipmongers surrounding us. *Worst plan ever.*

Trent laughed quietly, his long strides catching up to me in seconds. "You've been quiet ever since we left the game. Tell me what's wrong."

"It was a miserable game. I'm chilled to the bone and I have a headache." It was only half the truth. The game had started with a light drizzle that penetrated into the layers of my waterproof coat and wool sweater, and soaked into my jeans despite sheltering under Ava's massive golf umbrella. An umbrella she'd graciously shared with Trent.

He'd given her some bullshit story about being a scout for some obscure college I'd never heard of. He'd even jotted down notes and asked questions about the various players. But Ava wasn't stupid. Far from it.

"I see. You're angry I came." Trent let out a quiet groan, his hand brushing over his shadowed jaw. "What did you want me to do?"

I gave him a scowl but kept walking toward the garage. Mrs. Jordan was most likely watching. With the trees bare of leaves, she had an unobstructed view of our driveway. "First of all, learn to tell Mark no. You shouldn't have missed your nephew's birthday party."

Blaming Trent wasn't fair. As Mark's mother, I should have said no—I wanted to say no—but the last thing I wanted was an angry son flying off for a fun-filled birthday weekend with his father.

"Daniel's four. He was probably more focused on his bouncy house and the reptile guy." He leaned against the side of his car, arms crossed. I narrowed my eyes in doubt. Trent was more exciting than reptiles and some inflated amusement tent. But I wasn't four, or his nephew, so I kept my mouth shut.

"I promised Troy I'd swing by tomorrow and drop off his present. When I'll have his full attention. Probably better. This way we have until the morning together."

"Yeah, well... coming to Mark's game was a bad idea. People were taking pictures. Word will get out. Derek's bound to find out."

"They were taking pictures of their kids, not you." He frowned back at me. "And it wasn't like I could ignore Coach McDonald when Mark brought him up to meet me."

Trent had been selling the whole college scout thing until that point. But Mark's casual familiarity with him earned me Ava's curious stare, letting me know I could expect a call from her later.

It had been like a damn circus. I watched from a few yards down the bleachers as the team swarmed around Trent, asking for his autograph, posing for selfies. Mark grinning by his side.

"I'm sorry. I didn't think it would get out of hand. I haven't had anyone ask for my autograph in years." I melted into the warmth of Trent's embrace. We had one night before he was off again. A night I'd been looking forward to all week. I'd be damned if we spent it arguing in the garage.

"You're right. It's exhausting toeing the line, worrying about Derek's opinion every time I do something that might make him angry." I tipped my head up a fraction to look up at Trent. "You were flirting with Ava, though."

My friend's eyes had danced with interest the moment Trent arrived at the game. The man was pure sex appeal in his snug jeans and worn leather jacket, the scruff on his jaw lending a ruggedness to his already handsome face.

"I was deflecting everyone's attention away from you. Your friend is a bit nuts. And not at all my type."

Ava was everyone's type, with her ample curves and vivacious personality. I'd be willing to bet my next support check that she'd scrawled her number somewhere on Trent's notepad. "And what exactly is your type?"

"Leggy blondes who like to flirt with danger." He brushed his thumb across my bottom lip, his gaze molten. Over his shoulder and across the side yard, I saw movement in my neighbor's upstairs window. *Carol Jordan.*

"Not in public." I stepped back into the privacy of the

garage and then lifted onto my toes and kissed his scruffy jaw. "Not with my one-woman neighborhood watch watching."

Trent shot a glance over his shoulder, but there was nothing to see and he said as much.

"Carol Jordan's penchant for gossip is legendary. Interesting when it's not you, but when everyone on the lakefront is discussing your dramas..."

"I get it." Trent pressed a kiss to the top of my head, then pulled back.

"Come inside. I'll make us some cocoa. Or maybe some mulled wine?"

"Wine sounds good. But first I want to head off to the grocery store. I'm making you dinner tonight." His hands cupped my jaw, tilting my face up and kissing me gently on the lips. "Go inside and lock up, set the alarm. I'll be back shortly."

"I'll leave the garage door open for you." I gave him the alarm code, probably not necessary since he'd been standing next to me when I changed it this morning.

"No need. I might have programmed your opener into my car last night."

I barked out a surprised laugh, shaking my head in wonder. I should have been angry, but the man had my best interest at heart. "Trent..."

"What would have happened if you hadn't left the door open yesterday afternoon?"

My skin tingled uncomfortably at the thought. I had spent half the night imagining what would have happened if Trent hadn't barged in when he did. Wondering if Gabriel was as dangerous as Trent believed.

"Right." I turned to head up the three stairs leading from the garage to the mudroom. Even though the alarm light flashed red, my hand hesitated over the doorknob. Which was foolish. Gabriel didn't know the new codes. He couldn't even get through the front gates.

Trent's long strides brought him to my side. "You need me to go in with you?"

I sucked in a fortifying breath and unlocked the door. *Gabriel will not scare me out of my home.*

"Don't be silly. I'm fine." I smiled to reassure both of us. If I didn't confront my fears head on, I'd be jumping at everything.

I gave Trent a playful shove toward his car. "Just go, will you? I'm starved."

"Fine." He kissed me again and headed back out the wide garage door. I watched him pull away and then hit the button, closing all the bays.

Inside, I reset the alarm—no more forgetting for me—then headed toward the butler's pantry to raid Derek's prized wines. Their fate had yet to be decided in the divorce settlement, and possession was nine-tenths of the law. Or something like that. If he wanted the damn wine, he should have taken them when he moved out.

I pulled out a 2015 August Kesseler, a German pinot noir with a nondescript label. There were at least a half dozen bottles left. If Derek had bought a case, it was probably good. I grinned, thinking of the fit he'd throw if he saw me dumping the whole bottle into a saucepan and adding in spices.

I set the pan to simmer and contemplated the contents of the fridge. A couple of cheese wedges called to me, along with the fragrant saucisson sausage that had caught my eye from the deli counter yesterday. A frozen baguette went into the oven to bake while I sliced the sausage and cheese, my mouth watering from the scent of garlic and spices. A jar of artichokes and a bowl of olives went onto the platter along with some roasted red peppers.

The smell of cinnamon, cloves, and orange peel perfumed the air. I shut the flame off and let the fragrant steam from the wine waft over my face. The timer dinged. I pulled the baguette from the oven and set it onto the counter to cool. The yeasty smell of fresh bread added to the aroma of the mulled wine and sausages, making my stomach grumble.

Outside, rain dotted the French doors once again. A gust of wind buffeted the panes making me shiver. I shot a glance up the darkened backstairs, my imagination running wild. Perils of reading too many suspense novels. *Time to switch to something less violent, maybe?*

I shoved my runaway thoughts out of my mind and lit the fireplace. Maybe Gabriel would get hit by a bus or fall off a cliff. Not that we had cliffs on this side of the lake. But one could dream.

THE DELICIOUS SCENT of Trent's mother's beef stew perfumed the upstairs hall. My stomach gave an obnoxious growl, competing with the soft strains of piano and a woman's sultry voice drifting from below. While Trent started on dinner, I'd run upstairs to linger under a hot shower in an attempt to warm up—something I thought would never happen when we returned from Mark's game. Even with the heavy wool throw I pulled from the back of my car, and Ava's spiked hot cocoa, the bleachers had been freezing. As much as I hated to think winter was closing in, this was just the first hint. Halloween was only a couple of weeks away, and before long, Mark and I'd be shoveling heaps of lake-effect snow.

I shivered at the thought.

My attention landed on Trent as I rounded the landing. I paused for a second to appreciate the view. What was it about a man working in the kitchen? The simple grace in which he wielded a knife, the economy of his movements as he stirred the pot.

I could get used to this.

The thought came out of nowhere, and before I could analyze it, Trent looked my way and smiled.

I smiled back. "Something smells amazing." Then made my way down the final set of stairs, my feet encased in thick, fluffy socks I usually reserved for deep winter. I'd continued the casual fashion theme with a soft blue alpaca sweater and a pair of comfortable fleece-lined leggings I hadn't had the heart to toss with the rest of my old wardrobe.

He met me at the bottom, and I found myself cocooned in the warmth of his arms. "Feel better?"

"Getting there." In more ways than one.

His hands cupped my face as he brought his lips to mine in a soul-searing kiss.

I skated my still-cold hands under his sweater, appreciating the long muscles of his back. He shivered, but didn't voice any objection as I continued my exploration around front. The firm curves of his pectorals, the sharp tips of his nipples, the hard ridges of his abs. And lower, my fingers brushing against the shape of him behind his jeans, making him hiss.

My empty stomach interrupted the moment. Trent pulled back with a chuckle. Slipping his fingers through mine, he led me across the family room and into the kitchen. "Let's feed you before that becomes dangerous."

I wanted to complain, until he handed me a small plate filled with the savory goodies I'd laid out earlier. I could definitely get used to Trent's pampering.

I popped a briny olive into my mouth and then exchanged the plate for the footed mug of still-warm wine waiting for me on the counter. At the stove I lifted the lid off the Dutch oven, closing my eyes to inhale the heady combination of beef, vegetables, and spices. "Oh my God, Trent. This smells delicious."

He chuckled, pulling the wooden spoon from my grasp before I had a chance to taste his heavenly concoction. Dragging the heavy lid back over the pot, Trent tsked out his disapproval. "Patience, my love. In a couple hours it will be even better."

My love? It was only an expression, I told myself. Not a pledge of his feelings.

He handed me a hunk of baguette topped with a thick slice of sausage. "Eat this before you pass out. You've barely consumed enough to sustain a mouse today."

The urge to argue was strong. I had eaten plenty this morning under the watchful eyes of Trent and my son, despite—or maybe because of—the weird sense of normalcy at the breakfast table.

Instead, I raised my glass to my lips with a sultry smile. "A couple hours?"

There was a lot we could do in a couple of hours.

"Give or take." Pulling my glass out of my hand and setting it on the island, he slid the plate of food toward me. "So eat this, because you're gonna need your strength."

I fought a grin at his insinuation. "Is that so?"

Instead of answering, he lifted a slice of Gruèyre to my lips. His eyes darkened as I let my tongue graze his fingers before taking the pungent cheese into my mouth. Before I could tempt him further, he growled out, "Eat," and then turned away.

I couldn't help the goofy smile tugging on my wind-burned lips as I watched Trent putter around the kitchen, to keep from acting on his impulses I assumed.

"You're spoiling me, you know. I may not let you leave tomorrow," I said while forking an artichoke on top of a slice of baguette, then adding a piece of sausage to the stack.

While I'd slept, Trent and Mark had made breakfast. And the dinner simmering away on the stove, perfuming the room with its delicious scents, was all Trent. The last time someone had made me food was the peanut butter and jelly sandwich Brooke had prepared for Mother's Day when she was seven, or maybe eight. It had been adorable and messy.

I'd considered myself lucky when Derek thought to make coffee, but never expected him to do more. I'd never complained. It was easy to overlook the things you never had.

Trent set down the sponge and headed over to the stove, turning the burner under the pot of stew down to a low simmer. Then rounded the island and proceeded toward me, a crooked, bittersweet smile curving his mouth. "Believe me, I don't want to leave."

He pulled the almost empty wine glass from my hand, then wrapped his fingers around mine, tugging me off my barstool. The pinot had settled warm in my veins, leaving my limbs comfortably heavy and relaxed. He led me to the open space between the counters. I grinned as he slowly spun me into his arms with the grace of someone who knew how to dance.

"Why, Mr. Richards, you have some serious moves." I giggled as he dipped me with a confident grin. "If you are trying to seduce me, your plan is working."

"Good."

Soft, slow music filtered around us, and I followed Trent's lead, swaying easily in his arms. Happy goosebumps spread across my skin, and my heart swelled in my chest. I couldn't remember the last time Derek and I had danced— it definitely wasn't in the kitchen, or spontaneous.

Stop comparing the two men, a voice in my head urged. There was no comparison between Derek and Trent. One man had let me go, and the other…

Heavy words threatened to spill from my tongue. Words that would change everything between me and Trent. Words that would shift our relationship past casual. A small thread of fear tugged at my insides with the realization my feelings had already flown well past that point.

What if Trent didn't feel the same?

I swallowed the words down as doubt settled heavy on my chest. Once spoken those kinds of declarations couldn't be recalled. I had made enough mistakes this past month. From the start we'd agreed to keep things casual. Trent's schedule and the uncertainty of my divorce were reason enough. Was I even ready for something more than casual? Ready to plunge headlong into whatever was happening when I hadn't even terminated my marriage?

And what about Gabriel? Crazy as it sounded in my head, I needed to call him. Talk some sense into the man. Or I needed to come clean with Trent and trust he'd forgive me.

Neither option sounded appealing.

I ignored my own doubts and fears, and whispered, "Kiss me, Mr. Richards."

He reached up, placing his hands on either side of my face, and kissed me in earnest. I dug my fingers into his soft hair, holding on in desperation as he explored every inch of my mouth. God, what this man could do with his lips, his tongue. He kissed me like it was his sole purpose in life. Like his mouth had been created only for pleasure.

He seared a path along my jaw. His fingers dragging the high neck of my sweater aside, his lips following a path to my shoulder, making me tremble with need. I gasped his name on a ragged breath.

"I've wanted you like crazy since the moment we met," he whispered, pulling back, his pupils large and dark amidst a sea of green, his cheeks ruddy from more than just this afternoon's wind.

Wrapping my hand around his, I tugged him toward the stairs. "Show me."

CHAPTER
TWENTY-ONE

J ust inside the double doors of my bedroom, Trent halted.

"Wow." He let out a slightly unhinged chuckle.

I'd had a similar reaction almost twenty years ago. In the intervening years I'd become accustomed to the square footage of this room, with its high beamed ceilings, breathtaking views of Lake Michigan, floor to ceiling mullioned windows, and French doors leading to my private balcony. My gaze stopped on the pretty walnut sleigh bed I'd splurged on the day after Derek asked for a divorce.

"Stay focused here," I said while tugging on the hem of his sweater.

"Yes, princess," Trent said with an impish grin.

I rolled my eyes as he guided me toward the bed. Then he dragged both his soft sweater and T-shirt over his head while I fumbled to unzip his fly.

Trent stepped out of his jeans, and I gaped for a second at all the gorgeousness in front of me. Not that I hadn't seen it all before, but there was something ridiculously perfect about Trent that deserved gawking.

I could only remember seeing his type of muscle definition in movies. Everything about Trent defied my imagination. Actually, our whole relationship—sort of like this fantasy bedroom—was a bit surreal. But unlike this room, there was no way I'd take Trent Richards for granted. Even if we lasted twenty years.

"Stay focused here." He repeated my earlier request, and I was more than happy to abandon the trajectory of my unsettling thoughts. Whatever was happening between us, I wanted to enjoy every minute. Not think about some unknown future.

He kissed me deep, stealing the air from my lungs and making me forget everything except his mouth and his warm, slightly callus-roughened hands gathering up the fabric of my sweater. We separated only long enough for him to slip the soft wool over my head, and then he was kissing me again.

I wrapped my arms around his neck and pulled myself against him, lifting onto my toes and aligning myself with his impossibly hard body. Then his hands slid down the back of my leggings, cupping my ass and pulling me snug against him. He was hard and hot, the warmth of his skin penetrating into my still-chilled flesh.

He gripped my hips and lifted me onto the mattress with unexpected ease. I wasn't small, but with Trent I felt tiny.

I parted my thighs, allowing him room to maneuver. His hands tightened on my waist, pulling me in. My fingers dug into his shoulders, my legs encircled his hips. There wasn't even a whisper of air between us, but I wanted him closer. No, not wanted, *needed*.

Trent laid a trail of kisses from my lips to my jaw, then down the column of my neck. Sucking at the tender skin. Nipping. He flexed his hips, pressing his erection against me. I let out a whimper of pleasure, and he answered with a throaty groan.

"So good," he whispered against my skin.

"And we're not even naked yet," I said with a little giggle. "We're like horny teenagers."

"You make me feel sixteen again." He pulled back with a grin, then turned his attention to the front clasp of my bra. "Christ, my hands are shaking."

I couldn't help but laugh as I took over his fumbled attempts at the fastener. A moment later my breasts spilled out from their confines, the loose straps of my bra slipping off my shoulders.

"God, I've missed these." He slid the bra straps down my arms and tossed the undergarment over his shoulder. A second later my flesh overflowed his grasp, my nipples hardening under his searing touch. He dipped his head down, capturing one of the tips between his lips, sucking hard enough to make me gasp.

"Trent..." I pleaded.

His fingers gave the other side equal attention, while his free hand pressed me back into the mattress.

"Naked. I need you naked. Now. Before your phone rings or the doorbell chimes or the fucking roof caves in."

"My phone's on silent, and I plan on ignoring everything else until morning," I assured.

"Until morning... I can definitely work with that time frame," he said while slipping his fingers inside the waistband of my pants. I raised my hips, giving him access to slide the fabric down my thighs, down my calves, and then off. He tossed them onto the growing pile of clothes on the floor. His boxer briefs followed, and I couldn't help but gape. The image of him naked would never get old.

He stood, staring back, his hand slowly stroking up and down his shaft in a way that had my body clenching and my thighs growing slick with the anticipation.

I lifted my knees and spread them a fraction apart, giving him a teasing glimpse of what he was doing to me. "Please. I need you."

"I can see that, beautiful. Tell me exactly what you need."

"To finish what we started that night at your penthouse." I'd spent an inordinate amount of time reliving the moments before we'd been interrupted. His mouth devouring mine, his deft fingers stroking me, his thick cock stretching me.

He cupped my heel in his warm palm, bringing my foot to his mouth. His lips brushed over each of my toes, biting gently before he slipped my leg over his shoulder. Then he repeated the process with the other leg, leaving me open and exposed to his view.

"It's been torture, you know?" His gaze locked with mine, his eyes dark and hooded, his voice husky with lust. He pressed a kiss against the tender skin of my inner thigh. "Knowing how perfect you feel..." And then another kiss higher. "Your heat surrounding me..." His hot tongue flicked against my skin, so close to where I needed him, before retreating. "And then gone."

"Please," I said on a whimper. There was a good chance I would explode in the next minute, but I really wanted to enjoy his mouth on me before that happened.

He chuckled as his lips made their torturous path again, making me squirm with needy frustration.

"I love when you beg, but patience, sweetheart."

"I've never been exceptionally good with patience."

He smirked, his eyes twinkling with mischief. "I tend to approve of your impulsiveness, but not right now. Not when I need to find out if you taste as good as I remember."

I collapsed back onto the pillow, watching Trent slowly lower his head. His hands spread me wide, and then... *Oh hell.* My mind reeled with the sensation of his glorious mouth on me.

My world shrunk to the space between my legs and Trent's hot, wet tongue. I gasped, his name on my lips, begging him to *slow down, speed up. God. Just. Don't. Stop.* I would surely die. Nothing else mattered but the exquisite pleasure he coaxed from my body.

"So fucking good," he groaned out. The deep sound vibrated against my sensitive flesh, making my insides spasm and tremble. His talented tongue continued to push me to the edge with deliberate strokes. My breath caught. My skin tingled. Then I was gone in a rush of white-hot pleasure.

"Oh my God..." My orgasm crashed through me like a runaway freight train, leaving twitching limbs and shattered nerve endings in its wake.

Some moments later, Trent smiled up at me and a small laugh escaped his lips. I'd been incoherent—that much was painfully obvious. My face heated, and I closed my eyes as I struggled to recall what I had said. It was his fault. The man had no idea what kind of weapon he wielded. In all my life I'd never experienced an orgasm as intense as this.

Breath ragged and body trembling, I raised my heavy eyelids to find Trent still staring up at me. His mossy eyes locked on mine and my face flamed, blast-furnace hot with embarrassment.

He raised an eyebrow as a grin spread across his face. "I

want to be responsible for those sweet sounds of yours every damn night."

"Um..." I started, unsure what to say. *Every night?*

"Um?" Trent repeated, raising the other brow. *Cocky bastard.*

I closed my eyes tight while trying to compose myself. He was still staring when I opened them again seconds later. I'd never stop blushing if he kept it up.

"Now she's speechless..." he said, more to himself, then flicked his tongue lightly across the too-sensitive bundle of nerves that seemed to control my entire body. I flinched. Trent's face lit up. His lips curved and his eyebrows rose higher. A wicked gleam glinted in his eye. He lowered his head to his task again to the soundtrack of my feeble objections.

"Trent..." I cried out incoherently a few moments later as a second glorious orgasm crashed over me with equal intensity as the first. There was a good chance I'd be dead by dawn if he kept this up.

He pressed a closed-mouth kiss to my mound and then pinned me with a crooked smile that said he was damn proud of himself. "Fuck, you're addicting."

Trent allowed me no time to ponder his statement or anything else. The slow graze of his teeth and delicate swipes of his tongue along the tender skin of my inner thigh had me squealing.

"Ah, she speaks." He grinned wolfishly. "I was begin-ning to worry I'd damaged your brain."

I rolled my eyes hard at his words. "Trent..."

He laughed, his eyes sparking with boyish humor. "Yes, Nic?"

"Get up here."

"Yes, ma'am." Despite my demand, he moved forward

at iceberg speed, pausing to place a lingering kiss on my hip bone, then another on my stomach. I groaned as he continued his leisurely journey up my body, scattering hot, wet kisses at random.

"We only have until morning," I reminded. Not that I minded his attention to detail.

"Patience."

The hungry look in his eyes told me neither one of us had much use for patience at the moment. He brushed a quick kiss to my lips and then rose up between my thighs.

I stared for a moment at his gorgeous cock—*Hello again* —then reached out, almost unconsciously. My fingertips brushed over the curve of his impossibly hard pecs sprinkled with swirls of fine dark hair that converged in the center of his chest. His nipples pebbled on contact, and his whole body froze as I let my fingertips drift down the dark trail of silky-soft hair. Past what had to be a textbook definition of washboard abs. My fingers read each ridge and valley before returning to the downy trail and the final stop on my journey.

I swallowed hard and met Trent's gaze. He'd been statue-still the whole time, but obviously not unaffected. His chest rose and fell rapidly with his accelerated breath, and a dusky blush spread across his cheeks. In the dim twilight his eyes had turned almost black.

His tongue traced a slow path along his bottom lip, still glistening and slick from my orgasms, as he glanced down at my hands.

I followed his gaze, letting my touch drift lower.

He was a beautiful man, and this part was no exception. Long and thick and heavily veined, he was magnificent— and maybe a bit intimidating, if I were honest with myself. I brushed my thumb over the bead of slick moisture glistening at the tip, then slowly dragged it over the sensitive ridge at the base of his crown. His hips jerked and he gasped sharply, making me smile with satisfaction. He wasn't the only one who knew how to give pleasure.

My fingers curled around his circumference, stroking the silky, yet impossibly hard length.

He sucked in a deep breath, eyes closed tight as if in pain. "Fuck, Nic," he rasped, placing his hand over mine. "Stop, baby. Please."

It was my turn to grin. Talk about having the bull by the horns. "I like making you beg, too," I whispered, not letting go as I sat up on my heels.

Placing my free hand on the middle of his chest, I pushed him down on the comforter. His eyes widened a fraction and a grin spread across his lips.

"Nicki..." He drew out my name, his voice lowered with a hint of warning I chose to ignore.

Rising to my knees, I straddled his thighs and then leaned forward.

"Shush. It's my turn to play." I breathed against his lips as I continued to stroke him.

"Nic..." he groaned. "Neither one of us is going to win this game."

I slid forward, my slick folds slipping against his thick hardness, kindling my desire once again. Trent sank his teeth into his bottom lip as his hands settled at my waist, pressing my still over-sensitive flesh firmly against him. A third impossible orgasm danced just on the edge of the horizon. But I wanted—no needed—to experience all of him this time.

Shifting my angle, I reached down and brought him into my body, inch by slow, glorious inch, until he was seated completely inside me.

"That's it. Ride me sweetheart," he whispered as I rose up, delighting in the feel of his wide head stroking against my inner walls. Then lowering down just as slow, only to rise up again. Talk about addicting...

His hands tightened on my hips as he took control, guiding me up and down on his shaft at a pace only a bit faster than mine, but somehow it made all the difference.

Maybe it was the bite of his fingers in my flesh, promising bruises come morning. Or maybe it was the way his eyes locked on mine with an intimacy I'd never felt before. Or maybe it was this feeling of power he had over me, the way my body responded whenever he was near, whenever he touched me.

Trent was like a drug. A really nice drug that would leave me begging for more long after he left. My heart squeezed tight with the fear that this would never be enough. One night would leave me wanting so much more.

I pushed that thought aside, focusing on the moment. Focusing on Trent and the way our bodies fit so perfectly. The way he stretched me a hair past the point of comfort, into a place where pleasure mixed with pain to create something indescribable.

"Don't want this to end." He pulled me down, kissing me hard and deep, growling my name against my parted lips.

"Me neither."

His body trembled against mine as we fought against the inevitable. My release built heavy and hot, coiling inside me, making me whimper.

"Can't last... forever." He groaned, then kissed me harder, while sliding a hand between us, touching me in the one place that guaranteed I'd lose control.

My fingers dug into his shoulders and I screamed out

his name as hot, electric waves of pleasure swept through me until I was spent and boneless in Trent's arms. He shifted, turning me, guiding me down, and covering me with his warmth as I shuddered with the aftereffects of a third mind-blowing orgasm.

His fingers threaded with mine and his lips claimed me, soft and sweet.

"Wrap those sexy legs around me, sweetheart."

Finding a reserve of energy from somewhere I wasn't aware of, I obeyed, hooking my legs around his hips as he slammed into me with brutal thrusts, leaving me breathless. Once, twice, and again and again with increasing speed and a delicious roughness that promised I'd be sore for days. Moments later he stilled, spilling his release with a chant of my name on his breath.

He pressed his lips to my forehead, my eyelids, then my lips. Kissing me with a reverence that brought tears to my eyes.

"Someday. I promise. It will be me and you, like this, every damn night."

I grinned like a fool at his words. Because for once his promises didn't scare me.

CANDLELIGHT DANCED ON THE CEILING, the walls. The smell of Trent surrounded me, spicy, masculine with the tang of sweat and sex. Warmth filled my veins and my heart swelled, recalling every minute of the previous hour.

I love you.

A smile tugged at my lips, but the words stayed silent in my brain. I'd said those same words countless times over the years to Derek, and look where it got me. Teetering on the verge of bankruptcy and sleeping with a man a half dozen years younger than me.

I wasn't complaining about the second part. But obviously those words hadn't gotten me anywhere.

"Hey." Trent smiled, walking into the room in just a pair of low-hung sweats showing way too much of his body to be decent. The man didn't have an ounce of fat on him. "I thought we could eat up here. Unless you have an aversion to eating in bed."

It took a second to notice the tray in his hands, loaded with two bowls of stew, the leftover baguette, and a bottle of wine.

I scooted over toward the opposite side of the bed and he sat down, placing the tray between us. "Not at all."

"Good, because I don't plan on leaving this bed until my flight tomorrow."

I laughed, watching him set the tray on his lap and hand me a warm bowl of his mother's stew. "I like the sound of this plan."

"Good," he replied while pouring the wine into the two glasses sitting on the tray. It was another one of Derek's prized cabernets put to good use.

"I'm just being practical," he continued, settling back against the pillows. "I don't know when our schedules will fit so perfectly again. I plan on taking advantage of every second I have with you."

"I'm not complaining. A girl could get used to this." I sighed, taking a deep inhale of the beefy stew loaded with chunks of potato and carrots swimming in a thick gravy. It was the perfect meal after the cold morning at the game. "Especially this food."

"So it's just my cooking you're after?" He grinned over the rim of his wine glass, his eyes glinting with dark humor.

"Maybe not just your cooking," I admitted without shame before spooning a healthy bite of stew into my mouth. My eyes rolled back into my head and I moaned in pleasure.

Trent chuckled. "Anything that'll have you making that sound, sweetheart, is fine by me."

My cheeks warmed at his words. Or maybe the heat of the stew. Either way, I'd never been fond of pet names, but coming from Trent, I didn't seem to mind. I was more than happy to be his sweetheart. Or anything else he wanted me to be.

CHAPTER
TWENTY-TWO

The morning sun sparkled on the cut crystal wine glasses left on the nightstand. Trent's warm body pressed against my back, his arm snug around my waist. I smiled, for the first time not waking alone in this massive bed.

Randall would have a coronary, but I didn't care about him or the divorce at the moment. I was happy, Trent was happy, and nothing else mattered.

I turned slowly to face the man who'd left me sore in all the right places. He had been insatiable last night. And in the early hours of this morning after we'd indulged in way too much apple pie and ice cream. There was something to be said about youth.

At the moment he looked too young and innocent to have done the things he did to me. There wasn't a wrinkle on his handsome face. Unlike me.

Will he want me ten years from now? A doubtful voice whispered inside my head. The thought made my stomach clench. I never wanted to go through the betrayal and disappointment of the past month again.

Trent's arms tightened around my waist, and his lips pressed against my neck.

"What's got you thinking so loud, Nic?" he whispered, his stubble rubbing against my tender skin, making me shiver.

"Fear," I answered honestly.

His gaze met mine, soft with concern. "What are you afraid of?"

I held my fingers against his lips. "I just..."

Cynthia's voice echoed in my head, telling me to *stop worrying and enjoy your fling*. But was this only a fling to Trent when he threw out words like someday and forever? A braver me would have the nerve to ask.

He pressed a soft kiss to the center of my palm. "Just what?"

"Just... I don't want to get hurt again. This divorce—"

Trent silenced me with his lips, kissing me slow and deep. "I have no intention of hurting you. Trust me, I'm in this as deep as you."

Yeah, I needed clarification on what Trent's definition of deep was.

Before I could work up the nerve to ask, the coffee maker burbled to life at the far end of the bedroom. The scent of coffee drifted across the room, and the moment was lost.

"If I didn't have a flight in a few hours, you'd never get me out of this bed."

I never wanted him to leave. Never wanted this morning to end. Never wanted to leave this cocoon of warmth and safety his presence provided despite my fears for the future.

"It's early. We still have time," I said, chasing those impossible desires from my mind.

With Trent's busy schedule set for the foreseeable future and the uncertainty of my divorce, talk about the future would have to wait. Until then, I was going to treasure every minute before he left. Hold each second tight, not waste them with idle talk.

With that thought I wrapped my hand around his hard length, tight enough to make him groan.

"Looks like I'll be taking my coffee to go," he said while pressing me into the sheets with his warm body. My legs wrapped around his waist and he sank into me.

"You sore?" he asked, stilling as I tried not to wince. There was definitely a price to pay for too much fun.

"Only in the best way."

"Nic..." He let out a sigh and then started to pull away. "I don't want—"

I sank my fingers into the firm muscles of his ass, stopping his retreat. "Don't. I want to feel you all week. Every time I move I want to remember this moment."

His lips curved into a wicked grin. "I like the thought of you remembering me inside you."

He surged forward and this time we both gasped. Emotions threatened to overwhelm me as I stared into his eyes. Watching the signs of pleasure in his expression and storing it away in my memory like a squirrel and her acorns, for the cold and lonely nights to come.

My phone rang, breaking the moment. Unease mixed with frustration. *If it's a telemarketer, I swear...*

Trent reached over to the nightstand and grabbed the offending item. Then frowned. "It says Derek."

"Shit, Mark," I yelped, fear eclipsing my frustration, as Trent handed me the phone. My heart skipped a beat and my imagination played different scenarios for why Derek would be calling. None of them were good.

"What's wrong?" My voice trembled, full of panic as I spoke into the phone. Trent's arms came around me, pulling me against his solid frame and grounding me. "Where's Mark? What happened?"

"Mark's still asleep." Derek paused for a second while I frowned in confusion. "I asked you for one thing. One thing, Nicole. Keep fucking quiet. But no. You never listen."

I frowned at the phone. "What are you talking about?"

"Turn on the news."

He hung up and my spine tingled with fear. *Gabriel? Or possibly photos of me and Trent from yesterday's game?* Either option would be reason for Derek's call.

"Everything okay, Nic?" Trent's voice broke me out of my thoughts.

I scrambled out of bed, a heady mix of anxiety and irritation pulling me away from Trent when all I wanted was to stay in bed. To forget Derek's call. But something dark slithered under my skin, telling me not to ignore my husband's order.

"I need to see something." Stumbling over to the sitting area, I turned on the TV. A commercial played, some drug promising relief for some ailment or another. My knee bounced in agitation as I waited through three other commercials selling insignificant products. Then the weather and sports. Nothing dire. Nothing Derek would have called me at six forty in the morning for.

Trent wrapped a throw around my naked shoulders and sat down next to me, his dark gray sweatpants covering his lower half, his hand gripping mine. After what seemed like forever, the Breaking News banner flashed across the top of the screen. Then a dated picture of me appeared in the corner, and the news anchor's smile gleamed. Not one of my better ones, if I had to be honest. My mouth was half open and my eyes were half shut.

All thoughts of unflattering photos vanished when the reporter started talking. A clip of a video of Gabriel, in an expensive suit I would have sworn he couldn't afford, played. My stomach twisted with fear.

I switched the TV off.

"Shit."

"Was that…" Trent pulled the remote from my hands and turned the TV back on.

I turned to ice as I watched the rest of the report. *Fucking bastard.* I didn't need to hear anymore to know what had made Derek furious, but I was frozen in place.

The caption above my face blurred behind tears, and I collapsed back against the sofa, my muscles weak. I'd seen enough. The two anchors discussed my personal life like I was the day's entertainment. Like I had no rights to privacy or respect.

You're a public figure. You have to expect the scrutiny, I remember Derek's press secretary telling me ages ago.

But what about my kids?

"…no word to confirm or deny the scandal yet. Stay tuned for the stunning interview with Gabriel Roth, the man alleged to have had an affair with the wife of our beloved senator, Derek Robinson, tonight at nine." Trent shut the TV off while I shivered with shock.

He tugged the throw around my shoulders and then knelt in front of me.

"Nicki?" He frowned, his hands rubbing mine. "Tell me none of this is true. Tell me you haven't been having an affair with that man for the past five years."

"No. Of course he's lying," I spat out with disgust, and the muscles of Trent's face relaxed.

He let out a deep breath, shaking his head as if waking up. "I'm sorry. Of course I believe you. I should never have doubted..." He stood and paced across the carpet. "Fuck him. We'll get a lawyer. Sue for defamation."

I shook my head as tears spilled down my cheeks. "No, Trent."

"Nicki?"

"I'm so sorry," I whispered, my voice hoarse. This was it. Once I told him the truth, there would be no way Trent— or my kids, or my parents—would look at me the same way again.

"What?" He closed his eyes tight, rubbing at his temples as if in pain. "Why are you sorry? This man is obviously—"

I shook my head slowly, silencing his words with a desperate stare. "The day before I met you..." I waved a hand at the screen and dipped my head to avoid Trent's reaction. "It was only once. A complete mistake."

"What was a mistake?" An ugly silence filled the gap between us. "You fucked him?"

"Please. Just let me explain." I stood, walking toward Trent as he backed up, hands raised to fend off my words. Words I'd hoped never to speak. "You have to understand. I was angry—"

"Is that a yes?" He shook his head and spun away. "Jesus Christ."

"Trent. You have to understand—"

"Understand what?" he yelled, pointing at the TV. "You knew. I asked you two days ago what his deal was." He slowly shook his head, his eyes widening. "You knew, and you fucking lied to me."

"Stop, Trent. You're making more of this than—"

"I'm making more of this? Nicki, your affair with that— that, man is splashed across the morning news, for Christ's

236

sake." His sharp laugh filled the room. "Now I get why you didn't want to call the cops."

"Just stop, Trent. He's lying. It was one time, not a damn *affair*."

The way he crossed his arms and narrowed his eyes said I was wasting my breath. He didn't believe me. Or maybe it didn't matter. He didn't care.

"I... I need to go. I can't think right now." His eyes darted around the room for a second, and then he gathered up his things and stormed out of the bedroom.

STUPID, stupid, stupid.

Would I ever learn? Trusting men only brought pain. Derek, Gabriel, Trent. *God, Trent.* If he'd only let me explain. Given me the time.

Maybe you should have tried calling Gabriel sooner? But when? I'd barely had a second alone yesterday.

"Shut up," I sobbed, my voice echoing through the empty house. How was I to know the man was going to pull something so stupid so fast?

Trent was right. This stupid house was too big. Mocking me with its false sense of protection. No security alarms could keep me safe from scandal.

Gabriel knew just how to get me. Forty-eight hours ago my main worry had been the mediation. I laughed bitterly, shaking my head. *May as well have given him written instructions on the best way to destroy me.*

And Derek. Shit. With the final details of our divorce still unsettled, what was he planning? What could he do? We both wanted this over with. Anything he could do would prolong the process. He couldn't want that. Could he?

I didn't dare call him back. He'd been spitting mad earlier. And Randall said not to talk to him. Wise advice, but what about Mark? What would Derek tell him? If my son heard his version of the situation he might never want to see me again. And what about Brooke? Would she feel the same?

Those dark thoughts stayed with me until the limo pulled up later that evening when Mark walked in, eyes wide, mouth gaping.

"I'm so sorry," I blurted out before he could say anything.

"There's a crowd by the gate. Dozens of reporters." He shook his head. "What happened?"

"You don't know?" I silently thanked Derek for being a chickenshit this time.

Mark dropped his bag on the tile floor, his head shaking, his eyes rolling. "What did Dad do now?"

Of course there'd be reporters. There were always reporters. Smiling faces and cameras capturing the good deeds we'd done. All the times Derek fought for some social services program, every time I'd helped raise money for a homeless shelter, or the countless other charities we'd worked with or started over the years. They'd smiled just as wide when Derek's brother had been caught with a prostitute, or the time a hot mic captured his unflattering opinion of the sitting president, even though it was an opinion everyone shared.

Fair-weather friends who shoved their microphones in your face when they wanted to boost their ratings. I'd learned over the years. Reporters were not your friends and, like the men in my life, not to be trusted.

"They didn't harass you, did they?" My blood pressure spiked at the thought of reporters bothering my kids. There were lines I refused to let those vultures cross. *But what can you do about it?*

"No. Not really. So what's up this time?"

It disturbed me that my kids were barely fazed by the press.

"You'd better sit down." I sighed, then told him in as few words as possible about Gabriel. "I have never regretted anything more than this."

"Even when you were photographed with your skirt tucked into you underwear?" He grinned, making me laugh until tears pricked the corners of my eyes.

"That might come close."

We both grinned and then laughed some more.

"We all make mistakes." He walked to the fridge and pulled out a bottle of apple juice, retrieving two glasses from the cabinet. "The important thing is to learn from them."

I made a face. Nothing like having your children lecture you with the advice you'd given them at one time.

"Sage advice, my wise one." I rubbed at the headache that had lingered since shortly after Trent left this morning. Mark handed me the full glass of juice, and I motioned him to sit down again. "There's more."

"Oh boy..."

I didn't want to, but I had to tell Mark everything that happened Friday before he got home. Gabriel was unpredictable. And dangerous. Whether he'd go after Mark, I didn't know. But I wasn't taking chances. I'd underestimated him once. I wouldn't make that mistake again.

"I don't get it. Dad always told me that if a girl isn't interested, walk away."

239

"Your dad is a smart man." *Sometimes.* "Maybe Gabriel wasn't so lucky in the father department. Which makes Gabriel Roth even more dangerous. If you spot him, promise me you'll call the police. Don't take chances."

Mark nodded, his eyes shifting toward the stairs, like he had better things to do than listen to my lecture. My hands cupped his face to pull his attention back. "Please, Mark, this is important. Gabriel, the reporters. We can't be too careful."

"Okay, Mom." He nodded again. Message received, I hoped. "So now what?"

"Now, I go see Brooke."

CHAPTER
TWENTY-THREE

The next morning I strode straight into Cynthia's office, armed with two Ethiopian blends from my boss's favorite coffee shop along with a cinnamon-studded muffin—also her favorite. I had no intention of buttering her up. I deserved to get fired. *May as well end my employment on a pleasant note.*

"Well, good morning to you." She motioned to the guest chair without looking up from the documents on her desk. "To what do I owe this pleasure, at..." She glanced at her watch, then finally looked me in the eye. "Six forty-three in the morning?"

"I thought this would be better done before the rest of your staff showed up."

Her eyes narrowed as she reached for her coffee. "This?"

I sank back in the chair. Was she really going to make me spell it out? "My resignation, of course."

She stilled, setting her cup down slowly. "What the fuck are you talking about, Ms. Adams?"

I blew out a frustrated breath. She had to have seen the

news by now. "You have every right to fire me. I'm just saving you the trouble."

She laughed, loud. "Because some one-night stand decides to go all revenge on you? Believe me, in my almost fifty years on this earth, I've experienced much worse. I'll be the last person to judge you, my friend."

"Technically it happened in the afternoon. And both Derek and Trent are judging me. Why not you?"

Cynthia snorted. "Because I've been there. Scorned lovers aren't in short supply, I'm afraid. And as for Derek and Trent, they both can go straight to hell. We're in the twenty-first century. Women should be free to fuck any man they choose. Even if they regret it later."

"Yes, but I'm still technically married."

"Whatever..." She waved her hand, dismissing the idea like it didn't matter. For a woman who swore she'd never get married, it probably didn't. "Now tell me your side, so I can prepare."

In as few words as possible, I gave Cynthia the high points of Friday night.

"Have you spoken to Randall?"

I gave my friend a level stare over my coffee cup. "I'm sorta afraid of his reaction."

"He'll get over it." She turned her attention to the bag with the muffins. "Cinnamon?"

I nodded. "Why me, Cyn? Trent and I had a wonderful day Saturday and an unbelievable night. Then Sunday he flew out of my house as if demons were after him. He's disgusted with me. I honestly can't blame him, but I keep going back to something he said. 'We could pretend you didn't have a life before we met, but that would be unfair to both of us.' I mean, we were discussing my marriage at the time, but still..."

"Fragile ego." Cynthia scowled for a second while peeling the paper from her breakfast. "Did you see the photo on the news? It was grainy as shit, but someone snapped a picture of you and Trent kissing in some parking lot."

"We didn't kiss." The goddamn soccer moms. My stomach soured, remembering how I'd found Trent reclining against my car in the school parking lot. He'd leaned in to kiss me, but I'd pulled back at the last second.

"Maybe it was the angle." She shrugged. "It looked bad, though."

"I warned him not to go to Mark's game Saturday, but no. 'It'll be fine,' he said. 'We'll be careful,' he promised." I closed my eyes, forcing back tears. Randall was going to skin me alive, unless Derek beat him to it. "Listen, Cyn, if you want me gone, I'll understand."

"Don't be ridiculous. I need you and I don't give a damn what people think." She slammed her fist on the desk, and I barked a dry laugh. "I have a lot of lawyer friends. We'll sue the fuckers."

She took a bite of muffin, all calm while my stomach twisted at her words—practically the same words Trent had uttered before I told him the truth. So much for honesty being the best policy.

"I'm not suing anyone. I just want this all to disappear."

"It will. In the meantime, you need to keep busy. And I have the perfect solution." She grinned like a maniac, making my stomach tighten. Whatever solution Cynthia had, I had a feeling I wouldn't like it. "The Argyle."

"The Argyle?"

"The Argyle," she sang, then slapped the file for the musty old hotel in front of me. "It's all yours. A local buyer is interested in it for their club. I've worked with them for years. Great guys. Easy sale." She opened the file on the desk and spread out the photos of the dilapidated hotel she'd shown me weeks ago. "They've outgrown their current location and are looking for something larger. I immediately thought about the Argyle Hotel. Could be perfect for what they're looking for, and if you can remove that pile from my books, the commission is all yours."

I couldn't help but laugh. Weeks ago she'd called it a diamond in the rough; now it was a pile.

"Local guys? Don't you think I should lay low for a bit?" They would have to be blind not to have seen the news reports.

"I'm double-booked with the rescheduled Clybourn Avenue closing. Chin up. I'm pretty sure Gordon Knight wouldn't care if you fucked all the pool boys in the city."

My heart stopped and all the blood drained from my head, making the room spin. "Gordon Knight? Did you say Gordon Knight?"

"Yep. Knight, Jamison, Owens Ltd. They own exclusive clubs all over the country. I had dinner with Gordon Knight the other day. He told me they've outgrown their Chicago location, so I mentioned the Argyle. Then sent him the pictures the next day. He thinks it's perfect. It's almost a done deal. Deets are in here." She patted the file sitting on the desk between us. "Go make lots of money."

"Oh God." I buried my face in my hands.

"What's wrong?"

"Unless there are two Gordon Knights." *God, let there be two of them.* It wasn't that uncommon of a name. Was it? "He's one of Derek's biggest donors. Six-foot, dark hair, light green eyes. Mid-thirties. English accent?"

Cynthia's eyes widened for a moment. "Interesting."

"What's interesting?"

She popped the last of her muffin into her mouth, chewing slowly. I could almost see the thoughts swirling around her head. Then she took a sip of coffee and stood, handing me the hotel file and pulling her briefcase out from under her desk. "Nothing. Got to go. I have a date with a six-million-dollar commission. I'd love to pamper you, but I can't. Gordon Knight will be here at nine. Conference room two. I suggest you familiarize yourself with his file. It's an easy sale. I know you can be professional. Go powder your nose and then get the job done."

GORDON KNIGHT WAS EXACTLY how I remembered him. Young, handsome, and charismatic—well, I couldn't see his charisma through the conference room wall of windows, but he was blessed with an unfair amount of sex appeal and a magnetic pull I'd done my best to ignore. The man had been on the guest list of most of our private dinners, a fact I found most disquieting at the moment.

He started showing up to campaign events a handful of years ago. Soon after, Derek had started including him in our guest list.

What had Gordon Knight got out of the millions he'd donated to Derek's campaign? Certainly more than being invited to a bunch of dull-as-dishwater dinners. No one would submit themselves to hours of dry conversations about tax codes and foreign affairs without a good reason, besides gourmet food or high-priced liquor. No one at those dinners left without something.

I'd considered the possibility Derek was helping him out with a few building permits or zoning regulations. *You are who you know*, Derek always said. And he knew someone on pretty much every level of government in the state.

Exclusive clubs, Cynthia had stated as his line of business. But then why did Derek have him listed as the head of some architectural firm? Gordon Knight of Knight Consulting, it had read on the donor spreadsheet and all the invitations I'd sent out. Cynthia's file said Knight, Jamison, Owens Ltd.

Does it really matter anymore?

My hand hesitated over the doorknob as I gathered my courage, then prayed Cynthia was right. I needed to keep busy.

If only the man inside the conference room hadn't donated millions into Derek's campaign coffers over the years. If only my face hadn't been splashed all over the local networks yesterday.

I took a deep breath in an attempt to settle my nerves—the rich coffee on an empty stomach hadn't been a wise choice—then stepped into the conference room, prepared to face... whatever it was I was about to face.

Gordon Knight's eyes widened for a fraction of a second, then he stood.

"Mrs. Robinson?" His dark eyebrows raised with the question.

I stepped forward and offered him my hand. "Adams, actually. Nicole Adams, Mr. Knight. Cynthia asked me to apologize. She had something come up. Unless you object, she asked me to handle your account."

The corner of his lip quirked up as his eyes meandered down my body, making me wish I'd worn something different. The lacy red blouse and stiletto heels I'd chosen this morning were a far cry from the dowdy clothes I'd worn as a senator's wife.

"I have no objections whatsoever," he chuckled. "But do call me Gordon. I believe we dispensed with all those stuffy honorifics ages ago."

THE ARGYLE HOTEL looked the same as when Cynthia and I'd been here just... was it really over a month ago? Dust motes swirled in the dull sunshine spilling through the atrium's dingy glass ceiling, dancing with the echoed whispers of our conversation. It had been the Monday after I'd impulsively invited Trent over for a bit of skinny-dipping, and she had lectured me on the importance of safe sex.

Wasted words. Condoms don't protect the heart. Or safeguard the trust Trent and I had built over the following weeks.

"Obviously the seller will clear out the furnishings," I told Gordon Knight as we strode past the ugly plaid sofas, while I pushed my memories aside.

"They remind me of my university lounge. Fun times." He chuckled.

"I could ask to have them stay."

"Move them into my spare bedroom and relive my misspent youth? Tempting, but I think not."

We both laughed, and some of the awkwardness hovering over us the past two hours dissipated. Gordon Knight had been nothing but professional, focusing his attention on every detail of this property, from the musty basement all the way up to the slightly spongy rooftop that had my heart in my throat with every step.

I had almost forgotten his sharp, self-deprecating sense of humor. He had been a refreshing change from most of

Derek's donors, who barely cracked a smile and wouldn't have known a joke if it bit them on the ass.

"I did warn you this place needs a lot of work," I said while watching his sharp attention turn to the plaster walls, dark with water stains and missing in spots.

"The bones of the building appear in good order," he said, stopping for a moment to inspect one of the massive marble columns stretching to the ceiling six stories above us. The architecture in this place was stunning, if a bit tarnished.

We continued past the threadbare seating area earmarking the hotel's last heyday in the early 1980s. "We'll be gutting the upper floors, so a bit of water damage doesn't concern me. At least if it's not structural, which I don't believe is the case."

"That's what inspections are for," I reminded. The cost of this rehab would be enormous. "Cyn tells me you plan on turning this into a club. Not one of those stuffy places where men get together, smoke cigars, drink expensive whiskey, and bar women from entering, is it?"

His laughter echoed around the open space. "Definitely not."

Not for the first time today, a host of questions swirled around my head. Who was this man, and why had Derek spent so much time with him? Hours of phone conversations with his office door shut tight. Late night meetings. Derek made it his job to know everything about everyone. Why had he kept this side of Gordon Knight's business quiet? Something didn't quite add up.

We passed by the dated reception desk and through a set of double doors leading to one of the hotel's two ballrooms. Bits of flocked wallpaper clung to water-stained walls, and the ceiling was a skeleton of support beams and darkened wood planks from the floor above. The worst of the water damage had occurred on this side of the building and it showed.

"Maybe I should join, then." I ran a finger across one of the streaky windows leaving a trail behind. "Maybe find my next husband."

He flashed me an inscrutable glance before resuming his inspection of the room. "Try church, Nicole. I don't believe our club is for you."

"How about Derek? Is your club for him?"

"I couldn't tell you even if I wanted to. The price of our membership guarantees complete anonymity."

"Even from spouses?" My molars ground together at the implication of his comment. If he was trying to block my curiosity, he was doing a piss-poor job of it.

He sent me a smug grin. "You don't quite qualify as one of those do you, Ms. Adams?"

"The divorce isn't final, so yes, I still qualify," I snapped while heading across the marble floor to the other side of the room. "Cyn mentioned you own clubs in other cities. Including DC."

"I'm afraid you're wasting your breath with these inquiries." He stopped just inside the double doors, waving me forward. "Now do come along, Nicole. The mold in this room is unhealthy."

The mold or my questions? I thought but chose not to ask aloud. I was here to sell this hotel, not probe this man's knowledge of my husband. Even if the temptation was hard to resist. I had a gut feeling he knew a lot more about Derek than I did.

"Fine, then. Let's go see the bar. I've saved it until last for a reason."

"Are you going to buy me a drink?" He chuckled from a

few steps behind me. "It's a bit early, but I wouldn't complain."

"I wouldn't either. Unfortunately the shelves here are empty." I turned to face him. "And I think this property is best viewed without gin-colored glasses."

"You remember what I drink?"

Gin and tonic made with Gin Mare, a lot of ice and a twist of lime. Hard to forget when Derek had me chasing all over the city in search of the Barcelona-produced liquor.

"It used to be my job to remember everyone's drink preference." And now we were back to awkward. I turned back toward the direction I'd been heading, donning my professionalism like a cloak. "Prepare yourself for a pleasant surprise."

I ushered him through the frosted double doors marking the entry of the bar. Inside it showcased the real heyday of the hotel in the mid-1920s. Then the Depression happened. Then prohibition. According to Cynthia's notes, there were rumors the mob had taken possession of the building and filled the place with high-priced prostitutes, gambling, and bootlegged liquor in one of the basement rooms. Not that I'd share that bit of information with an upstanding client. Or the fact that numerous guests had spotted the apparition of a woman singing in the corner of the bar. Or the well-dressed man lingering in the fourth-floor hallway.

For the last decade the place had been neglected. The cramped rooms upstairs had been rented out as SROs for the less fortunate until the owner died. Now his children wanted nothing to do with this money pit. I didn't blame them.

Gordon's eyes lit up as we passed through the doorway to another time, not fazed at all by the condition of the property or the millions it would take to bring this hotel back to life.

"Everything in here is original." The hinges emitted a high-pitched squeak as I swung one of the doors open and closed. "With a little work, this hotel could be stunning."

He paused just past the open doorway, squinting into the gloom of the space. I headed across the room. Behind the bar I found a light switch and flipped it on with a prayer it still worked. The lights flickered to life, and the weak glow of the vintage fixtures—draped in years of cobwebs—chased away a bit of the gloom.

Gordon dusted off a couple of the art deco barstools and then sat, motioning for me to take the other seat.

"The photos Cynthia sent you don't do this place justice." I ignored his request, pointing out the original wood-paneled walls, the coffered ceilings, the marble-topped bar.

"Please have a seat, Nicole."

"Of course." I took a deep breath and then headed back to the bar. Cynthia was counting on me to be professional.

"I regret being unable to help you." He covered my hand with his, squeezing lightly, then letting go.

I nodded. "*I* should apologize. This is not the place to discuss my marriage."

"Agreed, but the two of us find ourselves in an uncomfortable position. Unless you prefer to ignore the situation."

I huffed an uncomfortable laugh. "What situation would that be?"

He glanced around for a second, and then those piercing green eyes settled on me. "Touché. Let's get out of here. I'm famished and there's a brilliant restaurant right around the corner."

I HEADED into Cynthia's office, my mind racing from too much coffee and too many random thoughts.

"Men." I groaned, recalling the ominous message left on my voicemail. I didn't have the patience to deal with whatever bad news my lawyer had at the moment. Setting that problem aside, I dropped into one of Cynthia's guest chairs and looked across the desk at my best friend.

"So, how'd it go?" She leaned back in her chair, dropping her reading glasses on the desktop.

"Weird. Uncomfortable."

She tipped her head to the side and frowned at me. "How do you mean?"

I sighed, kicking off my stilettos and rubbing my arches. If I'd known I was going to be walking miles today, I'd have worn different shoes.

"Never mind. It's something I'm learning to live with." I straightened and then gave my boss my full attention. "Gordon Knight needs to crunch the numbers with his partners, but he said if everything worked out, he'd stop by in the morning with an offer. Either way, he'll call me."

"Good. I have a feeling he'll see the value hidden in that hotel." She smoothed the crease between her brows with her fingertips.

I collapsed back into the chair, exhausted from a day spent climbing stairs and a night without sleep. "Answer me honestly, Cyn. Do you think Derek is a member of Gordon's clubs?"

Cynthia barked a sharp laugh. "Absolutely not."

I stared back at her for a long second, watching her clear off her desk with brisk efficiency. Her answer had come way too quickly to convince me. "Cyn..."

"What?" She glanced at her watch and stood. "Listen, I'd love to talk, but I have a date."

I stood as well, blocking her exit. "Cyn...what exactly do you know about these clubs?"

She huffed out an impatient breath and then stepped around me to close the door. Crossing her arms, she leaned against the doorframe. "You don't want to know, but believe me, Derek is the last person I'd expect to see at one of Gordon Knight's clubs."

"Why?" My eyes widened with realization. "Wait a minute. Are you a member?"

She snorted. "I have better things to spend a hundred grand on. But Randall is."

"Randall?" I prompted, hoping she would tell me more. If Randall could afford a hundred-thousand-dollar club membership, I was definitely paying him too much.

"And Derek is nothing like Randall." The way she emphasized both men's names had my thoughts reeling out of control. "So, no, I don't think your husband would appreciate the benefits of membership."

Don't get involved with him unless you want to be tied up and spanked. Cynthia's warning the night she'd given me Randall's card rang through my head.

I'd heard whispers of such places back in college. Murmurs of the things that went on inside. I wasn't naïve. Still... the Gordon Knight I knew didn't seem the type. But then who was the type to frequent those places? And how did Cynthia know Derek didn't fit the type? I barely knew him anymore.

But no.

Derek would have to be out of his mind to accept the kind of donations Gordon Knight had given if he was aware of these clubs. It would be political suicide if the press ever got a hold of that information.

Should I warn him? For the kids' sake, if not for my own. The kind of scandal this information would create would make the mess with Gabriel seem insignificant—which might be a good thing. But at the same time, it would ruin Derek—and any chance of receiving the alimony he'd agreed upon last week.

"Forget it. I don't want to know." I held up my hands in front of me to ward off any more information. Ignorance really was bliss sometimes. I had enough trouble at the moment. I didn't need to go searching for more.

"Know what?" Cynthia winked conspiratorially.

"Exactly. Listen, I'm planning on flying out to see Brooke," I said, changing the subject to a safer, more pressing topic. "She's still not taking my calls. And now this... mess. I need to fix this situation before it gets any worse. If that's possible."

"Get a signed offer on the Argyle tomorrow morning, and then take the rest of the week off. Tell Sonya before you leave to book your flight and hotel. Company expense."

"Not necessary, Cyn. My finances aren't that dire." They were worse than dire, not that Cynthia needed to know. My measly interim allowance had me stretched to the bare minimum. I wouldn't be comfortable until the divorce was finalized next month. "And Brooke has classes all week. I'll fly out Friday evening after work and be ready to face her bright and early Saturday."

CHAPTER
TWENTY-FOUR

"God, Mom. This stew... amazing," Mark mumbled through a mouthful as I stepped through the mudroom door after work on Wednesday evening. He pointed at the almost empty bowl in front of him with a hunk of bread before using it to mop up the thick gravy.

"Thanks," I said, setting my purse down on the counter, my heart twisting painfully. "Glad you liked it."

"I saved you some. If you want I can heat it up."

Mark acted like our conversation on Sunday night never happened. Which I appreciated. Unlike the stew Trent had left in the fridge. Every time I opened the door, I was accosted by the scent of beef and vegetables, and the memory of our dinner in bed. Followed by a marathon of lovemaking that I still felt the twinges of four days later, just like I had asked.

"Nah. Big lunch today. Can't even think about food. Go ahead and finish it off." At least my fridge would be a memory-free zone. Unlike my bed.

Mark grinned. "Lunch with anyone I know?"

I turned toward the sink to hide the emotions that surfaced. Trent was gone. That was painfully obvious by the silence of my phone.

So many times over the past few days I'd picked up the thing, tempted to call, to send an apology, but for what? Cynthia was right. Trent was being hypocritical. He'd been okay with my sexual history when it had included only my husband and him. God forbid I take offense over how many women had warmed his bed before we met.

Maybe I should have been upfront with him, but I was under no illusion he'd been living like a saint. For all I knew he could have taken someone home that night after Cynthia and I left the bar.

For all I knew he could be with someone right now.

That thought had tears stinging at the corners of my eyes.

"No. Aunt Cyn. She wanted to celebrate my first solo sale," I said, filling a glass with tap water in hopes the running faucet would mask my emotions. "Listen, I've booked a flight to Boston Friday night. I need to decide what to do with you."

"Congrats on the sale," Mark said with a chuckle. "You're taking me with, of course. I love Boston."

"I'm staying in Cambridge." I turned around to face him, forcing a smile. "I haven't talked to your sister in over a month. I think it's better if I make this trip alone."

He grinned. "Because a certain basketball team is playing at TD Garden this weekend? I totally approve if you want some alone time with Trent."

I took another deep breath as the staggering pain washed over me again. Funny, over the last month I'd fretted over how to tell Mark about Trent. Worried how my son would react to the possibility of another man replacing his father.

"Appreciate your approval, but I'm thinking this drama was a bit much for him."

Mark's smile vanished. "Oh, that's too bad. I really liked him."

"Yeah," I choked out. "Me too."

"He sent me a birthday card along with tickets to next week's game." He shoved the rest of his baguette into his mouth and then mumbled, "Was thinking of inviting Brian."

I forced a smile. "I'm sure Brian would appreciate it. But right now we need to solve the problem of where you're staying this weekend. Phoebe said they have plans." I lifted my glass to my lips, then paused. "How about Ava's? You and Sam—"

"No, Mom. We haven't been friends since eighth grade." He grabbed his dishes and headed over to the dishwasher, making me smile for real. In the past month he'd gotten used to cleaning up after himself. Better than me most days. "You know I'm old enough to stay home alone."

"Absolutely not. This whole thing with Gabriel, and then the reporters. I don't want you here alone."

"Mom..." he groaned.

"Let me think about it." It took two seconds of thinking for me to decide, but I wasn't in the mood to argue, so I kept quiet.

THE NEXT MORNING I settled myself at my desk and picked up my phone. I'd ignored Randall's messages all week. Not exactly ignored. With the negotiations on the Argyle Hotel offer, arranging my trip to Boston, and figuring out what to do with Mark, I had little time to call my lawyer. Or so I had convinced myself.

But now it was time to face the proverbial music.

Randall's assistant put me straight through without delay.

"Mrs. Robinson. We find ourselves in a bit of a mess." Never a jovial man, Randall sounded especially grim. "Your husband's lawyer is requesting some changes."

I'd been holding my breath ever since Derek's call Sunday morning, my mind running in circles. *What could he do to me?* I kept repeating those words all week, like a meditation chant, in an attempt to keep my blood pressure level. But a small knowing voice told me otherwise. Derek didn't make idle threats.

"What changes? Can he even do that?"

"Of course he can. We're still in negotiations. I *thought* I asked you to behave." His loud sigh gusted across the phone line. "Are you sitting down?"

I was and I told him so.

"The news reports don't paint you in a very good light, Mrs. Robinson. Your husband's lawyer wanted me to let you know how shocked and disappointed his client is."

"Shocked and disappointed..." I laughed sarcastically. "Imagine coming home and finding your husband packed and ready to move out. Imagine your life turned upside down in an instant. He waived his right to be shocked and disappointed once he asked for a divorce. Anything I've done after is none of his business."

"Are you done Mrs. Robinson?" He sighed again.

"Derek's the one who cheated, not me," I huffed back, not in the mood for his condescending tone.

"You have no proof."

"Well, let's get some goddamn proof, Mr. Harris. I'm paying you enough," I barked, the frustration of the past week leaking out. "I know my husband. He lied when I asked him if there was someone else. I also know he's been taking donations from less-than-reputable sources. If he wants to play rough, I'm more than ready to join in. Tell him I know all about his association with Gordon Knight, then see if he's interested in these changes."

My threat was a complete bluff. Derek had cleared out his home office, along with any records of Gordon Knight's donations, the day he moved out. I had no proof of that fact either.

"Hello?" I asked. The silence on the other end of the line had dragged on so long I thought we'd been disconnected.

Randall cleared his throat. "This is a delicate situation. Let's leave the counterthreats off the table for the moment and focus on our current problem. Your face was splashed across the news channels this weekend. This affair—"

"Lies," I interrupted. "It was one time, not an affair. Almost everything Gabriel Roth said in his interview was fabrication."

I'd forced myself to watch his ridiculous interview, but it wasn't easy. The sick story he'd shared with the world made me want to throw the remote at the TV screen.

I went on to describe Gabriel's visit Friday evening, and his very real threat of exposing me.

"With your permission, I'd like to get my investigator on this. Find out who Gabriel Roth is. Until then, hold off on the accusation about your husband. We don't want to do anything rash. But I will take your information on his donations into consideration. Now let's go over these changes."

"Fine."

"Mr. Robinson is now asking for sole custody of your dependent son, Mark. He feels you are no longer a suitable role model for a teenage boy. Therefore, obviously, they are requesting child support be removed and the terms of the alimony payments be shortened to twelve months—long enough for you to sell the house."

Black spots danced before my eyes. Even sitting down wasn't enough for this much of a shock. I lowered my head onto the cool surface of my desk. After a few deep breaths Randall's voice called from my phone.

"Mrs. Robinson?"

"He can't do that," I whimpered. "Mark doesn't want to move to D.C. His friends are here. His school. How do we stop this?"

"Try to stay calm," he replied, like it was the easiest thing in the world. "We'll file a counterpetition. Your husband felt you were competent enough to raise his children for the last nineteen years—virtually on your own. We will prove you still are and, at the same time, question your husband's competency. His schedule leaves him little time to commit to parenting a teenage boy. "Discuss this with Mark. His opinion will be important to a judge. It's possible this may drag on past his eighteenth birthday, deeming any custody matter void. But please, Mrs. Robinson, do not do anything without consulting me first. Do I make myself clear?"

I blinked back the tears stinging my eyes. I couldn't lose Mark. "I'm leaving for Boston tomorrow. They can't stop me from seeing my daughter."

"Fine. Just don't leave your son home alone."

"Of course not." To say Mark had been thrilled when I told him he'd be staying with Cynthia this weekend would have been an understatement. Derek would be less so, but I wasn't going to mention that to Randall. "What about Mark's visit next weekend with Derek? I don't want him going if there's any possibility his father won't let him return."

The thought chilled me, keeping me up every night this past week.

"That would be considered kidnaping. I think your husband is smart enough not to do that." He paused a second before adding, "I'll be in touch."

"I don't understand. Derek wanted a quick divorce. Why would he want to prolong it now? This makes no sense."

"Think about it logically. You've given him an escape from years of mortgage payments and support while still maintaining his squeaky-clean image. It's a win-win situation for him no matter how long the divorce takes."

No matter how long it takes. The thought soured in my stomach. I'd have an ulcer by then.

MY STOMACH TWISTED with the sight that was becoming all too familiar on the narrow stretch of Sheridan just before my drive. Lines of trucks and vans clogging the shoulder of the road, causing a backup of traffic. It had gotten only worse as the week wore on. *Isn't there a law preventing this kind of disruption?*

The situation with the reporters had become intolerable. They waited for me at the train station, blocked my way into Cynthia's building, and there was still the stalwart group greeting me every morning and evening outside my house. They'd rush from their toasty-warm news vans lining the street the moment I approached the gate, forcing me to inch forward so as not to hit one of them. Not that the idea wasn't tempting.

When will this end?

I was desperate enough to do just about anything to stop the crowd of reporters multiplying everywhere I looked. Maybe not mass homicide. But something.

"Come on Mrs. Robinson, just a few words, then we'll go," one promised the minute I turned off the street, his voice smooth, like a snake-oil salesman. I stared straight ahead ignoring the lot of them as I waited for the gate to open. I needed a faster gate.

Would they really go? A few words couldn't hurt, could they?

My lawyer's voice from earlier in the day rang loud in my head. *I thought I asked you to behave.*

A familiar woman in the back caught my eye. What was her name? *Carolyn something.* I'd done an interview with her last year at the opening of a women's shelter.

Randall will kill you.

Likely, but he wasn't here dealing with this every day. He didn't have his son driving past this circus every time he left home, knowing it was for his mother. It'd be worth the risk just so Mark wouldn't have to put up with this.

I rolled down my window, and after a second of stunned silence, they all went crazy. *Stupid idea.*

"You there," I yelled, pointing to the woman in the back. "Carolyn?"

She forced her way to the front of the crowd. "Sherilyn... Jeffreys," She corrected, shifting closer to me as the crowd closed in around her.

"Get in," I whispered, then unlocked the car doors.

"What?" She seemed hesitant, like she was weighing her options, and one was getting murdered and dumped in the lake.

"You want an interview, don't you?"

"Can I bring my cameraman?" She pointed to a man behind her.

"Oh hell. Fine. Him too." I sighed. *I'm regretting this already, and we haven't even started.*

"What about us?" a few others yelled, pushing their microphones in my face before I had a chance to close the window. Sherilyn climbed in the back seat while her cameraman ran back to the van. A moment later he returned, juggling enough camera gear to make me second guess my decision.

"Mrs. Robinson," someone yelled, rapping on my window with their mic. "Are you leaving Senator Robinson for your pool boy?"

"What do your kids think?" another reporter yelled. More questions followed, each more infuriating than the previous one.

Ignoring the flash of cameras, I drove through the open gates.

MARK LEAPT up from the kitchen counter the moment we walked in. Eyes wide, he took in the two strangers following me with a look of trepidation. I didn't blame him. My apprehension had only increased on the short trip down the driveway. If there was a special kind of hell for people who ignored their lawyer's instructions, I was definitely headed there.

"No pictures of my son." I pointed at Sherilyn and Cameraman Rick as they followed me into the kitchen. "Mark, honey, go to your room."

"Don't have to tell me twice," he said, grabbing his

sandwich from the counter along with his phone and then sprinting toward the stairs.

I turned toward Sherilyn. "Let's get a few things straight. No questions about my children. Actually, no questions regarding anything other than Gabriel Roth and his interview. I'm going to tell my side of the story, and then we wrap it up."

"Whatever you want." She held up her hands. "We can shoot anywhere you like."

"Great room works for me." I pointed to the seating in front of the fireplace while taking a deep, calming breath. "Would you like a glass of wine?" I definitely needed one.

Sherilyn flashed a surprised smile. "Sure."

I headed to the wine cellar as Rick set up his equipment, stopping in the powder room to touch up my makeup first. The person in the mirror told me I was nuts, but I ignored her. There was no going back now.

I grabbed two glasses and an eight-year-old Screaming Eagle cab from the red side of the cellar. It was one Derek's father had given him, so I knew it was expensive.

In the kitchen I uncorked the wine and headed into the great room. Rick had lights and a tripod set facing the fireplace and was fiddling with his camera. I handed Sherilyn her glass, then walked to the mantel and flipped over the kids' photos.

"Oh, this is nice," she purred, tasting the wine.

"Last bottle from my father-in-law's Christmas present last year." I gave her a stiff smile while pouring myself a glass. Then I set the bottle on the table between us, turning it so the label faced the camera. *Hope you're watching, Derek.* "Let's make this worth it."

She grinned. "I'll do my best."

"Are you married?" I asked, before taking a small sip of wine.

Sherilyn wasn't wearing a ring. Her age was close to mine. Smartly dressed and petite. She'd been on the local news for decades, and probably should have been an anchor somewhere instead of freezing her ass on a suburban road.

Her smile tightened a fraction. "Divorced."

I sat down across from her and sipped my wine while Rick attached my mic. Sherilyn asked if I was ready. I nodded, plastering on my public smile.

"I'm Sherilyn Jeffreys. We are in the home of Mrs. Robinson—"

"Please call me Nicki," I interrupted.

"Of course. Nicki Robinson is the wife of Senator Robinson, founder of the Literacy Cooperative and the Women's Empowerment Group, and currently the subject of the controversy surrounding the allegations last week by a young man, Gabriel Roth, of a long-running sexual relationship." Sherilyn turned to me. "Nicki, what was your reaction to these allegations?"

"Gosh, Sherilyn, my initial reaction to Gabriel's interview was complete and utter shock. Gabriel worked for our family for the past five years, but nothing more. That he could fabricate a story like that, it was beyond my comprehension." I gave the camera what I hoped was a sympathetic smile, shaking my head slowly.

"So you never had more than a working relationship with Gabriel Roth?"

"Have you ever done anything you regretted, Sherilyn?" I asked, taking control of the narrative.

Her eyes widened a fraction. Sherilyn was a seasoned reporter, but I wasn't a pushover. I'd done countless interviews, knew the tricks reporters used to slant a story to their benefit. But I wasn't going to give her something salacious to boost ratings at the expense of my reputation.

"Um, ah, probably." Her eyes shifted away with what I thought was guilt. "I believe everyone has done things they regret. What do *you* regret, Nicki?"

"Well, I'm gonna be completely honest with everyone out there." I turned my body away from Sherilyn, facing the camera full on. *Here goes.*

"For the past twenty years, I've loved my husband. Completely. With all my heart. So when he came home in September and told me he wanted a divorce—well, to say I was shocked would be an understatement. Words can't even describe the hurt and betrayal I felt."

Out of the corner of my eye, Sherilyn nodded.

"I wasn't in a good place, wasn't thinking straight. I could give a hundred excuses for my behavior, but let's face it, when you're hurt, you do stupid things. Gabriel was one of those stupid things."

"So you did have a relationship with Gabriel Roth."

I breathed out a quiet laugh and turned back toward Sherilyn. "Calling it a relationship would be a stretch. He caught me at a weak moment, then wanted more. I didn't. I tried to explain, but he wouldn't listen. He sent me notes, left messages on my phone. If I led him on, it was unintentional, but...

"My hope is everyone can look past this and remember the person you've seen for the past fifteen years of Derek's campaigns and my charity work. I still love helping others, I still support and love my husband, even though..." I sighed and pressed my lips together, looking away, letting the anguish of the past week color my voice. "...even though he doesn't return it."

I shifted in my seat, turning toward the camera again. "I know some of you out there are disappointed with me. I'd like to think we've all made at least one bad decision in our lives, and I hope you can find it in your heart not to judge me by this one moment of weakness. To all the people in my life I love, I am truly sorry to put you through this."

"What do you hope to get out of this interview, Nicki?" Sherilyn asked, her eyes narrowed in a way I didn't like. If she didn't believe me, how could I expect her audience to?

I paused to take a breath. "There's been a lot of ugly things said about me this week. My family, those I love, don't deserve this. The two charities you mentioned earlier —the Literacy Cooperative, which provides free mobile libraries to underserved neighborhoods, and the Women's Empowerment Group, which supports women entrepreneurs—along with several other charities where I've volunteered my time, don't deserve to be affected by one person's need for revenge, and the media's need to sensationalize it. I know this won't go away anytime soon, but I hope everyone can think of the impact these stories have on lives beyond mine."

"An important point for everyone out there to be aware of. Thank you, Nicki, for being brave enough to share your side of the story with our viewers." She ended with her station identification and a vague reference to our location.

"Perfect," she squealed. "Thank you."

I blew out a long breath, the knot in my stomach relaxing a fraction. "When will it air?"

"Not sure, but soon. I'll let you know when."

"Thanks. It'll give me time to hide from my lawyer." Randall was definitely going to kill me.

She narrowed her eyes in suspicion or possibly just curiosity. "Off the record, is that everything?"

"Regarding Gabriel?" I asked. She nodded as we headed back into the kitchen. The cameraman walked into the mudroom to pack his things. "Why do you ask?"

"I don't know. Women's intuition. Reporter's instincts." She shrugged into the coat she'd hung over the back of a barstool. "I watched the interview a half a dozen times, and I sense there's more there than an obsessed lover."

"Off the record?" I paused, more to gather my thoughts than confirm confidentiality. "In the five years Gabriel worked for my family, he'd been nothing but professional. Polite. Nothing like the angry man who showed up here last Friday, spewing threats and insults."

Sherilyn's eyes narrowed again, possibly with suspicion. Of course it would be easier to discount my less-than-tawdry tale. Dissatisfied workmen didn't sell advertising as well as juicy sex scandals. "He threatened you? Physically?"

I'd done my best not to think about the minutes with Gabriel before Trent had shown up. Or what would have happened if he hadn't. The way Gabriel had me trapped against the island. The moment he'd raised his hand to strike me. His sick smile after Trent had punched him. The man would haunt my dreams for a long time to come.

"He had his hands on me. Luckily a friend showed up, and Gabriel left before things had a chance to escalate."

She set her leather briefcase on the counter before turning her focus back to me. "But if your friend hadn't shown up, you think things would have escalated?"

"My mind refuses to follow that line of thinking."

"I knew there was something I didn't like about him. Smug bastard." She returned her notepad and recorder back to her case, then fastened the clasps. "Did you call the police? You didn't, did you? That would have been in the news."

I raised my hands, motioning toward her, Rick, and then the general direction of the driveway gate. "This was what I was afraid of. My life has turned into a circus. And honestly, what would I have told them?"

"Don't you worry about him coming back?"

"Of course. It's my waking nightmare. I changed the locks, the security code on my alarm. I watch for him everywhere I go. I don't know what else to do."

"Men like Gabriel don't give up."

"I get what you're saying, but..." I blew out a deep breath, looking down. "At this point who's going to believe me? I have too much shit going on right now to think about Gabriel."

Rick poked his head out of the mudroom, letting Sherilyn know he was ready to go. We exchanged business cards, promising to stay in touch. I drove them back to the gate and headed back home.

Mark stood in the kitchen doorway when I returned. He frowned at me, shaking his head. "I hope you know what you're doing, Mom."

"I'm just winging it most of the time, but not when it comes to you." I gave him a small smile, ruffling his hair, as I headed into the great room, grabbing the empty wine glasses and the half-empty bottle of cabernet, that was destined for the sink drain. It had served its purpose. "Pack up, buddy. Aunt Cyn said she's got plans for the two of you."

His laugh reminded me of a particularly sinister mad scientist cartoon he used to watch when he was younger. "Cool," he drew out the word, his grin a mile wide.

CHAPTER
TWENTY-FIVE

My best friend owned a large greystone in Lincoln Park. Very traditional, and contradicting everything one would expect in the home of a modern woman.

But when you live and sell high-rise Chicago every breathing minute, that's the last thing you want to see when you wake up in the morning, Cynthia had told me when she first bought the place years ago. Only the bold fabrics covering the vintage furniture gave away her hand in decorating the space. Her home was a rare gem among the neighborhoods of sterilized rehabs and new high-rise condos.

Cynthia opened her front door wearing a broad smile, martini glass in hand. Her expensive suit had been replaced with a vintage Blondie T-shirt and a pair of slim jeans. Led Zeppelin's "Kashmir" blasted through her expensive audio system.

"Come in you two," she yelled, then walked over to the cabinet housing her stereo components and lowered the volume on the music a bit. "Perfect timing. I just ordered curry from the Indian place around the corner. We have a few minutes."

Mark bent down to pet her giant cat, Nyx, who had slinked down the stairway to greet us, while I followed Cynthia toward the back of her house.

Her kitchen always blinded me with its whiteness. This was the only space lacking color. Everything from the floor to the ceiling was white. Even the princess-white granite countertops had only a slight mottling of gray.

"Soda?" Cynthia looked at Mark, who'd appeared in the doorway along with Nyx. "I bought all kinds. Tell me what you want."

Mark's eyes lit up as Cynthia listed off a dozen different brands.

"Easy champ," I cautioned, imagining the dentist bills as a result of a weekend's sugar binge.

"Let him enjoy, Nicki," Cynthia scolded, popping the top off a Mountain Dew for herself. "It's only soda. There's a lot worse."

"Yeah, Mom. It's not like I'm gonna die from the stuff." Mark scrunched up his face and stuck out his tongue.

"Mature." I scowled back.

"Okay, you two. Aunt Cynthia's in charge. We're going to have a pleasant evening tonight. No arguing. I have tons of fun things planned this weekend, but I can always take you to work and have you organize my file cabinets." She sent Mark a severe look, then turned it on me. "And you, Ms. Adams, won't be too happy on Monday if you don't trust me to take care of your son. Starting now. You have enough to worry about this weekend. I've got this."

"Fun things?" Mark asked, picking up on the important part of Cynthia's reprimand. "What fun things?"

"Ah, I've got your attention." Cynthia grinned. The

doorbell rang and she held up a finger. "Hold that thought. That's dinner."

By the time we filled our plates with enough fragrant curry and samosas and garlicky naan, Mark was squirming on his barstool for information.

"Now where were we," Cynthia teased, tapping her finger against her lip as if she had to think about it. "Yes, fun things... Well, to start off, tonight after your mom leaves, I thought we could download your choice of movie, make popcorn, and I could teach you how to make the perfect martini." I opened my mouth to protest, but Cynthia held up her hand. "For me, Mom. Who do you take me for? Every man should know how to make a decent martini. I'm teaching your son life skills.

"Then tomorrow, after the best French toast ever at my favorite place around the corner, we'll visit my friend who owns a rock-climbing gym. I got us both lessons. Later, Thirteen Zombies is playing at a nearby park. I thought you might like to see them." Mark's eyes got wider by the minute. "Then Sunday, old Aunt Cyn may want to sleep in a bit. After a late brunch, I thought we'd take it easy and do some indoor skydiving before your mom comes and picks you up. Sound good?"

Mark will never want to come home.

I sent another thanks to Cynthia on my phone and then powered down, settling into the first-class seat she had Sonya book. The woman—Cynthia, that is—was a godsend who had probably never flown coach in her life.

Someone dropped in next to me, an older gentleman. He quickly busied himself with some papers he pulled out of his briefcase, and I turned my focus to the orange-vested workers scurrying on the tarmac outside my window.

Our flight attendant stopped by with heated towels and then glasses of champagne. My neighbor gave me a brief greeting and a small smile before returning to his work.

I downed my champagne and then turned back toward the window as emotions threatened to pull me under. Under different circumstances, Trent might have been waiting for me at my destination, or possibly have been sitting next to me, but he wasn't. I glanced at my phone, now turned off, but it didn't matter. He hadn't called— probably wouldn't call. I had to face reality.

My heart squeezed painfully. Gabriel had destroyed everything. I'd spent the week replaying Trent's old voice-mail messages and reading the text messages he'd sent from the road. At some point I'd have to delete them, but at the moment they were my crutch. Proof that a happy life after divorce was attainable, even if it didn't include a hot basketball coach.

Did I feel this lost when Derek left? I'd been frightened, unsure, like getting lost while driving in a strange city. Maybe because Derek was gone so much, it was more his existence and not his companionship I missed.

He was already gone when he left.

Trent's schedule kept him away, but he always called. Every night, we talked. I knew he thought about me.

Is he thinking about me now?

Don't be ridiculous.

The plane paused at the end of the runway for a second and then lurched forward. Within seconds we were airborne, banking sharply as the plane gained altitude.

I sighed heavily, reminding myself whatever brief happiness Trent brought into my life, it was over. He was gone, and I really couldn't blame him. Watching the full interview with Gabriel had turned my stomach. And I'd been prepared for what he would say. Most of it. The man had a gift for embellishment.

Mark hadn't seen it, thank God. But Brooke on the other hand... had she? I would find out in the morning. If she hadn't, some of her classmates probably had.

After a while I looked around, stretching to relieve the cramp in my neck. The man next to me had fallen asleep. The first-class cabin was mostly dark; the glow of computers or overhead lights spotlighted a few workaholics.

Trent's schedule had him in Boston tomorrow. So close, but worlds apart. If only—

Stop.

It was over. Constantly wishing otherwise was just an exercise in self-flagellation. I needed to move forward. Tomorrow I would see Brooke. That was enough to think about for now.

I closed my eyes, letting the drone of the engines lull me to sleep.

THE CRISP OCTOBER morning air nipped at my cheeks as I made the half-mile trip from my hotel to Harvard Square. It was the perfect time of year for walking, the trees dressed in fall colors, the early morning walkers also dressed for the season in warm sweaters and light jackets. I loved autumn in Chicago, but there was something special about New England in the fall.

A wave of melancholy memories swept over me. Derek and I had walked these same paths over twenty years ago.

The place had barely changed, but so much of my life had.

The Wigglesworth dorms sat just ahead. My stomach twisted with nerves as I entered through the gates and then found door J. Dorm policy wouldn't allow me upstairs without permission, but an overly friendly girl in pajamas was more than willing to send someone to get Brooke. I stood in the spartan lobby to wait, listening to the drama of college life lamented by a group of girls passing by.

"Mom, what are you doing here?" Brooke stepped around the corner, a frown on her face. She was also in PJs and no makeup, and she looked about fourteen. My heart broke a little. What had she been going through alone and so far from home? *Damn you, Derek.*

"You wouldn't return my calls. What did you expect?" I gave her a hug.

She pulled back, her eyes widening as they scanned me from my head to my toes. A smile lit her face, and I chastised myself for not making the trip earlier.

"I love your hair... and are those my jeans? And sweater? You've been in my closet." She sent me a look of mock censure and then laughed.

"I needed a new look and I liked yours." I laughed back, and the knot of unease loosened. "I hear your dad's been here. I figured I better make sure you remember you have two parents."

I'd promised Mark I wouldn't reveal that little tidbit of information he'd given me a few nights ago, but I couldn't help the slip. It stung that Derek had been to visit our daughter, while I'd been ghosted.

"Mom." She huffed, rolling her eyes. "I don't want to get in the middle."

"Good. There shouldn't be a middle. This isn't a tug of

war for your approval and affection." I patted her back, shoving my emotions aside. This was a mission of peace. The last thing I wanted was to start an argument. "Go get dressed. I'm buying breakfast or brunch or whatever you're calling it."

We headed back down the sidewalk a short time later. Brooke frowned, looking around. "Don't you have a car?"

I laughed. Only my daughter would expect me to drive her a few blocks to breakfast. "No. My hotel is close and I figured I wasn't going anywhere except here. I'm only staying until tomorrow."

We walked a couple of trendy blocks to a café my concierge promised had the most decadent breakfasts. I knew my daughter. The way to her heart was through her stomach, and her wide smile told me I'd chosen correctly.

Inside, the smell of fresh-baked bread and cinnamon was so strong you could lean against it. The sign by the register instructed patrons to seat themselves. Clearly the rush had passed. Two tables stood empty among the six in the room.

Sighing with pleasure, I sat down at a small table by the front window where the bright puddle of sunshine warmed me instantly. Brooke sat across from me and then glanced toward the back. Her eyes went saucer-wide and she blushed to her blonde hairline.

"What is it?" I whispered, glancing around.

Small paper menus sat in the middle of the table propped in a holder. I pulled two out, casually handing one to Brooke while scanning the room over mine to see who she was looking at.

There was a group of giggling coeds occupying two tables that had been squished together. In the corner an older couple chatted. A bearded gentleman claimed the fourth table. He looked about my age, dark hair shot through with silver. His head was bent over a stack of papers, readers propped at the end of his nose, pen in hand.

"That's Professor Richards, my anatomy instructor. All the girls have a thing for him," she whispered back, trying to hide behind the small sheet.

Richards. It was a common enough name, but the pain it caused had me wincing.

I forced a smile while watching my daughter's blush fade. "Including you?"

"No... I mean he's okay-looking for an older guy, but he's just—old. But my friends..." She waved it off with a cringe. "It's embarrassing."

I glanced over again. From what I could tell he was more than okay-looking. "Thanks. You know he's probably about my age. So what do your friends do that's embarrassing?"

Her blush came back as she glanced his way. "Oh, it's horrible. They send him anonymous notes. He teaches anatomy, so... you can imagine. I thought only guys could be so crude. All I want is a decent grade, not..." She trailed off with a look of disgust. "But what if he thinks it's me?"

"Oh dear." I paused as the waitress informed us of the day's specials and took our drink order. "Maybe you should talk to him. Explain." Her eyes widened and her face went pale. "Or maybe not."

Brooke sat facing his direction, so it was easy for her to look at him—not that she seemed at all comfortable with the position. I pretended to pick something off my shoulder and glanced back. The professor looked up and smiled.

"Mother!" Brooke gasped and dropped her head onto her arms. "Oh. My. God."

"Sorry. Now tell me why you've chosen not to answer my calls for over a month?" I gave her my sweetest smile.

The waitress dropped off coffee for me and juice for Brooke, then took our order.

"I didn't want to talk to either of you until the semester was over. You did tell me to focus on my studies, and I was doing just that... but then Dad just barged in here." She threw her hands in the air, scowling.

"Your father didn't get to where he is by asking for anyone's permission." I gave her a tight smile.

She flashed me a wary look. "Fine. Whatever. But, just so you know, he wasn't alone."

The smile on my face froze. "Who did he bring?"

"Patty." She made an ugly face.

I concentrated on stirring the swirls of cream into my coffee until I had my emotions under control. I had more than suspicions there was someone else, but having the proof set in front of me was still a blow.

Patty Fucking Sullivan.

Patty was Derek's campaign manager. She'd been with him for... years. As long as I could remember. And married. Or at least she was as far as I knew.

Now, under the circumstances, everything made sense.

"—to say the least. How could you, Mom!"

"What?" Deep in thought, I'd missed the turn in the conversation.

She huffed. "I'm talking about you and Gabriel. Ew, Mom. Seriously, just no."

"Oh." I waved her off while taking a sip of coffee. "Don't believe half of what you see on TV. Haven't I told you that a thousand times?"

Her eyes went comically wide. "Half? I was hoping to believe none of it."

I sighed and gave her the same story as Mark, bracing for her disapproval.

"The next time you want to let loose, I'll introduce you to professor hottie over there." She discreetly pointed behind her hand.

I choked, coffee threatening to come out my nose. Grabbing my napkin, I dabbed my watering eyes.

"Jesus, Brooke," I wheezed. "Thanks, but no thanks."

She giggled. "You have to admit a professor is way more your style than our *pool guy*."

"You used to think that *pool guy* was hot." I sipped my coffee carefully, ready for more shocking words of wisdom. "You sound just like Aunt Cyn."

"I was sixteen. Hard muscles and a pretty smile are nice but, I don't know. I sometimes got a creepy feeling around him."

"Trust your instincts. They're usually right." The man was a snake.

The waitress returned with plates of greasy comfort food. My stomach growled in appreciation.

"Did you and Dad even love each other?" Her gaze locked onto mine, the desperation clear on her face.

I dropped my fork back on my plate. "Of course. What makes you doubt that?"

She gave a little shrug while shoving a forkful of French toast in her mouth. I waited while she chewed for the answer I wasn't sure I wanted to hear.

"I don't know. You two always seemed so distant."

"We had hundreds of miles between us most of the year. But I think we did. We were very happy for a long time." At least I thought so for twenty-some years. I shrugged off my confusion. Sometimes you never found an answer. "I'm trying really hard to focus on the good times we had as a family and not what's happening now. Anger is a waste of time."

She forked a potato aggressively. "We were *all* happy. Why did he have to go and screw everything up? I don't want to be one of those families where everything is *complicated*."

I shook my head, the sadness in her blue eyes crushing my heart. "I'm sorry. I promise to do my best to keep our lives uncomplicated."

"So what now?" She sighed, hopelessly. "What about you? Mark said something about a guy?"

"Of course he did." I let out a quiet laugh. I'd been stupid to think he wouldn't tell Brooke about Trent. "There's no guy. None worth mentioning." I rubbed her hand to comfort her. "Don't be so sad. I'm working with Cyn. She'll take care of me."

"Girl power," she said, reciting one of Cynthia Jacobs's mottos, tears glazing her eyes.

"That's Cyn."

"She would make a good general."

"Yeah." I pictured my best friend inspecting her troops, leather riding crop in hand to keep everyone in line. "I don't think she's interested."

"So when do you think you'll date again?"

"Not for a long time."

"No? Why?" She furrowed her brows in confusion.

"I'm forty-three. Where would I start? And don't say a dating app."

"I don't want you to become an old spinster with, like, dozens of cats." She gave me an exaggerated grimace. "I won't bring my family over if you do."

"How about you? Any men—your age—I should know about?" I asked, changing the direction of the subject.

"Please. I am so busy right now. So far the only guys who have shown interest are a few poly sci majors." I raised an eyebrow. Her nose scrunched. "Inquiring about an internship with Dad."

"I'm sorry." I grimaced at the thought of my daughter being used as a stepping stone for ambitious future politicians. Like her mother. "You don't want to get into politics. Find a nice guy who doesn't want the limelight. I'm sure there are some in your classes."

"Hard to tell when my face is stuck in books." She laughed. "Maybe I'll find Mr. Right once I'm settled in a decent practice."

I hated to think of my daughter postponing her personal life indefinitely. But she was an adult, and we'd grown past the point where my opinion would sway her.

"I should let you get back to whatever your plans are." I signaled the waitress for the check.

"Endless studying and homework. What about you?"

"Cyn sent me a to-do list." Besides a few contracts to go over, she'd instructed me to find a hot guy and make good use of my hotel room's king-sized bed. Like that was going to happen. "How about dinner?"

"That would be great. I'd reciprocate, but all this poor college student can afford is the Berg." She grinned, referencing the freshman cafeteria Annenberg Hall.

I grinned back. "Your dad is paying for it, so bonus."

As we waited at the counter to pay, a tall shadow fell across the floor beside me. By Brooke's stiff reaction I knew with certainty who was there.

"Brooke Robinson, right?" Professor Richards's deep voice rumbled, causing my stomach to drop. He wasn't Trent, I knew that much, but he was almost as tall. In my boots, I stood just shy of six feet, and he had a couple of inches on me.

"Um, yeah." She nodded.

He gave a warm chuckle. "I always feel like the year is progressing when I can link names and faces." He turned to me. "At least some. Brooke is one of my more attentive students. Never misses my ten-thirty class. Sits..." He squeezed his eyes shut. "First row, just left of the podium, correct? I mean my left, your right."

"Yeah." She laughed uncomfortably.

"It takes longer every year." His pretty gray eyes flashed to mine. "In my younger days I had it down within the first week. And this must be your..."

"Professor Richards, my mom. Nicki Robinson."

"Lovely to meet you. Please call me Travis. You look alike, and way too young to be her mother." His smile was surrounded by a neatly trimmed beard, and his steely gray eyes twinkled with humor. *Charming*.

I laughed at his flattery while searching his face for any signs of familiarity. Silly, I knew. Chances of this man being related to Trent were about as good as Derek and I getting back together. I could see why the female population was smitten, but besides being tall, and a man, there was no resemblance to Trent.

"Thank you, but I most definitely am," I said.

"I'm headed back to the yard. Are you ladies headed that way?"

"Yes, we are. Someone needs to study."

"Ah. My Monday quiz, I hope."

"As a matter of fact, yes," Brooke answered, relaxing as we walked out the door. "I did have a question about something, if you don't mind?"

"Of course not."

I held back, giving Brooke space to discuss her business. She had her father's habit of gesturing wildly when nervous or excited. Early on in Derek's political career, he'd been warned it was a distraction during speeches. For the most part he'd trained himself out of the habit, but watching Brooke was a little like déjà vu.

The sound of Professor Richards deep voice filtered back, but not the words. The man looked as if he'd stepped out of a fashion magazine for Ivy League professors, with well-fitted jeans, gray tweed jacket—sans elbow patches—and well-worn comfortable shoes and an equally worn leather satchel slung over his shoulder.

Brooke's suggestion that Professor Richards's would be a more appropriate lover made me smile. Not that I would act on her recommendation. It was just nice to know my daughter didn't expect me to pine away for her father for the rest of my life.

I dropped Brooke back at her dorm, and then I walked away, deep in thought over another man with the last name Richards. I'd spent way too much time thinking of Trent, but I'd yet to find a way to stop myself.

"Excuse me," Professor Richards said, catching up with me. I flinched in surprise. He winced, stepping back. "My apologies for startling you. I was wondering if you had plans this afternoon?"

"Not really." I shrugged, glancing around. Students gathered in small groups, walking slowly, not in a rush on this early Saturday afternoon. Like them, I had nothing pressing except Cynthia's contracts waiting at the hotel.

Staying cooped inside on such a beautiful day didn't appeal.

"If you're interested, I'd be happy to give you a campus tour."

I smiled at his offer. The opportunity to find out more about Brooke was standing in front of me, but I still hesitated. "Thank you, but I have been here before. My husband —ex, that is—he attended law school here. We had an apartment just a few blocks away. I'm sure you have more important things to do, but I appreciate the offer."

"I'm actually not busy. And the places I can show you definitely wouldn't have been common haunts for a law student." He glanced around and then shielded his mouth, whispering, "I happen to have access to some really interesting spots around campus many people don't know about."

I couldn't help but laugh. "I'm intrigued."

"Come on, then." He held out his arm for me to take. "There's a lovely little garden behind this building. It's in its fall splendor right now. You can't miss it."

CHAPTER
TWENTY-SIX

T doubted the places Travis Richards showed me were closely guarded faculty secrets. In fact, a few showed signs of student occupancy—a forgotten pencil, a discarded chip bag, which Travis, as he instructed me to call him, deposited into a nearby trash bin.

"If you want I can bring you back tonight," he offered, not winded in the least. I couldn't say the same for myself. We had already gone up eight floors of the science building by way of an elevator that, unfortunately, didn't reach the top. We were currently huffing our way up a staircase heading in that direction. Or, at least, I was huffing. A small sign at the stairwell entrance we had passed through helpfully pointed the direction, *To the Telescopes*. It being daylight, I assumed we weren't stargazing.

A wide-domed ceiling awaited at the top, along with a sizable telescope angled toward the heavens. Travis stopped and propped open a door leading outside, grinning. "Don't want to get locked out. We might not be found until dark."

"That would be unfortunate." The wind had a nasty

bite promising to be downright painful after any length of time. Although I was sure Travis would be more than willing to keep me warm. His interest was obvious, and would have been welcome if I wasn't still licking my wounds over another tall, handsome man.

Two flights down an outside stairway sat a set of smaller telescopes, a deck, and a stunning view.

"Oh my goodness," I whispered. Most of Harvard, Cambridge, and the Boston skyline stood before us. "This is amazing."

"Isn't it? At night the city lights are wonderful from this side. And if it's a clear night, you can see the stars from over there. Obviously." He gestured to the telescopes with a sweep of his hand.

"It's funny. My boss tells people every week how they are getting the best view of Chicago, but I think this is just as fantastic."

"You might be right."

I turned toward him with a grimace. "You've been to Chicago?"

He let out a chuckle. "Born and raised in Lake Bluff."

"You know Derek." I didn't phrase it as a question, but by his blank expression the answer would have been no.

"Your ex-husband? Not really. Brooke introduced me to him maybe a month ago. I may have voted for him, but that was... gosh, almost a decade ago. I've been here six years and before that North Carolina."

"Soon-to-be ex," I corrected while stifling a groan. "Tell me you don't watch TV."

If Travis had watched Gabriel's interview, why would he be interested in me? Or was his attraction all a front to score the next spot on national TV?

He turned, leaning against the railing. "Not often. Too

busy. But things tend to get through the campus rumor mill." He offered me a sad, understanding smile. "You don't have to explain yourself to me. I went through a divorce a few years back. It is such an emotional roller coaster. Anyone who judges you has not been in your position."

"Thank you," I replied while mentally reprimanding myself for being paranoid. The last thing a respected Harvard professor would want was to get involved in a scandal with his student's mother.

He turned toward me, a small hopeful smile on his face "You know, I just ran you all over this place. How about I buy you a late lunch. A burger and a pint sound good?"

"Sure," I said, ignoring the same reprimanding voice as it warned me this time against encouraging Travis. Returning to my all-too-quiet hotel room for an overpriced salad from room service and an afternoon of work didn't sound as fun as what Travis proposed. And I was actually hungry.

TRAVIS'S PUB looked like something straight out of Britain. Dark woods, rich leathers, and the smell of food, beer, and a sweet hint of ancient tobacco permeated the place. We sat in a cozy booth tucked behind a high private wall separating us from the sounds of the bar.

"So, what brings you here?" Travis asked, once the waitress brought us pints of a rich local brew and took our orders for what my companion promised were the best burgers on the East Coast. "Not that I'm objecting, it's just this isn't the usual time for parental visits."

"I hadn't heard from Brooke in a while. I was worried about her." I hesitated only a second before being completely honest. He was her professor. Another set of eyes would be useful in making sure she coped with the strain of her parents' drama. "Actually, she's barely responded to my calls since I broke the news of the divorce over a month ago."

"Ahh, I see. Well if it's any comfort, I don't think you have anything to worry about." He sipped his beer. "I can't really comment further, I'm afraid. FERPA and all that."

"I understand." I gave him a grateful smile and changed the subject. "Do you have children?"

"A daughter and two sons, Olivia is seventeen, Carter is fourteen, and Bryce is seven. They live in Chicago with their mother."

The waitress returned with two platters of juicy cheeseburgers and thick steak fries. Despite the large breakfast, I had worked up an appetite on our walk around campus.

"My son, Mark, just turned seventeen," I informed him while contemplating the best way to tackle my overly large burger. "I can't imagine being separated from him. It must be difficult living so far away."

"Yes. The divorce was for the best, but it wasn't pretty. Samantha has a... well, to be honest, she had a bit of a trust issue. I'm sure you can see where this is going. Every phone call, every student meeting, every time I left the house became an interrogation. I tried to reassure her. I mean, the things she suspected would have destroyed my career, and at some point I started to fear her insinuations would."

I swallowed down a bite of burger while offering him a sympathetic smile. *Professor hottie indeed.*

"I'm so sorry. I can't even imagine." I grimaced. Brooke wouldn't approve of me getting this involved with her professor, but I was here and... oh well. "Brooke might have mentioned something over breakfast. Not that she's a participant. She made it quite unflatteringly clear she has no interest in older men."

He laughed quietly and shook his head, his cheeks pinking. "I wish all nineteen-year-old girls thought of me as old. Let's just say I prefer women with a bit more maturity."

"I've never been the jealous type, but then I thought I had no reason." I set down my beer glass with a bit of a thud, my skin warming as the intention of Travis's loaded words and his intense gaze sank in. *Oh dear.* Brooke was definitely going to kill me. "Until now. I don't think I'm imagining the possibility there's someone else. But I really don't know. Right now I'm just trying to move forward."

He reached to touch my hand but stopped himself. "You seem to have a good attitude."

"Thank you." I took another sip of beer, trying not to laugh at the situation. Who knew men would be throwing themselves at me at this point in my life? "It's a work in progress. Have any words of wisdom from someone who's made it back from the front line?"

He popped a couple of fries into his mouth and chewed thoughtfully. "Give it time. Sam and I can talk now without yelling. Maybe it's the distance. But the trade-off of peace has been missing my kids grow up. I'm not sure it's been worth it."

"I'm finding seventeen a tough age for a single parent. I don't think I could juggle Mark so well if there were a few younger siblings in the picture." *Not if they all pulled the stunts he had lately*, I thought while taking a last bite of my burger.

"From what I've heard, Bryce has been having challenges in school. He's quiet. A sensitive soul. I'm not sure what I hate more, that he's having problems or that I'm not there to support him." He glanced around the small dining area, but we were the only ones left. "My brothers and sister will probably think I'm nuts. I'm a year from tenure, but I've make a few calls. I'm considering other options. Boston's nice and all, but..."

He leaned back, running a hand over his neat salt-and-pepper beard. The memory of Trent doing the same gesture in the back of the limo while he explained why he hadn't called formed in my mind. Not that Travis looked anything like Trent, besides his height and maybe a similar twinkle in his storm-cloud eyes.

You're losing it.

Shaking my head, I cleared my rambling thoughts. Before long, I'd be seeing Trent in every man I met.

Pushing Trent out of my mind, I finished Travis's thought. "...but it's not home. I get it, and I don't think you're nuts. I'd give up everything for my kids."

"Thank you." He sighed as if I'd lifted a weight off his shoulders. "Your understanding... it means a lot."

"It would be a shame if no one else could experience your special tours," I said, turning to lighter subjects and the few french fries left on my plate.

"I'd like to think it was custom made for you." He held up his glass. "So how did I do?"

Swallowing down my food first, I answered, "Quite well. I loved all the little gardens and quiet alcoves. This place is absolutely charming."

"So are you." He grinned, wide. "What are your plans for the rest of the weekend?"

By that twinkle in his eye and his confident grin, I doubted any woman would turn him down. But I wasn't any woman. And continuing this flirtation was a recipe for disaster.

"Tonight I'm having dinner with Brooke. Then

tomorrow morning I have an eleven o'clock flight. I'll probably say goodbye to Brooke tonight. She's not a morning person, hence the ten-thirty breakfast this morning. I doubt she will be up before I have to leave."

"Would you like to meet later this evening? You really shouldn't miss the observatory at night."

Tipping my head to the side, I frowned. "Travis, I'm probably just as dangerous to your career as your coeds."

"I like you. I like being able to talk to someone who is above their twenties and can converse about something besides their area of interest or department politics." He sighed, running his hand over his jaw again, making me second guess my thoughts. "I know this is awkward. At the moment I'm your daughter's professor. But I like you, Nicki. And who knows? Someday we might find ourselves in the same state."

I should tell him no. Starting something while my heart still beat for Trent wouldn't be fair to Travis. But I wasn't one for burning bridges. Who knew how I'd feel six months from now?

"Can we take this one step at a time? I like you, Travis, I really do, but this divorce and everything... it's such a mess. I'm not sure I can commit to my hair appointments, much less a relationship."

"Fair enough." He pulled out his business card and handed it to me. "Call me tonight if you're interested in stargazing with a friend. Say, around ten?"

"Sounds perfect."

"Wonderful." He stood up, leaving cash on the table. "Unfortunately, I have office hours shortly."

"And I have work waiting for me at the hotel," I said, following him out. "Then dinner at the Berg. Should I be worried?"

"Quite the opposite. The food is surprisingly good, and the architecture... well, you'll see. I would have added that to the tour, but I overheard you and Brooke." He winked. "Let me know what you think later, if you decide the stars are worth it."

"I will." My heart stopped as he leaned in and brushed his lips on my cheek, his musky cologne drifting around me like a warm cloud. Brooke was going to kill me.

ANNENBERG HALL, with its massive arching roof timbers, hanging gothic chandeliers, and glowing stained-glass windows, reminded me of a cross between a German cathedral and something straight out of a fairy tale. In short, it was nothing like the mundane dining hall I ate most of my meals in while in college.

Brooke found a semi-empty table for us to talk and eat in relative quiet. As Auguste Comte once said, *everything is relative*. The architecture may have been beautiful, but the acoustics had not been designed for private dining. The place rumbled with the sounds of hundreds of students all talking at once.

"So, Mom, what did you do today?" Of course the first question she asked was the one to cause the most trouble.

I breathed out a slow exhale. "Actually, your Professor Richards gave me an interesting tour of the campus. Did you know this used to be part of the underground railroad?" I offered a bit of trivia in hopes of diverting her from the heart of the subject.

Her eyes grew as big as saucers. "You did what, with who?"

"With *whom*," I corrected, smiling. "He invited me for a

tour after we dropped you off. It seemed rude to refuse. He is very nice, by the way."

"You know I was only kidding when I said you would be better off with him than Gabriel, right?"

I stirred my soup, a rich bisque that never would have graced the menu at my college cafeteria. "We live almost a thousand miles away from each other. It's not like we're going to date or anything. I think he's lonely. You know he's divorced too?"

She darted a glance toward the diners at the other end of our table, but they were immersed in their own conversation. Brooke frowned and lowered her voice anyway. "No, and I don't really want to know the private lives of my professors. It's uncomfortable, Mom. Plus if my friends find out—"

"How are they going to find out?" I rolled my eyes. "If they're busy obsessing over their professors, they aren't spending enough time on their studies."

"I don't know. It just feels weird. I prefer to think of him in the two dimensional, not a person who has wants and needs. Especially if those involve my mother." Her face scrunched up in disgust, reminding me of her brother just a few days ago.

"But, he *is* a person. It's unfair to think of him as a thing without feelings. You're no better than the girls who treat him like a sex object." I shook my head in frustration. I didn't teach her not to respect others. *More likely one of her grandmothers did that.* "Did I ever tell you about the first time I met the president?"

"I don't recall," she said while dipping a hunk of bread into her soup and then popping it into her mouth.

"I've met a couple over the past sixteen years your father has held office in Washington. The first time was the scariest." I couldn't help but smile at the memory. "It was at an inauguration party. I had gone to the washroom, and when I came out, there he was walking out of the men's room with his security detail. I had known him for some years, but this was different. He was so much more important, powerful. I was flustered. I'm sure he sensed it. And do you know what he said?"

"What?" Brooke asked.

"He said, 'You know, pardon my frankness, Mrs. Robinson, but I don't think I'm ever gonna get used to all these men watching me relieve myself. Guess everyone will know I wash my hands at least.' We both laughed, the tension of the awkward moment broke, and then he walked away. And I realized he was just a man, no different than your father. No different than your professors." I paused and gave Brooke a small smile. "You're going to meet some important people in your life, and some people are going to be nervous to meet you because of who you are. It takes just as much courage to be comfortable with either of those people."

"You know what, Mom?" Brooke squeezed my hand. "I think you are way smarter than Dad."

"Thank you."

After dinner, my daughter declined to join me at the observatory. I texted Travis and arranged to meet him in front of Brooke's residence. If he found employment at another college, he would likely be missed. Just like earlier in the day, every few steps someone shouted a greeting to him.

"You're very popular," I commented after a large group of students passed, all of them calling out to him.

He shrugged. "I try to be accessible to my students. I want them to succeed. If it requires a little more effort on my part, so be it. We aren't a state university here, churning out education on an assembly line. I'd like to think I'm giving what these kids are paying for."

"I don't see them cheerfully acknowledging all the professors."

"There's a few stodgy ones." He chuckled. "Old-fashioned in their ways. Wanting respect and distance. I don't see the sense in that."

"And that's what got your marriage in trouble?" I hated bringing that subject back up, but he didn't seem to mind.

"Probably." He stopped at the door to the Science Center, a thoughtful look on his face. "But I can't change the past. Come on, let's see what they've found tonight."

The observatory was busier than in the morning. Small clusters of students mingled along with who I assumed, by their age and clothing, were professors.

"Hey, Professor Richards! It's an awesome night," a student exclaimed, enthusiasm lacing his voice, when he looked up from the scope.

Travis took my hand and led us closer. "What are we looking at tonight?"

"Right now, M42." The young man grinned.

"Ah. The Orion Nebula. Fantastic. Is Marks coming?" Travis asked. "By the way, Vince, this is Nicki. Nicki, Vince is a budding astrophysicist. He's going to be running this place someday."

"Nice to meet you," I said, appreciating the first-name-only introduction.

"Me too." His eyes bounced between me and Travis with open curiosity. "I texted Professor Marks. He should be coming later. Had a meeting or something."

"So explain what we are looking at." Travis patted Vince on the shoulder, before stepping up to the scope.

Vince explained in technical detail, that soon had me lost, about what looked to me like an odd-shaped cloud of stars, and from Travis's less technical interpretation, *unborn stars*. I made what I hoped were intelligent noises when it was my turn at the lens.

While the Orion Nebula was quite impressive, the camaraderie between the students and faculty impressed me more. Not everyone here was a physics or astronomy major, but there was a shared interest in what they were doing. The lines blurred between the professors and the students. Everyone had a voice, an opinion, and they discussed their opinions without fear—as if everyone was equal.

Much later, Travis walked me back to my hotel. I should have been exhausted, but I wasn't. My mind whirled with today's successes. Things with Brooke were good, and I'd made a friend of sorts. Besides Mark and Cynthia, I had no reason to go home.

"Penny for your thoughts?" Travis asked, his voice soft in the quiet evening.

I pasted on a smile I didn't quite feel. "Just wishing I could hide out here forever. There are some unpleasant things waiting for me back home."

"We can't run away from reality, but you are always welcome here." He turned to me when we reached the entrance of the hotel.

The possibility of Travis being Trent's illusive brother, TJ, nudged into my thoughts once again, just like it had at a few points in the afternoon. Reason overrode panic. Odds of the two being the same man were less than slim. I didn't even know where TJ lived, besides somewhere outside of Illinois. Or what his occupation was. That left forty-nine states and millions of career choices.

Surely Trent would have said something when I mentioned Brooke attended Harvard.

Asking Travis outright if he and Trent were related would be risky. He'd probably say no, and then I'd have to explain who Trent Richards was. What if Travis connected Trent with that grainy photo all the news outlets had been circulating? The same Trent Richards who'd been a household name during his NBA career.

I might have been mad at Trent, but I wasn't about to betray him.

"What's your middle name?" I blurted out.

Travis gave me a confused look and then laughed. "It's Henry. Why do you ask?"

If Trent called his brother TJ, his middle name must've started with a J. But it didn't. At least this Travis's didn't. And it was likely Trent's brother wasn't even a Travis. Probably a Thomas or Theodore or something.

"Just curious. I have a thing for monograms. THR, very well thought out. Not all are. You have to be careful with middle names starting with vowels," I babbled, the relief inside me floating out with my words.

He laughed again. "I can't remember the last time I had this much fun."

"Thank you. I really enjoyed today." My heart beat faster as he stepped closer.

Before I could stop him, his soft lips met mine in a tender kiss. He slipped his arms around me, and I was immediately encircled in his warmth, his scent. He smelled of the outdoors, of fresh air, piney woods, and manly musk.

What Travis was offering would be perfect. A long-distance relationship with few strings attached. Perfect, except for Trent. My heart ached for him. Foolish, I knew. He was gone and I should move on. But how could I when his eyes haunted my dreams and I woke to the echo of his touch?

It would be unfair to string Travis along when my heart yearned for another.

We pulled away to catch our breaths.

But for me it was just from the lack of oxygen. It was a nice kiss, and probably a month or so ago it would have been a really great kiss. But now there was no heat, no sparks of excitement.

"I should, um, go." I motioned inside.

"Call me when you get home." He quickly kissed me one last time, as if the first one had done more for him than me.

"I will." I smiled and retreated through the glass doors of the hotel, sure if I turned around I would see Travis Richards watching me.

CHAPTER
TWENTY-SEVEN

I hadn't been kidding when I told Travis I'd been tempted to hide out in Cambridge. Randall Harris's message on my phone was reason enough to jump back on the plane.

"I need to see you first thing Monday morning. I've penciled you in at eight. Don't be late."

Great.

I could almost feel my savings account draining. This divorce should have been finalized at the end of the following week. Now Randall was calling me on a Sunday. Probably charging me double.

His front door swung open the next morning I as climbed the steps, and he ushered me in. My lawyer led me into his office, his assistant nowhere in sight.

"Mrs. Robinson—"

"I really prefer Ms. Adams—"

"And I prefer clients who follow my advice, Mrs. Robinson." His eyes narrowed and his voice lowered. "What part of *do nothing without consulting me first* did you not understand?"

"I understood you perfectly, but—"

"Then what possessed you to sit down and confess your affair on national TV?" His eyes swept the room as if looking for answers. "Seriously, you are undermining your case."

"The reporters were everywhere. I could barely leave my house, much less go to work or the store. I thought telling my side of things would get those vultures off my back."

He sighed, rubbing the crease between his eyes. "And did it?"

"There's fewer, I think."

I wasn't counting, but it did look like they were slowly peeling away. Maybe they would have anyway. Pondering those thoughts with Randall wasn't worth his hourly fees, and I probably wouldn't appreciate his opinion.

"Moving forward. Talk. To. No. One." He looked down, scratching something in my file with his Montblanc. The file had gotten considerably thicker over the past months. "Now, I have the documents here to file the counterpetition. In my opinion, we should stick with the terms of the mediation. This isn't a time to get greedy."

"Hold on." I winced at his glare. "You said this could take a long time. Maybe beyond Mark's eighteenth birthday. I can't live on the temporary support I'm getting. The mortgage alone. And winter's coming. The heating bills and snow removal."

The thought of begging to my parents made me queasy.

He flipped a couple of pages, then shook his head. "I'll negotiate for more, but it would be helpful if you followed my instructions. As I said in our first meeting, angry husbands are difficult to negotiate with. What were you thinking announcing he left you on national news?"

"I was *thinking* I needed the public—my family, my children's friends and their parents, my coworkers, my fucking hairdresser—to know the truth. The bastard cheated." Randall rolled his eyes, his expression all *not this again*. "No. I have proof. He took his campaign manager along to visit my daughter."

He stared at me for a moment. "Do you really think he'd be stupid enough to bring his mistress to visit his daughter at this point in the divorce?"

I'd pondered that question more times than I could count ever since Brooke had told me about Patty.

Before I could answer, Randall continued, "Now, as I was saying. My hopes are since the mediation agreement was signed by both parties, we can convince Derek that moving forward would be in his best interest. Maybe you recant the story you told that reporter. Take blame." I opened my mouth to object. No way in hell would I tell the world I'd been sleeping with Gabriel for years. Randall raised his voice, cutting me off. "But we need to prepare in case he doesn't. I'll be asking the court to appoint a social investigator to give their opinion on Mark's custody."

"I said I didn't want Mark involved." Did Derek really want some stranger invading his son's life? "And I'm not admitting to an affair with Gabriel Roth. Forget it."

"Mark's of an age where his opinion will be a deciding factor. This is important, I'm afraid." He swiveled a stack of papers toward me and handed me his three-hundred-dollar pen. Discussion over, his body language said. "I need your approval."

❧

"So TELL me about your visit to my goddaughter," Cynthia demanded, motioning to her guest chair, when I walked into her office later in the morning, drained and exhausted from sparring with Randall. "How is she?"

"Brooke is good. I think she just needed space to process, and focus on her studies of course. She seemed busy but happy."

Cynthia nodded, her eyes scanning my face. "And you? You seem... happier, maybe?"

"Getting chewed out by my lawyer must agree with me, then." I nibbled at my bottom lip—a new and annoying habit I'd picked up recently to the detriment of my lipstick. Happiness seemed like an arbitrary thing, like a sliding scale.

"Well, you look rested. Cambridge must have agreed with you."

I laughed quietly, and Cynthia's eyes sharpened.

"There was a man..." I grinned as Cynthia leaned forward.

"Do tell. *Details*. I want details. The juicier, the better."

I shook my head. "Sorry, no juice. He was polite, handsome, charming, but... not even a spark. I'm doomed, Cyn. I can't figure it out. I kept comparing the poor man to Trent. Even had myself convinced they might be related at one point. I just... it even hurts to breathe when I think about him. What's wrong with me? I didn't even feel this bad when Derek left."

She gave me a sad smile. "Love doesn't make sense."

"Love," I spat out the word as if it tasted foul. "I think you have the right attitude toward love. My heart needs to turn to stone, then I'll be able to appreciate men properly."

Cynthia laughed quietly. "How was Randall?"

My lips twisted into a scowl. "Angry. He said I'm making his job harder."

She waved a hand. "I'm sure you're paying him enough."

"Speaking of... I need to put the house on the market."

Cynthia frowned. "I thought you loved your house."

Tears burned the corners of my eyes. I did love my house, but it was starting to hold too many unpleasant memories.

"I have no choice. Derek's threatening to pay the mortgage for only one year. You and I both know it could take years to find a buyer. And the temporary support payments are barely covering the mortgage and utilities. I need to face reality, Cyn. It's really too big for me and Mark anyway."

She nudged her mouse and glanced at her screen with a huff. "Let me make some calls. If you're serious, I may have some ideas."

I stood and nodded. "I am."

CHAPTER
TWENTY-EIGHT

"Hey, Nicki!" Ava yelled as soon as I walked in the door of Rossi's Pizzeria, motioning me to the empty chair next to her. "Everyone, you remember Nicki. Be nice, she's still in the process of her divorce."

It's all I could do to stop the cringe.

The night I'd returned from Cambridge, Ava had called, inviting me to her monthly girls' night out. My first impulse had been to decline. The last thing I wanted was to face a bunch of strangers after Gabriel's interview. But Ava had a gift for persuasion.

Surprisingly enough, I did know most of the women by sight. Connie Miller, Bella Genova, and Kati O'Neal waved as I sat down. Between PTA and soccer, I'd worked with most of them on and off over the years.

"Unless you don't own a TV, you've all heard things." *May as well own my shame.* It wasn't like I could pretend the last two weeks hadn't happened. "I could sit here all night denying everything, but I'm sure you have better things to discuss."

"Honey, divorce is an ugly business and we've all sat in your seat. We're here to offer support, and a shoulder to cry on," Kati said. "Now who's up for shots?"

Everyone cheered while I adjusted my expectations for the evening.

~

"...so the guy—Chet—says, 'Awe, come on honey, you need to loosen up. That dinner cost me two hundred. I could have gotten a nice blow job for that much,'" Connie whispered, mindful of the family on the opposite side of the restaurant.

"Eew," Kati responded, her nose scrunching up.

"No way," Ava gasped before knocking back her shot and motioning to the waitress for another round.

Our table looked like it belonged to a frat party, not a bunch of middle-aged divorcées. Empty pizza trays, beer bottles, and enough shot glasses. If the press caught a photo of this, it would be just as embarrassing as a tell-all interview with a delusional pool boy. There was barely enough room for our next round, but somehow our waitress found space.

"Yep," Connie answered. "Told the fucker to spend his money more wisely next time and then walked out."

"Good for you," Bella said, glancing toward the door where the family was just leaving. "That's why I hate those online dating sites. Everyone sounds so nice until you meet them. Then wham-o." She banged on the table, sending a couple of bottles scattering as the waitress scrambled to clean up.

"Yeah, but where do you find the nice guys?" Connie pouted. "At our age it's not like they're falling at our feet."

"Well, there is this guy at work..." Bella grinned with a faraway look in her eyes.

Ava laughed. "You got to look out for those office romances... well, I don't. I don't think Mr. Henderson has the energy to make a pass at me. I pray every night he doesn't kick the bucket. Then I pray he hires some hot young attorney to take over his practice."

"Hot young attorney, now there's something to drink to," Connie said, holding up her shot glass.

"Nicki doesn't seem to have a problem with men, if the news reports have anything to say about it," Connie sniggered, sending me a wink.

I laughed. Over the last couple of weeks Gabriel, Trent, and a host of other men from the doorman at Cynthia's office building to the grocery store clerk, had featured as my latest love interest depending on which news network you followed.

"Please..." I tossed back the contents of my shot glass and then closed my eyes tight as the burn of—*What are we drinking again? Oh right, tequila.* "The least the reporters could do is pair me with someone interesting. Last night it was some guy that sat next to me on the train. The man had to be in his seventies, and he was wearing a wedding ring."

Coming out tonight was the best idea ever. And to think I almost turned Ava down. Almost chose to wallow in my self-pity and regret. And why? Why should I be sorry? None of this would have happened if Derek hadn't gotten some wild itch for his campaign manager. *Bastard.*

"Here's to Nicki," Bella said, lifting her shot glass in another toast.

Huh, where did you come from? I silently asked the fresh shot glass in front of me. Or maybe not so silently considering my friends' giggles.

Friends. I had friends.

My eyes flooded with tears. "You guys are the best."

Ava patted my arm in encouragement. "Nothing like a little tequila therapy."

I nodded in agreement while the conversation moved on. Something about Connie's sister or brother or something. I wasn't sure. I nodded at the appropriate places, trying not to focus on the slow rotation of the room. Closing one eye seemed to help for some reason, and I giggled at the thought of those old Popeye cartoons. *Whatever happened to those?*

My bladder suddenly demanded my attention and I stood, grabbing onto the back of my chair as the room tilted for a moment. "I need to pee, ladies."

Laughter sounded behind me as I tried not to bump into the bathroom doorway, with mediocre success. The stupid bathroom stall door also had a habit of moving.

I believe you're drunk, Ms. Adams.

The last time I'd been this drunk I'd slept with my pool boy. This wasn't quite as bad, but still...

Pulling my phone from my purse, I let out a groan. It was late, and Mark was going to kill me.

I squeezed my eyes shut in frustration, then immediately opened them. Bad idea. In the darkness behind my eyelids the stall spun. Opening them didn't help much.

How many shots did I have? Three, four. Maybe five?

The screen on my phone blurred, then doubled. I tapped on Mark's number. *Don't drop your phone in the toilet.* With one eye open and one closed, I typed out what I thought was an appropriate message and hit send.

The place was deserted except for our table when I walked out of the restroom. Connie's chair was also empty. How long had I been in the washroom?

A couple of minutes later Kati's and Bella's rides arrived and they left.

Ava sipped her coffee while we waited for our kids to pick us up.

Did Mark get my text?

What if he's asleep?

My thoughts sobered me up a fraction. My son was the heaviest sleeper.

The alternatives weren't pleasant. An Uber at this time of night, drunk and alone, wasn't wise. But neither was spending the night in the car. Walking from Wilmette to Kenilworth was also out of the question.

My phone buzzed with a text, and I almost fumbled the damn thing in my rush to read the message.

Here.

Short but sweet. He clearly wasn't happy about being woken up, but I'd make it up in the morning with banana-nut waffles—his favorite.

I thanked Ava for inviting me, and we both headed out of the restaurant in opposite directions. In the past few hours, a cold lake fog had rolled in. The streetlights glowed in their individual orbits, casting little illumination beyond the lamps and leaving long stretches in eerie darkness. Mark's car was nowhere to be seen, so I headed off to where I had parked in hopes he'd be there.

Just a few lungfuls of the cold, damp air had me sobering up quickly. Or maybe it was the atmosphere. Things rustled just out of sight. A dog yipped in the distance, or possibly a coyote? Whatever, the hairs on my arms stood at attention and my heart thudded hard against my breastbone. I picked up my pace, my anxious breath frosting the darkness in front of me.

I glanced around as the outline of my Cayenne emerged from the murky darkness, and frowned. Mark's bright blue Jeep Wrangler was nowhere in sight.

What the hell?

Movement caught my eye and I stopped. My car sat in the shadows between two lights, but as I got closer I could make out someone tall leaning against it.

"Mark?" I called, fear tingling down my spine. Whoever it was, he was way too bulky to be my son.

What if it's Gabriel? The thought had me halting in my tracks.

Go back to the bar, you idiot.

The figure looked up and my heart skidded to a stop.

"Nicki," Trent growled, pushing off from my car and walking toward me. My pulse rocketed and my skin tingled with relief as my knight in faded jeans and a leather jacket closed the distance.

"Oh God. W-what are you doing here?"

"You texted me." He huffed out a quiet laugh. "Who did you expect?"

"Huh?" I frowned, rubbing my forehead in confusion. "I didn't text you. I texted Mark."

"I beg to differ." He turned his phone to show me the message I sent. "'I know what you're going to say, but save it. I'm drunk and need a ride home. Consider this your get-out-of-jail-free card.' Are we talking misdemeanor or something more serious?"

"I... I don't know." The woodsy scent of his cologne and the cocky arch of his eyebrow had my thoughts spinning.

He tipped his head toward the car. "Let's get out of here."

His hand rested on my back and I melted into his

warmth as we walked the few steps to my car door. At the curb I stumbled, my hand pressing against his chest. He was close. Close enough to do all the things I had wanted to do over the past two weeks. But something held me back.

"Where's your car?"

He leaned against my door, his lips quirking in that half smile I loved. "Back at the house, I suspect. Unless Mark took it for a joyride after he dropped me off."

I forced out a laugh, my breath hitching as a pent-up sob threatened to break free from my chest. "I missed you."

"Get in." He shifted away, opening the passenger door. "Let's get you home."

I swallowed hard, fighting the disappointment settling over me like a heavy cloak.

A mistake brought him here. I tapped Trent Richards's number instead of Mark Robinson on my phone. He came out of obligation, not because he wanted to.

Silence filled the car on the ride home. I stared out the window at the expired Halloween decorations, trying not to notice how good Trent looked behind my wheel, or the way his cologne infused my car with his scent.

Even without looking in his direction, it was impossible not to acknowledge his presence. He was like the other half of my heart. For the past weeks, mine hadn't beat properly without him in my life. Tears ran down my cheeks as I sobbed quietly, my heart breaking all over again.

"Nicki..." He sighed.

"Why did you come?" I forced the words past the constriction in my throat, although I really didn't need his answer. I knew what it would be. He was a good guy. The kind of guy who could be counted on. The kind of guy who never turned his back on anyone. I was just an obligation, no different than Marcus Raburn or any of the other players who found themselves in a jam.

Trent pulled in the darkened driveway, next to his little red sports car glowing under the garage lights, and then turned toward me.

"You texted. I kind of assumed it was a mistake, but I'm not an asshole. Mark told me you went out with friends. At this time of the night, your son shouldn't have to go get you alone. Maybe think about that next time."

I shoved the door open and bolted away from the pain and anger threatening to choke me. Trent stopped me as I rounded the hood, but I shook off his hands.

"Fuck you," I spat, wiping at my face with the back of my hand. Stupid tears. He wasn't worth them. "I'm not one of your rookies who needs saving, so take your holier-than-thou attitude and shove it."

I spun and walked away from him.

He grabbed my arm, pulling me back to face him. "Holier than thou? I was sleeping. I could have ignored your text, left you waiting for Mark, who had no idea you needed him. The least you can do is thank me."

I pulled my arm from his grasp, taking a much-needed step away from him. "Don't save me anymore, Trent. It's too confusing, okay? I need to figure out how to get over you if you're not coming back."

He stomped away, then turned back, throwing his hands up between us. "You think this is easy on me? I keep replaying that fucking night, seeing that man pinning you against the island, the fear in your eyes. You could have told me why, but no, you lied to my face."

"I didn't lie. I just didn't volunteer the truth because I knew you would do exactly what you did." I turned away and headed toward the door. "Thank you for driving me Trent, but you need to go home now."

"Nicki, stop," Trent called as I reached the porch. "Nicki!"

"Please, Trent. Just go home."

CHAPTER
TWENTY-NINE

By the cold light of the next morning I regretted my harsh words. They *were* harsh, and angry. And stupid. Why the hell did I walk away from him? What would have happened if I'd swallowed my pride and stayed? Could we have worked things out? Those questions and more replayed in a continuous loop inside my head through the dark hours of the night and over the next several days until I was ready to scream.

Staring at my phone didn't offer any answers, or none I liked. I pushed aside my untouched salad with a sigh and tried to concentrate on my computer screen. I had a pile of work in my inbox that needed my attention. I didn't have time to go over my mistakes.

If Trent had things to say, he would have called, and he didn't. All Tuesday night did was rip open the scab on my heart, leaving me bleeding once again.

I shoved my phone in my purse with more force than necessary and then grabbed the top folder off the pile. Maybe Cynthia was right. I had to move forward.

If your dog dies, you get another fucking dog, she had told me just that morning.

I spun around, file forgotten. I stared out my office window at a blue-and-white tour boat as it meandered down the river, along with a hearty pair of late-season kayakers.

Maybe I needed another *dog*. Thanksgiving was almost here. Before long, I'd be headed back to Cambridge. I just needed to recognize all of Travis's really good qualities.

Spinning back to my desk, I grabbed a pen and my notepad. Another professor, years ago, taught me lists were good. They helped you see things clearly.

Smart. Well, that was a given.

Good-looking. I smiled, thinking about his storm-cloud eyes. Yeah, he was easy to look at.

Age. That was a big one. It would be nice to be with someone my age.

Well-off. Hmm. That was debatable. He certainly wasn't rich, but I'd had rich—

Inside my purse, my cell rang, and I scrambled to get it, Travis forgotten as hope sent my heart into my throat.

"Shit," I muttered. The picture of my husband displayed on my screen along with his Washington office number. *What the hell does he want?*

"I'm not supposed to talk to you," I answered, realizing I was doing just that.

"Then just listen," he replied.

Muffled voices sounded in the background, then came to a stop with the sound of a door snicking closed.

I instantly pictured his office. The muted colors of navy and rusty reds of the Persian rug spread out in front of his big oak desk, echoing the colors of the tapestry drapes and the pale blue walls. The photos of the kids on his desk—

keeping him grounded, he once told me. A Peale portrait of George and Martha Washington hung with prominence behind his desk, a birthday gift from my parents. And the antique German walnut and boxwood inlaid chessboard with bone pieces, sitting on his credenza, my gift to him on our fifteenth anniversary.

Derek had proposed to me over a similar board years earlier, said it was during our first game he knew he'd have to marry me. I was the only person skilled enough to beat him.

It was a different game we played now. With few winners and plenty of losers.

Lost in thought, I hadn't heard a word he said.

"I'm sorry, could you repeat that?"

His sigh came through as a gust of wind. "I'm talking about Thanksgiving, Nicki. I'd like to spend it with the kids. If the Germans and French could call an armistice during World War I, can't we do the same for one night?"

My laugh was short and lacked humor. "Would you prefer I tell you to fuck yourself in German or French? This isn't World War I or Christmas."

He sighed again, his chair creaking. I pictured him squirming. "How can I change your mind?"

"My lawyer would have my head for even talking to you." It was my turn to sigh. I was too exhausted to argue. "Okay, listen. I don't want to be the bad guy here. Once upon a time I had planned this to be a family holiday. You changed that, not me. Call your lawyer, increase my temporary support. When Randall Harris tells me I'll be able to buy groceries and pay the mortgage and heat the house this winter—Oh, and hire back Rosa. Mark misses her. Also, for your son's sake, stop with the whole custody nonsense. Then we can talk about Thanksgiving."

He made a choking noise and then no noise for a good minute. Had he perished from the thought of giving in?

"I want assurances there will be no more television interviews."

I managed not to roll my eyes. "Fine. I promise, no more talking to reporters."

"And you drop the trust-fund issue. The kids will get their share when I'm dead."

"I want their names on the settlement agreement. None of this equal division among your natural children bullshit."

He chuckled. "That was my lawyer's suggestion, but fine. Believe me, I have no intention of fathering any more children."

"Is that it?" I asked.

"That's it. Then I guess I'll see you at Thanksgiving?"

Happy tingles danced along my arms, and I pumped my fist in victory. "Good doing business with you, Derek."

Just as I slipped my phone back in my purse, it rang again. My stomach tensed.

Had Derek changed his mind already? Thought of a few more stipulations?

A quick glance at my phone told me otherwise. The number was unfamiliar, but I answered anyway.

"Ms. Adams, this is Sherilyn Jeffreys," the voice on the line said, giving me her station affiliation, and reminding me of the interview I granted her a couple of weeks back—like I needed any reminders. "Is this a good time to talk?"

I laughed to myself. "Probably not. My lawyer gave me hell for our last conversation, Ms. Jeffreys. I think he may put a muzzle on me if I give out any more interviews."

"I'm not calling for an interview, Ms. Adams. I have information for you. And I promise, no questions."

I sat up straighter. *Information?* "I'm all ears."

"After our interview, I decided to take a closer look into this story. The whole premise of your story. Gabriel Roth, scorned lover. It just didn't fit. Maybe if you did have a five-year affair, but a one-time fling? It just doesn't make sense. But this is what I do, you know, look for holes in stories."

My skin tightened uncomfortably. "You don't believe me? The man had some weird obsession for me all the time he was in our employ. I just fell into his trap."

She laughed. "Exactly, Ms. Adams."

"What?" I frowned at my phone, not seeing the humor in the situation.

"Relax, I believe you. Are you sitting down?"

I hated that question. "Yes."

"Gabriel Roth isn't who you think he is." She cleared her throat and then continued. "His name isn't even Gabriel Roth. It's Garrett Jacob MacKenzie. He's a con artist, Ms. Adams. He's been arrested several times for relationship fraud."

"Relationship fraud?" I had no idea what that even was.

"His whole pool-service gig is just a front. According to police records, he's scammed at least three other wealthy women in three different states. A real Casanova, our man Garrett. One minute he's convincing them he's in love, and the next thing the women know, he's drained their bank accounts."

My mind spun, trying to grasp what she was saying. "No. I... I don't understand. How can that be? He came with recommendations. Derek must have done a background check."

"Detective Cory Jackson at CPD had to dig to get the information on him. It was buried pretty deep. Garrett's father is a US Circuit Court judge. Might have had a hand in cleaning up his boy's record." Her voice rose with what I assumed was giddy excitement. This was the kind of story most reporters only dreamed about.

"H-holy shit," I sputtered. A dark chill slithered up my spine. Derek knew a lot of judges. But he wouldn't have...

"You said it." She huffed out a short breath and continued, "According to Detective Jackson, none of his arrests have led to convictions. But he told me it's quite common in these cases. Evidence is weak, victim's too embarrassed to testify... he said only about fifteen percent of these types of crimes ever get reported in the first place." She paused. "You dodged a bullet with this guy."

I collapsed back in my chair, my head spinning with confusion. "This makes less sense than the scorned lover theory. He was with us for five years and never made a single pass at me."

Sherilyn sighed over the phone. "I know. That bothered me too. But he had to have cleaning contracts with other homes in your area. You may have been a cover. A way to get referrals. Then you tell him about the divorce, and boom, you're suddenly a target."

A cold shiver danced across my skin. How many referrals had I given over the year? How many friends and neighbors had taken my word and trusted Gabriel, or Garrett?

"Shit." Closing my eyes I inhaled a shaky breath, but stopped as the scent of garlic made my stomach flip. I glanced at my Caesar salad with revulsion. Swiping it in the garbage, I strode across to the door to my office and set the wastebasket out in the hall.

"Detective Jackson is looking into this. I certainly wouldn't be surprised if he was scamming another woman right in your neighborhood. Men like Garrett MacKenzie, they're bold. Narcissistic. They believe they can get away with anything, usually because they have. I'm sure having an influential father doesn't hurt. His appearance on TV proves that. Although in the detective's opinion, he believes that was done out of anger. You'd shunned him, and he knew exactly how to hurt you."

"No kidding."

"Well, if it's any comfort, Mr. MacKenzie seems to have disappeared. According to the detective, his apartment has been cleaned out. The lease expired the first of November, and he didn't renew, according to the landlord. He left no forwarding address at the post office, and he closed out his bank account. It's as if he never existed."

"I'm not sure if that's a comfort or not. He's the invisible man. He could be anywhere."

"Anywhere but here. He's a con man, Ms. Adams. He's not going to stay where his cover's been blown. It's too much of a risk. I'll let you know if Detective Jackson finds out anything more." She paused for a second. In the background, several voices could be heard and phones rang. "Listen, I appreciate everything you've done for me, but this story has legs. I will do what I can to keep you out of it, but I can't guarantee anything."

Of course not. How had Derek not seen this coming?

I squeezed my eyes shut at the thought of my soon-to-be ex-husband. Ten minutes ago, Derek had been willing to negotiate. The last thing I needed was for my affair with Gabriel—Garrett—to blow up again.

But if Derek knew about his background... I'd kill him.

"Keep me informed. And thank you."

I dropped my head on my desk once the call ended. The satisfaction from my conversation with Derek moments ago had been steamrolled to dust. I stared at my phone for a long time. But it stayed quiet, offering me no more surprises.

I gave up on the file in front of me, stuffing it and its companions into my bag for later.

My mind kept going back to the same question. Had Gabriel—Garrett—fooled Derek as well as me? Cynthia would have answers or at least know where to get them. But she was out with clients.

I was alone. I'd been essentially alone since the beginning of September, but until this minute I had ignored the crushing loneliness and vulnerability of my situation. I ached for Trent's arms to hold me, for his lips to whisper that everything would be all right.

Where was he right now? Here, in Chicago? Likely somewhere else, looking forward to a night in some generic hotel. *Alone?* I could easily pull up their schedule and find out in seconds. But no. I wouldn't stoop to stalking him like some crazed fan.

I knew it was wrong, but the need for comfort had me dialing before I could stop myself.

"Hey, Nicki. I was just thinking about you." I smiled at the warmth in his voice, my loneliness evaporating even with the distance between us.

"Hi, Travis. Got a minute?"

CHAPTER

THIRTY

I had booked our Thanksgiving trip to Cambridge all the way back in August. Derek and Mark loved Boston's Harborwalk and diverse restaurants, and Brooke loved to shop. I had just wanted our family together during this short break. Little did I know last summer that everything would change in just a few months.

Cynthia instructed Sonya to get me a refund on Derek's plane ticket, but Mark and I were stuck with the oversized hotel accommodations I'd reserved on our joint credit card. *I must remember to thank him.*

Wednesday morning, I settled into my first-class window seat and glanced down the aisle for a moment to search for Mark. He hated being trapped, be it in a car or plane. He was not a fun travel companion. As soon as the seat belt sign turned off, he'd be up strolling the aisles to the frustration of the flight attendants. Early boarding was torture for him.

Before boarding, I'd noticed a family with daughters around his age—trading smiles and whispering in his direction. He'd taken off for the bathrooms, but more likely he was socializing with the pretty girls who waited with the other coach passengers.

I sat back and got comfortable, opening the nice romance novel I'd brought for the trip, not giving my son a second thought. He'd been traveling all his life. He would board eventually.

Or so I thought. Sometime later, I smiled as a frustrated flight attendant escorted him to his seat, just before the doors closed and the whine of the engines increased in volume.

"Cutting it close," I remarked, raising my eyes from my book to glare at my visibly winded son. "Really, Mark, I wouldn't enjoy explaining to your father how you missed our flight. He already thinks I'm a bad mother."

He snapped his seatbelt closed and the plane lurched forward. "Sorry, Mom."

I sent him a censured glare. The grin on his face negated his apology, but I chose to stay silent. We were going to have a pleasant holiday, even if it killed me.

I sighed and returned to the book. A guaranteed happy ending, that's what I needed, even if it was only fiction.

Immersed in the drama on the pages, I barely noticed the flight attendants safety spiel, or take off. Mark made a quick bolt from his seat as soon as the seat belt light dinged off. *Those girls must be something special.*

"That was quick," I commented, not looking up, when he plopped down a minute later. "No luck with the pretty—"

A familiar woodsy fragrance hit my nose and my voice faltered. I froze as Trent whispered in my ear, "The only pretty girl I want to get lucky with is you."

"W-what are you do-doing here?!" I asked, eyes wide as I took him in. "And where is Mark?"

"I happen to be delivering the world's most expensive apology." He gave me a flirty wink that was incongruous with the way we left things. "Thanks to Cynthia. And Mark."

"Cynthia gave you Derek's seat?" I gaped at him, the puzzle pieces slowly coming together.

"With conditions," he chuckled and I narrowed my eyes. "I never want to be on her bad side again."

I blinked slowly, my mouth dropping open. "Do I want to know about these conditions?"

"Definitely not." He threaded his fingers through mine. "Can we get back to this apology? I've been a stubborn ass, blind and possessive. Just plain stupid."

"Trent—"

He shook his head and held up his hand, stopping me. "Let me finish. I had no right, and I probably don't deserve you. The fact is, whatever you did before we met is your business. Not mine. It was just hard for me to think of you with that... that brute. I might have overreacted."

"Might?"

"I did overreact." He blew out a harsh exhale, looking down at his hands. "But... over the past few weeks I... I can't seem to remember how to breathe without you."

When he looked up, the pain in his eyes made my breath shudder because I felt it too—that gut-wrenching agony of our separation.

"I would have bought this damn plane, promised Cynthia anything, just to sit next to you. To tell you how much I miss you. Please, tell me what I need to do to get you to forgive me."

My hands found his face as tears blurred my vision. "Oh God, Trent. I did lie to you and I'm so sorry. It was stupid, because there were so many times that weekend I wanted to confess about me and Gabriel." I paused, shaking my head. His name wasn't even Gabriel. "Jesus, there's so much more to tell you. But I was a fool for not trusting you. I should've, but I didn't. So, I'm the one who's sorry. And you don't need forgiveness, or to buy airplanes, because I can't imagine—"

His hand slipped to the base of my neck and his soft lips covered mine, cutting off my rambling apology. And thank God. His kiss was better than anything I had to say.

A few moments later, Trent pulled back a fraction and whispered in my ear, "You realize we just had our first fight, *and* we just made up."

I leaned back and pressed my lips together to keep from kissing him again. It was tempting, but the sounds of other passengers and the hum of the jet engines reminded me we were far from alone. A quick glance around showed no one was watching, but still...

"Where exactly is my son?"

"Mark is sitting just behind us with a lovely girl. She looked much happier to have him entertain her than me." *Of course.* Cynthia planned this whole thing, that little sneak.

"And honestly, I think he is much happier too. Sorry, Mom." Trent gave me a little pout, like he was bringing me bad news.

"Don't worry. I know where my charms have their limits."

The flight attendant interrupted, dropping pastries and pretty fluted glasses of mimosas on our trays. I was pretty sure she glared at Trent. Obviously his charms had their limits as well.

He chuckled as she walked away with a huff. "There are no limits to your charms where I'm concerned." He glanced up and down the aisle, then returned his focus on me. His grin had me melting in my seat. "Maybe you could show me those *charms* right now."

I narrowed my eyes and set my glass down. I hadn't even taken a sip of the cocktail, but I was having trouble following him. "Charms?"

"Charms, sweetheart," he repeated, and then shot a glance down the aisle. Turning back, he raised a sexy eyebrow while drawing a finger up my pant leg. "We could slip into the lavatory, and you could charm the fuck out of me."

"Have you lost your mind?" I sputtered, smacking his hand away. He gave me a look that told me I really didn't want him to answer that. "My son is behind us, and no matter how engrossed in conversation he might be, he would definitely notice us slipping into the lavatory together. And so would the flight attendant. You know, the one you were arguing with?

"The last thing I need is to be the subject of the nightly news again. And one of us has standards including mattresses and privacy. Give me your hotel address. We'll figure something out later," I whispered, mindful of my son's very sharp ears behind us.

He scratched his stubbled jaw, reminding me of a certain professor. Oh hell. What was I going to do with Travis?

"What?" I asked, pushing that problem aside for now. I didn't have plans to meet with Travis Richards for a handful of hours. Trent's sheepish expression said I had other things to worry about at the moment.

"Well, Cyn did just pounce on me two days ago. God, that woman is scary when she's determined. I was busy trying to rearrange this flight with my schedule, and she sort of thought you'd let me stay with you." He raised his eyebrows, giving me a cheesy smile.

"She what?" My mouth dropped open. "Wait a minute. You don't have a hotel?"

He took a sip of his champagne cocktail and shrugged. "Not exactly. She did say you'd have enough room."

"I'm gonna kill her," I whispered through my clenched teeth while rubbing my eyes. She couldn't possibly think... but she probably did. Cynthia had no clue about parenting teenage boys, or managing suspicious soon-to-be ex-husbands.

He gave me a serious look. "You underestimate that boy's maturity."

I ignored his comment and all it implied. "What exactly would you do if I don't let you stay? Did you think that far?"

"TJ likes surprises. I can always crash at his place." He gave me a playful pout. "But you'll be missing out on the making up. I have some serious making-up plans."

An uneasy feeling settled in my gut. "TJ lives in Cambridge? Why didn't you ever tell me that?"

His shoulder lifted in a casual shrug. "Don't know. He's an anatomy professor at Harvard, genius IQ, and a fucking ladies' man." His brows lowered. "Not the kind of thing you share when you're trying to impress a woman with your stats."

I dropped my head into my hands and groaned. "TJ as in Travis Henry Richards?"

"Yeah..." His eyes sharpened and his brows furrowed as I peeked at him through my fingers.

How the hell do I get myself into these things?

"How do you know my brother's full name?"

Ignoring his question, I downed my mimosa in one

swallow wishing like hell it was something much stronger. "How do you get TJ out of Travis Henry?" I asked instead.

"Travis Henry, *Junior*. And you didn't answer my question, sweetheart."

"You think you would have mentioned something when I said Brooke is premed at Harvard," I blurted, my mouth drying up. *Fucking hell, his brother kissed me.*

"Sorry. Once again, impressing you with *me,* not—" He looked at me, eyes widening. "Oh shit. You didn't. God damn you, TJ!"

"No. *No!*" I denied, quickly realizing where his thoughts were heading. "Brooke and I ran into him in a café. He was very nice. Took me on a tour of the campus."

The flight attendant rushed over, her eyes darting between me and Trent. "Is everything okay?"

"Sorry about that." I glared at Trent. Before long we'd have an air marshal paying us a visit. "Everything is fine."

We both watched her walk away, then Trent turned back to me.

"I bet he *showed* you around." He growled, eyes narrowed. "What else?"

"Lunch. And later we went to the observatory to see the stars." Trent lowered his eyebrows, and I could almost see the romantic scene he was imagining. I grabbed his hand, talking faster to get everything out. "With about two dozen students and faculty. But later, he kissed me—"

"He what," he shouted, then sent an apologetic look to the front of the plane. It quickly vanished when he turned back to face me. Voice lowered, he continued, "He kissed you?"

"Might I remind you, we had broken up?" I covered his open mouth with my hand, stopping him from continuing to argue. "It was probably the most disappointing kiss I've ever had. I wanted you, and he wasn't you."

Behind my palm, his lips slowly curled up into a smile. I dropped my hand, my heart melting at the sight of his dimples. "Really?"

"Yeah." I nodded. "You've kind of... I don't know... grown on me."

"Sucks to be Travis." He laughed quietly.

"Trent, don't gloat. He's a nice guy. Do try and be humble."

"Humble. Hmm. I will have to look that one up." He slipped an arm around me. "You know we were hand-fed on sibling rivalry growing up."

I gave him my stern mother look. "Promise you will let me tell him."

"Fine." He looked around, his free hand sliding up my thigh. "Sure I can't talk you into joining the mile-high club? You kissed my brother. You kind of owe me."

"Gross," I answered, shifting in my seat to lean against him. He whimpered in my ear as I opened my book. This was going to be the longest trip ever, but deep down I was smiling.

AFTER UNPACKING I gave a quick rundown of our itinerary. Trent and Mark might have their own plans, but my schedule took precedence.

Brooke was busy until dinner, and I had arranged to meet Travis. Mark was free to explore the campus with the pretty new friends he'd made on the airplane, and Trent...

"You're not going with." I pointed a warning finger at him. He may or may not have noticed. He was busy tossing a chocolate bar—probably a ten-dollar chocolate bar—from the mini fridge to Mark and was heading back in for more. Derek was gonna shit when he saw the bill.

Raising my voice, I attempted to get Trent's attention. "I need to explain this to your brother as gently as possible. Go hang with Mark for a while."

"Not on your life." He sent me a stern expression, then bit into his candy bar. "Mark doesn't want me tagging along on his date."

Mark blushed. "It's not a date."

"Five minutes. Just give me five minutes to explain." I begged with my eyes as he walked over. "Don't make me the bad guy again."

"He kissed you," Trent whispered in my ear as he pulled me into a hug. "He'll be lucky if I don't walk out of his office with his nuts in my pocket."

"Trent..."

"Kidding," he growled, his lips finding a sensitive spot behind my ear.

"Son in the room." Mark cleared his throat and shoved half his candy bar into his mouth.

"Control yourself." I pushed Trent away, my face heating uncomfortably as I tried once again to bring order to our little circus. "Okay. Then we'll all meet back here. Brooke said she would stop by around six. There's a fabulous pub I was at back in October. It's just off the square—"

"O'Malley's. I know the place." Trent's narrow look told me I wasn't doing a good job at defusing the situation between him and his brother. Travis had mentioned O'Malley's was his favorite place.

Like walking a damn minefield.

"Great. I'm not sure if Brooke's been there, but I

thought it would be fun. I made reservations for dinner at seven tonight."

I groaned, slapping my head. "Dinner... oh hell."

"What?" Trent asked.

"I forgot Derek. He's coming for Thanksgiving dinner tomorrow."

"Dad's coming?" Mark chuckled while looking at Trent. "Wow, this should be *interesting*."

Trent shrugged. "I'll go to TJ's."

"No." Mark protested. "You should be here. For Mom."

I shook my head. As adorable as Mark's support was, Derek wouldn't be happy. And we'd just resolved most of the issues holding up the divorce.

"No, *Mark*... Sorry, Trent. If you can go to Travis's it would be best. I'm not even sure how to explain you to Derek without him going ballistic."

Mark huffed, dropping down on the sofa and crammed the last of his chocolate in his mouth. "You know Dad's gonna find out about him eventually."

Derek did ask for an armistice, but revealing my boyfriend might be pushing my luck.

"Don't talk with your mouth full." *How did we get here?* "And I know. But maybe let's not rub his nose in this. Not this weekend at least."

CHAPTER
THIRTY-ONE

T ravis's eyes lit up when I opened his office door, making my chest tighten with guilt.

"Are you busy?" I asked from the doorway.

"Not at all. Just catching up on some papers before relaxing for the holiday. I was counting the seconds since your text." He beamed while closing the file in front of him, then cleared off his desk. "Please come in and close the door. Don't want any students barging in."

Kill me now.

"If you're sure." I did as he asked and sat down, clasping my hands between my knees. "I'm sure a student's last-minute emergency is more important than me."

"Nonsense. I've been looking forward to seeing you all week. What are your plans for this holiday weekend?"

"Derek's coming, which should be a challenge." I sighed at my lack of courage. Like pulling off a bandage, I just needed to tell Travis about Trent.

"Always stressful, the holidays. Might I offer a little distraction? Say, dinner tonight?" He rounded his desk and was in the chair next to me in a heartbeat, his hand cradling the side of my face. "I know this romantic little place. White tablecloths, candles, champ—"

"We need to talk, Travis." I leaned back, breaking the connection and the impending kiss I could see coming. "I had a wonderful time in October, but I have to be honest. I had been seeing someone before I came out. Things went a bit wrong when... well, as you can imagine, the whole media debacle didn't sit well with him."

Travis's expression fell as I continued. "If I had thought when I came out here, there was any chance of us getting back together, I would have never encouraged things with you. I can assure you—"

"But you have gotten back together," he interrupted, finishing for me. I nodded. "I see. Well, I can't say I'm not disappointed, but—"

The doorknob rattled, then the door squeaked open. Travis's focus shifted up, his eyebrows furrowed.

"Surprise," Trent said with a laugh.

"Jesus, do you ever knock." Travis shot to his feet. "Please excuse the interruption, Nicki. This is my brother, Trent."

Shortest five minutes ever.

I glared up at the man who I planned on giving a new watch for Christmas. Or maybe a timer. One with really huge numbers. Trent stared back at me with a look of complete innocence.

"What's going on?" Travis asked.

"Well, you see..." I shot another glare at his brother.

Side by side, the resemblance between the two was— well, maybe not as obvious as Trent and Troy, but I must have been blind not to notice.

"I'm so sorry, Travis," I said, then gave him the high

points of my and Trent's relationship, omitting the more dramatic moments.

"Five minutes?" I shook my head at Trent before turning my attention toward his brother once more. "I asked him to give me time to talk to you *alone*. Obviously he doesn't listen very well."

"Ha. Good luck with that. If you have the next year I can tell you all the times this one didn't listen to instructions." Travis shifted his gaze back and forth between Trent and me. "Seriously, him?"

I looked at Trent and then nodded to Travis. "'Fraid so. He kind of grows on you."

"Hey—" Trent blurted out.

"I'm sure there's a cure for it. You should see a doctor," Travis cut in, grinning at his brother before giving him a sound hug. "It's good to see you anyway, Trent."

"You too, Teej." Behind his brother's back, Trent sent me a thumbs-up.

"So sit. Tell me what's up," Travis said, returning to the chair behind his desk while Trent claimed the one next to me.

"Long story short. I've come to set my brother straight on a few things…"

I gasped, slowly turning toward Travis.

"Kidding." Trent threw his head back, laughing. "Actually, I should thank you. You've given me something to hang over your head. Troy is going to love hearing this one."

Travis shook his head slowly as he sank back into his seat. "If there wasn't a lady in the room, I'd call you much worse than an asshole, you know that."

"And I'd probably deserve it. Ask Nic here." He patted me on the shoulder.

"Damn…" Travis sighed. "I'll try to be glad for you, baby brother."

"And I'll try to be humble," Trent said, and they both laughed.

A slightly awkward silence descended for a minute, then Travis said, "What are your plans tomorrow?"

Trent chuckled. "She's having dinner with her ex, but if it's okay with you, I was hoping to spend Thanksgiving with my big brother."

"If you don't mind serving food to the homeless, we'd be happy to have you tag along."

"We?" Trent asked. "Who's we?"

"Me, a few faculty members, and any students who don't have plans. We spend the day helping out at a local shelter run by a friend of a friend, maybe play a little football at a nearby park after, then head back for drinks and desserts for those who still have energy. It's my year to host the pies and booze. My fridge is packed."

"Very cool, Teej," Trent said. "Count me in."

Suddenly two boys burst through the open doorway, a pretty teenage girl trailing behind at a more mature pace. Too young to be students. Travis leapt to his feet a second before the boys tackled him with hearty hugs.

"Carter, Bryce, Olivia?" Travis whispered, his voice gruff. "I didn't think…"

If the names didn't clue me in to the two boys' identity, their looks did. It was like looking in a time machine. Bryce was a good foot and a half shorter than both men, while Carter was just shy of his father's height, with long athletic limbs. The older boy's hair was darker, like his sister's, and they both shared the same forest-green eye color of their uncle, unlike Bryce, who had his father's storm cloud-eyes.

All three were so beautiful my heart hurt.

"Olivia." Travis held out his arms and the pretty dark-haired girl stepped forward into his much more gentle embrace.

"Grandma gave Mom hell," Bryce said before launching himself at Trent with a squeal. "Uncle Trent."

"Bryce, my man," Trent said, catching him in his arms.

There was no half hug for this kid. Trent lifted the boy off his feet with as much enthusiasm as was allowed in the small room. And with just as much enthusiasm, he introduced the kids to me.

I laughed, watching the exchange. Travis with his pride, and Trent... he obviously loved these kids with everything he had.

He should have his own kids. The thought made my stomach knot. It was the only thing I couldn't give him.

Carter shook his head, his hands on his hips. "Man, Mom's gonna shit when she finds out Uncle Trent's here." The grin on his face said he looked forward to seeing that moment.

"Carter, language," Travis said.

"She calls him The Enabler," Bryce said with a frown, while his sister just rolled her eyes. "Why?"

Trent laughed. "I'm totally The Enabler. It means I make things possible."

Travis frowned at his younger son. "I don't think Sam means it in a good way, Trent."

"Perspective, big brother." Trent tapped his head. "All in the way you think about it. Superpowers can be used for good or bad, right Bryce?"

The boy nodded.

Trent ruffled his hair. "Then I choose to use my powers for good." He looked at me with a grin. "If it's okay with Nic here, what say you we all have dinner together tonight? I would love for you boys to meet her son, Mark, and daughter, Brooke. I think Mark's gonna be an enabler someday too, just like both of you."

Travis gave me a sympathetic look. "If you had plans for this weekend, forget it. The Enabler just took over."

~

"Okay, give it to me," Trent said once we left Travis's office.

"Don't know what you're talking about."

Leading me to a bench under an almost naked oak tree, he pulled me onto his lap. "Talk, Nicki. I saw the sunbeams that light up your eyes dim the minute TJ's kids showed up. Tell me why."

I let out a long, slow breath and thought of a million reasons not to tell him the truth. But we'd been there before. And Trent deserved the truth, no matter where it led us.

"You love them." I stared down at the brick pavers under the bench, unable to watch his reaction to what I was about to say. What if he didn't want me anymore? What if this was the end? I couldn't go through that again.

He barked a short laugh. "Of course I do."

"But they're not yours and someday—"

"I see where this is going." He tipped my chin up until our eyes met. "We've been through this. What do you want me to say?"

"What if you change your mind?" I whispered the question I feared the most.

His eyebrows rose. "Did you?"

I nodded as a lone tear fell from my eye. "Now. I'm changing my mind now, but it's too late."

Trent caught the tear with his thumb, then pulled me

into his arms. "Oh, Nic. Just tell me what you want. We'll figure it out."

"Figure out what? This is impossible." I collapsed onto his shoulder sobbing. I hated crying, but Trent's strong arms and whispered assurances somehow made it better.

"Nothing is impossible. And I've been thinking—" He pulled back, wiping my tears with the sleeve of his soft sweater. "Damn, now I know why men carry handkerchiefs. I'm sucking at this chivalry thing."

"No you're not," I said with a laugh that dissolved into another sob.

He settled onto the bench, pulling my back against his chest. I closed my eyes, feeling the rise and fall of his breaths and the warmth of his body seeping through the layers of our clothes. Birds twittered in the branches above us. Across the quad, a group of girls giggled. If only I could freeze time.

"You know, I've been thinking."

"You said that." I snuggled deeper into his warmth.

"I did. See, I'm getting old. Repeating myself. Practically geriatric these days." He sighed. "I've decided to retire."

I sat up and turned to face him. "What?"

"This is my last season. I want to retire. This lifestyle doesn't work for me anymore. I'm exhausted, traveling all the time." His large hand cupped my chin and he smiled. "I said I've been thinking."

I shook my head. "That's some pretty serious thinking."

"Yeah, well, there you go. Sometimes I'm a serious guy. Like right now, with you."

"Trent..."

"I know." He searched my eyes. "I know it's been barely two months, and you've got a lot of shit to work out. But I want us—with or without kids, I don't give a damn—because I love you."

O'MALLEY'S WAS CROWDED with a combination of rambunctious students and locals, their voices filling the air with cheers and boos as they watched the football game broadcast on the multiple screens hanging above the bar.

It was a rowdy crowd, but I was pretty sure we had them beat. Both Travis and Trent were well lubricated with the local beer and seemed to be doing their best to out-embarrass each other with tales of their youth. At the moment it was all PG, but things were ramping up.

"Remember when Troy shaved your head," Travis said with a gleam in his eye I was beginning to recognize as a family trait.

"Don't fucking remind me." Trent glared as if it had happened yesterday, not decades ago.

"Tell us, Dad," Bryce yelled, bouncing in his seat.

Travis took a sip of beer and pointed to Trent. "Language. You lose a point for swearing."

Trent scoffed. "What points? When the hell did we start scoring points?"

"Right now," Travis said, then turned to the table with a triumphant smile. "Young Trent here decided to join the swim team. You were what, seven?"

"Six." Trent scowled into his own beer.

"Troy and I had him convinced all serious swimmers shaved *everywhere*." Travis grinned. "The previous year had been the summer Olympics. I remember Troy using that as an example."

"And I bought it," Trent grumbled, glowering at Travis,

before taking a large bite of burger. "I hadn't grown wise to their ways. Yet."

"You're not telling him not to talk with his mouth full," Mark pointed out helpfully.

"He's not my child," I replied.

Trent gave me a sloppy kiss on the cheek. "Thanks, Mom."

"Please wipe your mouth before you kiss me," I said while wiping a combination of burger grease and condiments off my face. "Now be quiet and let your brother speak."

"Thanks, honey." Travis gave me a wink. "So we ushered him into the bathroom with Dad's electric razor..." Travis burst out laughing, pointing at his brother while tears glistened in his eyes. "We have pictures somewhere."

"Funny. Ha. Ha." Trent pointed back at Travis with a dark expression that said his brother would regret telling that story. "Call my girl honey again and I'll show you funny."

"Uncle Trent doesn't scare us, does he?" Travis gave Carter a fist bump, ignoring his brother's threat.

"Needless to say, I showed up at the pool to find I was the only bald kid there." Trent paused to take a sip of beer. "Even by the start of school I still looked like I was headed for boot camp, all because of my evil brothers."

I bit my lips, trying to keep the laughter from bubbling out. "Didn't your mom say something?"

"Well, not really. She was used to us doing odd things. The previous winter I had her shave the Bears logo into the side of my head for team pride day," Trent said with a sheepish smile. "I didn't want her to know my brothers had fooled me, so I didn't say anything."

Brooke and I shared a look that spoke volumes on the subject of male egos.

"That's okay. I was patient. Eventually, I got this one back." Trent narrowed his eyes at his brother. "Remember the video recorder?"

"You wouldn't." Travis glared. "Not in front of the kids."

Trent gave his older brother a wicked grin that said he definitely would, even without Olivia and Carter egging him on. Over the course of dinner the quiet girl had started opening up, maybe with a bit of help from Brooke. Cynthia would be proud.

"Well, you see, sometimes being the youngest has its advantages. I tended to get forgotten. I know it's hard to believe, but I *was* small once, and quiet. I think I was around eight and TJ was about Carter's age. Don't worry. I'm keeping this story PG. Even though what I witnessed between Casanova here and his girlfriend wasn't." He grinned, his eyes sparkling with mischief.

"I was either quiet or they were so busy, they... um... didn't notice me."

"Angela Wilson," Travis said in a dreamy voice. "We were studying, kids."

"That's why your father's so smart," Trent commented. "Anyway, I grabbed the video camera, hid under a blanket, and recorded his little... ahem... study session. Let's just say the next home movie night was a *little* unexpected. The looks on Mom's and Dad's faces were priceless. It was worth the pummeling I got from both of them a week later."

"Both of them? That's not fair," Mark protested, glancing at Travis, before shoving a handful of fries in his mouth.

"Yeah, well, Troy just wanted to prevent Trent from invading his privacy," Travis explained.

"Point, me," Trent said with a smirk.

Travis grinned. "Should I tell the cat story?"

Trent glared. In the middle of the silence, Brooke asked, "So when are you gonna marry my mother?"

"Brooke," I gasped.

Travis laughed. "She's got you there."

Trent chuckled, raising a hand to stop me. "Straight to the point. I like you."

He patted the pockets of his hoodie while grinning. My heart slammed against my breastbone. My mouth dried. *He wouldn't, would he?*

"Damn. You know, this trip was a little last minute. Didn't have time to buy a ring." Trent kissed my hand while giving me a lingering gaze that spoke of love and promises and a long and happy future together. "Let's just say you'll be the second to know when that time comes."

My heart swelled with happiness as everyone cheered.

A few minutes later, the kids were having a lively debate over the desserts menu, and my heart still beat a little fast. All I could think of was how to get Trent alone. I had assigned him to Mark's double room, but the heated looks he'd been giving me all day, and his very public declaration, had me rethinking that decision.

It'd been a long day. I'd caught Mark yawning several times over the last few minutes. Maybe he'd go to bed early. He was a heavy sleeper. Trent could probably sneak back into the suite at some point.

Brooke's phone rang, silencing the table.

"It's Dad," she groaned.

"Answer it," I said, even though it was the last thing I wanted. "And be nice."

She sighed and put the phone to her ear. "Dad," she chirped while pasting on a plastic smile, then paused. "No. I'm having dinner with Mom. And Mark. And..." Brooke sent me and Trent a wicked smile that had my pulse racing. I made a quick slashing motion across my throat to halt the words I could imagine coming out of my mischievous daughter's mouth.

"Friends," she finished. She paused to listen. "O'Malley's, Dad. And no, you can't come. I don't want any drama." She rolled her eyes, her face set in a scowl as she listened.

Mark reached for his sister's phone, but she jerked it back, giving him a cold glare.

"Fine..." She sighed and hung up.

"Your Dad's here?" I asked. He wasn't supposed to arrive until tomorrow.

"Yep." Brooke's lips twisted into something unpleasant.

"Did he mention his plans?"

"Not really." She pulled the dessert menu from her brother's hands. "Sorry, Mark. You're having ice cream at Lick's. Dad's picking us up out front in ten."

"What?" Mark's mouth dropped open. "Who wants ice cream when it's cold outside?"

Brooke's frown deepened, but I interrupted her response. "You can get a hot fudge sundae."

Mark sent me a look that revealed his opinion of that idea.

"Come on, sport." Brooke sighed and stood. "Nice to meet everyone. Professor Richards, it's been... interesting."

"And confidential," Travis said. "Everything said at this table, stays at this table."

"I won't remember anything once I walk out that door,"

my daughter said with a wave of her fingers, and then both of my kids walked away.

"Make sure your dad drives you back to the hotel," I called to Mark. "You have your key?"

He nodded sullenly and followed Brooke out the door.

"You know, I'm really full. And tired." Trent let out a fake yawn and sent me a look that threatened to have my panties bursting into flames. "I think we're going to head back to the hotel."

"Time to study?" Travis smirked.

"You bet." Trent dropped a stack of bills on the table and pulled me from my chair. "I need to compete with my older brother."

CHAPTER
THIRTY-TWO

Our lips fused together in a hungry kiss while Trent guided me through the entryway of my hotel room. Then pressed me against the wood-paneled door with his warm body, his hand at the back of my head to cushion it from the hard surface. The click of the dead bolt engaging filled the silent suite, and a small voice in my head wondered just how many times he'd performed that deft move. How many women had he taken to hotel rooms over the past decades?

He broke the kiss and stalked across the darkened suite, flipping the lock to Mark's adjoining room.

"You're thinking too much, Nic," he said, tossing his leather jacket onto the sofa and striding back to me.

"You just locked my son out of the suite," I said, choosing to keep my thoughts of other women to myself. He'd accepted my history with Gabriel—Garrett—I had to do likewise.

"You'd prefer he walk in on us?" Trent tugged on my hand, guiding me in the direction of the bedroom. "Your son has a key to his room. And if he knocks, we'll let him in."

I sent one last look toward Mark's door as doubts swirled in my head. *Should we really be doing this now?* The brisk walk back to the hotel had given me time to think logically. Derek probably wouldn't stick around long after they were done eating. Without me, the conversation between him and the kids had always been stilted.

Trent tugged off his sweater and glanced at his watch. "Relax, sweetheart. Lick's is on the other side of the square. And they're probably packed."

"I hope so." I let out a quiet whimper as Trent kissed me again, silencing the responsible voice in my head. I didn't want to stop, but I didn't want to be interrupted either.

"I need you." He groaned, his lips finding a particularly sensitive spot on my neck as his chilly hands slipped under my sweater. "I don't want to make this too quick, so stop talking."

"Trent," I sighed, every reservation vanishing with the next hungry kiss. My blood heated in my veins; the anticipation of this moment had kept me on a knife's edge all day.

"Shhh," he whispered, walking me backward through the door into my bedroom. "No time to talk."

"Mm-hmm," I agreed as he unzipped my jacket, yanking it off without finesse.

"Need to be inside you." He fumbled with the hem of my top for a second, gathering the knit fabric in his impatient hands.

"Oof, wait," I giggled as the neck of my sweater snagged on my chin. In his haste he was about to take my ears off. I backed up, my fingers working to unsnag my necklace that somehow got hooked into the open weave, without much luck.

"For fuck's sake, let me." He stepped forward to untangle the pendant in the dim light coming from the bathroom. Once freed, he tossed my sweater onto the dresser.

"Red," he breathed out the word, and I glanced down at the red bra I chose this morning because it matched my sweater. Trent flashed me an approving grin before tugging his T-shirt over his head. "I love you in red."

"I'm aware." I grinned back while teasing my thumb across the scalloped edge of my lace bra.

He sank down on the edge of the mattress. "Undress for me, Nic."

I flicked open the button on my jeans and dragged the zipper down with as much sex appeal as the few inches of teeth would allow. I'd never performed a striptease before, but Trent's hooded gaze was all the encouragement I needed.

Maybe too much encouragement.

I wrestled my skinny jeans down over my hips and then down my thighs. The fabric bunched at my knees, refusing to slide any lower. I might have wanted to take my boots off first. *So much for sexy.*

The next moment my balance deserted me and my ass hit the soft carpet with an undignified thud. Trent laughed, and I threw my hands up to cover my embarrassment.

"Need some help, sweetheart?" He peeled my fingers from my face, his amusement obvious.

I let out a pitiful sigh. "I guess sexy isn't my thing."

He knelt down to unzip my boot and then tugged it off with a chuckle. "Sexy is definitely your thing."

"Really?" I asked, watching him remove the other boot,

then drag my jeans down my legs. "Which part was the sexiest, the struggling or the falling?"

He guided my leg over his shoulder and kissed the inside of my thigh. "The on-the-floor part."

"I think that's a really good part," I said, and then gasped as Trent traced the center of my panties with his nose. Heat flooded my core, and my body clenched with the need for him to fill me.

"You smell so fucking good." Trent groaned, and then stood. "I wish I had time to do everything I want to you, but..."

"We don't," I finished while watching him undress with brisk efficiency.

Then he dropped back to his knees and dragged my panties down my legs.

"Oh, fuck. Just a quick taste," he said before burying his face between my thighs. "Missed you so much..."

He mumbled out a curse and something about dessert in between licks that had me spiraling.

"Time," I gasped out. "If you want more than this..."

Trent dragged his teeth across my clit, and I lost my train of thought in the spiral of pleasure he was giving me.

"How long?" he whispered before doing it again.

"Brooke's slower, but Mark... not long," I managed to get out before letting my head fall back with a whimper. The things this man could do with his mouth...

Trent's chuckle vibrated against my sensitive flesh. "Not them. You. How close?"

"Oh... *oh*," I screamed as my orgasm crested, sending pleasure all the way to my fingertips.

Before I could catch my breath, his hands cupped my bottom and he lifted me to him. I wrapped my limp legs around his waist a second before he thrusted all the way in, making me cry out again.

"Next time I promise this will last for days."

His words were a promise and a warning as he steadied my hips and then pistoned forward with a punishing thrust. And then another and another. My body stirred with pleasure as another orgasm built. His tempo was far from gentle, but at the moment I didn't want gentle. I needed this exquisite pain to prove this was real and not another dream. I needed to feel him when I woke, alone in the middle of the night. I needed to feel him with me tomorrow when we parted for the day. He off to his brother's, and I to spend the day making nice to Derek.

"Tighten your legs around me, sweetheart," Trent whispered, then kissed me hard and deep with the flavor of my pleasure on his lips and tongue.

His hands clamped around my hips as he shifted the angle of his thrusts. My head tipped back and my eyes closed, my orgasm teasingly close.

Trent's lips brushed mine. "Open your eyes. I need to see you come."

I need you. The thought should have scared me, but it didn't. And neither did the intensity of the emotions reflected in his eyes, or the trembling of his body.

I gasped his name and he shouted mine as both of our orgasms crashed together.

"I love you," I panted out on a shuddered breath, knowing no matter how many times I shattered, Trent would always be there to put my pieces back together again.

THIRTY-THREE

I woke to the sun streaming through the sheer bedroom curtains and the smell of coffee wafting through my hotel room. Male voices rumbled in the suite next door, along with their laughter. The door to the suite was closed, but I clasped the sheet to my naked chest on instinct. It had been years since the kids had barged into my bedroom, but I wasn't about to take the chance.

I moved to sit up, wincing at the reminder of last night. Then smiled. If that was make-up sex, Trent and I should argue more often.

After a long hot shower, I dressed and then slipped into the suite as discreetly as possible so as not to disturb the male bonding happening on the sofa. Mark and Trent sat side by side, one dark head, one light. Trent's shoulders were several inches broader than my son's, but they were close in height. The Macy's Thanksgiving Day parade played out on the TV. Mark had always loved parades, and we'd often seen this one in person.

My son's focus remained on the giant balloons floating down Sixth Avenue, but Trent turned as if he could sense me standing in the doorway. He followed my every step like a predator, his smug grin doing a better job of heating me than the steaming coffee waiting in the pot.

"Hey, beautiful," he called out, and Mark turned, a wide smile of his own spread across his face.

"Hey, Mom. How was your night?"

A knock at the door saved me from answering my son. Before he'd returned, Trent had tucked me in bed and I'd fallen asleep—and I assumed Trent migrated to his and Mark's room.

Brooke stood in the doorway, her cheeks ruddy from the cold and her hair still damp from her shower. Her eyes zeroed in on Mark and narrowed.

"Hey, sport, you tell Mom about last night?" She turned to me, eyebrows raised.

I shook my head and glanced at my son. "I just woke up," I replied. "Tell me what?"

Mark turned back to the TV. "She was in bed when I got back. Now *you* can tell her."

"Nice." Brooke shook her head and growled while rummaging through the fridge, then pulling out an orange juice. "Make me do the dirty work."

"What dirty work?" I poured a cup of coffee while frowning.

"You're older." Mark grinned over the back of the sofa at his sister. "And smarter."

Brooke turned toward me and rolled her eyes. "You might want to sit down."

I let out a lungful of air, shaking my head. "I'm getting tired of people telling me that. What's going on?"

My gaze narrowed in on my son. His shoulders hunched as he returned his focus on the TV. Trent shrugged. Obviously whatever happened Mark hadn't shared it with him.

"What did he do?" I shifted my attention back to my daughter. "What did your brother do?"

"Not Mark. Dad." Brooke scowled while glancing at Trent. "I don't get him, Mom. This was supposed to be a nice family holiday, but—"

"Please tell me what's going on," I interrupted, a cold dread sinking in my stomach.

"You know... I'm just gonna step out." Trent gave my shoulder a squeeze, and then headed out the door.

"Sorry, Mom," Brooke said, and turned. "Hey, asshole. Get over here. I'm not doing this alone."

Mark slunk over, his eyes on his feet. "I'm here. Now tell her."

I huffed. "If someone doesn't tell me something in the next two seconds, I'm gonna lose it."

"Dad brought Patty," Brooke said with a sigh.

"Oh. Well, that's..." I closed my eyes and counted to ten. *Stay calm.* Brooke and Mark needed a mature role model, not the screaming lunatic that threatened to take over at the moment. "Hmm. That's interesting. What does he plan on doing with her?"

I had a good idea what he'd done with her already, but hell would freeze over before I sat at a table with the woman who destroyed my marriage.

"Plan?" Brooke frowned at me.

"Thanksgiving." This was supposed to be a family dinner. Patty Sullivan was definitely not family. "She's not coming, is she? Hang on..."

Grabbing the hotel phone, I confirmed with the concierge what I had suspected, hoped, wished, whatever. There was no way I could sit at a table with that woman. Luckily, the dining room was full.

I dug my cell phone out of my pocket and dialed the

bastard, doing my best to keep the smugness out of my voice.

"Derek?" I laughed quietly into the phone. Okay, maybe there was a little smugness. "The kids just told me you added a plus one for dinner tonight."

Trent peeked around the door, a concerned look on his face. I waved him in just as my husband answered.

The other end of the line was silent.

Trent's eyes narrowed on me and I shrugged, waiting for my husband to find his voice. He was still on the line, I could hear his breath gusting across the speaker.

I stepped away, turning my back on my family's expectants stares.

"Derek?" I singsonged. "Say something."

"Patty's mother died last month. Her kids are with her ex-husband. I thought—"

I could almost picture his eye twitching. "Cut the bull-shit, Derek. I'm not stupid."

He sighed. "I invited her. I'm not uninviting her. What do you want me to say?"

The fucking truth would be nice, but it was a bit late for that. "This isn't going to work. The dining room is full, and unless there's a cancellation... hold on."

I put my phone on mute and turned toward my kids. "Unless you want to have dinner with your father and Patty?"

Both of my children shouted, "No."

"I'll eat out of the vending machine at the dorm first," Brooke blurted while Mark said, "I'm not having Thanks-giving dinner without you, Mom."

"Nope, sorry, Derek. I guess she'll be having room service. Maybe you could bring her leftovers."

Derek had the nerve to huff. "Really, Nicki? That's a bit uncalled for."

"No. Inviting your girlfriend to our Thanksgiving dinner at the last minute is uncalled for," I said, then waited for a response. "Admit it, Derek. No more bullshit. Let's just get everything out in the open."

"She's not my girlfriend."

I burst out laughing. Did he really think I was that gullible?

"Invite everyone to TJ's thing," Trent whispered in my ear once I recovered.

I spun around, my eyes widening. He gave me an encouraging nod. I shook my head and mouthed, *No way*.

Brooke's eyes went horror-film wide. "No. No. No. Absolutely not."

Trent motioned to Brooke and the two wandered a few feet away. Far enough away I couldn't make out what they were saying over Derek's rambling in my ear, but whatever it was had my daughter gesturing wildly.

"What's going on?" Derek asked.

"Not sure," I replied, my attention split between the phone call and what was happening in the room.

My daughter scowled. "Fine. Whatever. It's only my life at stake here."

Trent chuckled. "Invite Derek, Nic."

Brooke stomped away and flopped down on the sofa next to her brother. "But if anyone misbehaves, I'm never speaking to any of you again."

"Who the fuck are you talking to?" Derek barked in my ear.

"A friend. A man friend," I stumbled.

Trent chuckled. But what did a forty-three-year-old woman call the man she was sleeping with? Boyfriend sounded so teenager-ish. Not that man friend was any better. "Not that it's any of your business. But he has a solution to our problem. If you're interested."

"This is either going to be a complete disaster, or interesting. Or... both," I muttered from the middle back seat of our hired SUV that had driven us to Serenity House.

"Positive thoughts," Trent whispered in my ear before exiting from the passenger side.

I followed him out while Mark got out on the driver's side of the back seat and made his way around the front of the vehicle toward the sidewalk.

Brooke sat in front, and was currently finishing up her conversation with Thad, the driver—also a Harvard student, and a handsome one—about some campus event. I sensed Thad had been waiting for this moment to talk to my daughter without an audience.

"Yeah, Mom. Positive thoughts," Mark repeated while skirting past me and Trent.

At least someone was eager. The same couldn't be said for Brooke, whose wide smile vanished the second she got out of the car.

She'd lectured us numerous times on behaving ourselves since my phone call with her father this morning. At the moment she had stalled, her hand on the open car door, as if she was contemplating climbing back in. I wouldn't blame her.

"It's going to be fine," I said with way more confidence than I felt. Derek wouldn't dream of causing a scene here. Not with the Boston Daily reporter due to show up for the photo op Derek's team had arranged.

All it had taken for my soon-to-be ex to agree to this crazy plan was to suggest he invite the press. Nothing elaborate, nothing disruptive, of course. But what better way of showing the public our divorce was amicable than to give them a picture of us spending Thanksgiving together helping those less fortunate.

Trent once again voiced his promise to behave. Brooke hesitated a second longer, but then followed her brother up the aging concrete walk that led to the stout brick building that was our destination.

Once my kids were out of earshot, Trent added, "At least while the cameras are rolling, I promise to behave. After..."

I sent him a warning glare. Over the past couple of months Trent had threatened everything from bodily harm to thanking Derek for leaving me. Neither of those things would get Derek to forgive me for the whole Garrett MacKenzie fiasco.

Not that I was completely at fault for the mess caused by our pool boy turned con man. At least not one hundred percent at fault. But whatever...

"Joking." Trent offered me a reassuring smile and then took my hand, pulling me forward.

I gave a quick scan of our surroundings. Wouldn't do for anyone to witness Trent and I holding hands, but at the moment the street was quiet.

"Here they are," Travis called out the minute we walked in the door.

He was accompanied by an older man who resembled Santa Claus, if St. Nick were wearing blue jeans and a flannel shirt. Derek stood on the other side of the jolly fellow wearing his usual man-of-the-people uniform of pressed tan khakis and a blue oxford shirt with the top two buttons undone revealing a white cotton undershirt.

A handful of people shuffled around the large, rectangular room that was crammed tight with tables. A few volunteers laid down tablecloths in a variety of autumnal colors. Mark made a beeline toward Olivia, who was setting decorative pumpkins and small flower arrangements on the tables, while Brooke looked to be in serious conference with a few girls.

The place smelled delicious. Turkey and sage and onion and yeasty bread. My stomach growled despite my sudden onset of nerves.

Patty strode through a doorway on the far side of the room, then paused, her gaze shifting from me to Trent and back with a look of disgust I was more than familiar with. I dropped Trent's hand and wiped the moisture from my palms on the sides of my jeans.

Ever since Brooke tipped me off to her father's relationship with his much younger campaign manager, I tried to envision them together and failed. Patty Sullivan was the complete opposite of me in every way. A petite thing with long dark hair, warm brown eyes, and a curvy figure. She also had a sharp tongue and a mercurial temper. I remember her being warned early on not to scare off the volunteers. Derek kept her on only for her keen sense of voters' attitudes and her superior organizational skills—or so I'd thought.

Obviously, I was wrong.

Trent bumped me with his shoulder and offered a smile. "It's going to be fine. I'm here for you whatever happens."

His assurance was only mildly reassuring. I was sure Patty had Derek's—and his career's—best interest at heart, but the woman could be unpredictable. *Better keep tabs on the sharp utensils.*

"Uncle Trent," Bryce called out, and then we were ambushed by the exuberance of Travis's youngest.

"Dad, Uncle Trent's here!" he announced to the room.

"Easy, Bryce," Travis instructed, wandering over, a grin on his face while pulling his son off his brother. "Don't hurt your uncle."

He gave Trent one of those one-armed hugs and a smack on his back, then offered a slightly less violent hug for me that had Trent growling.

"I want to be on your team, Uncle Trent," the boy shouted.

"You got it, pal." Trent laughed, giving his nephew a fist bump.

"He's on my team." Carter narrowed his eyes at his brother in challenge.

"He's on my team," some guy shouted from the far end of the room.

"I seem to be on everyone's team." Trent gave his brother a slightly confused smile. "What are we talking about?"

"Football," both Carter and Bryce yelled.

"Later," Travis directed at his boys, then turned to us. "Let me introduce you to Les."

Les Norton turned out to be as jolly as the famous man he resembled. He even had the red suit, and planned on donning it later for the children.

"May as well put this big belly and beard to good use," he said while patting the former.

"Derek," I said, pasting on a smile and introducing him to the handsome man standing next to me. Derek stared at

Trent's hand for a moment as if he'd offered him a handful of shit, before shaking it.

"And this is Patty Sullivan," Derek said.

At some point she'd wandered over to our little group, looking smug and ridiculous in a cream-colored bodycon dress and four-inch heels. Obviously Derek hadn't advised her on what to wear. Or maybe he had, and this outfit was intentional.

"Nice to see you." I practically choked on the words, but years of dealing with unpleasant people had prepared me for these situations. *Well, maybe not this situation.*

"You look familiar," Derek remarked, his brows drawn into an arrogant scowl while giving Trent a thorough inspection.

"My brother was in the NBA. Played point guard for Boston, LA, and Chicago before taking a coaching position in the Windy City," Travis supplied, throwing an arm over his brother's shoulder.

"And you're Nic's soon-to-be ex." Trent's eyes sparkled and his grin was off the charts. "I'd like to personally thank you for your contribution to my happiness. You're doing a fine job for us citizens of Illinois."

Derek narrowed his eyes at me and mouthed, *Nic?* I shrugged.

Probably sensing the tension, Les clapped his hands together and said, "If you'll follow me, we'll get your coats hung up, grab some aprons, and I'll assign you your stations."

CHAPTER
THIRTY-FOUR

After standing on my feet, dishing out food for the past few hours I should have been tired, but I wasn't. It had been invigorating. I'd always enjoyed volunteering, talking to people whose life experiences and viewpoints were different than mine.

It didn't hurt that Patty was sporting a bright pink smear of cranberry sauce on the bodice of her dress. *Not my doing, I swear.*

Or that *somehow* Derek ended up sandwiched between Trent and Travis in what Les called the chow line. A surprising number of people recognized Trent from the time he'd played for the Celtics. And Travis was more than happy to be his brother's cheerleader, spouting his stats and accomplishments. I could almost feel Derek's annoyance grow every time someone asked Trent to pose for a selfie, which he was more than happy to do.

After an amazing turkey dinner provided by our host, we'd made our way to a park a few blocks away. Haphazard teams were assembled with Trent as captain on one side and Travis on the other. Everyone agreed putting both brothers on the same team would give them an unfair advantage.

Watching them play, I had to agree. At the moment, Bryce was clinging to his uncle's back, while Carter made a grab for his legs. Somehow he still made it to the end zone, where an argument ensued over the play. Travis's team thought the ball stopped when Trent was tackled. Trent was accusing the boys of holding and unnecessary roughness. Two things I would have known nothing about before meeting Trent.

I took a deep breath of the crisp fall air mixed with sandalwood and amber from Trent's sweater, along with the faint, lingering scent of the sage and onion dressing he'd been serving. As soon as we'd arrived at the park, he'd shucked off the fisherman's knit, handing it to me for safekeeping. I was doing my best not to bury my face into the still slightly warm wool, but the temptation was strong.

I gave a loud cheer from the sidelines, where I insisted on staying. I was well aware of my abilities, and they didn't stretch as far as football.

The same couldn't be said for Derek. Although I had to give him an A for effort. His khakis were destined for the trash, and the shoulder of his coat was sporting a gaping tear. I almost felt sorry for him, but his wide smile said he was enjoying himself.

"Enough, Scooter," Travis yelled at his brother when his touchdown celebration stretched on too long. "Get back in the damn game, you strutting peacock."

I shivered in my long wool coat as Trent jogged back to his side of the field, accepting high-fives and fist bumps along the way. Just the sight of his exposed skin and thin T-shirt was making me cold.

A thick layer of angry-looking clouds blanketed the sky,

causing the field's lights to turn on. The earlier sun was gone. A brisk wind swirled dead leaves into the sky, along with a few flakes of snow.

Patty shivered a few feet away. A more charitable person might have offered her Trent's sweater, but all my charity had been used up earlier.

Travis drew his arm back and rocketed the ball across the field straight into Mark's hands.

"Go. Go. Go," I screamed, jumping up and down until my son crossed the imaginary line into the end zone.

"You've moved on fast," Patty muttered. "Two men in how many months? Or is it three? I can't tell which of the brothers want you more. Maybe you've had both?"

Ignore her, a quiet voice told me, but I disregarded the voice of wisdom as angry heat bloomed under my skin. "At least none of them are married."

Her sharp laughter grated on my nerves. Involuntarily, I balled my fists. I'd never punched someone in my life, but I was willing to give it a go.

"Whatever you need to tell yourself to sleep at night. Although... I'm thinking you're not doing a lot of sleeping these days."

I turned to face her, giving her a narrow look. "You're one to talk. You fucked my husband."

Nearby, a woman gasped, reminding me we were far from alone. I took a deep breath and silently ordered myself to cool down. *She's not worth the frustration.*

"I haven't a clue what you're talking about," she said with a smirk.

I scoffed. *Please...*

Before I had a chance to come up with a suitable response to her hilarious attempt at innocence, the sparse sideline crowd burst out in laughter, and I watched as Trent broke away from his brother's hold and ran into the end zone. Everyone cheered as he made the final touchdown, and victory, for his team. I smiled and clapped, then turned back to Patty.

"You know what they say. Once a cheater always a cheater... and Derek's a really good cheater. You won't even see it coming," I said, and then walked away, heading toward the field of celebrating players without a backward glance.

TRENT RAN UP TO ME, eyes bright and cheeks flushed from exercise and the chilly autumn air, his exuberance making me disregard Patty's unpleasant words.

"God, that was fun. Did you see me?" He bounced alongside me, a grin stretched across his face.

I brushed at the few flakes of snow that hadn't melted in his damp hair. At some point during the game it had started to snow. Flurries at first, but now it was coming down in earnest.

"Of course I saw you." I offered him back his sweater, but he waved it off.

"Keep it. I'm hot."

I couldn't agree more. The man was pure sex appeal with his damp hair falling over his forehead and his under-shirt clinging to his sweaty chest.

"You were fun to watch." I refolded his sweater and hugged it to my chest like a teenager in possession of her boyfriend's letterman jacket.

Trent breathed on his knuckles, then buffed them on his jeans. "I still got it, although I might be grabbing the ibuprofen later."

The younger players lingered on the field, tossing the ball back and forth. I watched Brooke stiffen as her father approached, Patty trailing behind like an eager puppy. Derek shouted to Mark, and a second later, our son wandered toward the group, dragging his feet every step of the way. It conjured up a memory of a much younger Mark, reluctant to return home after a day spent with his little buddies at the park.

I had hoped at some point Derek and I could bury our grievances and, at least for the kids' sake, maintain a cordial relationship. But as long as Patty Sullivan was a fixture in his life, I couldn't see it happening.

A moment later the kids sprinted off toward their friends and Derek headed our way. *Suppose I should stop touching Trent.* But it was too late. They'd already seen us, and I couldn't muster up the will to care anymore.

"We're leaving," Derek said to me, then turned to Trent. "Thank you for inviting us. It was a lot of fun."

The expression on Patty's face said she didn't share Derek's sentiment. *Too bad.*

"Thank my brother. He arranged all this," Trent replied. Derek turned his gaze toward the field, probably in search of Travis, but Trent added, "He ran home to set up dessert."

"Then tell him thanks for me," Derek said while Patty huddled deeper into her flimsy but fashionable trench coat.

"You're not coming back for pie?" I asked. "From what I hear, Travis is putting out quite the spread."

I mentally patted myself on the back for not choking on my words. *I'd almost think you want them to stay.*

"Have to head back to DC. I've a meeting first thing in the morning. Our car is waiting." Derek motioned toward a big black SUV idling at the curb halfway down the block and then turned back to face us. "Good to meet you, Trent."

The two exchanged pleasantries and shook hands. Then Derek and Patty headed toward the waiting car. I couldn't help but grin as I watched her heels totter over the uneven ground.

"Is it wrong to be hoping she turns an ankle in those shoes?"

"She's a piece of work." Trent laughed. "I probably shouldn't tell you what she said to me earlier."

"Mom, Mom..." Before I could inquire further Mark ran up, just as bright-eyed and glowing as Trent. "Can we keep playing? They're about to start another game."

"Okay. Just..." What was I gonna say? Be careful? Don't stay out too late? He wasn't a little boy anymore. In a year and a half he'd be off to college himself. "Have fun."

He gave Trent an expectant look.

Trent held up his hands. "I'm toast, man."

Mark laughed and ran off, joining his sister and Travis's kids amid whoops and hollering and we headed in the opposite direction.

I kicked at the growing layer of fluffy white snow on the sidewalk. In the last few minutes the light flurries had increased to huge white flakes that were quickly accumulating on the ground. You could still make out Travis's footprints, along with the others who'd left before us, but just barely. My tennis shoes weren't quite as bad as Patty's heels, but the cold had started penetrating the flimsy fabric, and the rubber soles did little as far as traction.

Once Mark was out of earshot, I returned to our previous conversation. "Okay, spill it. What did Patty say?" When Trent hesitated, I added, "You can't drop a bomb like that and expect me to forget it."

His breath fogged the air. "You're not going to like it."

I gestured for him to go on.

"She tried to slip me her business card. Said basically I was wasting my time with someone your age, and when I wanted something fresher, I should give her a call."

"I'll kill her." I spun around intending to head back to the park. Not that she was there anymore. But before I could think through the haze of anger and realize as much, my feet slid out from under me. Everything slowed. Naked tree branches stretched across the leaden sky above me. A giant snowflake landed in my eye, blurring my vision with its icy wetness. I pinwheeled my arms in an attempt to regain my balance.

Trent's arms tightened around my waist, steadying me. "Easy, tiger."

"And that bitch called *me* a whore? Not in so many words, but..." I let out a primal scream.

"Shit." Trent looked around, but everyone in front of us had disappeared in the haze of snow. Grabbing my hand, he pulled me behind a large oak on the parkway. "Fuck her, Nic. Her opinion doesn't matter."

I tugged at the front of Trent's T-shirt, dragging him closer. "I'd rather, um, fuck you, Mr. Sexy Football Man."

Trent's eyes danced, his lips lifting into a wicked grin. "You think I'm sexy?"

He brushed at the snow that collected on my eyelashes, then his fingers trailed down my cold cheeks a second before he pressed his warm lips to mine. The icy wind and snow vanished as our bodies fit together. Trent's tongue tangled with mine while he slipped his hand inside my coat.

I sifted my fingers through his thick hair liberally sprinkled with snow, and warm and damp from his exertions, as his fingers found their way under my sweater. A naughty thrill flamed inside me, leaving me just as warm and wet.

Here in this upper-class neighborhood, with only the haze of snowflakes shielding us from the houses, anyone could walk upon us.

I didn't care anymore. My only thought was of Trent's chilled hands exploring my warm skin, and the heat of his thick thigh pressing between mine. I gasped as he tweaked my already hard nipple, sending jolts of desire to my core. Visions of him taking me against this tree flashed through my mind.

"Come on, before we get arrested." Slipping his arm around my waist to steady me, he pulled me back onto the sidewalk at a reckless pace.

I contemplated calling for a ride back to the hotel, where Trent and I could enjoy a few uninterrupted hours alone and naked. But as nice as that fantasy was, my kids wouldn't stay at the park forever, and somewhere up ahead, Travis was expecting us.

Trent guided me up a short sidewalk that led to a stately brick colonial with pretty mullioned windows flanked by raised panel shutters painted a dark navy blue. Travis's home, I presumed.

Trent pressed a finger to his lips before easing open his brother's sunny-yellow front door. I got a quick glimpse of a small foyer. High ceilings and scarred wood floors. A large hall tree dominated the wall to my left, its wood barely visible under an assortment of coats. To my right was a wide doorway into what looked like a formal living room. The muffled sounds of conversation and laughter came from somewhere in the back of the house. *Travis's guests.*

Trent tugged me past the coats and then made a left down a short, dark hallway. "Trent..."

"Shhh." This time he put his finger to *my* lips while giving me a devilish grin.

A tiny powder room stood at the end of the hall. Trent ushered me in and closed the door behind him.

Wide-eyed, I turned to face Trent as the click of the lock broke the silence. Before I could make a sound he crushed his lips against mine in a demanding kiss that consisted of tongues and teeth. Light on finesse but heavy on intention.

My coat hit the floor, and then he shoved my sweater over my head. His attention shifted to my jeans while I fumbled with his fly with cold, numb fingers.

He tugged the waistband of my pants past my hips and boosted me onto the tiny pedestal sink. My shoes hit the floor with a too-loud thud and my jeans followed.

"We'll have to be quick," Trent whispered, taking over my failed attempts at his zipper.

"Um-huh." I nodded my agreement and then reached into his boxers. He swore through gritted teeth as my icy hands touched his oh-so-hard and heated flesh. Before he could voice his complaints, I tugged him out of his underwear and gave him a firm stroke.

He yanked my panties to the side and we both guided his crown against my folds. Then he impaled me with enough violence to make me squeak. The warmth of his hands burned my skin as he guided my legs around his waist, then pistoned his hips forward until our bodies met.

I fell back, my head hitting the mirror with a loud thud that had us both giggling.

"Shhhh, woman," he snapped while looking over his shoulder at the door.

"Sorry." I giggled again, then gasped against his shoulder as he thrusted forward.

Trent bent down and captured my lace-covered nipple between his lips. I leaned back, slower this time, until my head rested against the mirror again. I felt filthy in the best

367

way possible. Practically naked in a strange bathroom, legs spread, the man I loved between my thighs, fucking me with abandon. Where had that prim and proper senator's wife gone?

Wherever, I was glad of her demise.

"Two weeks. Two fucking weeks until I can be inside you again," he said while delivering long, measured strokes, alternating between slow and gentle, then fast and hard, that had us both gasping for breath.

A bead of sweat rolled down my spine as pleasure coiled tight in my core. I was so close.

"Me too, sweetheart," Trent murmured, making me realize I'd said those words out loud.

The dainty pedestal sink creaked under me with the force of Trent's thrusts. Travis would kill both of us if we broke it.

A knock sounded on the door behind us and we both froze. Trent covered my mouth with one hand while reaching behind me to turn on the water. My eyes widened in surprise as a blast of chilly wetness soaked into the back of my panties for a second, before Trent lowered the pressure of the tap.

"Just a minute," he called out to whoever was on the other side of the door, his eyebrows raised in question. I nodded under his hand.

"Touch me," I whispered.

He slipped his hand between us, his digits finding my clit. I tightened around him as he slowed his pace, keeping the creaks from the sink beneath me to a minimum.

"Come for me, sweetheart," he whispered against my lips, his thumb pressing circles hard against my sensitive flesh.

I gasped as my body exploded into a million pieces

around him, while sinking my teeth into the soft cotton of his T-shirt to muffle my scream. Trent issued a guttural sound of his own as his release followed mine, filling me with liquid heat.

His dark green eyes locked onto mine and he kissed me, soft and sweet this time. "God help me, Nic. I love you."

"I love you, too," I whispered back as happy tears welled in my eyes.

Knuckles rapped on the door again. This time harder. I groaned against Trent's shoulder, praying for my knees to stop wobbling. Praying it wasn't one of my kids on the other side of the door.

"Keep your pants on, man," Trent yelled, and then dragged a washcloth under the faucet before turning off the water. "There's a bathroom upstairs. Third door on the right if you're desperate."

We froze for a second, for a response, but all was quiet.

"Sorry," Trent whispered. "Didn't mean to yell. Persistent asshole."

Before I could protest, he had the washcloth between my legs. I blushed, my face burning with embarrassment at the intimacy, which was stupid after what we just did. But somehow this was more.

"Best clear out before someone else knocks," he whispered, his eyes tender. He set me back on my feet and handed me my sweater and jeans.

I dressed quickly, or at least as quick as I could in less than twenty square feet of floor space shared with a six-foot-five man, a toilet, and a sink.

"You're a little wrinkled, not that anyone will notice."

Embarrassment forgotten, my heart warmed at the sight of his boyish grin and deep dimples.

Then I turned around and groaned at the image staring

back at me from the mirror. *No one will notice?* Makeup smeared, lipstick gone, my hair... like hell no one would notice.

Cynthia would be proud.

Trent gave me one last kiss and then opened the door. He laughed.

Travis glared back at us from the darkened hall. His posture tense, his arms crossed, he heaved a heavy sigh and shook his head.

"Better, you two?" He raised an eyebrow, his stern expression at odds with his shaking shoulders. He pressed his lips together, while the corners of his mouth quirked up.

"Her, um..." Trent waved a hand toward me.

"Something in my eye." I nodded like a fool.

"Yeah." Trent said, "Bug," at the same time I said, "Dirt."

Travis laughed. "Dirty bugs. Gotta watch out for them. Real loud bastards. Can hear them thumping around all the way in the kitchen."

As I walked away with what was left of my dignity—which wasn't much—Trent growled, "Were you listening, you fucking pervert?"

The dull thud of a fist meeting flesh and a muffled curse sounded from somewhere behind me just before I turned the corner. *Boys...*

CHAPTER
THIRTY-FIVE

The office quieted down in the weeks leading up to Christmas. We had few closings scheduled and even fewer showings.

"The rich are off celebrating their wealth at this time of year," Cynthia informed me the Monday after I'd gotten back from Cambridge. "Things will ramp up in January. Until then, have fun. I know I will."

To say my boss had a thing for Christmas would be like saying snowmen had a thing for the carrots. The woman was certifiable. Every bare inch of the office sparkled, blinked, or glittered, as if manic elves had thrown up all over the place.

Small presents, ornately wrapped, appeared on my desk at random every few days, unmarked, but I knew exactly who they had come from. It wasn't like anyone else in the office would be gifting me a Limoges box or a Montblanc pen—almost identical to my lawyers save the engraving.

Derek had been a man of his word, and our court date was set for the second week in January. He'd also increased my allowance enough that the next few weeks would be comfortable—not comfortable enough to be handing out expensive pens, but enough to pay the ever-increasing gas bill.

The weather had turned frigid shortly after returning from Cambridge, and we'd received a thick layer of lake-effect snow that promised to stick around for the upcoming holidays. Inside the house, it was warm and toasty with the heavenly scent of Rosa's Christmas cookies perfuming the kitchen.

If I learned anything over the past few months, a house this size could not function without a housekeeper. Rosa was irreplaceable, and I'd assured her she would be staying on even after we moved.

Both Mark and I agreed it was time to move. Every time I walked into the kitchen my eyes went straight to the patio door, sure I would see the ghost of Garrett MacKenzie staring back at me.

I received a call from Officer Charles Archambault of the Terrebonne Parish Sheriff's office, Detective Jackson had told me just a few days ago. *They've found Garrett MacKenzie aka Gabriel Roth.*

The man who'd cleaned my pool for the last five years was dead—shot in the head and then dumped into a Louisiana swamp. But even though he couldn't hurt me anymore, the memories lingered.

Derek, Trent, and I had been taken in for questioning over the murder, then released. I'd been instructed not to leave town—not that I had plans to—but the command left a hollow feeling in my stomach. Until Garrett's killer was found, I was a murder suspect.

"Mmm," Cynthia groaned, biting into a large, frosting-covered snowflake. She had appeared, like some wayward elf, on my doorstep a few minutes earlier, wearing a bright red sweater that said, *Spank me, I'm naughty*.

"Frosting's still wet," I warned as I set the piping bag into the sink where Rosa was doing the dishes. "Why are you here?"

"Merry Christmas to you, too," she mumbled around the crumbs. "These are fucking delicious. I knew you'd be baking. You always bake when you're stressed."

I raised my eyes at my gray-haired housekeeper, but she didn't flinch over Cynthia's language.

"You've got..." I handed her a napkin, ignoring her comment and gesturing to the side of her face where blue frosting had smeared.

Of course I was stressed. In just a few days I'd be meeting Trent's family, Brooke was due home this evening, and just yesterday I'd sank a fortune into retaining another lawyer. A ballbusting defense attorney, Fiona Jamison. I was beginning to hate lawyers, or at least my need for them.

"What brings you, besides eating all my cookies?"

"Shopping." She dabbed at her face, totally missing the mess. "I need to spoil your children mercilessly."

Rosa sent me a warm smile. We were all looking forward to Brooke coming home. I grabbed a towel, ran it under the faucet, and cleaned up Cynthia's face.

"Thanks, Mom." She laughed. "I'm taking another, so keep that thing handy."

I rolled my eyes as she bit the head off Santa.

"Shopping?" I scrunched up my face at the thought. I hated crowds, hated lines. Hated that Trent had a long day of practice and then a game before I could talk to him. I'd rather pipe frosting on cookies and worry. I had honed my worrying skills over the past twenty years of motherhood. They were razor sharp. But Cynthia knew that, and *no* wasn't in her vocabulary.

"It'll be fun." She grinned, before shoving the rest of Santa in her mouth. Red frosting tinted her lips, making her look like a bloodthirsty vampire. Not far from the truth. She was one of those people who'd trample innocent folks in order to get the hottest gift. Shopping was a blood sport in her opinion. "And it'll keep your thoughts off this mess for a little while."

She had a point. I could use the distraction, even if it involved standing in long checkout lines.

"Fine." I sighed and handed her the towel. "Go to the powder room and fix your lipstick."

She gave a little cheer while walking away.

I blew out a breath, giving Rosa a small smile. "Keep the kids from eating all the cookies. I'd like Trent and his brothers to get some when they get back later tonight."

Mark was in the basement playing billiards with Olivia, Carter, and Bryce. The boys had become fast friends over the Thanksgiving weekend, and the shy smiles and fleeting glances passing between Mark and Olivia were impossible to ignore. According to my son, he and Kennedy were a thing of the past, but getting involved with Trent's niece?

Maybe Rosa should keep an eye on those two as well as the cookies.

Before I could contemplate that dilemma, Cynthia dashed out the front door, leaving me in her sugar-fueled wake.

I gestured to the empty driveway with a frown. "Where's your car, Cyn?"

"Not here, obviously. Anthony dropped it off for maintenance and a good cleaning this morning. I instructed him to pick me up later."

My shoulders deflated in despair. "I'm driving?"

"Who else? Now go open the garage and stop acting like a baby, for God's sake," she said, shooing me back inside.

"Says the woman who can't keep frosting off her face," I shot back before disappearing behind the front door.

How did I get talked into this day?

"Your car's a fucking pigsty," Cynthia remarked as we pulled off the expressway.

"Thank you. Some of us have been busy and can't afford professional detailing."

"The real world uses cup holders for *cups*, Nicki." Turning around she snagged an empty bag off the back seat. "I'm cleaning this shit out so I can have someplace to put my coffee later."

"Suit yourself." Only my boss would pay to have her car cleaned, but clean mine.

I blocked out Cynthia's tuts and complaints while she dug through the chaos that had accumulated over the past few months. Those cup holders were symbolic of my life. I'd never been a particularly organized person, but ever since Derek asked for a divorce, things had slipped a bit more than usual.

"What the hell is this?" She held up a small ziplock bag that had seen better days. Inside was a flash drive.

"Oh, God," I groaned, the events of that awful day coming back in bright technicolor. The thunderstorm, the dry cleaners, Garrett MacKenzie's threats. I still hadn't come to grips with that situation. Latent anxiety curdled my stomach.

I shook my head and focused on the road, the bright sunshine, anything to chase the memories back where they belonged. "That's Derek's. The dry cleaner found it in one of his slacks. I was going to return it to him, but I forgot."

"You haven't looked at it?"

"Of course not." I sent her a sharp look before turning my eyes back on the road. "I've had more pressing matters to deal with."

"Aren't you even curious what's on it?"

I pulled up to a red light and then gave her a longer look. "Not really. Do you know how many of those damn things I've found laying around the house over the years? He was always misplacing them. The man made backups of his backups."

"Maybe I'm just more curious than you, but I'd want to know what's on these little fuckers." Cynthia chuckled while pocketing the flash drive.

"Suit yourself," I repeated, then let out a tortured whimper. The mall parking lot was jammed-packed. It would take hours to find an open spot. "Why are we doing this again?"

"Christmas. Get in the fucking spirit."

CHAPTER
THIRTY-SIX

On Monday morning I found Cynthia sitting at my desk—never a good sign, at least if my goal was to be productive. The gleam in her eyes and the Cheshire cat grin on her face advised me to back away slowly. I frowned, remembering her threat at the mall, gifting me with a Santa stripper if I didn't embrace the holiday spirit a little more.

I glanced down the hall, half expecting some kind of X-rated Yuletide ambush, but everything looked innocuous. Just the Christmas tree standing innocently in the alcove, the strings of lights hanging non-threateningly from the ceiling. My office looked fairly harmless as well, except of course for Cynthia and the small box wrapped in chartreuse plaid and sporting a hot pink bow sitting in the middle of my desk.

"Cyn, you have to stop this." I sighed, exasperated. "I can't afford to reciprocate."

Last week she had given me a Tiffany letter opener and an exquisite Lalique starfish paperweight that was destined for Trent's office, once he had papers that needed weighing down.

"I've been waiting over an hour for you." She nudged the small box toward me. "Open it."

"Sorry, I'm late." A surprise blanket of lake-effect snow, and my procrastination in finding a snow removal company, had me and a frustrated Mark cleaning a rudimentary path down the driveway before I could leave for work.

I stepped into my office and hung my coat on the hook behind the door, before sitting down across from my boss.

"If you must know, this little gem cost me nothing." She lifted the box off the desk as I leaned closer, and shoved it into my hands. "Just open it for fuck's sake."

I sent her a confused look, taking the wrapped box from her hand and giving it a little shake. The hollow rattle and insignificant weight held no clues. Cynthia heaved an impatient sigh while I peeled the taped edges from the expensive paper.

Underneath sat a mundane white box, no expensive label or embossed hallmark. I lifted the top off and then frowned.

"Is this Derek's flash drive?' I huffed a small uncomfortable laugh as I peered down at it again. If this was a joke, she'd lost me.

"You really need to be more inquisitive, Nicki. How many of these things did you say he misplaced around the house?"

I shrugged, shaking my head. "I can't recall. Dozens probably."

She leaned forward and picked up the flash drive with two fingers as if it might transmit a deadly pathogen. "I'm surprised he didn't rip the house apart looking for this one."

My skin tingled with the memory. A week after Derek had asked for a divorce, I'd discovered him in his home office. The ruckus I'd heard from the kitchen had my heart in my throat, my phone in my left hand, 911 already dialed in, and my thumb poised over the send button. In my right hand, I gripped a can of pepper spray I scavenged from the bottom of my purse.

I thought I left something here, he'd said when I'd burst through the office door to find him rummaging through his empty desk. Later that night I'd found my underwear drawer open and one of my new heels lying on the carpet, but had brushed it off. Surely Derek hadn't been up there?

"Why? What's on this thing?"

She let out a sinister laugh, waving the little black rectangle back and forth. "Evidence."

I narrowed my eyes at her cryptic tone. "Evidence?"

"Close the door, and then sit back down." She raised her brows, motioning to my open office door. "Prepare to be shocked. I know I was."

I let out a nervous laugh but did as she asked. Nothing ever shocked Cynthia. Whatever was stored on the drive had to be something interesting.

Cynthia plugged the flash drive into my computer, swiveled the monitor around to face me, and sat down in the chair next to mine. *I think*. She could have sat in my lap, dropped a bomb in the room, anything really and I wouldn't have noticed. All my attention was on the screen in front of me.

I gasped for a breath, every hair on my body standing on end as I stared at the dead man on my screen. Well, he wasn't dead yet.

"Senator Robinson." Garrett MacKenzie tsked. "I'm hoping you find this video as interesting as I did. I'm holding the original for safekeeping, of course, so destroying your copy would be useless."

"What happened to his southern accent?" I asked. *Stupid question.* The man had a half dozen different names.

"The details of my demands are in the envelope in front of you. If you are a wise man, you will do what I ask. I'd hate to have your pretty wife find out what kind of man you really are."

My stomach knotted with dread. *What kind of man does Garrett think Derek is?*

The screen went dark for a second and I fell back in my chair as if a thread pulling me toward the monitor had been cut.

"Jesus Christ. He was blackmailing Derek?" *Another stupid question.*

"Just wait," Cynthia said a second before the screen flickered back to life.

Music blared out from my monitor's speakers. Loud, with a heavy base, making me flinch. The screen flashed with light. On, then off, then on again. A strobe light. Memories of my younger days when my friends and I frequented dance clubs before I'd met Derek popped into my head for a brief second.

Derek's not being blackmailed for going dancing.

Whoever was holding the camera stopped and turned. I blinked a couple times to make sure I wasn't hallucinating. Strobe lights could be disorienting, at least from what I remember, causing vertigo and possibly seizures in those sensitive to such things. Unfortunately, I wasn't suffering from either.

"What the hell?" I whispered, my voice failing to reach

full volume. The people in this video definitely weren't dancing.

Under a spotlight, a woman lay naked on a white leather chaise. The light went out and then on again, but I'd seen enough to recognize her. Nancy Brockhorn was about my age, with long dark hair that she religiously colored to hide the gray. She was spread across the upholstery, an expression of pleasure on her face. A balding man I couldn't get a good look at, was performing oral sex while her husband stood by watching and stroking himself.

"Holy shit, that's—that's Senator Brockhorn," I said, stumbling over my words. The last time I'd seen Roger Brockhorn, he was hosting a barbecue in his Maryland back yard. Fully clothed. Here, not so much. His wife, Nancy, had promised me the recipe for her peach cobbler. Now I was watching her in the throes of an orgasm given by another man.

At least the music was too loud to hear her.

A second later the bald man looked up and I let out another gasp. The satisfied grin on Tom Morgan's face was unmistakable. Although I was more familiar with the Supreme Court judge displaying that smug smile while winning at croquet.

Before I could process this, the camera moved on. From what I could tell, the room was huge, with black walls and white furniture scattered around the space. I'd never seen so many naked body parts in my life. *Orgy*, a voice in my head whispered.

"Does anyone know they're being videotaped?" *Enough with the stupid questions.* No way would any of these people want video evidence of what they were doing. It would destroy their careers.

"My guess is he's wearing a hidden camera. Some kind

of pendant or maybe a pair of eyeglasses," Cynthia answered. "These places usually don't allow phones, and whoever is taping this would stand out if they were clothed."

But where's Derek?

Before I could voice the question, the video panned again, giving me the answer.

I closed my eyes and let out a groan of... betrayal, anger, maybe resignation? It was going to take a while to process how I was feeling at the moment.

The light flickered off and then on again, highlighting Jack Mitchell.

Derek and Jack had known each other since childhood. The two had gone to Harvard together. Jack had married a year after me and Derek. Their kids were the same age as ours. Jack stayed in Congress a half dozen years longer than Derek but eventually claimed the second Senate seat for the state.

Jack's wife, Hannah, had lost her battle with pancreatic cancer a year ago in June. A devastating blow for the family. Derek had even stayed with him for a few weeks that summer, concerned for his friend's mental state.

Derek's concern and the nature of their friendship took on a whole new light as I watched my soon-to-be ex-husband kneeling between Jack's spread legs. His back was to the camera, but if Derek's thick, honey-blond hair wasn't proof of his identity, the port-wine stain on his shoulder blade was.

It was obvious what he was doing, and a small part of me was thankful for the camera angle and the fact that Derek's head shielded me from the view of Jack's privates. Even if I'd never see the other men in the video, there was a good chance I'd be seeing Jack Mitchell again.

Even in this setting, I could tell there was more between the two men than carnal lust. The way Jack's half-closed eyes gazed down at his lover, the way his hand caressed the side of Derek's face...

"They're in love." I whispered the obvious secret while covering my eyes with my hands. "Please stop the video, Cyn."

Even though everyone in that room could have watched the pair, I hadn't received permission to, and I was sure Derek wouldn't want me seeing this.

As soon as the music stopped I dropped my hands and stared at Cynthia. "I don't know what to think."

Actually, I was thinking too many things.

Cynthia stood and patted my shoulder. "I have no doubt."

I pointed at the blank monitor. "I didn't think anything could top my shock the night Derek asked for a divorce, but this... Jesus, Cyn, a week ago I accused Patty Sullivan of having an affair with him."

My stomach soured, thinking back to the argument I'd had with Derek's campaign manager. I'd been so stupid.

"I think you're missing the bigger issue here." Cynthia stepped away, returning with a glass of cool water from the pitcher on the credenza Sonya filled every morning. "That video is a pretty good motive for murder."

My eyes widened at her insinuation. "No way. Derek's a lot of things, obviously more than I was aware of, but a murderer?"

"Could be Senator Mitchell or one of the other guys. Who did you say they were?"

"Senator Brockhorn and Supreme Court Justice Tom Morgan," I said before chugging down half the glass of water.

Cynthia shook her head and let out a whistle. "You might want to watch the rest of the video. There's others he focuses on later. I don't recognize them, but you probably will."

I'd rather Christmas shop for all eternity than watch more of Derek's colleagues having sex.

"What I don't understand is why Garrett sent the whole video? Why not edit out the parts that didn't pertain to Derek?"

"What would you do if your friends had a video of your deepest secret and you had theirs?"

It was too early on a Monday for me to contemplate such things. Instead, I asked, "Was Garrett behind the camera, or did he have an accomplice?"

It was a chilling thought, the possibility someone still had the power to destroy my family. My kids wouldn't have a moment's peace if this video went public.

"Possibly." Cynthia's sympathetic look said her thoughts followed similar lines to mine.

"And if Garrett had the original, where is it now?" I wondered out loud while setting the water glass down on my desk with trembling hands.

"We have an appointment with Randall this evening at seven."

I sent Cynthia a look of horror. "Randall? Enough people know about my husband's sexual orientation. We shouldn't be adding to that list."

Cynthia returned to the chair next to me, clasping my hands between hers. "With this video, you move way down the list of suspects in Garrett's murder. So does Trent."

"No way, Cyn. No way am I sacrificing Derek's future, my children's future, to save my ass."

Cynthia snorted, her lips pursed in what was probably disappointment. "You think Derek would save your ass?"

THAT EVENING, I followed Cynthia straight into Randall's office. It was late, the waiting area dark, Randall's handsome young assistant gone.

Randall strode though his office doorway, then gave Cynthia a tender kiss on her cheek. "How are you, beautiful?"

"Fine, Randall. Did you read my email?"

Just like his waiting room, his office lights were off, save the green desk lamp shining on the polished work surface. *Top secret meeting*, the atmosphere screamed. Randall's eyes landed on me, and he heaved out a loud sigh. I was getting tired of seeing him as well.

Apprehension prickled my skin. The last time I was here there'd been only two chairs facing his desk. Now there were three. If Randall was anyone else, anyone less anal, I would have thought the third chair had been left from his previous appointment. But I didn't think that was the case.

"I did. Please have a seat." He waved his hand in the direction of his desk and confirmed what I feared. "We're just waiting for one more to start this meeting."

"One more?" I glared at Cynthia and then Randall. "I thought—"

Not for the first time today, Cynthia grabbed my hand in sympathy. "She's in a bit of a shock, Randall. Try going easy on her."

"Seems fine to me," he quipped, giving me a quick once over before motioning once again for us to take a seat. This time a bit more brusque. He sank down into his chair surrounded by the dim circle of light cast by his lamp.

"I am fine. I'm just not happy adding to the list of people who know about this video," I said while taking the farthest of the three chairs sitting in front of Randall's desk. "But then it's only my children's opinion of their father on the line here."

Before I could go on with my rant, the specter of Gordon Knight entered the office. At least he looked like a specter in an immaculate black suit, charcoal dress shirt, and matching tie. Or maybe an undertaker. A very stylish undertaker.

I sprung up from my seat. "*Him?* Why him?"

Gordon claimed the seat on the other side of Cynthia while ignoring my question.

"He's here because the video was taken in one of his clubs," Cynthia answered, her voice calm.

"So?" I asked, my gaze fixed on Gordon Knight.

"So, Ms. Adams." Gordon shifted in his chair to face me. "This video is evidence of a serious security breach. Believe me, I have a lot more to lose if this video leaks to the public, than you do."

Anger heated my skin. Of course this pompous man thought his stake in this situation was greater than mine.

"If we can get started, Mrs. Robinson. I've better things to do with my time than play *calm the hysterical woman*," Randall said with an abrupt gesture for me to sit down.

I sat, sending Cynthia a look that said, *See what I've been putting up with?* Or at least I hoped it did. Either way we'd be having words later regarding her lawyer friend.

"Now, I've taken a look at the video in its entirety," Randall continued. "Quite a twist, I have to say, and one we need to handle with the sensitivity it deserves. Over a dozen people's privacy has been violated."

"My clients' privacy," Gordon inserted in his British accent, pronouncing privacy with a short i.

Funny that Randall's not scolding him for interrupting.

"Forgive me, gentlemen, but to hell with privacy. Nicki is a suspect in MacKenzie's murder. This video proves there were plenty of others with a motive to kill the man," Cynthia said.

I patted her hand, letting her know I appreciated her support. But…"As much as it kills me to say it, Randall's right. The privacy—and career—of everyone of those guests are at stake here. As well as their right to reveal their sexual orientation at a time of their choosing. I don't want this video going public. Sorry, Cyn, there has to be another way."

Cynthia gave a sharp shake of her head. "Your defense of Derek is all well and good, but remember this is only a copy of the original video—"

"The police have done a thorough search of MacKenzie's apartment," Randall stated, his dark gaze settling on my best friend. "If they'd found a video, we'd know about it. The whole fucking world would know it."

"There's more copies. Everyone on that video may have been blackmailed," I pointed out.

Gordon Knight cleared his throat. "I will be contacting the other club members in the video. Discretely, of course. By the end of the week, I should have all copies in my possession. Once there, they will be destroyed."

I had to laugh at his confidence. The man obviously didn't know politicians. "Good luck getting them to turn the videos over. Or even admitting they're in possession of them."

Gordon sent me an arrogant smirk. "Trust me, Nicki, I always get what I want."

"But—" Cynthia started, but Randall held up his hand.

"I'm not putting this meeting in my books for obvious reasons, but I'd appreciate you not wasting my free time."

Cynthia burst out laughing. "I promised you dinner, Randall."

His teeth flashed in the gloom, his grin suggesting she'd promised more than food. "You asked for my advice. I'm here to give it to you." Cynthia breathed out a sigh, but Randall went on. "The destruction of Derek Robinson's career does my client no financial good. I've spoken with Fiona Jamison and she assures me the evidence against Nicole is thin at best. Given MacKenzie's habit of swindling and blackmail, there are too many people who'd benefit from his death to pin it on Mrs. Robinson. Unless the police discover concrete evidence to indict her, this investigation will die a natural death."

"You're withholding evidence," Cynthia sputtered, her pale skin flushing with what I knew from experience was anger. "You could be disbarred. Or worse."

"Only if you tell someone." He narrowed his eyes at my friend. "Are you planning on telling anyone?"

"No," Cynthia said with a pout. "But for the record, I'm against letting a murderer goes free."

"Noted," Randall said. "Truth is, whoever killed MacKenzie did the world a favor. The man was a menace to decent society."

Cynthia opened her mouth to say more, but once again Randall held up his hand. "Enough. My job is to advise my client. Which I plan on doing unless you would prefer to do it for me."

"Go ahead, Randall," Cynthia said after a moment of silence.

"I believe it is in the best interest of Mrs. Robinson for Mr. Knight to destroy all the videos. Do not discuss this situation with anyone. Forget it exists. Mr. Robinson has agreed to every one of her demands, including a very generous financial settlement. Unless there is anything else, I will see Nicole next month in court, and Cynthia at Bagatelle next week where I plan on being very hungry." He stood.

Cynthia laughed.

"For the record, this meeting did not happen," Randall added.

Fine by me.

I stood as well, once again following Cynthia as she led the way out of the office. Gordon Knight stayed seated, but I was done worrying about him. At least until he was in the market for another hotel.

Randall held the entry door open, and my best friend passed through.

I paused and gave my lawyer a smug smile. "I knew my husband was cheating."

Randall shook his head, his gaze skirting past me. "Cynthia, if she wasn't a friend... I swear to God..."

Cynthia cackled while tugging me out the door and down the steps onto the sidewalk.

CHAPTER
THIRTY-SEVEN

A week later I paced the front hall, waiting for my almost ex-husband to arrive.

Cynthia thought I was crazy, and Trent...

"No way, Nic," he said on the phone a week before, when he'd finally calmed down enough to form sentences. I could almost feel his angry breaths all the way from LA. "I'm too far away to save you this time. Don't make me worry about you when I'm helpless to do anything about it."

I tried to explain, but neither of them understood. There was a time Derek was my world, and on some level I still loved him, and for Brooke and Mark's sake, I had a duty to protect him. That included keeping him out of jail.

Gloria, Derek's secretary, called me that morning to let me know he'd be stopping by. Flash drive in my sweaty palm, I contemplated how my soon-to-be ex-husband would react. I would have placed my bet on his usual steely stoicism. But I also would have bet he'd been sleeping with his campaign manager, so what did I know?

What if I'm wrong? What if I'm making a mistake? What if Derek really would do anything to save his reputation? What if he murdered Garrett? Those questions and more had run through my mind on an endless loop ever since hanging up with Gloria.

By the time Derek rang the front doorbell, I was sick with uncertainty.

"You changed the locks," he grumbled, walking in.

"Problem with the pool service," I replied. "I'm sure you understand. Didn't think you would want a key."

"Where's Mark and Brooke?" he asked, following me back to the family room.

"Out. Mark's at the Richards's house and Brooke's visiting Emily Lang. You remember her. Little dark-haired girl. She's back from—"

"What did you want to talk about, Nicki? I don't have all day," Derek huffed, cutting me off.

"No wine?" I asked as we headed toward the kitchen. *Wine would be good.* "I opened one of your favorites. You can take some of the bottles with you if you want. I've never been as big a fan as you."

"I have more in DC. I've yet to find a place locally, so I'd have no place to put them," he said, walking away from the island. "What's on your mind?"

"Please, sit." I gestured toward the sofa, taking the bottle and glasses with me as I followed. Derek sat and I poured two glasses of wine, and then took a hearty swig. To hell with him, I needed it.

He chuckled. "You just said you didn't like wine."

"I said I wasn't as big a fan as you, not that I don't drink it." I shrugged, taking another sip. "I found the video."

His glass stalled halfway to his lips. "What video?"

I sent him a knowing look and then raised my hand to stop the lies from tumbling out of his mouth. "After twenty years of marriage, I think I deserves some kind of explanation, don't you?"

His perpetually tanned skin paled.

"I'm not here to judge. Just... how long have you known?"

"Jack and I..." He sighed. "We'd been friends... I don't know how long. It's hard to explain. Just one day we went from best friends to something more."

"You love him?"

He nodded while pouring himself another glass of wine. "Always."

"Then why marry me?" I sort of knew the answer, but I wanted him to tell me.

Derek laughed, hard. "I had no plans on marrying. Believe me. But then one afternoon—we'd gotten sloppy—my mother walked in my room and there we were."

"Bit of a shock, I imagine." Not that I had to imagine. I'd lived that surprise.

"Shocked. Livid. Of course she told my father. And Jack's parents. We were told it was a phase. *Boyish curiosity.* Then threatened if it ever happened again, we'd be cut off. Out on the streets without a penny. No education. No support. Nothing."

Sympathetic tears burned the back of my eyes. I could never imagine being that cruel and heartless to our kids.

"We had two choices, poor and happy or follow the path our parents' arranged for us."

"Oh my God, Derek." I'd always joked with my friends about being in an arranged marriage, never realizing...

He picked up the flash drive from where I set it on the coffee table. "Who's seen it?"

"Me, Cyn, Randall Harris—although he'll deny it if asked. And Cyn's sworn to secrecy." I paused for a second, then added, "Gordon Knight."

Derek scrubbed his face with his hands. "Shit."

"He targeted us, Derek. For the past five years. Waiting for an opportunity to strike." I had no room to point fingers. We'd both fallen prey to MacKenzie's charms.

Derek sat back in his chair, deflated. "I know."

"Did you kill him?"

His eyes widened. "No. Never."

"Hire someone to do it?"

He laughed, the sound sharp and caustic. "Thought about it. The Monday after his interview about you, he'd called for another fifty grand. Said the media attention was addicting, and how much he'd enjoy giving them the video if I didn't pay up. But no. I did not kill him, nor did I hire someone."

Not even a fraction of a twitch at the corner of his eye. Unless he'd gotten better at lying over the last few months, he was telling the truth.

"Same for Jack? Was he being blackmailed too?"

"Jack's the least violent person I know."

I took a sip of wine while considering Derek's nonanswer. "It looks bad, though."

"For all of us. You too, sweetheart."

His use of his standard endearment made me wince. I wasn't his sweetheart anymore.

"Yeah." I drained the last of my wine, then set the glass down on the table. "Just so you know, I only slept with Gabriel—Garrett—once. The day after you walked out. I had been angry and stupid and drunk. It's no excuse, but in case you were curious, there you have it."

He raked his fingers through his golden hair streaked

with more silver than the last time we'd sat in these seats. My heart squeezed. The man I'd once loved for over twenty years was getting old.

He set his glass on the coffee table and stood. "We all make mistakes. If you can find a way to forgive me, I most certainly will forgive you."

A small part of me wanted to argue. But once again, I told myself it didn't matter anymore. Both of us owed it to our kids to at least remain cordial. They didn't deserve the drama.

"Of course."

Derek headed toward the foyer, meeting obviously over. I followed behind, those unwanted questions still swirling in my mind. *Would I ever get answers?*

He brushed his lips against my cheek, the familiar scent of his Tom Ford cologne filling my nose.

"I'll always love you, Nicki. Just not the way..." He trailed off with a shrug.

"I get it." I forced my lips into a smile I didn't quite feel. Then scolded myself as wistful tears pricked the corner of my eyes.

"Tell that new man of yours to be good to you. You deserve happiness."

I nodded, my emotions threatening to choke me. "Same to you."

Derek turned, then strode across the curved walkway to the driveway. I watched as he climbed into his trusty Cadillac and headed back down the driveway, the hollow pit in my stomach intensifying after his car disappeared behind the snow-covered pine trees.

It wasn't like I'd never see him again. We had the court date, and then Mark's graduation in less than two years. Brooke's, and then Mark's college graduation, and eventually weddings, and grandchildren... Our lives would always be linked by the kids.

Trent descended the front stairs and wrapped his arms around my waist as I swiped at my irrational tears. Of course he canceled his trip to LA to stay and protect me. My only stipulation in allowing it was for him to keep out of sight. "You are a remarkable woman, Nicole Adams. I don't think I would have let him off that easy."

"I have more important things to focus on."

I turned to face the man I'd come to love with all my heart over the past few months. I hadn't planned on falling for someone else so soon, or maybe not ever. The thought still scared me, but I had faced a lot of my fears since the night Derek asked for a divorce. I'd learned to stand on my own two feet. Learned to accept my mistakes and to celebrate my successes.

"Like us?" he asked.

"Like moving forward, like taking care of myself, like watching my kids turn into adults, and us. Definitely us." Trent's lips curved into a smile as I said the final two words. "I want you in my life."

"And I want you in mine. Through the good and bad."

"There's a lot of bad at the moment, so I hope you're—" He cut off my words with a brush of his lips.

"Don't you know, babe, you can't truly appreciate the good without some bad?" His forest-green eyes settled on mine while his fingers traced over the tracks of my tears. "I'm so fucking in love with you, nothing can chase me away at this point. You're mine forever, Nicole Adams."

My heart swelled with his words and, once more, tears filled my eyes. Trent pressed his lips against mine again, lingering this time. My fingers found their favorite spot, tangled in Trent's thick, soft hair, as we swayed in the open doorway, not giving a damn about Mrs. Jordan and her binoculars or the chilly December breeze blowing through the house.

No, I hadn't planned for Trent Richards to enter my life, but now that he was here, I planned on keeping him.

EPILOGUE

TRENT

"Hey, Trent, you look like you need a beer. Or two," Troy said, handing me an ice-cold bottle, then glancing around the yard. "Every time I'm here I have to pinch myself. I mean, I'm not struggling financially, but this..."

"Know what you mean." I scratched my chin and nodded. A year-and-a-half since I first met Nicki and I still wasn't used to this much... opulence.

We grew up normal. Dad was a contractor, Mom ran a florist. Pizza on Fridays, peanut butter and jelly in our lunchboxes. Camping in Wisconsin when my parents' schedules fit.

Not that I was begrudging Nic's kids for their trust funds, or this house, or the swimming pool that looked like it belonged at a resort, not a private back yard. Hell, if we'd had a house this big growing up, there probably would have been fewer arguments.

But at least when my parents sold the family home a few years back, it hadn't taken almost two years to find a buyer who could afford the price tag.

397

Troy laughed. "What about your condo? Have you put that on the market yet?"

"Last week."

"And TJ? How's that going?"

My gaze drifted to the man in question, who was currently splashing around in the water, not at all fazed by his sorta-homeless status. "We'll see."

Two weeks ago my oldest brother had shown up at my front door. He'd resigned from his prestigious faculty position at Harvard and sold his house. No explanation, no excuse.

Fuck off, he'd grumble anytime one of us would give him shit.

We'd all come to the conclusion that TJ lost his mind. He was the least impulsive of any one of us, but he'd yet to give an adequate explanation for his rash decision.

"Good luck, brother?" Troy lifted an eyebrow in challenge.

Not that he would be the one kicking TJ out. Faced with one of the three options, moving back in with our parents or surrounding himself in the chaos provided by Troy's two boys—I was willing to bet his ex, Samatha, hadn't offered him a room—TJ had jumped at my invitation to take one of my condo's two spare bedrooms.

Actually, it was kind of nice. Being ten years younger than Travis, we never really bonded in the same way Troy and I had. By the time I outgrew the obnoxious little brother phase, he'd moved halfway across the country. The past couple of weeks had given us some bonding time.

"You're brave to allow him and Nicki under the same roof. I know I wouldn't have trusted my girlfriend around TJ. Didn't you say he kissed her?"

"Once. Over a year and a half ago."

Whatever jealousy I'd suffered from the incident had long faded. Not that I didn't have a few reservations on how things would go when Nic moved in with me once this place closed. But those concerns had more to do with privacy than jealousy. Nic and I had enjoyed our fair share of naked time in her house. At least when Mark wasn't home.

But in two weeks we'd all be sleeping under my roof. Me and Nic, Travis and Mark. With the occasional addition of Carter, Olivia, and Bryce.

I continued, ignoring Troy's annoying chuckle. "She loves me, you stupid asshole."

At the moment Nic and my mom were sharing a laugh, and my frustration eased. My two favorite women were as thick as thieves, always scheming about something or another. Like this graduation party for Mark and Olivia.

"I'm not worried," I added for good measure.

"You sound very unworried. Might want to lock things down before then. You've been dicking around too long with this woman. It's time to get serious." He slapped my back with enough force to jerk me forward. My beer foamed down the side of the bottle, watering the slate patio. *Asshole*. "Now if you'll excuse me, I promised to teach my kids how to execute the perfect cannonball."

Troy rushed toward the pool, screaming like the ten-year-old that he still was whenever he took off his fucking suit. Ashley and Audrey, my sister Teresa's two youngest, along with Brooke, squealed from the lounge chairs as my brother's giant cannonball splash soaked them. The mid-May air temperature was hovering around seventy-six, but Nic had cranked the pool water heater up to a balmy eighty-six.

I chuckled, then turned away from the fun in the pool.

I'd proposed to Nic the previous spring, shortly after her and Derek's divorce was final. She'd said no at the time, offering a half dozen logical excuses. To sum it up, she needed time, and I was willing to be patient with her.

My gaze landed on Nic's ex and his husband, Jack, who were deep in conversation with Teresa's husband, Bennet. The couple's presence here attested to how far Nicki and Derek's relationship had come since their divorce.

Derek and Jack had married last winter in an intimate ceremony, after they'd both announced their retirement from politics. Probably best, Nicki thought. Last we had heard, Gordon Knight had destroyed every copy of the video he could get his hands on. But as far as we knew, no one had found MacKenzie's original. Had it gone down in the swamp with the man, or was it still floating around somewhere, waiting to destroy careers?

But that was someone else's problem. MacKenzie was dead. The killer caught, or at least the Houston socialite who'd hired him had been caught. Diana Colburn had been one of MacKenzie's many victims. According to court testimony, she'd been compelled to end the man after watching his prime-time interview claiming a long-standing affair with Nicki. Not because of jealousy, but to protect future women from falling for MacKenzie's charms. Rumor had it, a certain dark-haired real-estate mogul covered Ms. Colburn's legal expenses, but Cynthia wasn't admitting to anything.

On the corner of the patio, my dad stood guard over the massive barbecue setup. The scent of grilling meat wafted on the warm, early-summer breeze, bringing on a wave of nostalgia.

"I can take over if you want," I offered to my dad in vain, while keeping a cautious eye on the long-handled spatula he had been known to wield like a weapon. My old man had taken one look at the high-end outdoor kitchen attached to the back of this place and claimed instant ownership.

"Don't you dare," he said with a grin while flipping a half dozen burgers with his *weapon*, then slapping cheese on the sizzling meat with the experience of decades of backyard grilling. Mom was in trouble if she thought he'd be satisfied with the rusty old Weber in their backyard after today.

Mark and TJ's boys ambled over, still dripping from the pool. Dad pulled a platter of burgers out of the warmer before the words were even out of their mouths.

"Thanks, Mr. Richards," Mark said before shoving half the sandwich into his mouth.

"Thanks, Grandpa," Conner and Bryce added a second later, before the trio took off again.

"You want one of these?" Dad asked, sliding the new batch of melty burgers on the waiting buns and transferring them to the now empty platter. "They're disappearing fast."

"Nah," I answered. "I'm good."

"I'll take one, Dad," Nicki said, tucking her thumb into the waistband of my shorts. "I'm starved."

I slipped an arm around her sun-warmed shoulders and smiled. It had taken two seconds for Nic to blend into the Richards clan. Two seconds for her to become one of us.

"You think there's something going on over there?" She wiggled her eyebrows, pointing her chin toward a spot just over my shoulder. I turned just as my oldest brother let out a loud laugh. He and Cynthia looked to be having a flirtatious conversation.

401

"Maybe they're discussing real-estate," I suggested. Although I doubted it.

Nic's expression said she did as well.

"He's way over his head if they're discussing anything else, babe." I chuckled at the thought of my brother and Nicki's spitfire of a boss. Maybe a little time with Cynthia Jacobs was exactly what TJ needed. He'd been a moody motherfucker lately. Getting laid might help. Certainly couldn't hurt.

"It's a good thing, getting in over your head with a woman," my dad said, his eyes dancing between me and Nic.

She glanced up from the burger she was doctoring up, eyes narrowing at the flirty pair. "I'm not sure about that..."

I was definitely in over my head as I let my gaze wander over the skimpy red bikini that showed way too much of the woman I loved. Not that I was complaining, but I'd rather have this view all to myself. Somewhere quiet. With no interruptions.

My attention snagged on the dab of mustard she was sucking off her finger while flashing me a wicked smile. *You're envious of a damn condiment now?* I had firsthand knowledge of what the inside of her pretty little mouth felt like. And I was definitely envious.

I blinked back into the moment, having lost complete track of the conversation. Something about fishing?

I swiped the residual smear from the corner of her mouth and sucked the sharp mustard off my thumb. Then I offered her my beer.

My mouth dried as I watched her wrap her lips around the bottle in a way that had my thoughts drifting back to the forbidden land—at least in front of my father. *Have some control.*

Nic turned and walked away, my beer still in her hand. Tossing a wink over her shoulder, she let me know she was aware of exactly what I'd been thinking. My cock twitched while my eyes focused on the way her hips swayed as she walked.

"You better put a ring on that woman's finger," my dad offered with an uncomfortable cough.

"I'm working on it, Dad. Working on it." Pushing off the counter, I propelled myself across the patio, watching as Nic headed inside. I was two seconds behind her and getting harder with every step. *Okay, so maybe I don't have that much control.*

The door slammed behind me, and I wrapped my arms around her waist, pulling her against me. Nic giggled, grinding her luscious ass into me. Instantly, I was hard as steel, pressing between her ass cheeks to ease the ache.

"You better have something planned to take care of this, 'cause it's not going away on its own, sweetheart," I rasped in her ear.

"Powder room," she whispered, making me laugh. This woman and her thing for bathrooms. TJ's tiny powder room had been just the beginning. I'd yet to convince her of the benefits of the mile-high club, but we knew quite a few semiprivate spots in the city intimately. My girl liked to live dangerously.

I'd barely stepped inside the first-floor washroom when she slammed the door behind me. She engaged the lock and then dropped to her knees. Fucking hell, I loved this woman —and not only because there was never a more beautiful sight than her baby blues looking up at me while she was freeing me from my shorts.

Slamming my fists into the door, my eyes squeezed shut, and I groaned out a shuddered breath, then watched myself disappear into her mouth. Fingers wrapped around my base, she worked me over with her tongue and teeth and lips until my knees threatened to buckle. I was in fucking heaven, but by the pleasure building at the base of my spine I knew I couldn't last much longer.

I pulled her mouth off me and lifted her to her feet. She made a slight sound of protest, or maybe consent as I spun her around to face the vanity mirror.

"So fucking gorgeous with your lips swollen and your eyes bright with tears," I whispered into her ear. "I want to see you come on my dick, sweetheart."

Dragging those tiny bottoms down her hips, I groaned at the site of her perfect ass while squeezing the base of my cock to prevent myself from coming. Tracing a finger down her crack, I watched as she sucked her bottom lip into her mouth in anticipation. Then I tapped my foot against her ankle.

She widened her stance and I pressed her forward. Then slid my eager cock between her slick folds with a quiet groan, mindful of the multitude of people just outside the frosted window to my left. The last thing I wanted was an interruption. Or an audience.

My thighs shook as her heat enveloped me and the pleasure of my impending orgasm slithered down my spine. No, this wouldn't take long, and I needed Nic with me.

"Touch yourself."

Her eyes widened a fraction, meeting mine in the mirror as if to protest, but in the next second she slipped her fingers over her clit. I watched for a second as her hand moved and her eyes fluttered shut. My grip closed around her hips, then I pulled back and thrusted all the way home. Once, twice, and again. She was tight and hot, and it took only seconds to find the natural rhythm that pulsed between us. I buried my face at the base of her neck, teasing her with my tongue, savoring the taste of sunshine and sweat and the addictive flavor of her skin.

Everything about Nic was addictive, a drug I'd never get enough of even if we lived to one hundred. She was more than sex to me, probably from the beginning even though I'd been too stubborn to realize. She was my everything, my sole excuse for existing. We fit together in ways I would have never thought possible three years ago. But now that the possible was in front of me, I planned to never let go.

"Come for me." My whispered breath against the damp skin of her neck made her shiver, or maybe it was my words.

She gasped out my name, her body squeezing me as I pounded into her heat. I watched, mesmerized by the blush tinting her chest, slowly spreading up her throat, and pinking her cheeks. Her gaze locked on mine as her mouth dropped open in a silent cry, and her pussy pulsed around my cock. My release rushed through me and I came hard, my vision darkening at the edges.

I was pretty sure this woman was going to eventually kill me. But at least I'd die a happy man.

THE SUN HAD SET SOMETIME AGO, LEAVING the backyard in the glow from the pool and the light from the fire pit flickering on the happy faces. Perfect end to a perfect day.

"Maybe I should just buy your condo," TJ said, laughing for the first time in days. Maybe weeks. "You'd give your big brother a discount?"

I laughed back, shifting Nic a fraction on my lap. She

didn't weigh that much, but the small box hiding in my pocket dug uncomfortably into my thigh. Like I needed the reminder.

"I still can't believe you gave up Harvard," Teresa, scoffed, shaking her head. "I thought you were the smart one, Teej."

My parents shared a look, confirming my suspicion that they were in on whatever was happening with my eldest brother.

"Leave him alone," my dad said.

"Thanks, Dad, but I think I can take care of myself," TJ replied, sending our sister a scowl. "Maybe Teresa is afraid to have me living so close again."

"Probably." Ashley laughed. "At least with Uncle Trent away half the year, all Mom had to deal with was Troy. Now with all three of you around, there's gonna be nothing but trouble."

"I think there was plenty of trouble without these two." My sister glanced at her youngest son with a speculative look. He and Brooke had moved off to a shadowed spot just to the side of the fire pit. Their cozy conversation hadn't escaped his mother's notice. "At least Trevor seems to be enjoying himself, and his uncle's female friends."

"Mom," Trevor grumbled, his pale complexion darkening in the firelight. Brooke settled a few inches away from him, giving everyone a wide-eyed innocent look.

"Friendship?" Troy asked, a wicked gleam in his eyes. "Is that what they're calling it these days?"

His wife, Amanda, smacked him on the shoulder, imploring her husband to behave.

Whatever they called it, it seemed to be in the air tonight.

"I've heard it called a lot worse." TJ chuckled, taking over with the good-natured ribbing. "Right, Olivia?"

While Brooke and Trevor had been discreet, it was quite obvious Mark and Olivia had a thing for each other. But that was for TJ and Nic to worry about. I had enough on my mind without adding teen romance.

"Well, whatever it is, it's time your brother made my mother a respectable woman," Brooke chimed in, her eyes narrowing on me. "We were taught better than this, Mom."

"Brooke." Nic sighed, crossing her arms. "We've discussed this..."

"Seriously, Mom." Brooke pointed a finger at Nic. "Someone's got to stand up for our morals. You're the only role model we have left."

Jesus, this girl's honesty.

"Yeah, Mom," Cynthia called from her spot that was conspicuously close to my eldest brother. "Where are your morals?"

"Both of you are right." I nodded to Brooke and Cynthia who were in on my plans. "Heaven forbid I allow this lovely woman to fall into moral decay."

Nic turned toward me, but before she could protest, I pulled her to her feet. Her expression was a mixture of confusion and fear, her blue eyes wider than I've ever seen them.

Please let this be right.

My heart skipped a beat. I'd stopped breathing, but somehow I was still standing.

"Kneel, you idiot," Teresa yelled.

"Shush," Mom returned.

I let out a strangled groan, sending my entire family a frustrated glare. Then dropped to my knee. *Maybe this would have been better done in private.*

407

"I love you," I whispered, digging the box out of my pocket. "I know you're freaking out right now, but I'm not. So trust me to take care of you, to protect you, to stand by you. I want you to be mine, officially. Whether by a minister in a church or on some faraway beach or by some damn Elvis impersonator in Vegas."

My mother gasped. Chances were she'd have my head if we eloped.

I sent her a wink. "Okay, maybe not the last option..."

"I like the beach," Nic whispered back in a shaky voice, and my heart started beating again.

"Say you'll give me forever, sweetheart. Say you'll marry me."

Tears streamed down her cheeks, sparkling in the firelight. Beautiful. This woman was fucking beautiful and I was a wreck. My clumsy fingers fumbled to open the tiny velvet box. Six months ago, I'd been torn between letting her pick out the ring and surprising her. TJ said go with the surprise. Not that he was the best person to give advice, but the ring I picked out was pretty fabulous if I did say so myself.

"Ask her, dummy," Troy shouted, breaking me out of my anxious thoughts.

Nic chewed on her bottom lip as the corners of her mouth twitched. *Definitely should have done this in private.*

"Marry me, Nic?" My voice crackled like an adolescent boy's. "Please."

She swiped at the tears trickling down her cheeks and then bobbed her head. A quiet *yes* ghosted from her lips.

Pandemonium erupted all around us, but I barely noticed. I stood and kissed the hell out of the woman I would cherish for the rest of my life.

· · ·

THANK you for reading Separation Game! Want to know more about me and stay up to date on my new releases, sales, and promotions? Sign up for my newsletter at darciannbaker.com

Sign up for my newsletter!

ACKNOWLEDGMENTS

Back when I was a fledgeling writer, one of my greatest fears was coming to this section of the book and have no one to acknowledge. It wasn't an unfounded fear. I'm an introvert. All my life I've had maybe one or two close friends. No long list of people to fill up pages and pages of acknowledgements that's for sure.

What I didn't know then was it would be impossible to write and publish this novel without finding friends along the way. To those who joined my on this journey, you have my endless thanks!

My early beta readers, MaryLynn, Eileen, and Amy. Thank you for suffering through some truly horrible plot points and rusty grammar. The care and time you took to read this story and offer your advice has been invaluable.

Dr. Mardelle Fourtier and my fellow writing students at the College of DuPage. Thank you for keeping me on a weekly (mostly self-imposed) deadline to get the next chapter written.

The awesome members of Chicago-North Romance Writers. It's impossible to express the gratitude I have for your support, resources, critiques, and friendships over the years.

My sister Trish, for offering your honest feedback even though reading my intimate scenes was a "bit disturbing." Thanks for suffering through!

My fabulous editor, Lila. I'm so glad I found you! Thank

you for making the whole editing process fun and not at all painful, and for transforming this manuscript into something fabulous.

My husband for not noticing when I'm still in my pajamas when he comes home for work or the dust bunnies lurking everywhere. Who's initial response to my informing him I was writing a book was "That's awesome" and then telling everyone he was the inspiration for all my leading men.

My son and daughter, who were the original inspiration for my writing way back when I foolishly thought I could write for a younger audience.

And last, but not least, I want to thank my readers. Without you none of this would be possible.

About the Author

Darci Ann Baker spent her childhood imagining faraway lands and damsel-rescuing knights. She was always getting in trouble in school for daydreaming. Now she gets to day dream for a living, and no one is complaining.

Separation Game is Darci's debut novel.

 instagram.com/d.a.baker.author
 bsky.app/profile/dabakerauthor.bsky.social

www.ingramcontent.com/pod-product-compliance
Lightning Source LLC
Chambersburg PA
CBHW020928020726
47495CB00002B/394